Stories for Improvisation

Stories for Improvisation

in primary and secondary schools

Peter Chilver

B. T. Batsford Limited London

© Peter Chilver 1969
First published 1969

Printed in Great Britain by
Bristol Typesetting Company Limited
for the publishers B. T. Batsford Limited
4 Fitzhardinge Street, Portman Square, London, W.1
7134 2060 x

Contents

Group II   Older Junior—Younger Secondary

All these stories are adapted and retold. Their sources appear at the end of each story.

Foreword

This book is intended to be of value to teachers and pupils in primary and in secondary schools. 'Drama' in the classroom may assume many forms, but of all these the improvising of stories occupies a leading place. The stories in this anthology are drawn from a wide variety of sources. Most of them are folk stories or legends, but some of them are stories drawn from ideas which I have worked on with various groups of pupils and which I have here written down as stories in their own rights. In collecting all this material I have tried to select tales which are not just interesting and enjoyable unto themselves but are also highly suitable for classroom dramatisation—and the two do not necessarily, of course, go together. In the retelling of the tales I have aimed to bring out very clearly the specific points in the story which can be improvised, and for this reason I have tried as far as possible to tell all the stories in dialogue rather than in descriptive prose. Chiefly I have used stories that are light, comedic, and good-natured, and where the dramatic element is expressed very clearly and vividly in some form of verbal battle—battles of wits, in fact. For I believe this is the kind of story which all of us, whether child, adolescent or adult, most enjoy and, in particular, most enjoy improvising.

I hope, incidentally, that, quite apart from their usefulness for classroom drama, these stories will be enjoyable to read, to tell and to listen to.

Introduction

1 The layout of the book

The stories are in three main groups:

I   for older infant and younger junior
II   for older junior and younger secondary
III for older secondary

This grouping is meant to be helpful to those who are not too confident of their way around this particular subject, and not to be either rigid or in any way 'scientific'. Once a teacher and his or her class have got to know each other and are really confident with each other and have done plenty of creative drama, then a story which lends itself well to dramatisation will work just as well with one age group as with another. So once a rhythm has been established, the teacher should experiment freely with stories from all the three groupings in this book.

It must also be stressed that no two classes and no two teachers are alike, and that what a particular teacher may regard as suitable for dramatic material for a particular class may—in the early stages at least—be quite unlike what the class can in fact work with. The first couple of attempts may be fairly unsuccessful. This again is good reason for experimenting with the choice of stories and moving around from one 'group' to another.

At the end of the book, there is a section of notes covering in brief all the stories. These notes are meant as very simple pointers for the kind of work that can be done with the stories. They are meant to be helpful but not exhaustive in any way of the story's possibilities.

2 Telling a story

Most teachers will agree that pupils enjoy listening to stories: it is one of those marvellous 'highlights' in schoolwork which—like a really good session in music, or physical education—cannot fail to bring pleasure and relaxed concentration. There is a big difference, though, between *reading* a story to a class, and *telling* it. The latter is infinitely the more enjoyable. It is, obviously, a more difficult thing to do well: it needs plenty of practice, confidence, and, of course, great familiarity with the story. It needs a certain kind of histrionic talent also, for the good story-teller must also be something of an actor. But children, like adults, so obviously revel and delight in listening to someone *tell* them a story as opposed to reading it, that it is a skill well worth working at and developing.

Not all teachers, though, will have the time to get to know all stories sufficiently well to tell as opposed to read *all* of them. Indeed it is probably a good idea to vary one's style, and to read out some of them, and to tell others.

It is worth repeating here, that children enjoy hearing stories many times over. This applies to older as well as to younger children. And they also enjoy working over and again at improvising the same story. It is in this way that teachers are often able to guide and encourage children to develop their improvisations into quite elaborate and well worked out exercises.

3 The pattern of the lesson

Perhaps the most flexible pattern for such a lesson is:
(i) Teacher or pupil tells or reads the story to the class;
(ii) Class and teacher discuss the story (see below);
(iii) Class divide into small groups of perhaps four or five and each group works at the story independently of the other groups;
(iv) Those groups who wish to do so, show their improvisation to the rest of the class;
(v) The class discuss their 'improvisations' and then proceed to various kinds of 'follow-up' work, including writing and painting around ideas suggested by the story.

4 Discussing the story

Before getting down to the improvisations, the class will discuss the story with the teacher. There should be discussion about:
(i) The scene or scenes in the story which are genuinely *dramatic*. What does this mean?—very simply, a scene is dramatic when it contains a clear conflict. Basically this means that X wants something from Y, which Y is not prepared to give. This may take the form of Lady Macbeth urging her husband to murder the king, or of Hamlet struggling with his own conscience in order to resolve a complex political dilemma, or of a small boy trying to outwit a giant, or of a prince trying to solve a difficult riddle and so win the hand of the princess. Sometimes the end in view, the reason for the conflict, may seem insignificant. This is the case, for instance, with most types of domestic argument, such as the wife nagging the husband over breakfast and the husband making the occasional verbal riposte between the bowl of cereal and the plate of bacon and eggs. Child and

8

adult alike are very familiar with this kind of drama, and are well aware how extremely trifling incidents can suddenly become almost excessively ' dramatic '. In fact, melodramatic. In situations of this type there is a clear difference between the apparent drama and the real one: the apparent one may be to prove that Mrs Brown is a better judge of human nature than Mr Brown, and that she said five years ago that the woman in the flat opposite would eventually leave her husband. The real one may be the need for Mrs Brown to show her children that she is cleverer than her husband, and Mr Brown's need to show his children that she is not. Most children are much better able to grasp these various levels of meaning in situations than adults generally seem to imagine.

One other point should be made about this process of selecting the moments that are dramatic, and which therefore lend themselves to improvisation:

It is not necessarily the most *impressive* moments that are the most *dramatic*. Take a story such as the first one in this collection: ' Johnny the Giant-Catcher '—clearly the most impressive moment occurs when Johnny ties up the two giants and takes them back to the king and claims his reward. But this is not a particularly good point to take as the basis for an improvisation. The argument between the boy and his mother as to whether he can afford to give up his work as a tailor, and the argument later on between the two giants, are much richer and more rewarding scenes. They contain real conflict.

Once the story has been discussed in this way, then the class should decide whether the groups are to take different scenes or the whole story. In their early work in drama, classes usually want to take the whole story at one time. Later they become more interested in working at specific points of the story.

(ii) How the story is developed, and how it *might* have been developed. Could it have ended differently?

(iii) How the characters talk, think, behave, move, dress, live.

5 The improvisation

Encourage pupils to *use* the story rather than follow it faithfully and accurately. Perhaps ask one group to recreate the story just as they have heard it, another group to contrive a different ending, another group to introduce one new character, and another group to begin the story at a different point in time—for example, after the story has ended, say ten years after the prince has so joyously wedded the princess.

Above all, encourage them *to put themselves into the characters,*

9

to use their own speech and to recreate real dialogue and conversation.

6 The group

Some teachers like to appoint 'group leaders' who direct their groups. Other teachers find this unnecessary. The group should in any event become used to working efficiently, and to going on from one idea to another and to welcoming ideas from all its members. There should be plenty of talking about the story. If a group is too inhibited to 'act' the story, then they should be encouraged simply to 'tell' the story to each other, and then to retell the story, acting out small sections of it. Encourage the groups to get down to the various 'follow-up' work as soon as they have completed their dramatisations, and without waiting necessarily for the rest of the class to catch up.

7 Listening to the story

It is worth stressing that one of the educational values of this kind of lesson is that it trains pupils to listen. But this particular value is undermined if pupils are asked to respond actively *at the same time* as listening. Some teachers, for instance, ask children to 'act out' a narrative poem while the teacher is reading it to them. The trouble is that this confuses two quite distinct processes: listening, absorbing, comprehending on the one hand, and actively responding on the other. By and large, one should be encouraged to *listen* first, and to respond —actively, that is—later.

8 Hall or classroom?

Many teachers are given no choice in the matter: the hall is only available at certain very limited times, and all drama work has to be done in the classroom. Ideally, the place for all drama is wherever there is space, whether it be in the gymnasium, or the hall or the playing ground, or—if the desks can be moved around easily—in the classroom. But human nature, child's or adult's, is infinitely resilient and adaptive, and excellent work can be done in drama even in the most old-fashioned of classrooms, such as the four-tiered classrooms with fixed benches.

Small rostra can be useful, if there is space for them, and children can come to use them very imaginatively to convey dramatic points, to give shape to a scene, and to devise the basic kinds of setting and scenic design. But rostra are not essential.

A costume box, with various oddments of materials and colourful props, can be useful and can also be distracting. Each teacher will discover his or her own best policy on this subject.

9 What kind of standards?

The kind of standard we look for as teachers in our pupils' improvisations will depend on what we see as the educational aim of the drama lesson.

Very often we lose ourselves, and perhaps our pupils also, in a welter of vaguely psychological ideas about 'achieving personal integration' and 'releasing our inhibitions' and 'acting out our fantasies'.

It is possible that spontaneous improvisation does achieve such ends, but we cannot, simply as teachers, know whether it does or not. Only a psychologist or psychiatrist who has conducted extensive research into this field, could even begin to know.

Also, it is possibly very dangerous for anyone who lacks specialist qualifications and precise academic knowledge to even begin to encourage children—or adults—to act out their fantasies or relieve themselves of their inhibitions. This is not to deny that an intelligent and properly trained teacher will observe a great deal of his or her pupils' characters from the work they do in the drama lessons. And from these observations it should in many cases be possible to throw light on various problems that children may be encountering elsewhere in their schoolwork and in their private lives. But this is not the same thing as seeing the drama sessions in terms of some form of anarchy. After all, when children are improvising we expect them to observe the same personal code as is expected of them elsewhere: we do not give them permission to hurt, harm or injure. Or if we do, we show remarkably little respect for the children themselves. The drama lesson should not become a form of tyranny where one child acts out his fantasies at the expense of the feelings of another.

I think we are on much firmer ground when we see the aims of the drama lesson as being (a) *verbal* and (b) *social*:

(a) On the *verbal* level, all work in drama adds to the child's verbal experience and his verbal powers. He *listens* to the story, he hears it and he responds to it. He follows the development of the narrative. He then *talks* about the story, discussing this aspect and that. He shares his imaginative understanding of the story with the rest of his group. He then *acts out* the story, creating dialogue, sustaining ideas, modifying the story, responding and reacting to the others around him. In the *follow-up* work, he carries all this oral activity into some form of written work.

In other words, improvisation plays an important part in the growth of the child's oracy—his ability to talk, listen and to understand. Indeed it is so fundamental that children do of course improvise with each other quite spontaneously. But in the classroom the teacher can use this instinctive enjoyment of ' acting out the story ' so as to extend much further the child's oral powers.

It is worth adding that this educational value stems not only from the literary value of the stories themselves, but also from the literacy that children acquire simply from talking, listening and working with each other. It is only quite recently that we have come generally to accept that children educate each other—and it can be fairly claimed that the drama lesson utilised this process even before most of us were quite aware that it was going on.

(b) On the *social* level, the child learns from the improvisations of the class an immense amount about the society around him. He sees, in some cases for the first time, how other people behave. The walls surrounding his own individual life begin to disappear. When for instance, he sees two of his friends improvising a breakfast scene between the King and the Queen, he learns that other parents beside his own have their domestic problems, that they argue, row, and moan at each other, that they run down their neighbours, and lament the decline in the ' tone ' and ' class ' of the neighbourhood. This is all part, however elementary, of one's social education. More than this, the child also learns a great deal about what is acceptable and what is not. The spoilt Prince can brag and sulk and show off, and the group can adapt to this quite easily and keep the story going. But if he bashes the King and Queen on the head, then the improvisation takes a drastic turn for the worse and may well come to an immediate end!

The child is able to see and to explore in his improvisations the experiences of other children. Without knowing it, he is observing other people's lives. He is hearing what other people say, and seeing what they do. Without being invited to anyone's dinner table, he is seeing into the life of the community and discovering that other children's mums, dads, grannies, in-laws, relations and friends all have problems much like his own. This, of course, will only be the case if children are encouraged to improvise in their own language and utilising their own experiences. Otherwise they will merely produce rather fragmentary renderings of how people appear to behave in ' literature '.

We can now perhaps answer the question presented at the beginning of this section: what sort of standard are we looking for?

As teachers we hope that in their improvisations pupils will extend their verbal powers—their vocabulary, their skill in the use of words, their confidence in the use of words.

We hope also, that this development will spill over into everything else they do: that their verbal powers will manifest themselves in the rest of their schoolwork and in their personal confidence and poise and relaxation.

And as a postscript, we may add that we hope, as teachers, that from their improvisations we may be able to observe something of the background, character, and problems of each child, and to a greater extent than we have previously been able to do.

10 What do you say about it?

The chief thing is to encourage the class to talk freely about each other's improvisations. The teacher's aim should not be to 'mark' or 'grade' improvisations in any way, but to see what can be used in each improvisation as a point for discussion or for further improvisation. Take, for instance, a very interesting point in the improvisation and ask another group to develop the scene from that point. Or ask the group to re-enact a particular moment.

Very few improvisations will be *totally* successful—in other words, they will not add up to complete scenes. This does not matter. Nor does it matter that the dramatisation never reaches a real ending. Some teachers, very wisely, tell pupils not to worry about the ending. The great thing is that at some point in the scene, all the group become really involved in what they are doing.

11 Follow-up work

The actual improvising of a story is only a part of the whole operation: the follow-up work is equally important. Some of the following ideas may be useful:

(i) Pupils write the story in their own words, perhaps as a piece of narrative prose, or as a piece of verse (free or otherwise) or as a play. Children often take to the dramatist's way of story-telling with both ease and flair.

(ii) They paint a scene from the story, or the 'background' of the story. Some teachers ask one group to do this while the other groups are working on their improvisations.

(iii) Extend the story into a project, with essays, plays, poems, friezes, paintings and any other ideas that come to hand, such as choosing suitable background music, writing life stories of the characters, and adding different scenes together to make a complete play.

(iv) Pupils collect stories for improvisation, tell them, and improvise them.

(v) Group story-telling: i.e. a group work on a story, and then partly tell it to the class and partly act it out.

(vi) Improvising stories out of anecdotes and ideas suggested freely around the class or the group.

The improvising of stories is a basic part of all ' language ' work. ' English ' as a subject is incomplete without ' Drama '.

Group I

Older Infant and Younger Junior

B

1 Johnny the Giant-Catcher

An English Folk Tale

'I'm fed up with being a tailor,' said Johnny one day to his mother.

'And that's a foolish thing to say,' said his mother. 'A lad must have a trade. How else do you think you can make a living?'

'There must be better ways than this,' said Johnny.

'It's been good enough for your father, heaven knows, and for his father before him.'

'But I get so bored,' said Johnny. 'I'm fed up with the sight of needles and thread and buttons. I want something more from life.'

'No good will come of saying things like that,' said his mother.

Later that day, Johnny saw a notice posted up in the village square.

'Wanted,' said the notice, 'any brave man who thinks he can rid the kingdom of the two great giants who have terrorised the countryside since last Easter. Reward: 5,000 pieces of gold and the hand in marriage of the beautiful Princess Sophie. Applicants should report at once to the King.'

Johnny was not at all sure that he was brave enough or clever enough to handle one giant, let alone two, but he was absolutely sure that he didn't want to be a tailor all his life, and so this was too good an opportunity to miss.

'I want to see the two giants,' Johnny told the King.

'You seem rather small for the job,' said the King.

'He looks like a tailor to me,' said the Princess.

'Nevertheless, I want to see the giants,' said Johnny.

'One never knows, he may be braver than he looks,' said the King.

Johnny was directed to the district where the giants lived and off he went to find them. He still had no idea what he would do when he found them, and he had no weapons of any kind. Then he thought that if he was ever able to capture them he would need a good length of rope to bind them with, so he went into the nearest village and bought some rope.

He was walking across some fields when he first saw them, or rather when he first heard them. There was an enormous roar, like twenty lions demanding their supper, and Johnny shivered with fear and climbed up the nearest tree to hide himself.

The roar he had heard was of one of the giants blowing his nose.

Then he saw them: at least nine foot tall and as wide as oak trees. One was just a little bigger than the other.

They were digging an enormous ditch, big enough to drop a palace into.

'And when we've finished,' said one of them, 'this'll be my bedroom.'

'Then we'll dig another ditch in the next field, and that'll be my bedroom,' said the other one.

'Then we'll think about building the rest of the house.'

'Maybe we'll have to knock down the village over there,' said the smaller one.

'That'll be easy,' said the bigger one, and they both giggled.

Johnny climbed down from the tree and picked up a small stone, threw it at the bigger one's head, and then hid himself away again.

'What was that?' asked the bigger one.

'What was what?' asked the other.

'You threw a stone at me,' said the bigger one.

'I did not,' said the other.

'Oh yes you did. You just watch what you're doing. You may be little, but don't you start taking advantage of the fact. I like a joke, just like the next man, but enough's enough. Understand?'

'I don't know what you're talking about,' said the smaller.

'Maybe,' said the other ominously.

They continued digging.

Johnny climbed down again, threw a slightly bigger stone this time, and again hid himself away.

'Ouch,' said the bigger one.

'What's the matter now?'

'You devil.'

'I haven't done anything.'

'That hurt me.'

'What hurt you?'

'You know what hurt me.'

'I don't.'

'Nasty little devil you are. Always have been. But you don't like it when people play jokes on you.'

'You're going mad, that's what you are.'

'Really?'

'Yes. Always have been a bit mad now I come to think of it.'

'You just behave yourself, you hear me? The next time you'll know it. And that's that.'

And they carried on digging the ditch.

Johnny climbed down once more, threw an even bigger stone, and hid himself away again.

'Ouch. Ooh. Ah. Oh,' said the bigger giant.

'What's the—'

'Take that you devil,' said the bigger one, and they started to fight, grumbling at each other all the time.

'You never did know when to stop, always went too far,' said the bigger one.

'You were always half mad,' said the other one. 'Now you're completely crazy.'

They fought for the rest of the day, neither of them winning. Then they both flopped down exhausted.

'I'm so worn out,' said the bigger one, 'that a little mouse could beat me now.'

'And I'm so whacked,' said the smaller one, 'that you could pinch the money from my pockets and I wouldn't have the strength to stop you.'

Whereupon Johnny climbed down from the tree, tied them both together with the rope and led them off to the Palace.

'I've brought you the giants,' he said to the King, 'and I've come to claim my reward.'

And that's how it happened that Johnny never worked again as a tailor for the rest of his life.

Adapted from the story 'Johnny Gloke' in *More English Fairy Stories* by Joseph Jacobs 1894.

2 Leah and the Tiger

A West Indian Folk Tale

Leah was exceedingly beautiful, but strangely enough, she had no wish whatever to get married. She was quite content with the company of her two parents, both of whom adored her, and so all her many suitors were turned away. But no matter how many times Leah said, ' No, I have no intention of marrying you or anyone,' still the young men queued up outside her door to ask her to marry them. In fact they were quite a nuisance, for it was impossible to move in or out of her house without bumping into them. Even the neighbours complained, for the street was never less than crowded. So eventually Leah's father said to her, ' Now Leah, my darling daughter, if you do not wish to get married, so be it. Far be it from us to force you to get married. But are you quite sure that you will never ever wish to take any man for your husband?' Leah was absolutely sure, so her father continued, ' Then your mother and I have devised a very simple plan for you. As you know the street is never free of young men wanting to marry you, and the neighbours are getting fed up with the noise they make and so are we, and so something must be done. This is what we propose. We shall buy you a little house, all of your own, way up the hill and over the other side, and nobody will know you are there, and the suitors will leave you alone and we, and the street, will have peace at last. And every morning we shall bring you breakfast, your mother or I, and every afternoon we shall bring you tea, and every evening we shall bring you supper, and we shall sit and talk with you as before, and you will never be lonely and never be hungry. Does that seem like a good plan to you?'

Leah thought it an excellent plan, and so, without wasting another day, Leah moved into her house up the hill and over the other side, and nobody knew where she had gone. Some even thought she had at last gone off and married, and so the suitors stopped coming to her door, and peace returned to the street. Leah and her parents—not to mention the neighbours—were delighted. Her parents took turns to take the meals to her, and everything worked out just as splendidly as they had hoped, and Leah never had a dull moment looking after her little house and looking forward to her mother's or her father's next visit.

Now as we all know from bitter experience, nothing perfect lasts for ever. And so it was with the beautiful Leah. Her mother brought her breakfast one morning at the usual time—in a beautiful silver tureen by the way—and stood outside her front door and called out the special signal that they had arranged:

> Leah, Leah, let me in
> Honey at the door dear
> Sugar at the door dear
> Ting a ling, ting a ling.

And Leah, hearing the signal, and knowing that all was well, opened the door. It was, as always, an excellent breakfast, and after she and her mother had chatted about this and that, the two said their good-byes at the garden gate.

'Thank you for coming, Mother,' said Leah.

'And don't forget,' said her mother, 'tea at the usual time.'

'I won't forget,' said Leah.

And so the mother went home.

But all this time a tiger had been hiding in the trees just across from the front of the house. He had seen the mother arrive with the silver tureen and had heard her call out the secret signal and had seen Leah let her mother in. And in a flash he understood what had happened. For like almost everybody else, he had always admired Leah and her great beauty, and so now he thought to himself, 'So this is her secret, eh. Well, well. I have always wanted to marry a really beautiful young girl like her, and now I shall. I shall make her marry me, whether she likes it or not.'

The only trouble was that the house was an especially good one, and there was no way of getting into it except through the front door, and the tiger understood that Leah would never open the door except to her mother when she came next time with food—tea-time, didn't she say?—and spoke the secret signal. And the tiger had such a gruff deep voice that Leah would never for one moment imagine that it was her mother. The tiger thought about this for a moment and then decided that great opportunities—like the chance to marry Leah—demanded great sacrifices, and so he made his way down to the black-smith and said to him, 'Blacksmith, is it possible for you to change my voice? Now it is deep and gruff, but can you make it soft and tender?'

'That depends how brave you are. It can be done, but it's a terrify-ing operation.'

'No one's as brave as I am,' said the tiger, hoping that he was as brave as he'd always thought he was.

21

'Very well then. Open your mouth—wide.'

The tiger did so, and the blacksmith plunged down his throat a great red-hot poker, and there was a tremendous sizzling noise as the blacksmith removed the poker a second later.

The tiger meanwhile had not moved, thinking all the while of the beautiful Leah so as to stop himself from showing fear.

'You're a brave one, and that's a fact,' said the blacksmith. 'Now say something, and we can see if the operation's been successful.'

And the tiger said, 'Well I certainly hope it has. I wouldn't like to have gone through all that for—' And then he stopped, realising that his voice had suddenly become a beautiful soft voice, just like the voice of Leah's mother. And so he bounded off delightedly back to Leah's house, and he waited till just a few minutes before tea-time and then he knocked at Leah's front door.

> Leah, Leah, let me in
> Honey at the door dear
> Sugar at the door dear
> Ting a ling, ting a ling.

And Leah heard the tiger's soft voice, and thought, 'That sounds just like my mother. Something's wrong here. It was my mother who brought my breakfast, so it should be my father who brings my tea. No. I am sure this is a trap. I shall refuse to open the door.'

And the tiger repeated the secret signal, but still Leah did not open the door, and he said to himself, 'What's the matter with the wretched girl? Has she gone deaf, or has she suddenly lost her appetite?'

Then he saw her father approaching the house, so he crept stealthily round the corner and watched and waited. And Leah's father called out the signal, and then Leah opened the door, and let him in. An hour later, her father left her, calling out from the gate, 'And dinner at the usual time, my dear.'

Then the tiger realised his foolish mistake. But he was never a man to give up easily, so he bounded back to the blacksmith, who was just about to close up his shop, and said, 'I know how enormously clever you are, blacksmith, you've proved it once today already.'

'Sorry,' said the blacksmith, 'I've finished work for today.'

But the tiger pleaded with him to perform just one more operation: change his voice back to its normal gruffness, so that he could sound like Leah's father. In the end the blacksmith did the job, for the tiger quite sensibly offered him the biggest fee he'd been offered for years and years.

The tiger bounded back to Leah's house, and once more he called out the secret signal to Leah, and once more Leah refused to open the door, for this time, she reminded herself, it was her mother who should be bringing the meal. And a few minutes later her mother came while the tiger, in his fury, was hiding round the corner. This time, when she was leaving, the mother called out, ' Breakfast the same time tomorrow, my dear.'

The tiger was immensely depressed, and debated whether it was worthwhile going down to the blacksmith's again, asking him to change his voice yet again, so that by breakfast time he would sound like Leah's mother. Leah was so beautiful that he finally decided that it was well worth it, even though the blacksmith would have to be woken up in the middle of the night, would create a great fuss, and would demand even more money. And as you can imagine the blacksmith was indeed furious.

' Who do you think I am?' he demanded. ' I run a business like any other man, and I keep business hours, like any other man. And my shop's closed now. Away with you.'

But the tiger begged him to change back his voice. ' After all,' he said, ' I'm an especially good customer. Think how many times I've done business with you today.'

' I know,' the blacksmith called out from his window, ' and you're driving me crazy with all these changes of voice. One minute you want a soft voice, then you want a deep voice, now you want a soft voice again—whatever's the matter with you, man? I suggest you go home like a good sensible fellow, leave other people in peace, and decide once and for all what sort of voice you definitely want—and stick to it.'

But at that very moment, the penny—as they say—dropped. ' But of course,' said the tiger to himself, ' what a fool I've been. Now I understand. Her mother and father take turns. One takes breakfast, the other takes tea, and so on. What a fool I've been. All I have to do is keep my own voice, and in the morning I shall call the secret message from outside the front door, a few minutes before her father arrives, she'll open the door and that will be that. I'll make her marry me—for no one ever argued with me—and I shall live happily ever after with the most beautiful bride in the world.'

The tiger did as he had planned and at breakfast time stood outside Leah's house and called the secret signal. But Leah never came, even though he stood outside the house calling her all morning. And this is why. Leah had heard the tiger calling her first in his soft voice and then in his gruff voice, and though she did not know who it was, nevertheless she had the sense to realise something dangerous was going on. So that night, while the tiger was calling on the blacksmith, she thought everything over very carefully. 'What a terrible situation I am in,' she said, ' living all on my own with no one to look after me.' And the more she thought about it, the more foolish her present way of life seemed to her. ' Really it's ridiculous, living all alone like this when I could have a fine handsome husband to love me and protect me.' And since she was never a girl to spend very long making up her mind, she packed up her things that very night and walked all the way over the hill and up the other side and woke up her parents with the very unexpected news that enough was enough: she had decided to get married.

And so it happened, that when the poor tiger had eventually tired himself out, calling the secret signal to Leah without any success whatsoever, he walked back down the path with his tail between his legs, feeling very sorry for himself. It was then he noticed a sign in the upstairs window:

House for Sale. In excellent condition. Owner recently vacated property in order to get married.

Most people would have sat down and wept with frustration, and the tiger nearly did just that, but he didn't. He thought about it for a while and then he got up very cheerfully and made his way back into the world, saying to himself, ' Ah well. Things could be much worse. After all, I'm still a bachelor. And not only that, I've still got my own voice.' And with that he let out a magnificent roar, just to prove it.

Adapted from the story 'Why Women Won't Listen' in *West Indian Folk Tales* by Philip Sherlock, Oxford University Press 1954.

3 The Tiger, the Brahman and the Jackal

An Indian Folk Story

A tiger was prowling through the jungle when he was suddenly caught in a trap. He was there for several hours, calling out all the time for some good soul to come and help him, and eventually a Brahman came by.

'Dear Brahman,' called out the tiger, 'I'm caught in a trap, and am almost dead with the pain of it. I beg of you, good kind man that you so obviously are, to climb up and release me.'

'Oh no,' said the Brahman, 'I am indeed a good kind man but I'm not a foolish one also. If I were to release you, the first thing you'd do would be to seize me and put me by for your next dinner. I have learned not to trust tigers.'

'But I'm an especially good tiger, and I never hurt men, never. I give you my word of honour as a tiger of quite exceptional honour and integrity, that if you are so gracious as to set me free, I will never under any circumstance harm you.'

'Sorry. I don't believe you,' said the Brahman, who proceeded to walk away.

'Please, dear good kind Brahman, please do not leave me here to die. Is that a kindly thing to do? Is such an action worthy of a man famous for his charity—such as you are?'

'Famous? Did you say famous?'

'I did indeed. We animals are for ever hearing news of your great good deeds. We hardly ever talk of anything else. And imagine how we will talk about this kind deed you are about to do for me.'

The Brahman thought about this for a minute, then he said, 'Very well. But you must first promise not to harm me.'

'Promise,' said the tiger.

'Say it again, louder,' said the Brahman.

'I promise never to harm you,' said the tiger, loud enough for everyone in the jungle to hear him.

'Very good. Now I shall release you.'

But no sooner had the Brahman released the tiger from the trap than the tiger sprang upon him, gripped him tight, and cried out, 'Ha, ha, and now I make another promise, and this one I shall definitely keep, to eat you for my supper this evening.'

'You wretch,' cried the Brahman in despair, 'is that how you keep your promises?' But the tiger only laughed in reply.

25

'You'll be delicious,' said the tiger, 'and after supper I'll put your bones in the pot and make a lovely stew of you. Brahman stew. Ha, ha.'

'You dreadful creature. What a way to repay my kindness.'

And the Brahman carried on grumbling so much that the tiger became quite fed up with it.

'Oh do stop grumbling for heaven's sake. I cannot bear grumblers.'

'But it's so unjust, that's why I'm grumbling,' insisted the Brahman.

'What's so unjust about it?' asked the tiger. 'You're the only one who thinks it's unjust. Ask anyone else and they'll tell you that you're getting exactly what you deserve. Everyone knows that you mustn't trust a tiger.'

'Very well then, let's ask someone.'

'Very well.'

And the first person they met was an old horse.

The tiger explained the problem to him.

'Well,' said the tiger, 'do you think I'm being unjust?'

'Not at all,' said the horse, 'the Brahman is being repaid for his kindness in just the same way that I have been repaid for the hard work I did for my master. I toiled for him for many years, faithfully and industriously, and then when I grew old and grey he threw me out. Said I was too expensive to keep. That was the thanks I got. So the Brahman is no more unjustly repaid than I have been.'

'Excellent,' said the tiger. 'Now I shall eat you,' he said to the Brahman.

'Let us ask someone else,' begged the Brahman.

The next person they met was an old dog. He too had been turned out by his master after working for him faithfully for years until he'd grown too old to work any longer. 'In fact,' said the dog, 'he meant to sell me to be slaughtered, for meat. But I ran away. That was the thanks I got. So the Brahman is no more unjustly repaid than I have been.'

'Wonderful,' said the tiger. 'Now I shall eat you,' he said to the Brahman.

'But I beg of you, let us ask just one more person.'

'Only one,' said the tiger, 'for I'm getting hungry.'

And then they met a jackal. The tiger explained the problem to him, but the jackal did not seem to understand.

'I see,' said the jackal, 'so the Brahman was caught in a trap and you—'

'No no,' said the tiger, 'the tiger was caught in a trap. I mean I was.'

26

' Ah yes. You were caught in a Brahman, and a trap came along—'

' No, no, don't be so ridiculous: I was caught in a trap, and along came a Brahman.'

' Where?'

' Here. This Brahman.'

' Oh yes. I understand.'

' And what do you think?'

' About what?'

' Why! about my eating the Brahman?'

' How do you mean?'

So the tiger explained it all over again, but still the jackal did not understand.

' Perhaps I would understand it better if you could show me how it all actually happened.'

So they all three went back to the tree where the tiger had been caught.

' I was up there,' said the tiger.

' Oh yes. You were up there,' said the jackal. ' Where?'

' There. In the tree.'

' Oh yes. Which tree?'

' This tree.'

' Whereabouts in the tree?'

' In the trap?'

' Which trap?'

By now the tiger was getting short of temper.

' You simpleton,' he said to the jackal, ' this trap up here.'

And so saying he climbed up into the trap.

' This trap. Like this.' And now the tiger was caught, just as he had been at first.

' Ah now I see,' said the jackal.

' But now the Brahman lets me out. And that's when I decide to eat him.'

' Ah yes. Well that's a very easy one to answer. I'd advise the Brahman not to let you out.'

And with that, the Brahman and the jackal walked off, leaving the tiger still calling out for help.

Adapted from *Indian Fairy Tales* by Joseph Jacobs 1892.

4 The Boy who had everything

An African Folk Story

We all of us want more than we have, and unhappy is the man who has everything. This story proves it.

There was once a young prince who was the apple of his father's eye, and since his father was the King, then, as you can imagine, the young prince was wickedly spoilt. He had everything he wanted. He had only to say to his father, 'Father, I want that,' and he got it. For his father thought his young son the best that ever was—the most handsome, the best behaved, and the finest in character. Every now and again one or other of the wise men would be so bold as to suggest that the prince was just a trifle rude, or just a little greedy, or just slightly ill-tempered, but the King would hear nothing of it. 'My son is perfection,' the King would say, and he would heap him with yet more gifts of every description.

One day the Prince was playing with some of his friends when he lost a game of—tennis I believe it was. The Prince was furious, for he hated to lose anything.

'It's absurd,' said the Prince. 'How can I possibly have lost? Someone must have been cheating. Or there's something wrong with the rules.'

'There was no cheating,' said one of his friends, who was well aware that the only person who ever cheated was the Prince himself.

'Well there's something wrong, for I couldn't possibly lose otherwise.'

'But even you must lose sometimes. You can't always win.'

'Of course I can. For I am the most powerful person in the whole land. Everybody has to bow down when I walk past. I am the best person living, my father often tells me so, and I believe him. And if that is true, how can I, the best and most powerful in the land, ever lose such a little thing as a game of tennis?'

The friends thought it best to let him carry on with his boasting.

'After all, if I went to fight the enemy I would be sure to win, wouldn't I? Or if I went to do battle with some hideous giant or some ghastly one-eyed ogre, or an enchantress, then I would win. Wouldn't I?'

They all agreed that he would undoubtedly vanquish any enemy, giant, ogre or enchantress that might ever have the misfortune to meet him.

28

' So how could I ever possibly lose a mere game of tennis?'

And since no one disputed what he said, he concluded triumphantly, ' Therefore I say someone has been cheating, and I by rights have won the game.'

But not all of his friends were frightened of him, and one of them, the one who had spoken up before, said, ' There is one person who is more powerful than you are. You are not the greatest in the land, and therefore you do not have to win every game you play.'

The Prince was furious. ' Nonsense. Who is more powerful than I am?'

' Your father. The King,' said the friend.

' Are you sure?' said the Prince, greatly surprised.

' I'm positive,' said the friend. ' When the army goes out to fight the enemy, it is your father who leads them, not yourself. While you are playing games like this, it is your father who goes out to fight the giants and ogres and enchantresses. If your father walked into this room now, all of us would have to bow, including yourself. He is the King. He is more powerful than you are. For we are all his subjects —yourself included.'

With that the Prince went into a great sulk, as he always did when something happened that displeased him.

' I don't believe you,' he said.

' It doesn't matter whether you believe me or not. It's true, and that's that.'

' I still don't believe you. And I'm not playing any more.'

And with that he ordered his servants to take away the tennis rackets so that nobody else should be able to play after he'd gone.

' They're my tennis rackets, and you're only here as my guests.' And with that he stormed off to see his father.

The King was in the middle of a great council meeting where all the wise men of the land were assembled. But the Prince took no notice of this, and instead rushed in as though the King was in the middle of nothing more important than a tea party.

' Father, father, I am terribly upset,' he said. ' And I feel like sulking for the rest of the year.'

' Ah, my wonderful perfect son, star of the firmament, what can be distressing you? Nothing that is in my power shall ever cause you grief. Come, tell your poor father,' said the King.

The wise men grumbled quietly to each other that the Prince was a confounded nuisance and the King a great fool to be so much the slave of his own son. In every other respect he was such an excellent king—as all the wise men agreed. And what would become of them all when the King died and the Prince became King in his place?

29

The Prince explained why he was so upset. ' One of my friends says that I am not the most powerful person in the land—he says that you are. And I'm dreadfully put out, because I've always thought nobody the equal of me, and now I find that you're not only my equal, you're my superior. My friend says that we are all your subjects and that I don't have any subjects at all. It isn't fair. I want some subjects too, and I want more than you have.'

' But that would be difficult, my son. However, it is only a matter of patience, for when I am dead, then you shall have all my subjects for yourself, for you will be king in my place.'

' That may not happen for years and years, I can't wait that long. I want some subjects now.'

The King turned to his wise men. ' What is to be done?' he asked. ' How can I satisfy this little wish of my dear and perfect son?'

The wise men fidgeted and were reluctant to reply.

' The Prince will have to wait until he is King,' said one of them.

' I don't want to wait,' said the Prince. ' I won't wait.'

More fidgeting, and someone called out from the back that the Prince could do with a good walloping, and then perhaps he'd have a little more patience. There were murmurs of agreement, but the King pretended not to hear.

' I have an excellent idea,' said the King. ' I think this will make you perfectly happy, my wonderfully perfect son. I shall give you all those of my subjects who are unmarried, and I shall keep all the married ones. Now. Does that please you?'

The wise men fidgeted again, and there were more murmurs of disapproval.

' Does that mean that I shall have more subjects than you will have?' asked the Prince.

' Most certainly. For every husband and wife in the land have children, or most of them do. And most of them have more than two children. So the unmarried must outnumber the married.'

' Then I am the greatest in the land.'

' Decidedly so.'

And without waiting to say thank you, off went the Prince to tell his friends.

' So you see—now I am the most powerful in the land.'

With that he ordered the servants to bring back the rackets so that they could resume playing. And although the Prince cheated like mad, for he always did, nevertheless he again lost the game. And again he was furious.

' I won't have it. I simply won't have it. How can it happen that I who have everything, could possibly fail to have the highest score?

30

I ought by rights to be the winner.'

' Well you aren't, and that's that,' said the same friend who had been so outspoken previously.

' It isn't fair,' said the Prince.

' It's perfectly fair,' said the friend.

' But don't you see,' insisted the Prince, ' since I now have every-thing—for my father has given me more subjects than he has himself —then I must obviously win at everything I do. For I am the most powerful in the land.'

' But you don't have everything,' said the friend.

' I do,' said the Prince.

' Rubbish,' said the friend.

' Very well then. Name one thing that is not mine.'

' The moon,' replied the friend simply.

' Oh dear. You're quite right. I don't have the moon, do I? But I shall have. I shall go to my father immediately, and ask him for it.' And he did.

The King was still in the middle of his council meeting when the Prince rushed in.

' Father, I have discovered something that is not mine, and I am dreadfully unhappy,' he said.

' I shall not allow you to be unhappy,' said the King. ' Tell me what it is that you do not have.'

' The moon,' said the Prince.

Great consternation among the wise men.

' The moon? But dear wonderful son, prince of total perfection, nobody has the moon. Not even I.'

' That doesn't matter. I still want it.'

' But I cannot give it to you. It would be impossible.'

' If you loved me as you say you do, then you would give it to me, even though it is impossible.'

' I certainly love you very much, for you are so perfect that every-one loves you. But how can I get to the moon in order to give it to you?'

' Think,' said the Prince, ' and tell your silly wise men to think too.'

' Yes,' said the King, ' what an excellent idea. Wise men. Think for once.'

And the wise men murmured among themselves. ' The moon he wants, does he? I'd give him the moon, I would. If he were my son I'd give him something to think about, that's a fact, I would. The moon, indeed.'

' Dear son,' said the King, ' is there not something else I could give you? Something just as wonderful as the moon. A great forest perhaps. Or a herd of elephants. Or a beautiful island. Any of these I could give you.'

' Yes I'll have all those,' said the Prince, ' but I must also have the moon.'

' It's impossible,' said all the wise men.

' No. It is not impossible,' said a voice from the back of the council chamber. It was the friend with whom the Prince had been playing tennis. ' Your gracious Majesty, most high, learned, and famous wise men, may I be humbly permitted to speak?'

' If you have a good suggestion to make, then speak on,' said the King.

' There is only one way for the Prince to get the moon. We must build a great tower that will reach up to the moon, and then the Prince can himself climb up the tower and bring the moon back with him when he comes down.'

' And can such a tower be built?' asked the King.

' Give me the men, and the right to cut down all the trees I need, and I will build the tower.'

' Very good. You will have all the men in the land, and all the trees in the land, if you so need them.'

And so it happened that the friend ordered all the men in the kingdom to start cutting down all the trees in the forest, which they did. Then, slowly, carefully, they built a great scaffold by tying the tree-trunks together with strong rope, and each day the scaffolding got higher and higher. Soon the top of the scaffolding was completely out of sight, and people came from lands far away just to look at it. Still the friend and all the men under him worked at building the scaffolding higher and higher, and in this way a year and a day passed before the friend came to the King, and said to him, ' Your Majesty, the tower is ready.'

' It is a wonderful thing,' said the King. ' I have never seen such a tower.'

' Now the great Prince can climb up the tower and seize the moon.'

The Prince needed no telling. He couldn't wait to go. A great ceremony was held to mark the moment when the Prince began his climb, for no one could tell how long the Prince would be away. The King made a speech, in which he told the people how lucky they were to have such a wonderfully perfect prince who one day would reign over them. ' Surely we shall be remembered in history for the perfection of our prince,' he said.

The chief wise man made a speech, in which he praised the King and the Prince, but discreetly hinted that everyone hoped that once

the Prince had obtained the moon he would be content and want
nothing else, at least for a few years. Then the Prince made a speech,
in which he said how wonderful he was, and how he was the greatest
prince that ever was, and how he was about to prove it to all the
world by climbing up the tower and bringing the moon back home with
him. 'And when I am home,' he said, 'then shall no one ever again
dare beat me at tennis—or at anything else.'

So saying, the Prince walked boldly towards the tower. The trumpets sounded, the people cheered, and the Prince began to climb.
He climbed and climbed and climbed. Eventually he climbed so high
that he was completely out of sight. And since it might be ages before he came back, the people went about their work and life went
on as usual.

Months passed. Then years. And still the Prince never returned.

The King grew very old. Though still a good king, he grieved
bitterly for his son, and could hardly concentrate on matters of state.
He died, and since the Prince had still not returned the wise men
had to elect someone to rule in his place. Now the friend who had
suggested and planned the building of the tower had made such a
good impression on everyone that he was elected to rule over the
kingdom until the Prince returned. He made an excellent ruler. He
was practical, fair, good natured and understanding. His people loved
him, and in time they forgot altogether about the prince who'd climbed
up in quest of the moon.

One day the wise men suggested that the scaffolding should be taken
down, but the ruler would hear nothing of this. 'Who knows, the
Prince may yet return,' he said. 'He may be on his way down right
now. And if he never comes back, then perhaps the scaffold will serve
as a vivid reminder to all of us, not to want too much, and more
especially, not to want everything.'

Well, the prince never came back. And so the scaffold is still there
to this very day. And, incidentally, so is the moon.

Adapted from *My Dark Companions* by Henry Stanley 1893.

5 The Death of Abu Nowas and His Wife

An Arabian Folk Tale

Abu Nowas, poet to the great Sultan of Baghdad, was very keen to get married and he told the Sultan so.

' There must be plenty of suitable young ladies,' said the Sultan.

' I particularly want someone who is almost as amusing as I am, almost as witty, almost as clever, and almost as lazy,' said Abu Nowas.

' Why only " almost "?' asked the Sultan.

' Because no one could ever be more than " almost " as amusing, witty, clever or lazy as I am,' explained Abu.

' I'll speak to my wives,' said the Sultan. ' There must be many such ladies in my harem.'

' I only want one,' said Abu.

' I'll see what I can do,' said the Sultan.

And he debated the matter with one of his most beautiful wives, Narefta, who said, ' I know the very girl. Her name is Parenista, and she is really rather amusing, and rather clever, and rather lazy. She would be perfect for Abu Nowas.'

And so Parenista was presented to Abu Nowas—and Abu Nowas was delighted with her. She was everything he looked for in a wife. He was even more pleased when the Sultan sent fifty pieces of gold as a wedding present, and the two lived happily on the gold for months and months. But they also lived very very expensively and soon the gold was completely used up.

' And what will we live on now?' asked Parenista.

' We shall have to use our wits,' said Abu Nowas.

That same afternoon Abu Nowas went into the Sultan's palace, weeping bitterly, and crying out to the gods for comfort and consolation.

' What on earth is the matter?' asked the Sultan.

' The matter, the matter—oh do not ask me,' said Abu Nowas, weeping even more bitterly than before.

' Come now, it can't be as bad as all that,' said the Sultan.

' My wife, my poor dear wife—' said Abu Nowas.

' And what about your wife?'

' She's dead—oh alack the day, woe is me, why cannot I die too?' said Abu Nowas.

' Come now, it's very tragic, I know, that your wife should die so

34

soon, but you must not think of ending your own life as well. Here. Take these few pieces of gold as a token of my esteem for your dear dead wife.'

'But I couldn't possibly take them, your Highness,' said Abu, immediately pocketing the gold pieces—'how kind you are.'

Meanwhile, Parenista had entered the chamber of Narefta, and she cried out, 'Oh, why do I live still? Why cannot heaven call me too? Oh—oh.'

Narefta asked what was the matter with her.

'My poor dear beloved and loving husband, he is—oh I cannot bring myself to say it—he is—dead. Oh. Oh.'

'But how dreadful. My dear, it is a terrible thing to lose a good husband, but here, please accept these few pieces of gold as a token of my high regard for your husband.'

'I couldn't accept them, your Highness,' said Parenista, immediately taking the gold pieces, 'you are too kind.'

And after Narefta had again comforted her, and Parenista had again declared that life was not worth living, Parenista returned home, where she and Abu Nowas roared with laughter at the success of their excellent trick.

'But it is not finished yet, my dear,' said Abu Nowas. 'You must now go to your bed, and lie there pretending to be dead. I shall sit outside the door wailing hideously. Go. Do as I tell you.'

And when the Sultan met Narefta that evening he said to her, 'How terribly sad, the news about poor Parenista.'

'What news?' asked Narefta.

'She is dead. Poor Abu Nowas came to me this afternoon, beside himself with grief. He was inconsolable.'

'Oh no. You must be mistaken. It is Abu Nowas who is dead. Parenista came to me this afternoon, beside herself with grief. She was inconsolable.'

'Ridiculous. Abu Nowas came to me.'

'No. Parenista came to me.'

'There is one way to settle this.' And with that he told one of his attendants to go straight away to Abu's house and see who was dead, the husband or the wife.

The attendant reached the house and there was Abu sitting outside weeping and wailing.

'My poor dear wife, my poor dear wife,' he said, 'no doubt you have come to pay your respects to her. She is in there on her bed. She is—oh how can I say it?—she is dead.'

And the attendant looked inside the door and saw Parenista lying there, presumably dead.

He went to the Sultan and reported what he had seen.

' You see,' said the Sultan. ' I was right.'

' This is absurd,' said Narefta, and she ordered one of her attendants to go at once to Abu's house and report back to her.

By the time the attendant had reached the house Abu and his wife had changed places, and Abu was lying motionless on the bed while Parenista was weeping and wailing at the door.

' My poor husband, my poor husband—he is dead. Oh. He is dead. My poor perfect wonderful irreplaceable husband.'

And so the attendant reported back to Narefta.

' There is only one thing to do,' said the Sultan, ' we must both go down to Abu Nowas's house, and see for ourselves.'

' An excellent idea,' said Narefta.

And so, with all their attendants they went down to the house, and by the time they had got there, both Abu Nowas and Parenista were lying motionless, side by side on the bed, as if dead, and their servants were weeping and wailing over them.

' But this is almost unbelievable,' said the Sultan. ' If they are both dead, how does it happen that both Narefta and myself have been told by the husband and the wife that the other one is dead?'

And the matter puzzled him so much that he added, ' I demand to know, and will give 100 pieces of gold to the person who can tell me.'

Whereupon both Abu Nowas and Parenista his wife sat up in the bed and said, ' Your Highness, give us the gold, and we will tell you.'

And the Sultan was so delighted with the joke—for he was both good natured and honourable—that he paid the 100 pieces of gold twice over, first to Abu Nowas and then to his wife.

' Ah well,' said Abu Nowas, ' that will help us to keep going for another few months.'

And it did.

Adapted from *Fairy Tales from the Barbary Coast by* Peter Lum, Frederick Muller 1967. Copyright Lady Crowe.

6 The Nun's Priest's Tale

From Chaucer's Canterbury Tales

Chanticleer the cock had seven wives, all of whom were exceedingly beautiful, but the most beautiful of them all was Dame Partlet, a hen as fair to behold as any hen that has ever been born. It is not surprising that Chanticleer loved Dame Partlet more than he loved his other wives.

One morning he told her, 'Partlet my dear, I've just woken up from the most dreadful dream.'

'Really,' said Partlet, not greatly interested, 'I never take much notice of dreams. They're rather foolish things.'

'But this one was especially dreadful. I'd like to tell you about it. It would make me feel better.'

'Very well. If you insist,' said Partlet.

'In my dream I was pursued by some evil creature who sought to kill me. It was all quite terrifying. I woke up feeling almost dead with fright.'

And Chanticleer was still in a highly nervous state.

'What nonsense,' said Partlet. 'What will people think of me, if the news is spread around that my husband shakes with fear because of a mere dream? Be a man for goodness' sake, and behave like one —with courage and spirit.'

'Then you don't think I should be worried at all by my dream?'

'Only if you are an old coward. As for myself, I never take the least notice of dreams. There's nothing in them.'

'I'm sure you're right, my dear,' said Chanticleer. 'It was just a dream. And besides, it is a fine summer's morning, and with you here at my side, how could I be less than happy?'

And with that he jumped down into the yard and started showing off as he always did, giving orders to the hens, and generally behaving like the lord of the farm, which indeed he was.

'That's more like it,' said Dame Partlet, 'that's how I expect a man to behave.'

And she was happy too, and she also went round the yard showing off and putting everybody else in their place.

Then Chanticleer saw the fox. He was crouching only a few feet away from him, half-hidden by a bush. He was about to run away when the fox called out to him, 'Good morning, good Chanticleer. A fine morning it is.'

' Why—yes, it is.'

' Surely you would not run away from me? A brave fellow like you? Besides, I only called in for a chat, to pass the time of day. I used often to call in to chat to your dear father.'

' Oh—I see—well, if you just want a chat—'

' Of course I do. Everybody knows that you're the most interesting person to talk to for miles and miles around.'

' Really?'

' Most decidedly.'

' Then by all means let us talk,' said Chanticleer, delighted. And with that he walked over to the fox who, without wasting another second, snatched up poor Chanticleer between his strong jaws and ran off with him towards the woods. The hens cried out in alarm, and the farm hands put everything down and, calling out to the fox, started to chase after him.

' Let Chanticleer go, you old devil,' cried one.

' You villain,' cried another, ' release Chanticleer this instant, or I'll have you shot, you see if I don't.'

' Please let him go,' cried all the hens.

' I order you to bring him back this instant,' called the farmer in a very commanding voice.

But the fox never stopped or looked back.

Chanticleer recovered sufficiently from his fright to think for a few moments.

' What a cheek they have,' said Chanticleer to the fox, ' to shout out their orders at you. Really—who do they think they're talking to? If I were a great fox like yourself I'd give them a piece of my mind. I'd let them know who's who.'

' You're absolutely right,' said the fox, ' what a confounded impudence of them to speak in that tone of voice to a great fox like myself.'

And with that he put Chanticleer down for a moment and called out to the farmer and his farmhands. ' How dare you shout out your orders to me. I'm a great fox, and take orders from no one. If you had come to me, cap in hand, and begged me as a very great favour to let Chanticleer go free, then I might have obliged. But not now— I shall never—'

And then he stopped, for he realised that while he'd been talking Chanticleer had fled up the nearest tree and was safely rid of him.

' Oh dear,' said the fox. ' Surely you don't think I was going to kill you, Chanticleer. Be a good fellow and come down from the tree so that we can have our chat, just like you promised.'

' Not again,' said Chanticleer, ' you've made a fool of me once, but not twice.'

'And now you've made a fool of me too, so perhaps we're both the wiser. I've learnt something today, even though I haven't caught myself a delicious meal.'

'And me too,' said Chanticleer. 'In future I shall listen to my own counsel, and not be ruled by my wife.'

'And I,' said the fox, 'won't open my mouth in future without thinking a little beforehand.'

'Well then,' said Chanticleer, 'the day's not been wasted after all, has it?'

And the fox agreed.

Adapted from *The Canterbury Tales* by William Chaucer.

7 The Twilight of the Gods

An Icelandic Legend

The greatest of all the gods was Odin, and he had many sons of whom the most handsome, the most noble and the most loved by all men, was Balder. But one night Balder had a terrible dream in which he learnt that he would soon die, and when he told the dream to the other gods there was much sadness and alarm.

'Why should we allow this dream to come true,' said Balder's mother, the goddess Frigg, 'surely we are powerful enough to devise some plan so that Balder will be safe for ever.'

And this is the plan that Frigg thought of: 'We shall go to everything there is, man, animal, stone, or tree, and ask for a promise that they will never harm Balder. And then he will be safe.'

That is exactly what the gods did. And so, in course of time, everyone, including Balder himself, believed that the dream would never now come true and Balder would be safe for ever. And because even the stones had promised never to harm him, it soon became the custom for everyone to pay their respects to Balder by throwing things at him, and no matter what they threw it would glide off him and do him no harm.

Who knows, Balder might well have lived for ever had it not been for the jealousy of another of the gods, Loki, the god of fire. He could not bear to see everyone admire Balder so much and pay him such homage, and so he thought of a way of doing him some awful injury. Now Loki also was handsome and so no one ever suspected him of wicked thoughts, and when Loki went to Frigg and said to her, quite pleasantly, in conversation—'And did everything promise never to hurt Balder?'—she quite unthinkingly said, 'Well, no, not everything.'

'Really?' said Loki.

'Everything except a small mistletoe bush. It was too small at the time to be worth bothering about, but some time I must go back and find the bush and make it promise.'

Without discussing the matter again, Loki went out and found the mistletoe bush, broke a twig from it, and then went to join the others. They were throwing stones at Balder who stood smiling and chatting and letting the stones glide off him.

'Here,' said Loki to a blind man, 'I see you have nothing to throw at Balder. People will think you have no respect for him.'

' I know,' said the blind man, ' but I am blind and cannot see to choose something to throw.'

' Then throw this,' said Loki, and he put into his hand the twig from the mistletoe bush. And the blind man threw the twig and the end of it cut into Balder's flesh and pierced his heart and killed him.

And Balder had been so great a god, and it had seemed so impossible that he should ever die, that even the gods themselves believed that the world could not survive this awful disaster. And so Odin sent another of his sons, Hermod, to take the long journey to Hel, the Goddess of the Underworld, to ask if they could have Balder back. And though the journey was perilous Hermod went willingly and did in time come face to face with the Goddess herself.

' I come to beg the greatest favour of you, Goddess,' said Hermod.

' I know the favour that you come to ask,' said Hel, ' for I have heard all the weeping, and know of the sorrow of the gods. Yes, you can have Balder back, but on one condition.'

' Name it, Goddess,' said Hermod.

' You can have him back provided everyone and everything in the world will weep for him. Then he can return.'

And so it happened that the gods went all over the earth asking everyone and everything to weep for Balder, the most splendid and best loved of all the gods that ever were. And the trees wept, and the stones; and so did peoples of all manner of strange lands who had only heard of Balder and his goodness, and soon it seemed that Hel's condition had been fulfilled. But there was one old witch who had no pity in her, and she said, ' Why should an old witch like me weep for Balder? What did he ever do for me?' And even the power of the gods could not move her to weep.

So Balder never returned from the underworld, and the gods knew that without the greatest of them all, they themselves would in time disappear, and that the world—their world—would never be the same again. And so it was.

Adapted from *Book of Legends* by Jacynth Hope-Simpson, Hamish Hamilton 1964.

8 The Husband of Rhiannon

A Celtic Legend

Rhiannon was such a beautiful princess that almost every man in the land, and certainly every prince, wanted to marry her. There were two suitors who were even more anxious than any of the others that Rhiannon should be their bride. And though only one of these is the hero of the tale, yet both of them loved Rhiannon more than most men ever love any one. Prince Pwyll was one of these suitors. The other was Prince Gwawl. Now Prince Pwyll was exceedingly handsome, and so it happened, not unnaturally, that the Princess was madly in love with him. But Prince Gwawl was exceedingly rich and so it happened, not unnaturally, that the father of the princess decided that he should marry her. Or rather I should say, her father thought he had so decided—until the news was taken to the Princess, and she protested so strongly and pleaded so appealingly with her father that he quite changed his mind and announced a magnificent feast where Pwyll and Rhiannon were to be betrothed.

The feast was quite the happiest event in the whole life of the Princess, and there was much eating and drinking and merriment. And Pwyll had no doubt been drinking and eating and laughing as much as the rest when he suddenly noticed a stranger standing in front of his table. The stranger looked pale and poor and wretched.

' Gracious Prince,' said the stranger.

' Throw the beggar out,' cried one of the courtiers.

' Yes, get rid of him,' cried another.

' We don't want to see wretches like that at such times of merriment. Out with him.'

' Wait,' said Prince Pwyll. ' We must not be so uncharitable. What is it you want, stranger?'

' And if I tell you what I want, will you promise to give it to me?' said the stranger, in piteous tones.

' If it is in my power to give, surely I will give,' said the Prince.

' Aha,' said the stranger, and then and there he threw off his cloak and revealed himself as the rejected suitor, the rich Prince Gwawl. ' You promised, and everyone heard you promise. I want the hand in marriage of the beautiful Princess Rhiannon, and if you are a man of honour then surely you will give her to me.'

The Princess fainted away with horror and disappointment, and

42

the Prince had no alternative but to say, ' Truly, I promised you whatever you asked for, provided it was in my power to give. And as I am a man of honour I am trapped.'

And so another feast was planned for a week hence, at which the Princess was to be betrothed to Prince Gwawl. All that week the Princess was inconsolable; even though her father was full of high spirits and kept on saying to her, ' Really my dear, I cannot see why you make such a fuss. Gwawl may not be fantastically handsome, but I've seen worse, and even I wasn't much better looking when I married your dear mother. But he is quite stupendously rich, and believe me my dear, when you're as old as I am you'll know that riches last far longer than good looks.'

' Oh how ridiculous,' said the Princess. ' I shall never be as old as you are, and even if I were I would still remember how much I loved Prince Pwyll and how handsome he was.'

And so the week passed and the feast was all ready and all the nobles and their ladies gathered to witness the betrothal. And there was much drinking and eating and merriment and Prince Gwawl drank and ate quite as much as everybody else and so was feeling exceptionally happy when suddenly he saw a tramp standing in front of his table.

' Gracious Prince,' said the tramp.

' Throw him out,' cried the courtiers.

' How dare a tramp enter a festivity such as this?' cried one of the ladies.

And Prince Gwawl thought to himself, ' This must be a trap, like the trap wherein I caught poor Prince Pwyll.' But at that moment the beautiful Princess shouted out, ' Attendants. Throw out that wretched old tramp. How dare he spoil our celebrations with his wretched presence? Out with him. Off with his head.'

And so the Prince Gwawl thought again to himself, ' But if the fair Princess wants to be rid of him, then surely it cannot be a trap, so this will be a marvellous chance to show the court what a generous good-natured fellow I am.'

' No, wait,' he shouted. ' Do not throw him out. My dear,' he said to the Princess, ' what will our people think of us if we show no pity for this poor old tramp?'

' Very well,' said the Princess, smiling secretly to herself.

' Now then,' said the Prince, ' what do you want, my good man?'

' Food,' said the tramp, ' food enough to fill my poor sack here.'

' I knew it,' said the Prince. ' The poor man wants food for his sack, nothing else. Go take him into the kitchen and fill his sack until it is full, and then, my good man, you can tell all the people wherever you

go, how good and kind a man I am. You know who I am, don't you—
Prince Gwawl.' And so that there should be no mistake he spelt out
the name slowly to the tramp.

'Thank you, kind Prince,' said the tramp, 'and I promise I'll tell
all the people wherever I go, how good and kind you are.'

And with that the tramp went into the kitchen, taking his sack with
him.

'You see, my dear,' said the Prince, 'it always pays to be nice to
the poor. It does marvels for one's reputation.'

'How clever and wise you are,' said the Princess. 'How lucky I am
to have you for my husband.'

'Yes you are rather lucky,' said the Prince.

'Dear Prince,' called out the tramp, returning with his sack still
empty, 'I've just remembered. My sack is enchanted, and nothing
will go in it until a man of high birth has climbed inside it.'

'What nonsense,' said the Prince.

'No, 'tis true, I swear it,' said the beggar.

'Oh very well, one must humour these poor simple folk. I am of
exceptionally high birth, and I shall stand inside your sack and then
that will break the spell.'

'That's right, your Highness,' said the tramp. 'That would break
the spell most certainly.'

'It's all absolute nonsense, my dear, and you mustn't believe a word
of it,' said the Prince to the Princess, 'but it will impress the people,
and give me an even better reputation.' And with that he climbed into
the sack as the tramp held it open for him. And no sooner had he
done so than the tramp closed up the sack and lifted it high on to his
shoulders and shouted out, 'You made a fool of me last week, and
now I make a fool of you this. For I am Prince Pwyll, and unless you
agree to let me marry the beautiful Princess I shall take the sack and
you inside it and drop both into the river. And believe me, dear
Prince, I shall tie the sack so tight that the water will more quickly
get into it than you will ever get out of it.'

And the Princess clapped her hands with delight, the King, her
father, was greatly confused, and the unfortunate Prince Gwawl called
out, 'No, no, do not take me to the river. I beg of you. I surrender.
You can marry the fair Princess.'

And he did.

Adapted from *More Celtic Fairy Stories* by Joseph Jacobs 1894.

9 The Foolish Weaver

An Indian Folk Tale

There was once a young weaver who could find no place to work at his weaving, so he had to make up his mind to do any other kind of job that might come his way. He did not like the thought of this in the least because he enjoyed his weaving and he doubted very much whether he'd be the least bit of good at anything else. And years before, when his father had taught him the trade, he had said to the young weaver, 'Well now my son, at last you know something. Your mother and I were thinking that happy day would never come. For surely, you are the most simple-minded son two sensible and honest parents did ever produce.' So as I say, the weaver set forth to look for other work with very little faith in his heart. And in fact he went without work—and so, without wages—for a very long time until, one fine summer's day, a farmer took pity on him and said, 'Why, there must be some simple little job I can find for a young fellow like yourself, something that doesn't require too much in the way of brains, something where you just have to do what you're told. Now do you reckon you *can* do what you're told? Do you listen well? and can you remember things properly?' Naturally enough, the young weaver assured the farmer that he was very good at doing what he was told, and so the farmer gave him the job of minding the sheep. 'Now listen carefully,' said the farmer, 'if ever a tiger comes near the flocks, you just take a great big stone and you throw it at the tiger. That'll frighten him away. You understand?' The young weaver's face assumed a puzzled expression, just as it had done years before when his father had tried to explain to him the craft of weaving, or when his mother had tried to tell him the goods he was to buy for her from the market and how much he was to pay for them. So the farmer, being a patient and kindly person, said, 'Why now, young fellow, it couldn't be simpler. You know what a tiger is?' And the young weaver nodded. 'Well now, when you see a tiger coming near my sheep, you just pick up a good big stone, like this one here '—and the farmer picked up a big stone from the farmyard—' and you throw it at the tiger. You understand that now, don't you?' The young weaver smiled with delight. 'Yes, I understand that,' he said, and the farmer was delighted and the young weaver went up into the hills with the sheep, determined to guard them as carefully and as well as any sheep had ever

45

been guarded in all history.

Well it wasn't very long before the young weaver saw a tiger hiding in one of the bushes on the hillside, waiting to pounce on the poor, unsuspecting sheep. So without a moment's hesitation he ran for all he was worth back down the hill to the farmyard and looked for the very stone the farmer had picked up when he was explaining to the young weaver what he had to do. Needless to say by the time the young weaver had got back to the hill and to the sheep, the tiger had made off with several of them, and the stone was quite useless.

The farmer was furious, but being a kindly man, and an extremely patient one, he didn't do what most of us would have done—he did not sack the young weaver there and then. He determined to give him another chance. 'I can't think why I'm so good natured,' said the farmer sincerely, 'but my father is, and so was his father before him. And talking of father,' said the farmer, 'here's your next job.' And he took the young weaver into the garden at the back of the farm, and there, sleeping soundly, was the farmer's elderly father. He looked extremely contented, except when one of the flies—and there were many of them—landed on his nose, and then the father would grunt irritably in his sleep and he would try to flick the flies away. 'Well now,' said the farmer, 'your job could hardly be simpler: keep the flies off my father's face, so that he can sleep peacefully and not be disturbed in his old age.' No sooner had the farmer gone than a fly settled on the end of the old man's nose. Quick as lightning the young weaver ran into the farmyard and picked up the same stone that the farmer had used earlier to show him how to frighten tigers away. 'Now I shall be able to show the farmer that I know how to do what I'm told,' he said to himself proudly. And with that he ran back into the garden and hurled the stone at the fly, which was still passing the time away very contentedly on the end of the farmer's nose. As luck would have it—and it was very great luck, as I'm sure you'll agree—the stone missed both the fly and the old man's nose, but instead it went flying into the huge windows at the back of the farm house, smashed them completely and then made yet another explosive commotion as it came to ground inside the farmer's kitchen. The old man woke up with a start, and started to shout angrily and excitedly at the young weaver. The old man had never seen him before, and he was convinced he was one of those idle young ne'er-do-wells who like nothing better than going round the country, spoiling decent folks' property. 'I'll have the law on you,' he shouted, 'I'll have the law on you.'

The young weaver decided there was no time to stop and explain so he took to his heels and flew up the hillside and out of sight as

46

quickly as he could. And while he was running—and he had no idea now where he was, or how far he had journeyed—he saw four young men sitting by the wayside and looking very sad and sorry for themselves.

'And why do you look so sad and sorry for yourselves?' he asked them.

'Because we're four young weavers,' said one of them, 'and nobody will give us work to do.'

'Why then,' said our young weaver, still a little out of breath from having run so far and so hard, 'I'm a young weaver too, and if I may I'd like to join you. Then there'll be five young weavers instead of four. And who knows, maybe that'll bring us luck.'

'Truly,' said one of the four, 'five is a much luckier number than four. My grandmother always used to say so, and she was never wrong in such matters for she was the unluckiest person that was ever born.' And with that all their faces cheered up tremendously, and they went on their way, all five together, convinced that any moment now their luck would change and someone would offer them work.

But sadly enough, their luck didn't change at all, for they walked up hill and down dale and through this village and that, but they found no work. Eventually they sat down to think it out. 'Now how does it happen?' said one of them, 'there are five of us, and my grandmother always said that five was a lucky number, yet still our luck doesn't change.'

They thought about this for a minute or two.

Then our young weaver had a brilliant thought. 'But are you sure,' he said, 'that there are five of us?'

'But of course there are,' said another. 'There were four of us before you came. So now there must be five of us.'

'But let's be sure,' said another. 'Let's all count, and then we'll know definitely.'

And so they all counted up how many of them there were. And of course each of them forgot to count himself, so at the end of all this counting they all came to the conclusion that there were only four of them. 'But,' said our young weaver, 'when I first joined you, there were five of us. I'm sure of it.' And the others were sure of it too. 'So,' he said, 'somewhere, one of us must have got lost. We must have left him somewhere.'

'And,' said another, 'if we could only find him, then there would be five of us again, and then our luck would change.'

And so they went all over the hills looking for the weaver they thought they had left behind, and asking for him everywhere. And eventually they came to the very farm where our young weaver had

D

47

been working earlier, and although our young weaver was so busy looking for his lost friend that he did not recognise the farmer, the farmer very certainly recognised him.

'We're looking for a young weaver,' said one of them.

'Are you really?' said the farmer, 'and what does he look like?'

'We're not quite sure,' came the reply, 'but you see, when we set out on our travels there were five of us, and five is a lucky number. But now there are only four of us and we can't think where we've lost the other one.'

'And show me how you count, then,' said the farmer.

And they demonstrated how they counted, and again each of them forgot to count himself.

'Well now,' said the farmer, taking up a big stick he always kept handy in the farmyard, 'I think I can find the fifth one for you.' And they all assured him they'd be grateful to him for ever more if he only could. So the farmer struck the first weaver with the stick and said, 'There, Number One,' and striking each one in turn he quickly reached number five. The poor young weavers could not decide whether the surprise was greater than the hurt inflicted by the farmer with his stick. 'And perhaps you would like me to count you again, just to make sure,' said the farmer, but the weavers were sure enough, thank you very much and took to their heels as fast as they could. The farmer and his stick may have been a nasty experience, but at least there were five of them again, so now their luck was bound to change.

Adapted from *Folk Tales of the World* by Roger Lancelyn Green, Purnell 1966.

10 How Finn was Married

An Irish Folk Legend

Finn had long been in quest of a perfect wife when he saw the beautiful daughter of the King of Ciarra. He knew at once that she and she alone was the wife for him.

But she was so beautiful that every other prince in the land was in love with her, and she had rejected all of them. Some people said she was too proud ever to marry anyone. There was perhaps some truth in this, for it was announced at about this time that the Princess had devised a means of testing all her many suitors. There was a wide and deep cleft in the side of the mountain where her father's palace stood, and any man who wished to marry her had to jump across this cleft and land safely on the other side. If he failed in this, he would fall to his death. If he succeeded, she would marry him.

Naturally enough, this announcement had the effect of cutting down the list of suitors, but it didn't discourage Finn. He went to the mountainside to look at the cleft that he would have to jump, and he realised at once that there were few men in the entire world who could do it. He was about to inform the King that he wished to test his skill for the hand of his daughter, when there was a fanfare of trumpets and a great prince appeared, splendidly robed. He too was brave enough to dare try to leap the cleft and win the princess. Finn was furious with himself for not having come earlier. Suppose the prince should succeed: the princess would then be lost to him for ever. And certainly the prince looked splendid and bold as he walked over to the cleft and looked down and across it without any trace of nervousness. His numerous attendants meanwhile fussed around him, offering him encouragement and advice, and the Prince ran up and down and limbered his muscles in preparation for the great event.

A vast crowd gathered, and finally the Princess herself arrived. She was haughty and proud and magnificent, and Finn would have jumped across the ocean itself had she so requested.

' The Prince is ready,' said the King.

' Very good,' said the Princess.

And they gave her a special seat where she could see everything comfortably.

The Prince bowed to her. She smiled coldly back.

' Great and beautiful Princess,' he said, ' if I die, let it be known that I die bravely and gladly, seeking the love of the fairest maiden in the whole world.'

'Very good,' said the Princess, 'we shall let it be known, if you should happen to die, that you died gladly.'

'And if I live,' said the Prince, 'then I shall be the happiest man in the world.'

'No doubt,' said the Princess, who clearly was not much interested in speech-making.

'And now I shall leap the chasm,' said the Prince proudly.

'I hope you do,' said the Princess.

The Prince bowed again, and so did all his servants.

There was another fanfare of trumpets, and the Prince was about to make his great heroic bid for the hand of the Princess, when the King interrupted him, saying, 'Wait, wait, you mustn't jump yet. We must first have the names of your next of kin. We can't have you falling to your death without us knowing where to send the message of sympathy. Clerk, take down the names of his next of kin.'

This held up the proceedings for quite some time. For the Prince clearly came from a distinguished line, and the names of his parents were apparently quite long. Finn all this time found himself hoping, and yet not hoping, that the Prince would drop to his death, and so leave him the chance of winning the Princess.

And now another fanfare, and again the Prince bows to the Princess, who smiles coldly back, and again he runs boldly towards the cleft. The crowd gasp. Will he do it? Will he?

Not this time. The Prince stops, just before he reaches the edge, and walks back to the starting point.

'I'll do it this time,' he explains rather nervously to the Princess.

'I'm sure you will,' she replies.

Another fanfare, and off he goes again. The crowd gasp as before. Everyone is standing up to see what will happen—except for the Princess. Will he do it? Will he?

Not this time either.

'Dreadfully sorry, your Highness,' he explains, 'my foot slipped. Better luck next time, eh?'

'Truly.'

More preparation. More limbering up. Another fanfare. Another bow. And he's off again. Gasps. Expectancy. Everyone standing—except the Princess. Will he do it? Will he?

Unfortunately not. Too embarrassed to return to the Princess, he picks up his cloak, and his attendants bustle around him as he leaves the field.

'Are there any more contestants today?' asks the King.

Now it is his moment.

'Yes—me,' says Finn.

'You look an extremely poor contestant,' says the King. 'Most men who come in quest of my daughter are as rich and royal as she is, and their fine robes bear witness to it.'

'I'm poor,' says Finn, 'but I shall leap the chasm.'

And he looks at the Princess, and she is even more magnificent than he had first thought. And now she looks at him for the first time, and the coldness and the haughtiness and contempt vanish from her face.

'Are you ready then?' asks the King.

'I am,' says Finn.

'Your next of kin,' says the clerk. 'Give me their names and addresses.'

'I have no next of kin,' says Finn. 'If I die, that's that. You can forget all about me.'

And Finn prepared to take the leap, but then the Princess called out, 'Be careful. Be careful.'

She had never taken the least interest in any other of her suitors, and so this caused quite a sensation among the crowd.

'I shall be careful,' said Finn, looking calmly back at her.

'You do not have to take the test,' said the Princess, 'we could devise some other way of finding me a husband.'

'No. This is the test you laid down. This is the test I'll perform.'

And with that, while the crowd were deadly silent, Finn took a mighty leap and cleared the cleft easily and landed on the other side. The crowd cheered with delight.

'And now,' he cried out to the Princess, 'will you be my wife?'

'That I will,' replied the Princess, her face flushed with joy.

With that Finn did another mighty leap and was back on the other side.

'If you want me to, I'll do it all again.'

'No you won't,' said the Princess, 'now you're to be my husband, you'll need to take more care of yourself.'

And that's how Finn got married.

Adapted from *Finn and His Companions* by S. O'Grady 1892.

11 Sana, the Cowardly Prince

An Arabic Folk Tale

There are thousands and thousands of legends about princes, and almost all of them are princes who are strong and brave and did brave and wonderful things. This, however, is about a prince who was an absolute coward. But the one thing to be said in his defence, though perhaps you will disagree about this, was that he never made any bones about being a coward. ' I have not an ounce of courage in me,' said Prince Sana whenever anybody asked why he wasn't out killing dragons or giants and saving beautiful ladies in distress. At first nobody would believe him, for Prince Sana was as handsome as a prince should be, and his father was as brave a warrior as any king should be, but in time it became common knowledge, even among ordinary folk, that Prince Sana was just as big a coward as he had always said he was. Once, at a royal banquet for a visiting princess whom everybody hoped Sana would marry, a mouse was seen to run across one corner of the hall. Sana leapt on to the table and screamed for all he was worth until the mouse was out of sight. Then he was so pale and upset that he had to leave the table and go straight off to bed. Before he did so he doubled the number of guards posted at his bedroom door, in case the mouse should in some way manage to get from the ground floor banqueting hall to his magnificent bedroom at the top of the tallest turret in the castle. The Princess was scandalised that Prince Sana was such a coward and walked out in a great huff, and all her attendants, of course, had to follow her. And that was the end of any plans for marriage.

Eventually the situation grew desperate, for Prince Sana, though as handsome as ever, was known for miles around for his lack of courage, and so no self-respecting princess would ever consider marrying him. ' There's nothing for it,' said his father, ' but to send you far, far away, where nobody knows of your cowardice, and to give you so many rich and wonderful presents that any king would be only too pleased to marry you to his daughter.' Immediately Sana fainted away, for fear of having to travel such a great distance. ' But father,' he protested the following morning, when he had more or less revived, ' just think of all the dreadful things that may happen to me on the way. Think what all those foreigners may do to me.'

' I know,' said the King, ' but I have guarded against that. I am

52

sending an entire regiment of my army to watch over you. Nearly a thousand of the best soldiers in the land.'

'What,' said Sana, turning pale, 'only a thousand? But suppose there are more than a thousand foreigners, then they would outnumber us.'

'A good point,' said the King. 'According to my magicians, there are likely to be several thousand foreigners, if not more, dotted about all over the world. One of my magicians even went so far as to claim that once you leave the country you'll never be free of them. Of course I don't doubt that he was exaggerating, you know what these magicians are, but there may be some truth in it.' And with that he doubled the number of soldiers that were to accompany Sana on his journey. Sana remained extremely pale, and in the following weeks he lost a little weight—though not much, for he was a passionate eater. When it came to the day of departure, Sana said to the King: 'Father, I should feel much happier if everyone were to come on my journey with me.'

'Everyone?' said the King.

'Yes,' said the Prince. 'All your subjects. Every single one of them. Then I would feel much safer. I might even get some sleep on the way.'

'What nonsense,' said the King, who decided that enough was enough. And so, full of fears and apprehensions, Prince Sana went on his long journey in quest of a distant land where news of his cowardice had never reached.

And happily enough, he did find such a land, and he did marry a beautiful princess who was overwhelmed with his fine good looks and whose parents were delighted with the great riches he brought her. And Sana lived in this foreign land and loved his princess very much and was quite remarkably happy until one dreadful day the country was attacked by a band of awful brigands.

'Oh how happy I am,' said the Princess as she told Sana the news.

'Why on earth should you be happy?' said Sana.

'Because now you can lead our men into battle, and you will prove how brave you are, and how worthy to be a prince and to be my husband.'

'But my dear wife,' said Sana, already beginning to turn pale, 'I am an absolute coward. I could no more lead soldiers into battle than I could turn fire into water.'

The Princess smiled. 'Oh what a jester you are. How you love to tease me with your jokes.'

'But I assure you,' said Sana, 'I've never been more serious in all my life. I am a coward. I always have been.'

'You mean, you won't go to lead our soldiers against these brigands?'

'I'm sorry, my dear, but it's out of the question.'

'Oh the disgrace,' said the Princess, 'oh the shame of it. I shall be the laughing stock of all the world.'

'Well I'm terribly sorry my dear,' said Sana, 'but there's nothing I can do about it. I wish there was.'

'But there's something *I* can do about it,' said the Princess. And without more ado, she dressed herself in the armour that the Prince should have worn, and went out to battle carrying the Prince's standard just as if she were the Prince himself. And hidden beneath all this armour she was impossible to recognise. And she fought like six brave princes rolled into one, and when she got home to the palace the Prince was hailed as the bravest prince in all history.

A week later the brigands, who were a bloodthirsty lot who could never get enough fighting to satisfy them, demanded another battle, and again Sana declared he could not go, and again the Princess went in his place. And when she came back the people sang the praises of their courageous Prince. But unfortunately the Princess was injured that time in her right arm and it was not possible for her to go to battle yet again the following week when the brigands demanded their third and final battle.

'This time you really must go,' said the Princess.

'It's impossible,' said Sana.

'But if you really loved me, you would go,' said the Princess trying to be clever.

'My dear, it's nothing to do with love,' said Sana, 'it's all to do with courage, and I have none of it.'

And they had a great argument there and then, or at least the Princess tried to have one, but Sana remained quite unconcerned. At length the Princess calmed down.

'I have a very clever idea,' said the Princess.

'I knew you would have,' said Sana.

'Now listen very carefully. You don't mind riding a horse, I take it.'

'Not if it's very old and can't move very far or very fast,' replied Sana.

'Very well then, I shall find the oldest horse in the country. You will put on the armour, and you will ride the horse at the head of the army, and then, when you are leaving the city I shall pretend to be seriously ill, and send a messenger after you to bring you back, and then my younger brother will have to lead the army in your place. That way you shall be safe and we will both keep our honour and our good name. Do you agree?'

Sana was reluctant at first, but being a good-natured Prince, always willing to oblige any one, and especially his beautiful Princess, he agreed. And so he put on the armour and rode out of the city at the head of the army, cheerfully patting his dear old horse on the neck to keep him steady.

But as you have already guessed, the Princess had not given him an old horse but a very lively and quite young one who had often ridden into battle before. And when the messenger came riding up to the Prince as he was reaching the outskirts of the city he did not bring any message about the Princess. Instead he lifted a trumpet to his mouth and blew three fierce and warlike blasts, which was a cue for all the horses to charge for all their worth and not to stop until they'd reached the enemy. So the Prince found himself carried forward at the head of the army right into the very encampment of the villainous brigands. And since the Prince had never before ridden any but the oldest and weakest of horses, he could think of nothing to do but to hold on tight and close his eyes and pray. And so instead of drawing his horse to a halt as they approached the brigands, he rode straight on at them. The army, being loyal and brave and true, had no alternative but to follow him. The enemy were so terrified when they saw this mad horseman lead the army right down into their very ranks that they turned and fled as fast as their legs could carry them.

And so it happened that Prince Sana was declared the bravest Prince that ever was. His father-in-law retired to lead a quiet life in the country, and Sana became King. The Princess was overjoyed.

'You see,' she said, 'you really are brave, and you only needed the chance to prove it.'

'No,' said Sana, 'you can deceive men, but you can't deceive the Gods. I am the biggest coward that ever was.' And with that he cried out in such alarm that every attendant and every soldier in the palace came running in to see what was the matter. And there was Prince Sana swinging from the chandelier, his face as white as a sheet, and there in the corner, not quite sure what he was doing or where he was going, was a mouse.

Adapted from ' The Coward ' in *Folk Tales of the World* by Roger Lancelyn Green, Purnell 1966.

Group II

Older Junior and Younger Secondary

12 The Peasant and his Mother-in-Law

A Russian Folk Tale

Not so very long ago there was a young Russian peasant whose name, not surprisingly, was Ivan Ivanovitch. Now Ivan Ivanovitch was a good hard-working man and he looked after his wife and his two children, and he never grumbled and he hardly ever sulked or showed off. And in fact, he was near perfect as you could ever ask anyone to be. So you would expect his wife to be grateful to him, and to treat him well and try to keep him happy. But his wife did nothing of the kind. She never stopped grumbling and sulking, and criticising him and telling him off. If he worked twelve hours in the field she'd say he neglected his wife and children. If he worked eleven hours the next day, she'd say he didn't work hard enough, and that before the year was out he'd surely leave his wife and children to go hungry. There was no pleasing her, and for miles around the peasant's wife was known as the shrew, and tales were told about her by mothers to their sons, to warn them of the consequences of a careless marriage.

But sadly enough, the shrewish wife was only half our peasant's troubles. For the wife's mother was even more of a battle-axe, and every week the peasant had to take the long walk through the forest to take a present to her. These presents were always food of some kind, a partridge, perhaps, or a wild fowl, that the peasant had shot down while hunting. And though he never was fond of his nagging mother-in-law, indeed she never once said thank you for his presents nor made him feel at home after his long journey through the forest, he never once complained or refused to go. Nor did he answer back when his mother-in-law grumbled at him, as she always did: ' I cannot for the life of me imagine how a girl like mine, who could have married the richest and the handsomest man in all the Russias, if she'd so wished, should disgrace herself with marrying a penniless, ugly rascal like yourself. What a grief for my old age, what a grief for my old age.' And she'd be saying this while she took the present from him and her mouth fairly watered at the delicious thought of cooking it and eating it. Then ' Off with you,' she'd cry, ' you lazy good-fornothing.' And the peasant would bow humbly and take his leave. ' For it is true enough,' he would say to himself, ' my wife is a beautiful creature, even though she does tend to be a nagger, and if she had so wished, she could probably have married the richest and the handsomest man in all the Russias. And yet she married me, who's neither rich nor handsome. Poor woman. How it must grieve her poor mother. Poor woman.' And he could never make up his mind which one he felt the more sorry for: the wife, who'd given up all her fine chances to marry him, or the mother-in-law who'd witnessed her daughter's downfall. And when he got home from his long journey, the wife would take up the same tune as her mother: ' And why has it taken you so long, you wicked man, to walk through the forest? I know what you've been up to, so don't start making excuses. Ah, why did I ever marry such a worthless man? And why did I not listen to my poor dear mother who warned me how bad it would be?'

But one fine day, things changed, for ever. And this is how it happened:

While he was out one Saturday morning, hunting for a gift to take to his mother-in-law, the peasant saw a magnificent crane sitting on the branch of a tree. The bird seemed too good to kill, but it had to be done, so the peasant took aim and was about to shoot when the crane suddenly called out to the peasant, ' Don't shoot me, please don't shoot me.'

The peasant was so surprised to hear a crane talking that he could think of nothing to say.

' If you don't shoot me,' said the crane, ' I will do you a great favour. The greatest favour you could ever wish for.'

' Well,' said the peasant, slowly collecting his thoughts, ' I hate killing anything at any time, specially a magnificent-looking creature like yourself.' And with that, he put down his gun and said, ' Ah well, I suppose I'll just have to tell my mother-in-law that the forest was empty. I dread to think what she'll say, but she's said plenty of things before now, and I'm not dead yet, so I daresay I'll survive this one too.' And he turned to go.

' No, don't go,' said the crane. ' Didn't I promise you a great favour if you spared my life? Well, I'm not the sort of crane who makes a promise and then breaks it. Here. Here's the favour, the greatest you could wish.' And before the peasant knew what was happening, there at his feet was a great big carpet-bag.

' Well, thank you very much indeed,' said the peasant. ' I don't really need a carpet-bag just at this moment, but I'll take it home with me, and no doubt it will come in useful some time or other.' But the crane walked over to the bag and called out, ' Fie, fum, diddly dum, Chief Cook and Head Waiter, both, out you come.' Whereupon the bag opened up and out stepped a fine-looking Chief Cook and an equally impressive Head Waiter, and they proceeded to lay a magnificent table in front of the peasant and to serve him the best meal

60

he'd ever had in all his life.

The peasant was highly impressed, and thanking the crane many times over for this magnificent present, he told the cook and the waiter to put everything, including themselves, back in the bag, and off he went to his mother-in-law's. Needless to say, she scowled when she saw him. ' Don't you bring any grubby old carpet-bags in my house,' she said.

' But, dear mother-in-law,' he said, ' this is a very special carpet-bag. Watch.' And with that he set the bag down, and called out:

> ' Fie fum diddly dum,
>   Chief Cook and Head Waiter, both,
>   Out you come.'

And sure enough, the cook and the waiter leapt out of the bag and proceeded to lay the table for the mother-in-law and to serve her the most delicious meal she had ever tasted. The mother-in-law was over-come with delight. ' What a marvellous carpet-bag,' she said. ' And what a marvellous son-in-law you are,' she said, ' to bring me all these wonderful presents. Oh I do appreciate you,' she said, ' for you're the finest son-in-law in all the world, and I'm always telling my daughter how clever she was, and how lucky she was, to marry you.' And with that she even kissed him, very lightly, and very quickly, on the left cheek. The peasant was overcome. ' And now, while I'm finishing off my meal,' she said, ' you must be tired out from your long journey through the forest, so why don't you go to the wash-house and give yourself a nice fresh bath? I've just had a lovely new copper bath put in, the very latest model, the only one you'll find in any house this side of Petersburg. It won't take you long to boil up the water.' The peasant said he'd be delighted, for he'd never had a bath before in a brand new copper bath, and he didn't doubt that he'd be the first peasant ever to do so. And just as he was going, his mother-in-law called out, ' But tell me, my dear, when you want to put away your chief cook and your head waiter, what do you have to do?'

' Oh, there's nothing to it,' said the peasant, ' you just tell them to go back.'

And with that he went out to the wash-house and boiled himself ten buckets of water and admired the beautiful new copper bath before climbing into it and scrubbing himself as clean as a new pin. And he was as happy as any man could ever be, for now that he had the crane's magic carpet-bag he need never worry again about feed-ing his wife and his mother-in-law and his children. And he lay in the beautiful copper-bath singing to himself,

61

> ' Fie fum diddly dum,
> Chief Cook and Head Waiter, both,
> Out you come.'

But while he was in the beautiful copper-bath the mother-in-law went up into the loft of her house and found an old carpet-bag that looked exactly the same as the magic one. So after telling the cook and the waiter to get back in the magic bag she put it away and left the old and useless one in its place. And when the peasant came back from his marvellous bath, for which he thanked her a thousand times, the mother-in-law gave him the old bag and sent him on his way. When he got back home to his wife she told him off in no uncertain terms for being so late. ' But my dear wife,' he said, ' a most wonderful thing happened to me today,' and with that he told her all about the crane and the magic bag. ' What nonsense,' said the wife, ' to think I've been married all these years to a man who isn't only a lazy good-for-nothing, but a raving idiot as well. What have I done to deserve it, what have I done to deserve it?'

' But it's true,' said the peasant, when he was at last able to get a word in edgeways, and with that he put down the old bag and called out to it,

> ' Fie fum diddly dum,
> Chief Cook and Head Waiter, both,
> Out you come.'

And of course nothing whatsoever happened.

' There, what did I say?' said the wife. ' I've married a total nincompoop. Why did I never listen to my poor dear mother? Why did I never listen?'

But the next day, when the peasant was on his way to church, he saw the crane again in the forest.

' Never mind,' said the crane, ' I haven't forgotten you and the good turn you did for me. Here's another favour for you,' and with that the crane placed in front of him, another carpet-bag, very similar to the other one.

' And what does this do?' said the peasant.

' Look,' said the crane.

And the crane called out,

> ' Hi, ho, riddle de ree
> Beat as hard as hard can be.'

And two enormous sticks came out and started beating the peasant for all their might.

'And when you want them to go back,' said the crane, 'you just call out,

> 'Hi ho, re mi doh
> Into the bag, now, both of you go.'

And with that the two sticks jumped back into the bag and the crane was gone.

But the peasant needed no one to tell him what to do next.

'Dear mother-in-law,' he cried, as he stood at her doorstep later that morning.

'And what do you want, troubling me on the Sabbath Day like this? Off with you,' she called from her upstairs window, for she feared he might have come back to have his revenge on her for taking his magic bag.

'Dear mother-in-law,' he said, 'I've brought you another present. Since you liked the other bag so much, I thought this might please you also.'

And with that she cast covetous eyes on the bag he was now holding.

'I'll be down, dear son-in-law,' she said, 'don't move, don't go away. I'll be straight down.'

And within seconds she was at his side.

'It looks a very ordinary bag, dear son-in-law, but then so did the other one.'

'Just watch,' said the peasant.

And he called out,

> 'Hi, ho, riddle de ree
> Beat as hard as hard can be.'

And the two sticks leapt out of the bag and started beating the mother-in-law for all their worth. And while they were at their task, the peasant went into the house, looked for the other magic bag, found it, had another hot bath in the copper bath, and eventually went out back to his mother-in-law.

> 'Hi, ho, re mi doh
> Into the bag, now, both of you go.'

The sticks did as they were told.

'And now, dear mother-in-law, I must be getting back to your dear and lovely daughter. I love her just as I respect you, but she too has a lesson to learn, and it's high time she learnt it.'

And he made his way, with both his magic bags, back to his wife.

'And what's this you're bringing into the house now?' said the wife. 'More such nonsense—and on the Sabbath Day too. What have I done to deserve such a husband? Oh why did I never listen to my dear mother? Why did I never listen to my dear mother?'

And the peasant put down the two bags and he called out,

> 'Hi, ho, riddle de ree
> Beat as hard as hard can be.'

And the two sticks leapt out and started beating the wife, until she called to her husband, 'Oh dear husband,' she cried, 'save me from this terrible beating.'

'And if I do,' said the peasant, 'do you promise never to nag me again?'

'Yes, I do,' said the wife.

'Your word of honour?'

'My word of honour.'

And the peasant called out the magic words and the sticks went back into the bag and that was that.

Then the peasant decided that one week-end of magic was quite enough in anyone's life, so he took the two bags back into the forest and left them where he had met the crane.

And as for the wife, she never nagged her husband again.

And as for the mother-in-law, she spent the rest of her days telling her neighbours how clever she had been to find such a wonderful husband for her daughter.

And as for the crane, neither he nor his magic carpet-bags were ever seen again.

Adapted from 'The Wishing Table, the Golden Ass and the Cudgel,' by Grimm, and from a Russian variation.

13 Urashima the Fisherman

A Japanese Folk Tale

The young fisherman Urashima was coming home from work one evening when he saw a crowd of youngsters beating the shell of a turtle. The poor creature could not have survived much longer, for though its shell was tough the youngsters were merciless and were beating it for all they were worth, and laughing as they did so. 'But it is wrong to hit those who cannot hit you back,' said Urashima. 'You must stop your wickedness immediately.'

But the youngsters only laughed the more and carried on beating the turtle.

'What would your parents think of you if they could see you now?' said Urashima, but even this made no effect upon them.

'Very well then,' he said, 'if I give you money, then will you stop?'

'Money?' said one of them. 'How much money?'

'As much as I can afford,' said Urashima.

'How much is that? Is it enough to compensate us for having our fun spoiled?'

'A strange idea you have of fun, I must say. But here—this is all I have with me,' and so saying, he gave them all the money, and it was not much, that he had made from selling the fish he had caught that day.

'Very good—now you can have your stupid old turtle, and much good may he do you,' said one of the youths.

'He must be a little mad to think an old turtle worth all his hard-earned money,' said another.

And they left Urashima, and went off to spend the money he had paid them.

'Come, you must be too weak and upset to make your own way back to the seashore, come, let me carry you,' said Urashima to the turtle. 'It's dreadful what some people will do to poor animals—quite apart from what they will do to each other. But you must not imagine,' said Urashima to the turtle, 'that all of us are as bad as the rest.'

And he carried the turtle down to the sea and placed him carefully down into the water.

'Now another time,' he told the turtle, 'remember to keep to the water, that's where you belong, just as I belong to the land. Remember what I say—for another time I may not be here to help you out.'

And with that the turtle swam out into the sea and Urashima went home and went early to bed, as he usually did, so that he should be up again first thing next morning.

But the following day when he was out fishing, the same turtle came swimming up alongside his little fishing boat.

' Do you remember me?' said the turtle.

' I do indeed,' said Urashima, ' but I never expected to see you again. And I had no idea you could speak. You said nothing yesterday.'

' Today I have been given special permission to speak, by my mistress, the Dragon Princess.'

' I have heard a great deal about the Dragon Princess,' said Urashima, ' about how beautiful she is and how kind, but she lives in her magnificent palace at the very bottom of the deepest sea, and so, naturally enough, I never thought to meet anyone who knew her.'

' The Princess was most impressed when I told her how kind you had been to me, and how you saved my life. And she wishes to meet you.'

' Is such a thing possible?' asked Urashima, greatly interested.

' If you are willing to come with me, to her palace beneath the sea? If you are not afraid then I can take you to her. You will be quite safe. I shall make sure that you come to no harm.'

' I am a little afraid, to be quite honest,' said Urashima, ' and I'd be a terrible liar if I were to pretend otherwise. But I've heard so much about the Dragon Princess, and I would dearly like to see her for myself. Just think, I would then be the only man for miles and miles around actually to have met her. Now there's something for me to tell my grandchildren.'

' Then you will come?' asked the turtle.

Without saying another word, Urashima climbed out of his fishing boat and on to the turtle's back, and away they both went, out far away from the shore. Then, when the land was right out of sight, the turtle called out to him, ' Now hold on tight, and trust in me.' And the turtle dived down beneath the waves, with Urashima holding tightly to him, and down and down they went, so far that Urashima could not believe that the sea was anywhere so deep. And then he saw the palace. It was more beautiful than he had ever imagined or men had ever said. And when he got down from the turtle's back and an attendant called out his name, Urashima found that although he was deep beneath the sea he could breathe as freely as if he were on the land, and that although he had travelled a great distance with the turtle he did not feel in the least tired or exhausted. But all this surprise was nothing compared with the surprise when he saw the Dragon Princess, for he had never seen anything anywhere so lovely. Not only that, but she was clearly so good-natured and pleasant, and easy to talk to. He had expected to be shy and clumsy—a mere fisherman meeting a princess, but instead he found himself completely at ease and relaxed.

'It was brave of you to come,' said the Princess, 'but then it was brave of you to rescue the turtle. And like you said, it was really his own fault for wandering up on to the shore where he does not belong. The sea is his rightful element, and there he should always stay.'

She showed Urashima all over the palace, and he marvelled at the great size of the building, and the exquisite rooms that stretched mile upon mile along endless corridors. And then when he had seen all the palace, the Princess took him out into the sea itself, and showed him the great and beautiful colours of the sea, and showed him how the seasons change beneath the sea just as they do upon the land. And indeed there were so many wonders for Urashima to behold that he almost forgot the little village from which he had come, and his parents and his brothers and sisters. But not completely, for one day he said to the Princess: 'It seems such a long time since I last saw my people. I must go back to let them know how well I am, and how happy I am. They are sure to be worrying about me.'

The Princess was not at all keen for him to return, and urged him to stay a little longer. She used every possible argument to convince him that his home and his family were all quite safe, but still he insisted on going to them. 'I shall return, Princess, I promise you that. Nothing could ever keep me there for ever.'

'Very well then, before you go,' said the Princess, 'you must accept this little present from me. You must keep it with you always. It will protect you from all harm, and it will make sure you come back safely to me when your purpose is accomplished.'

And with that she gave him a very small box, beautifully lacquered and exquisitely painted.

'I shall keep this with me always, until I come back to you,' said Urashima, taking the box.

'But you must promise me that you will never, whatever may happen, open the box.'

'Yes, I promise,' said Urashima.

'And remember what you said, you will return to me when you have seen your old home again,' said the Princess.

And so it happened that one of the Princess's attendants—another turtle—delivered Urashima back to the shore, and he ran joyfully up on to the beach, leaving the turtle to swim away back into the sea.

Urashima was even more pleased than he had expected to be back once more upon the land, but as he looked about him he remembered how foolish he had been to let the turtle go without asking him where this place was. For it certainly was not the village where his family lived. In fact, it must have been a long way from his home, and probably some foreign country. For Urashima had never seen such a strange collection of buildings, and as he peered up at them a crowd of people gathered, all dressed in the strangest of clothes. When he called to them they cried out in alarm and first moved away and then ran away from him. Only one remained, a very small old lady, who looked as though she was too tired to be scared of anyone or to run away.

'Good lady,' said Urashima, 'please tell me where I am. I was hoping to find the little village that I left a few months ago, but this is a strange place to me, and I cannot think where I am.'

'This is the town of Urashima,' said the old lady. 'Have you never heard of it?'

Urashima was amazed to hear of a town that had the same name as himself.

'What an extraordinary thing,' he said, 'I never heard of a town with such a name.'

'Well it's had that name for over three hundred years, ever since a young fisherman was enchanted away from his little fishing boat and went to live with the Dragon Princess beneath the sea. And his name was Urashima, and so, when the village grew into a fine big town like it is now, they called the town after him, as a warning no doubt to other young men.'

'Warning? What kind of warning?'

'Why—a warning to stay where you belong and not to go seeking danger where you have no business to go. That's the way parents always end the story when they tell it to their children.'

'And did all this really happen three hundred years ago?' asked Urashima.

'Who knows? Perhaps there is not really a Dragon Princess and perhaps the poor young man just fell into the sea and was drowned. But it is certain there was such a man for my grandparents were told by their grandparents who were told by their grandparents who were told by their grandparents, who actually knew the young man, and who looked after the fisherman's mother as she lay dying from grief.'

And seeing the great sorrow that had come into the eyes of Urashima, the old lady said to him, 'It is a sad story, is it not?'

'It is indeed,' he replied, and truly it seemed to the young fisherman that there was nothing left for him in life now. He had lived so far beyond the years by rights allotted him, and had brought such cruel grief to his poor dead mother whom he had always sworn to care for and protect in her old age, that he could see no joy in anything now.

'Here,' he said to the old lady, 'you have been good to me, and dared to stay and talk with me when all the others ran away. You remind me of another old lady whom once I ran away from, without meaning to. This is the only gift I can offer you, but please, accept it from me.'

And so saying, he gave her the lacquered box that the Dragon Princess had given him and the old lady gasped to see how finely it was made. But by the time she had thought to thank him, Urashima had wandered back down to the shore, and stood there looking out at the sea, and thinking of the time that had passed while he wandered through the rooms of the Princess's palace and marvelled at the beauty of the world beneath the sea. And still the old lady looked admiringly at the box the stranger had given her, and when her friends came back to hear what conversation she'd had with the stranger, she told them, 'Look. This is what he gave me. Although he was so oddly dressed, he was a very pleasant and good-natured young gentleman—and this is what he gave me.'

'It's a beautiful box,' said one of them, 'perhaps there is something of great value and beauty inside it.'

'Open it,' said another.

'Yes, open it,' they all cried.

And the old lady opened the box, and as she did so a very thin wisp of smoke floated up out of it, but no one noticed it, and there was nothing else in the box.

'But it's empty,' they all said. 'What a silly gift—a box with nothing it it.'

'Not in the least,' said the old lady, 'it is a beautiful box, and I am just as pleased that it is empty as if it had been full of gold. I shall treasure it always. And so shall my children after me.'

But down on the shore, just as the old lady opened the box, Urashima suddenly weakened, and stumbled and fell towards the waves. His body grew old, very, very, old, in just a few seconds, and his face wrinkled and the strength fled from him. And as the waves lifted him and carried him out into the sea, he was already dead. For the box that the Dragon Princess had given him, contained the spirit of his youth, which now was gone for ever.

Adapted from the story in *The Japanese Fairy Book* compiled by Yei Theodora Ozaki 1903.

69

14 Jack Frost and the Sisters

A Russian Folk Story

There was once a peasant-woman who worshipped her two daughters but despised her step-daughter, whose name was Mara. Perhaps one of the reasons why she felt so ill-disposed to Mara was that her step-daughter was extremely beautiful, while her own two daughters were exceedingly plain.

She made Mara do all the work about the house: she had to get up early in the morning to light the fires and to get breakfast ready for all the family, and if there was any outing or social occasion Mara was always left out of it.

One day the peasant-woman said to her husband, 'It is time for our daughters to marry. Fanny is eighteen and Annie is nineteen and all the boys in the village have been making eyes at them for I don't know how long. There'll be no difficulty finding them good husbands, for they're wonderful creatures both of them, as lovely in character as they are in person.'

Neither Fanny nor Annie believed this, for although their mother was foolish, they were themselves sensible and knew very well that whatever virtues they might or might not possess, neither of them was beautiful.

'It's not true, Mother,' said Fanny, 'we're not wonderful creatures like you say we are, and the boys haven't been making eyes at us, not that I've ever seen. It's Mara the boys all look at.'

'Don't talk such silliness,' said the mother. 'As though any self-respecting boy would look at a plain thing like Mara here.'

'Plenty of them do,' said Annie.

'I don't believe it,' said the mother. 'But like I said, it's time our Annie and our Fanny here were getting wed, and so I think you ought to tell them what dowry you'll give them.'

'There'll be no dowry for Fanny or Annie until our Mara finds a husband,' said the father. 'She's the oldest, and the oldest must be married first. She's twenty and not until she's wed can Fanny or Annie even think of getting married.'

'But who'll ever marry Mara? No decent class of person would. And if she married a beggar off the streets that would bring shame on her dear lovely sisters.'

'I don't care who she marries, but she's got to get married first. It's traditional.'

' Oh dear,' said the mother.

' Yes, it's traditional,' repeated the father, and with that he made his way off to work.

' Oh dear, as soon as your father says a thing is traditional then that's that. He'll never break a tradition, not your father. Never has, never will.'

' Surely someone will marry our Mara,' said Annie.

' Anyone will do,' said Fanny.

' Doesn't matter how old he is,' said Annie.

' Oh no,' said Fanny.

' Of course it doesn't,' said the mother, ' anyone's good enough for her.'

Mara meanwhile had said nothing and been asked to say nothing. But for all that, she must have overheard the conversation for she was waiting on them all the while and serving them their breakfast.

' And she's going off to find herself a husband this very day,' said the mother.

' Today?' said Fanny.

' So soon?' said Annie.

' Mustn't waste a second, my girls. By the time poor Mara here has found herself a man, why, the bloom of your youth will have faded.'

The thought of this made all three very sad.

' I'd hate the bloom of my youth to fade,' said Annie.

' Me too,' said Fanny.

' All blooms fade eventually,' said the mother philosophically, ' mine faded long ago.'

' Oh Mum, what a shame,' said Annie and Fanny together.

' But I'd found a husband by that time, so it didn't matter.'

' What a blessing,' said Annie.

' Wouldn't it be awful,' said Fanny, ' if our bloom faded before we'd found a husband?'

' That won't happen, my girls. Now then, Mara, put on this cloak. Wrap it around you. Say good-bye to your pretty sisters for you're never going to see them again.'

' Won't she?' said Fanny.

' Then who'll do the work around the house?'

' You will, the pair of you, until you get married,' said the mother.

' Where am I going?' asked Mara.

' Listen to the child. Just listen to her. The way I've looked after her and cared for her all these years, now she wants to know where she's going. What impudence.'

' But where is she going?' asked Fanny.

' I'm taking her over the hill, right out into the countryside. And there I'm leaving her.'

'But it's the middle of winter, dear mother,' said Fanny, 'and the snow's a foot thick. She'll catch the death of cold.'

'Well, either she catches that, or she catches a husband. I don't mind which. Either way, your father then can't stop the two of you from getting married, and that's all I'm interested in.'

And so she took Mara from the house and led her up over the hill and into the countryside. It was freezing cold and the snow was just as thick as Fanny had said.

'There you are, child,' said the mother harshly, 'you can stand just here and wait. Some folks say you're pretty. If you are, then no doubt Jack Frost himself will come along and marry you.'

And so she left her. Mara called out to her, begging for mercy, but the mother paid no attention.

'If you don't stay where you are, I'll tell folks you're a witch, and then they'll come and burn you. You just see if they don't.'

The following morning, the mother said, 'Well Father, your daughter Mara went off yesterday and found a husband. A farmer's son who lives over the hill.'

'Good,' said the father, who wasn't much interested. 'I'm glad to hear it.'

'Now we can think about getting Fanny and Annie married,' she said.

'I suppose so,' he replied, without enthusiasm.

'All the boys in the village will be queueing up for my two girls, you just see if they don't.'

'Mm,' said the father, concentrating on eating his breakfast.

'I think Fanny ought to marry a rich farmer, and Annie ought to marry a lord.'

'I don't think any rich farmer would want to marry me,' said Fanny.

'And I can't imagine any lord wanting to marry me,' said Annie.

'We just want a man who'll look after us properly,' they both said, realistically.

'It'll be a rich farmer for you, my dear, and a lord for you. Nothing less will do.'

'I had my eye on young Boris,' said Fanny.

'Never,' said her mother, 'he's just a silly peasant.'

'And I like young Rudolf,' said Annie.

'And he's an even sillier peasant than Boris, I wouldn't hear of it,' said their mother.

At that moment a neighbour came rushing to their door.

'Have you heard the news?' said she.

72

'What news?' said the mother.

'About your Mara.'

'What about her?' asked the mother.

'She's married a prince.'

'I don't believe it.'

'Believe it or not, it's the truth, the whole truth and nothing but the truth.'

'Then tell us all about it.'

The neighbour, unfortunately, was one of those people who cannot tell a story without going all the way round the houses and back again before they get to the point of it. But in the end, they all understood what had happened.

Mara had stood in the snow, just as her mother had left her, and within five minutes who should come along but a fine, handsome prince, who asked her why she was waiting there cold and lonely. He was so impressed by her beauty and fine character that he fell in love with her there and then, begged her to marry him, and took her straight back to his palace to get his parents' permission. No sooner was this permission given than Mara and the prince were married.

'So Mara's a princess, and one day she'll be a queen,' ended the neighbour at long last.

'Well you took a mighty long time telling the story, and you went a very long way as well, but it was worth telling for all that,' said the mother. And then, turning to Fanny and Annie, she said, 'Right, my girls. What's good enough for Mara is good enough for you. Put on your hat and coat, both of you, we're going out.'

And so, despite their protests, she led both her daughters to the very same spot where she had left Mara the previous day.

'You wait here, both of you. And before five minutes are out, there'll be handsome princes come along and marry you. Just like it happened to Mara. You wait and see.'

Both Fanny and Annie protested vigorously, but their mother would not listen to them. Off she went.

Five hours later, Fanny and Annie had seen no princes, but they were both exceedingly cold.

'Oh Fanny,' said Annie.

'Oh Annie,' said Fanny.

'I'm cold.'

'I'm freezing.'

'I'm frozen.'

'I'm going.'

'So am I.'

'Our mother's got no sense.'

73

'None at all.'

'As though princes come riding this way every day.'

'As though they'd want to marry us even if they did.'

Then who should they see running towards them but Boris and Rudolf.

'We heard you're looking for husbands,' they said. 'Will you take us?'

'Our mother doesn't think you're good enough for us,' said Fanny.

'She thinks there's a couple of princes going to ride over the hill and take us off with them to some great big beautiful palace,' said Annie.

'That's what your mother thinks,' said Boris and Rudolf, 'but what do you think?'

'We think,' said Fanny and Annie, smiling, 'our mother has no sense.'

And so Fanny married Boris, and Annie married Rudolf, and the last we heard of them, they were happy with their husbands, just as Mara was happy with her prince.

Adapted from *Russian Fairy Tales* by W. R. Ralston 1873.

15 Robin Hood and the King

An English Folk Tale

'Go now,' said Robin Hood to his men, 'and bring me a guest for our dinner table.' For it was the custom of Robin Hood and his Merry Men that they would not sit down to dinner without a guest to share their meal with. The men would seize the first stranger they could find, and if he was a poor man then he would have his dinner for free, and if he were a rich man then he would pay enough—or be made to pay enough—to feed not only himself but Robin Hood and all the men as well.

And so Little John led the men from their hideout in the forest and out on to the highway, and the first people they saw were a small group of monks.

'Good day to you, good Holy Fathers,' cried Little John.

The monks looked apprehensively at the tall monk who was leading them and said nothing.

'Good day to you, Sir,' said the leader, 'may the Lord bless you.'

'I'm sure He will,' said Little John, 'and right now He is blessing all five of you, for my master invites you all to be his guests for dinner.'

'Your master is most kind,' said the leader of the monks. 'And may we know your master's name?'

'Robin Hood is our master,' said Little John, 'and no man in England has ever dared refuse his invitation.'

'Why should we refuse?' said the monk. 'My brothers here are hungry, and your master's invitation is most welcome.'

'Well they look more scared than hungry,' said Little John.

'Not scared,' said the monk, 'just lost in prayer.'

'They certainly don't look as if they're praying,' said Little John. Whereupon all the monks began to pray out loud and call upon the good Lord to protect them from robbers and outlaws.

'And now you can lead us to your master,' said the leader. 'I have always wanted to meet your good Robin Hood.'

'He is a fine man,' said Little John.

'It's good to hear a man speak well of his master. It is not common nowadays. Most people seem to take pleasure in abusing their masters, and running them down behind their backs.'

'All the men speak well of Robin,' said Little John, 'and so shall you, good Father, if you are a good poor man. 'Tis only the bad and the rich who speak ill of him.'

'Well, I must confess I am quite a good man, and quite a poor one too. So no doubt I shall like him very much.'

And with that they came to the hideout and Robin stepped forward to greet his guests.

'Good monks, you are most welcome,' he said. 'As you can see from the tables laid out before you, my simple meal is good and wholesome. And though we shoot the King's deer to provide meat for our table, the King will never miss it, and we are always pleased to greet strangers to share it with us.'

The monks crossed themselves hastily before seating themselves at the tables.

'You are most kind,' said the leader. And he led the company in prayers before they started on their meal. Robin and all the men were amused to see how heartily the monks proceeded to eat.

'It's good to see the holy life does not spoil a man's appetite,' said Little John.

'A really holy life never does,' said the leader. 'In fact, the holier the monk, the greater his appetite.'

'Then truly you must all five be the holiest monks in Christendom,' said Robin.

'We like to think we are,' said the leader, 'and surely the venison is good. Well worthy of a king.'

'It's because it's so good that the King will not allow his people to hunt the deer and shoot them for their food. But how else can most poor folk live but by hunting?'

Then, raising his goblet filled with wine, the leader of the monks said, 'And now I propose a toast. Gentlemen, I call on you to be upstanding with me and drink to the health of—' there was a pause, and then the monk continued, 'and drink to the health of His Gracious Majesty, King Richard of England.'

'We are not great lovers of the King Richard, as you well know, Sir,' said Robin Hood angrily.

'I know, Sir,' said the monk, 'but this is his country, his kingdom, and this is his venison we are now eating, whether he likes it or not, and whether he knows it or not. Besides, with all his faults, and I grant you, they are many, there have been worse kings, and no doubt there will be worse to come. So let us be thankful for small mercies, and let us drink a health unto His Majesty.'

'Well I must say, Holy Father,' said Robin Hood, 'we've got so used to cursing the King for not letting ordinary folk go hunting his deer, and for making us outlaws for disobeying his wretched laws and commands, that we've never thought about him in the way you say.

But now I come to think of it, there's much truth to it—the King's not as bad as he might be, nor so good as he might be, and that's about all you can say for most men. So let us all be upstanding, and drink a health to His Majesty.'

And so to their amazement the Merry Men found themselves, for the very first time, drinking the health of the very man they had grown so used to cursing and abusing, King Richard himself.

' It was an excellent dinner,' said the monk, when the meal was finished.

' And can you pay for your dinner, good monk?' asked Robin Hood.

' I'm but a humble monk,' said he, ' my means are slight, my status lowly.'

' Exactly how slight? and exactly how lowly?' asked Robin.

' In my saddle I have forty pounds. The savings of a lifetime. I beg you not to take it all.'

' Go see how much he has,' said Robin to one of the men, and in the monk's saddle was found just as the monk had said, forty pounds.

' And this is all you have? These are your life's savings?'

' Indeed they are,' said the monk.

' Then you shall leave me none the poorer. Indeed you shall leave me a richer man than I found you.' And with that Robin told the men to double the money in the monk's saddle. The monk was most impressed and told Robin Hood that he and his four brothers would pray for the soul of Robin and the Merry Men for the rest of their days.

' And now,' said Robin, ' for a little entertainment.' And he and the men gave the monks a magnificent display of archery. They were all good, but Robin Hood was the best of all.

' Have you ever seen better archery, anywhere?' asked Little John.

' When I was a boy,' said the leader of the monks, ' I was rather good at it myself.'

They all laughed.

' In fact, I may still be rather good at it. May I see if I am?'

And as they all laughed, Robin gave him his bow and the monk stepped forward and took aim. But as he did so, the cowl that covered his face fell back, revealing that he was not a monk at all, for his hair had not been shaved away as a monk's is, and indeed the face, now that one looked at it properly, was that of a fighting man. It was Little John who recognised him.

' It is the King himself,' said he.

' Yes, and these are four of my knights.' And seeing that his knights and Robin Hood's men were about to leap at each other and have a great battle he called out, ' No, there is no need for fighting. For

77

haven't we shown what excellent friends we can be?'

'We've never yet thought ourselves friends of the King,' said Robin.

'But then, until this moment you had not met the King. Nor had the King met Robin Hood. And at least you must give the King credit for one thing: he did come all this way to meet you. And all his advisers and all his friends said, "No, Robin Hood is a villain and a criminal and he will shoot you in the back and rob you and leave you in the wayside to rot and perish." But the King thought more highly of Robin Hood than anyone else did; and so he came to meet him for himself.'

'That was very bold of you, Your Majesty, and now that you have met him, what do you think of him?'

'I think that he is too good and clever and courageous—and so are all his men—for him to be wasting his life away here in the forest, leading the life of the outlaw.'

'Then what would you recommend him to do instead?'

'I would recommend that he accept the King's invitation to go with the King, and serve him and defend him against his enemies—and believe me, there are many enemies, and the King is much in need of protecting.'

And Robin conferred with his men, and they all agreed to follow Robin Hood and serve the King, if that was his wish. And so it happened, that after being hunted down as robbers and outlaws, Robin Hood and his Merry Men became the loyal servants of the King and remained so for many years. And so they might have remained for the rest of their lives. But times changed. King Richard died, and the next king was such a tyrant that Robin Hood and his men left the service of the King and returned to Sherwood Forest, and there again they robbed from the rich and gave to the poor and were hunted down by the King's men and the Sheriff's men. And as you will probably know, in time Robin Hood was betrayed and died most sadly—but that is another story, and will keep for another time.

Based on a medieval ballad, 'The Gest of Robin Hood.'

16 The Prince who lost at Cards

An Indian Folk Tale

There were once two princes who were twin brothers, and they looked so much alike that it was difficult to tell them apart. But one of them, David, was very keen to travel, while the other, Henry, was quite content to stay at home. So, when they were eighteen, Prince David told the King and the Queen that he was off in quest of adventure, while Prince Henry said that he would stay behind to look after his parents in their old age.

' But you must let us know if you are ever in need of help,' said Henry to David. ' Adventures are all very well, but who knows, you may be in a tight spot some day and I may be able to assist you.'

So the court magician was consulted and he planted a special kind of fruit tree just outside Prince Henry's window, and this tree, he said, would bear fruit all the year around, for years and years to come, but all the fruit would wither away if ever Prince David was in danger. Then Henry would know that his brother needed help and would ride off to find him.

David travelled for many days without finding any adventures at all, and he was greatly disappointed. Then, half-way up a desolate mountainside he met a hideous old witch.

' Greetings, good Prince,' said the witch.

' Greetings,' replied David coldly.

' I'm glad the Prince has come at last. I've waited a long time.'

' How could you have known that I was coming this way? I didn't know myself until a few moments ago.'

' Aha. I knew. I have the cards ready on the table. Won't you come in?'

' Cards?'

' A pack for you. And another for your brother.'

' For my brother? But he is not with me.'

' He will come. Be sure of it.'

' And how do you know I have a brother?'

' Like I said, I have been expecting you for a long time, Prince David.'

' You know my name as well. You are a strange creature.'

' And do you know what I like best in all the world?—a good game of cards. And up here on the mountainside, there are so few people I can persuade to play with me. But you will, won't you—young

Prince in quest of adventure?'

'Well it would certainly be an adventure to play cards with a witch. I've played cards with my brother often enough. And he always wins. Perhaps if I play with you, then I shall win for a change.'

'Perhaps,' said the witch. 'Will you come in?'

And she led him to a miserable old hut. 'This is my little palace,' she said, 'I'm extremely fond of it. So elegant, don't you think?'

'I've seen better,' said the Prince, unimpressed.

As she was dealing the cards, the witch said, 'What stakes shall we play for?'

'I don't play for stakes, only for the fun of playing,' said the Prince.

The witch was furious. 'I always play for stakes, the higher the stakes the better I like it.'

'And like I said, I never play for stakes. I don't approve of gambling.'

'You don't approve of gambling? And yet you have the effrontery to call yourself an adventurer? What sort of adventures do you think you'll ever meet if you never gamble?'

Prince David thought there was some truth in this, so he said, 'Very well. But the stakes will be something small and unimportant. I'm not going to gamble away all the money I possess, or my title, or anything of any value.'

'For the first round,' said the witch, 'the stakes will be—your hat. It's a pretty one. I like it. If I win, I get your hat. If I lose I give you another one, exactly like it. Agreed?'

'Agreed,' said the Prince. 'My hat's a very unimportant thing indeed. I can always buy another if I lose this one.'

And he did. He lost the round, and the witch, chuckling wickedly, took his hat from him.

'And for the second round, the stakes will be—let me see—'

'Nothing of any importance or value,' interrupted the Prince.

'Very well then—the stakes shall be your gloves. If I win, I get your gloves. If I lose I give you another pair exactly like them. Agreed?'

'Agreed,' said the Prince. 'But I promise you, I shan't lose this time.'

But he did, and the witch, chuckling even more wickedly than before, took his gloves from him.

'I've played enough cards for one day,' said the Prince, 'I must be going.

'No,' said the witch, 'you shall not go until you've played your third and final round.'

But the Prince got up to leave.

' Are you an adventurer, or just a coward?' taunted the witch. ' Because you're losing you want to go. If you were winning you'd be begging me to let you stay. Ah, I've met your sort before. Very well. Be off with you. You'll never meet any adventure, you don't have the nerve for it.'

' I'm no coward,' replied David, infuriated by her insult. ' I shall stay and play one final round.'

' And the stakes this time, will be your freedom. If I win, you are my prisoner for life. If I lose, I will give you your double.'

' That would be impossible,' said the Prince, ' to give me my double. The only person in the world who looks like me is my brother.'

' I told you, if I lose I shall give you your double. I never break a pledge. And neither will you.'

' A man's freedom is a very big thing to play cards for,' said David.

' You're afraid again, are you, adventurer?' sneered the witch.

' Never,' said David.

' Good,' said the witch, grinning, as she dealt the cards.

' I shall win this time,' said David. ' I promise you.'

But he didn't. He lost again. And the witch said, ' Now you are my prisoner for ever and ever.' And she locked him away in a cave behind the hut.

And at that moment the fruit tree that had been planted outside Prince Henry's window in the palace, withered and died, and so everyone knew that David was in danger. The same day Prince Henry rode off to rescue him and after a long journey came to the same desolate mountainside where the witch lived.

' Greetings good Prince,' cried the witch.

' I've come in search of my brother,' said Henry, ' he looks exactly like I do. Has he passed this way?'

' I've never seen him, or then again, perhaps I have.'

' Can't you be sure?'

' I could be sure—after a game of cards. There's nothing like a game of cards for sharpening my memory, that's what I always find,' said the witch.

' I'm delighted to hear it. Then let us have a quick game, so I can make my way again in search of my brother.'

' I only play cards if the stakes are high,' said the witch.

' I'd call that gambling,' said Henry, ' and I never gamble. My parents disapprove of it.'

' Then I shan't play cards with you at all,' said the witch. ' And then you'll never know if I've seen your brother pass this way or not.

But, I'll tell you what I'll do, for the first round we'll play for something that's not important. Shall we say your hat? If I win, I get your hat. If I lose, I give you another exactly like it.'

' There's only one hat in the world exactly like mine, and that was worn by my brother the day he rode off to seek adventure.'

' Is that so?' said the witch, giggling fiendishly to herself.

' It is indeed.'

And the two played the first hand of cards, the Prince concentrating with all his might, determined that he should win and discover what news, if any, the witch might have of his brother.

' I seldom lose, if ever,' said the witch.

' I never lose,' said the Prince.

And he won.

' Very good,' said the witch, ' I like to lose a game every now and again. It gets monotonous to win every time.'

And so saying she gave him his brother's hat, an exact copy of his own.

' And now tell me where my brother is,' said Henry. ' It's clear you've seen him, for this is his very hat. He must have passed this way.'

' I still can't quite remember, but it's coming to me. Play one more round and then my memory will come back properly and I'll be able to tell you. Sit down, and play one more round.'

This time they played for his gloves, and again Henry said, ' There's only one person in the world whose gloves are the same as my own— my brother.'

The witch giggled, and said, ' Let's see who wins this time.'

And they both concentrated on the game, the witch murmuring wickedly to herself all the time. And Henry won again.

' Here's the gloves,' said the witch.

' They *are* my brother's. He must have passed this way. You must have seen him. Now tell me which way he went.'

' I still can't remember, not quite.'

' You've wasted all this time. He might be dying.'

' Give me one more round of cards, and then I'll swear I'll tell you. And the stakes this time will be your liberty.'

' How can I be sure that you'll tell me. For all I know you may be trying to keep me here for ever.'

The witch laughed and said, ' I am. But never mind, I'll keep my pledge for all that.' And so saying, she dealt the cards.

' If I win this round, you will be my prisoner for life. If I lose, then I shall give you another exactly like yourself.'

' And that,' said Prince Henry, ' can only be my brother.'

They both concentrated on the third and final round, and even the witch was silent.

And Henry won.

'Here is your brother,' said the witch, taking Henry to the cave where David had been imprisoned. The two brothers were overjoyed to be reunited.

'It is a happy occasion for me too,' croaked the witch, and at that very moment she was changed into a beautiful princess.

'Some time ago,' she explained, 'an evil spell was cast over me. I was made into a witch, and I was given only one way of ever returning to my real self: to lose a game of cards to a handsome prince.'

Henry and David were so delighted that both of them asked for the princess's hand in marriage.

'I am the one who beat you at cards,' said Henry, 'so I am the one you should marry.'

'And I am the one who lost,' said David, 'so I have no claim upon you.'

The Princess thought about it a long time and then said, 'It is David I choose. For he's just as handsome as his brother, and just as strong. But at least I can beat him at cards. And every woman likes to be better than her husband at something.'

And so she married the brother who lost at cards. And they were extremely happy.

Adapted from *Folk Tales of Bengal* by Lalayihari De in 1883.

17 The silliest thing you can think of

An English Folk Tale

Sam's mother despaired of him, for he was the silliest boy in the town, and she told him so.

'Eee, Mother,' says Sam, 'if I be the silliest in town, will I be getting a prize for that, do you think?'

'No, son,' says his mother, 'they give no prizes for silliness, I'm afraid.'

'Why not, Mother?' says Sam sadly.

'Now that's a silly thing to ask,' says his mother, 'for everyone knows that there aren't any prizes for being silly.'

'Then it's a hard world, Mother,' says Sam, 'for if I be the silliest, that means I'm the best at being silly, and so I reckons I ought to get a prize for it.'

'Poor boy,' says his mother. 'Whatever will become of you when your father and me have gone—I dread to think.'

Sam's mother went to see his schoolteacher and asked her why Sam was so silly.

'That's something I've been meaning to ask you for a long time,' said the teacher rather sternly. 'The boy can't concentrate. And he won't sit still. And he never does stop talking.'

And at that very moment Sam was talking at the back of the classroom.

'Stop talking,' said the teacher.

'Beg your pardon, Miss?' said Sam politely.

'I said, stop talking,' said the teacher.

'Ah,' says Sam to the boy at the side of him, 'Mistress sees I been talking. Mistress don't miss much, do she?'

'I said, stop talking,' said the teacher, getting even more annoyed.

'Beg your pardon, Miss?' said Sam politely.

'You heard me,' said the teacher, 'I said, stop talking.'

'Aye, Miss, I heard you the first time. I was just begging your pardon.'

'Very well then. Just stop talking.'

So Sam turned to the boy again and said, 'Sorry, Walter, I won't be speaking to you again for a while yet. Mistress just told me to stop talking.'

'You see what I mean,' said the teacher to Sam's mother, 'he just can't stop. He's no brains whatsoever.'

So his mother decided to send him to the local witch. In actual fact she was not really a witch at all: she was just an old lady who had a lot of common sense and sometimes could suggest remedies that other people never thought of. Even so they called her a witch.

The witch was busy when Sam visited her.

'There's a lot of things I have to do,' said the witch. 'It's the time of year when everyone gets a cold and expects me to cure it. So come on. Don't just stand there. Tell me what you want.'

'Ah,' said Samuel.

'Yes, and what else have you got to say?'

'Ah,' again said Samuel. 'I ain't never seen no witch before.'

'And now you've seen one you can go, can't you. I have work to do,' said the witch.

'I be Samuel,' said Samuel.

'Really,' said the witch.

'No, not Samuel Really. That's not my name. I'm Samuel Roehampton.'

The witch nodded in irritation.

'That's 'cause my father's name was Roehampton,' said Sam.

'I'm glad to hear it,' said the witch. 'And now if you'll excuse me—'

'Leastways, I think that be his name. I ain't never asked him if it were,' said Sam, growing quite perplexed by the thought of it.

'Now,' said the witch, holding open the door, 'tell me your business or out you go.'

'Please,' said Sam, trying to gather his wits together, 'I think I want something.'

'No doubt you do,' said the witch, 'and what is it you think you want?'

Sam paused to think, and then with sudden inspiration, he remembered. Proudly he stated, ' 'Tain't me as wants it, it's my mother.'

'Very good. Now we're getting somewhere, and what is it she wants?'

Another pause.

'I think—I think she wants me to get some brains. She says I'm the silliest boy in the town, and that I won't get no prize for it. So she wants me to get some brains.'

'I'm not surprised,' says the witch.

'Well, can you give me some?' said Sam.

'Mercy on me, do you think I can just pull brains out of the cupboard and give them to you? I wish I could. I can't give you brains my boy. But I'll give you something to tell your mother. Do you think you can remember it?'

' I'll try,' said Sam.

' Tell her: you'll never have any brains till you've done the silliest thing you can think of.'

' I'll tell her that,' said Sam, and he ran straight off to his mother.

' And what did the witch say?' asked his mother.

' She said, you'll never have any brains till you've done the silliest thing you can think of,' said Sam.

' You silly boy, she meant *you'll* never have any brains, not *me*. But it's the silliest advice I ever heard. You're for ever doing silly things. Who's to judge which is the silliest?'

But Sam wasn't quite so silly after all, for he remembered what the witch had told him and he decided that very day that he would do the silliest thing he could think of. So he ran down to his uncle's farm and asked to see Betsy the farm-girl. She was seventeen and none of the young men thought she was in the least pretty and folks said poor Betsy—who was just a poor orphan girl—would never marry.

' Hello Betsy,' said Sam.

' And what do you want?' said Betsy, none too pleased to see Sam, for the young boys were always teasing her.

' I be Samuel,' said Sam.

' I know that, you great oaf,' said Betsy. ' You're the master's nephew.'

' Aye,' said Samuel, grinning foolishly at Betsy.

' And what do you think you're doing, coming here to waste my time? I've got work to do.'

' The witch said as how I'd never have any brains till I'd done the silliest thing I could think of,' said Sam.

' The impudence of it; and you think coming here to see me is the silliest thing you could think of,' said Betsy, quite upset.

' Maybe so, maybe no,' said Sam, still grinning.

' It's too bad, 'cause I'm not pretty and got no riches, you boys think you can say what you like to me,' said Betsy.

' You're not silly, are you?' asked Sam.

' That I'm not. I've got a head on my shoulders, even if it isn't a pretty one.'

' Then—when I've grown up—when I'm seventeen like you are—will you marry me?'

' Mercy on me—how old are you now, then?'

' Mother reckons I'm fourteen. So it shouldn't be too long afore I catches up with you,' said Sam.

' You great goose,' said Betsy, ' when you're seventeen I'll be twenty, won't I?'

' I don't know,' said Sam, ' you understand that sort of thing better than I do. You're the one with brains.'

'And with the arithmetic too, by the looks of things,' said Betsy.

'Well, what's your answer then? Will you marry me when I'm a man?'

'Do you love me?' said Betsy.

'I don't know,' said Sam. 'Like I said, I don't have any brains. I don't know anything.'

'But will you keep your word when you're a man? That's the important thing,' said Betsy.

'That I will,' said Sam.

'Well, you're not exactly handsome,' said Betsy, 'but then, handsome is as handsome does. And you're not exactly rich, but then I'm not either. And you're not exactly clever, but that doesn't matter, for I'll be clever enough for the two of us. Right you are then, Samuel, if you ask me again when you're seventeen, why then I'll say yes. And I'll be proud to be your wife.'

And with that Samuel let out a great 'yippee' of pure joy and rushed out to tell his friends the good news. Most of them only laughed at him and said, 'Who wants to marry old Betsy? No one in their proper senses wants to marry her.' But then Sam called again on the old witch, who was still extremely busy, and he said to her, 'Witch, I've done the silliest thing I could think of, so now I should have some brains.' And he told her the whole story.

'It's like I said,' said the witch, 'now indeed you'll have some brains. For young Betsy's true to her word: she's got enough brains for the two of you.'

Adapted from *More English Folk Tales* by Joseph Jacobs 1894.

18 The Ghost who was afraid of being bagged

An Indian Folk Tale

Mr Mukerjhee was henpecked. He loved his wife, and always had, but in twenty-five years of married life, she had never stopped nagging him. Finally he decided that he'd had enough of it and he determined to leave home and never see his wife again. But before he did so he decided to tell his wife exactly what he thought of her.

It was breakfast, and as usual, his wife was nagging.

'You were five minutes late coming downstairs,' she said. 'I've never known such a thing. Other men treat their wives with a bit of respect. If their wives have the decency to get up in the morning and cook a good breakfast for them, then they have the goodness in them to get up in time to eat it while it's still hot. But not my husband. Five minutes late he is. And now his breakfast's cold, and then he'll start grumbling and say it's all my fault.'

In actual fact Mr Mukerjhee had never grumbled in his entire life, and it was impossible to grumble to his wife, even if he wished to, for she never allowed anyone to get a word in edgeways.

'I wasn't going to grumble about the breakfast, my dear. I was just going to tell you—'

'Not grumble? Not grumble? I should hope not. So you come down late for your breakfast, you lie up there in that bed of yours while I'm down here working myself to the bone trying to feed you decently, and you tell me you're not going to grumble? I should hope not indeed. I'm the one who should be grumbling, though heaven knows it isn't in my nature to grumble. Heaven help you if it had been. Heaven help you, Bharat Mukerjhee, if you'd married the sort of woman who grumbles. Though heaven knows, you deserve a woman like that, indeed you do.'

She paused to get her breath back.

'I wasn't going to grumble, my dear, I was only going to tell you—'

'It's just like my mother always said: marry that man, and you'll live to regret it. They were her exact words. I swear it. That's what she said to me. Marry that man and you'll live to regret it. Well, I didn't believe my dear mother then, but I've lived to regret it. She was right. She could see what I was letting myself in for. She said to me, Daughter, she said, Daughter, you've a sweet and innocent and trusting disposition—and I have, I always did have—and there's not a man who's ever been born who's good enough for you. Marry that man, she said, marry him, and you'll never have a minute's peace, for he'll be grumbling at you and moaning at you all day long, and you'll never get a word in edgeways. They were her very words. And oh, it's all come true. It's all come true.'

She paused to wipe the tears from her eyes.

'Like I said, my dear, I was not going to grumble, for we all know how good you have been to me, I was only going to tell you that I am—'

'And look at us. You're so lazy you've never earned enough money to look after me. I might as well be a widow for all you care. What clothes do I have? Even if I was invited to a fine banquet I wouldn't dare go, for I've nothing good to dress myself in. And when I was a girl I was for ever being invited out to fine houses. I was very popular when I was a girl, maybe you didn't know that, but I was. My mother used to say to me, why, you're the most popular girl in the town, you really are. And I was. Do you know I had so many invitations I couldn't accept half of them? That's the truth. I swear to it.'

She paused to drink some tea.

'I'm sure you were the toast of the town, my dear, before you married me, but all I wanted to say was that I have at last decided to—'

'So you can imagine how surprised everyone was when I decided to marry you. No one could believe it. After all, I could have married the handsomest as well as the richest man for miles around. Oh why didn't I listen to my dear mother? Why didn't I listen to her? I could have been rich and fashionable and happy, and now look at me. Poor, miserable and unappreciated. You've never appreciated me. I've slaved for you, given you the best years of my life. And what have I got in return? Why, you won't even sit and talk to me.'

'I merely wanted to say that I have at last decided to—'

'Oh don't talk to me,' said Mrs Mukerjhee, 'I don't want to hear. You never say anything nice or kind to me. You only notice me when you want to grumble or criticise me. Don't talk to me.'

'Well, before you interrupt me again, let me just say—'

'Interrupt? Interrupt? I'm the one who's always being interrupted. I'm the one who never gets a word in edgeways. Don't you dare come grumbling to me about *my* interrupting *you*. Don't you dare.'

Mr Mukerjhee put on his hat and coat and went to the door.

'And where do you think you're going?' she asked.

'I've no idea,' he said. 'All I know is that I'm leaving you. Now and for ever. I've had enough. Good-bye.'

And before his wife could argue back at him, he had walked out of the house.

'Oh, dear,' shouted the wife tearfully. 'Why didn't I listen to my poor dear mother?'

And she ran to the door to call out to her husband and order him back. But he had already disappeared down the street.

He walked and walked and walked, with no idea where he was going. He just wanted to get as far away as possible from his nagging wife. At midnight he found himself in a vast dark forest, and there he settled down against a tree-trunk to get some sleep.

'It's bliss,' he said to himself, 'for the first time in twenty-five years there's no one to nag me. It's sheer beautiful bliss.'

But at that moment a ghost appeared out of nowhere and crept up behind him and made a hideous noise, intending to frighten him out of his wits. Mr. Mukerjhee however had never been much afraid of ghosts. As a general rule he found them far less troublesome than wives.

The ghost repeated his hideous noise.

'I'm sorry to disappoint you, old chap,' said Mr Mukerjhee pleasantly, 'but I've never been afraid of ghosts. You'll have to find someone else to haunt.'

The ghost found this difficult to believe, so a few moments later he crept up again on Mr Mukerjhee and made an even more hideous noise. Whereupon Mr Mukerjhee decided to make use of this unexpected acquaintanceship.

'And now,' said he to the ghost, 'I have you in my power.'

'You have?' said the ghost, greatly surprised.

'I have indeed. I have magical power over ghosts. I can do with them whatever I will.'

'Really?' said the ghost, more and more surprised.

'You see this bag of mine here? Inside that bag are twenty-five ghosts I've caught already today.'

'Twenty-five. That's a big number for such a small bag,' said the ghost.

'Have you never heard of us ghost-catchers before? We creep out in the night and we capture nasty silly little ghosts like yourself, and we put them in our bags and we take them home and sell them.'

'I've heard of ghost-catchers, certainly, but I've never met one before,' said the ghost, now greatly frightened.

'Look. Do you want to see one of the ghosts I've captured?'

'Perhaps, perhaps, just a little peep,' said the ghost nervously.

'Here,' and so saying Mr Mukerjhee took his mirror from his bag and held it up to the ghost's face. 'Do you see it?'

'Indeed I do,' said the ghost, now absolutely terrified.

'Good. And now I must put you in my bag too.'

'Oh please don't. Spare me, I beg you.'

'Spare you? It wouldn't be worth my reputation as a ghost-catcher if I were to spare you.'

'But if you do, then I'll give you anything you may ask for.'

'Anything?'

'Anything.'

Mr Mukerjhee thought for a moment.

'My wife is always nagging me, because she thinks we're not rich enough. So, Mr Ghost, bring me a pot of gold and then I'll spare you. Can you do that?'

'Well, my uncle has a pot of gold that he stole from someone years and years ago that he nearly frightened to death. I could go to my uncle and ask him.'

'You do that, and mark my word. If you break your promise and you don't come back with the gold, I'll go and fetch all the ghost-catchers in the land and we'll all come out together and hunt you down.'

'I'll come back, I promise you.'

And the ghost went off, and Mr Mukerjhee decided to get some sleep.

As you can imagine, the ghost's uncle, who was quite an enormous ghost, was not at all keen to part with his pot of gold.

'What do you want it for?' he demanded, and he was furious when the ghost explained.

'A man frightening a ghost? I've never heard of such a thing. If news like that gets around we ghosts will be laughed out of existence. Come. I'll show you what to do with men like that.'

And so the uncle crept up on Mr Mukerjhee and gave forth the most horrific sound that any ghost ever made. But Mr Mukerjhee simply turned round, as calm as you like, and said, 'Why you must be the ghost's silly uncle. And if you haven't brought the gold with you, I'll have to bag you and your nephew as well.'

And with that he took the mirror from his bag again, and said, 'Here's one of your brethren that I've caught today, and there's twenty-four more in the bag with him. Do you want to join them?'

The uncle was as terrified as his nephew and said, 'Nephew. Go home this instant and bring back the pot of gold with you.'

That's how it happened that the following day Mr Mukerjhee returned to his wife and said, 'Mrs Mukerjhee, my dear, I meant to leave you and never return. But you're my wife, and I love you and I can't live without you. And that's that. So here I am. And here's a little present for you.'

And before Mrs Mukerjhee could say anything he presented her with the pot of gold. For a minute or so she was speechless with wonder as she counted out the great fortune he had given her.

' How rich we are. How rich we are,' she said.

Then her mood changed. ' So, you've come back, have you? So you find you can't get along without your slave of a wife after all? I knew it. Isn't it just like my mother said? Didn't she always say to me—'

And so Mrs Mukerjhee started grumbling again, and Mr Mukerjhee smiled to himself. ' Ah well. I managed to tell her I was leaving her, and I managed to tell her I've come back. So I must be contented with that.'

He never got another word in edgeways for the rest of his life.

Adapted from *Folk Tales of Bengal* 1883.

19 The Farmer's Pot of Gold

An English Folk Tale

Old Jack was a rogue, and a clever one, and this is how he cheated the farmer of his pot of gold.

' I've got to go into market,' said Farmer Giles to his wife one morning. ' Be sure to look after the place properly while I'm gone.'

' You know I'll find it very difficult to do that,' said the wife. ' I'm no good at looking after things.'

' Then you must concentrate, and not let your attention wander,' said the farmer. ' And pay special care to the pot of gold.'

' Ooh dear, the pot of gold,' said the wife, greatly worried by having to be responsible for it.

' Don't you dare let anyone touch that pot of gold,' said the farmer.

' Couldn't you take it with you?' asked the wife. ' I'm sure it would be safer with you than it will be with me.'

' No. Don't be so silly. How could I go to market with a pot of gold under my arm? Everyone would think I'd gone mad.'

' Very well. If you say so.'

And off went the farmer, and the wife said to herself, ' I shall pay attention and not let any harm come to the house, or to the pot of gold.'

At that moment there was a knock on the door.

' Goodness me,' thought the wife, ' who can this be?'

' Good morning, ma'am,' said the stranger at the door, smiling pleasantly.

' And who would you be?' asked the wife.

' Old Jack they call me,' said the stranger, ' and I've come miles and miles to give you a message.'

' Miles and miles, you say?'

' Aye, miles and miles. From Paradise.'

' Paradise? That must be a very long way away. I've never met anyone from there before.'

' Oh no, you wouldn't have. Very few are willing to make the journey.'

' And you say you have a message for me?'

' Aye—from your dear sister.'

' Sister? I don't have a sister. I have a brother, but not a sister.'

' I meant your brother, not your sister.'

93

'But my poor brother's dead. He has been for five years.'

'Of course he's dead. That's why he's in Paradise.'

'Of course. Mercy on me. And what's the message?'

'Well your brother's hard up and wondered if you could lend him some money.'

'Well—I could manage a shilling or two, I suppose.'

'Oh no. Must be more than that. And must be pure gold. That's the only money they use in Paradise.'

'Gold?'

'Aye gold.'

'Well I have *some* gold.'

'How much, my dear?'

'A whole pot of it actually, but I don't know that my husband would approve of my letting you have all of it.'

'Remember it's only a loan. I'll bring it back to you with interest.'

'Yes, I'd forgotten that. Very well. I'll lend him the whole pot. Returnable with interest at the end of the year.'

So saying, she brought out the pot, gave him all the gold in it, and then made Jack a cup of tea. They chatted a while about Paradise and about her brother, and then Jack went on his way.

Then the farmer returned, and was furious when he heard what had happened.

'You fool,' he shouted angrily, 'the man was a crook, and you fell for his knavery like a little child would. Now we may never see that gold again.'

'Oh dear,' said the wife, 'I knew you shouldn't have left me to look after it.'

And the farmer rode off on his horse to see if he could find the stranger somewhere on the road. He couldn't have got far away.

Indeed he hadn't—for there was Jack just down the road, with the pot of gold carefully hidden beneath the coat he carried on his arm. Jack realised who the farmer was, so as the farmer rode up to him on his horse, Jack lay down on the road and stared up to the sky.

'What's going on here?' asked the farmer.

'A marvellous thing,' said Jack. 'A truly marvellous thing. A minute ago I met a strange man riding along this road, and he was carrying a pot of gold he was.'

'He was?' said the farmer.

'Aye,' said Jack. 'And I asked him where he was going, and he said he was going to Paradise. And he'd no sooner said it than he called to his horse, and the horse leapt into the air and rode off with him to the clouds. I can still see him.'

'You can?'

'Aye, he hasn't disappeared yet—though he will in a second or two. He's just about to ride into the clouds.'

'Let me look,' said the farmer.

'By all means,' said Jack. 'Just lie down on the ground here, and look straight about you.'

And Jack got up as the farmer laid down.

'I can't see him,' said the farmer.

'You will do. Keep looking,' said Jack. And he got on to the farmer's horse and rode away.

'I still can't see him,' said the farmer.

Then he realised that Jack had gone and had taken his horse.

'Did you find him?' asked the wife when he got back.

'No, my dear,' said the farmer. 'I didn't find him—but I did manage to learn something very interesting.'

'And what's that?' asked the wife.

'Well, you may be a silly woman, but you've got a silly husband too, so we're well matched.'

And they found they were just as happy without the pot of gold as they had been with it. And no one knows whether Jack was happy or not, for he was never seen again.

Adapted from the story 'Jack Hannaford' in *English Fairy Tales* by Joseph Jacobs 1890.

20 Emrys and the Ghost

A Welsh Folk Tale

Young Emrys was a good hard-working lad, but his father never gave him thanks for all the work he did. Instead he insulted him and mocked him and criticised him and eventually, not surprisingly, Emrys decided to leave home. He packed together his few belongings into a red bag which he threw over his shoulders and away he went. He had no money and so he had to find work wherever he went to pay for food and lodging, and it was not always easy to find work, for times were bad. He had many adventures but the strangest of all was the adventure that ended his wanderings.

He'd walked a long way that day, and a fierce wind was blowing up when he came to an old farm house. As he knocked on the door he could hear the sound of laughter and music from inside the house.

'Forgive me for interrupting your celebrations,' said Emrys when an old farmer opened the door to him, 'but I am looking for food and shelter for the night. I have no money, but in the morning I would be pleased to work for you to repay you for your hospitality. I'm strong and I can work well.'

'My dear boy,' said the farmer, 'I would be only too pleased to give you all the food you wish and a comfortable bed as well, but I am having a great party here tonight. There is hardly any food left, and there are so many guests that there is not a space, not to mention a bed, where you would sleep. I wish there was.'

'Well thank you for trying to help me,' said Emrys, 'I shall walk on up the hill and try to find some other place.'

'But there's not another place for miles around, and the wind is blowing itself up into a great fury and soon it will be night.'

'That does not worry me,' said Emrys, 'I've been wandering now a very long time, I'm used to dark and windy nights.'

'But wait,' said the farmer, 'are you really as brave as you seem?'

Emrys laughed. 'I have need to be,' he said, 'a wanderer's life is not an easy one.'

'Well then, if you are really brave, then perhaps I can help you. I have another house, the only other one for miles around. It is over there in the middle of the forest. You can sleep there and welcome. You will find food in the kitchen and a good, comfortable bed up-stairs, but you will find no company of any kind—save for—save for—' And the farmer hesitated.

' Well?' said Emrys.

' Save for the ghost.'

' Ghosts have never greatly worried me,' said Emrys, lying some-what, for he no more liked ghosts than most men do.

' This one worried everybody else who has ever seen or heard him. I use the house in the daytime, that's why there's food there, but never at night. But if you say you are not worried by the thought of ghosts, then you can sleep there, and good luck to you.'

And so Emrys followed the path indicated by the farmer, and came at last to the dark and empty house. And there in the kitchen he found all the food and drink he could wish for, and upstairs was the most comfortable bed he had seen since leaving home. And he had no sooner undressed and climbed into bed than he heard a strange tapping on the window outside. Emrys ignored it at first, but the tapping continued.

' You stupid ghost,' called out Emrys, ' can't you see I'm tired and want to sleep?'

And the ghost was so furious to hear Emrys address him in this way that he stopped tapping on the window, leapt into the room and created an awful howling noise such as to make the flesh of any ordinary man creep and his hair stand on end.

' Oh really,' said Emrys, ' what a noisy ghost you are. Don't you know that it is quite out of fashion for ghosts to make so much noise?'

The ghost howled the more hideously, shaking with rage.

Emrys replied by pulling the blankets over his head and pretending to fall to sleep.

Furious beyond all belief, the ghost now changed himself into a dragon-like monster and breathed fire all over the room.

' Really you should be ashamed of yourself. Don't you realise you could burn the house down, breathing fire all over everything? It's careless people like you who cause forest fires.'

And with that Emrys leapt out of bed, ran downstairs for a bucket of cold water, and running back to his room threw the water all over the monster. As he did that, so the monster changed into a little goblin with a funny hat and a long nose.

' Now the truth is out at last,' said Emrys, sitting down on the bed. ' Now I see you for what you really are. A silly mischievous little goblin. To think how you've been troubling people all this time with a fear of ghosts, and you're nothing but a little goblin.'

' I got fed up with being a goblin,' said the goblin. ' So I ran away from home and came to live here. And I knew how people would never allow an ugly old goblin to live among them, so I learnt all sorts of wicked magic to scare them away, so I could keep the house to myself. And now you've come, and you're so calm and brave that you have spoiled it all for me. Now I suppose I shall have to go back to my old home that I ran away from, and that I hated so much.'

'I ran away from home too,' said Emrys. 'So I'll have pity for you. Let me have a good night's sleep and then in the morning I'll see what I can do for you.'

And in the morning the farmer came to see if Emrys had been scared away by the ghost, and was so impressed when he learnt how the goblin had been frightening people all these years and how he and Emrys had come to an understanding that he invited Emrys to keep the old house for himself, and to farm the land around it. And Emrys, true to his word, allowed the goblin to stay there too, for as long as he chose.

Adapted from the story 'The Little Red Bogie Man' in *Welsh Legendary Tales* by Elizabeth Sheppard-Jones, Thomas Nelson 1959.

21 A Man among Men

An African Folk Story

Tommy was a fine, big fellow and was very fond of telling everyone,
'Why, I'm a man among men and there's none in the whole world
who is my equal. Look at the muscles of my arms. Has anyone ever
seen better? Look how tall I stand in my socks. Has anyone ever seen
taller? Look how broad and strong are my shoulders. Has anyone
ever seen stronger?'

And as I say, Tommy really was an impressive figure of a man and
no one ever contradicted him. Except his wife. 'You're a foolish
fellow, Tommy,' she'd say. 'There must be plenty of men in the
world who are the equal of you, and better. If I were you I'd keep
my mouth shut and go my way and do my work.'

'You're just jealous,' Tommy would say.

'Jealous?' Annie—his wife—would ask.

'Yes, jealous.'

'And why should I want to be strong and tall and broad in the
shoulder? In a woman it would look ridiculous.'

'Even so, you're jealous. 'Cause all the other women admire me so.'

'Not those with any sense.'

'Ah. That's what you say.'

'It is indeed,' Annie would reply. 'And you mark my words. No
good will come of all this showing off. One day, someone will hear
you and say, "Who do you think you are? Can't you see I'm a better
man than you are?" And then there'll be trouble. Just you see.'

'I'm a man among men,' repeated Tommy. 'There'll never be
another like me.'

'Why, you're as vain as the young girls who think there never was
a beautiful woman till they were born. No matter how pretty a woman
is, there's always someone prettier. And no matter how strong a man
is, there's always someone stronger.'

'I'm a man among men. Everyone says I am,' repeated Tommy.

'Then everyone has no more sense than you have.'

And indeed it happened one morning that Annie went down to
the market and saw a fine big lad carrying his mother's shopping.

'That's a fine lad you have there,' said Annie to his mother.

'That he is,' said the mother proudly. 'He takes after his dear
father.'

'And is he as strong as he looks?' asked Annie.

'Stronger,' said the mother.

'How strong?'

'Why, he's almost a man among men, and that's a fact.'

'Only " almost "?' said Annie.

'Well his dear father's still alive, and he's much stronger than my son. A real giant is his father. He's the man among men.'

'Can the boy show us how strong he is?' said Annie, for quite a crowd had now gathered round.

'That he can,' said the mother. 'Here Dan,' she said, calling the boy to her, 'this lady here is admiring your strength. Let us all see how strong you are.'

'Eh?' said Dan slowly.

'I said, show the lady how strong you are.'

'Oh mother,' said Dan, after a pause, 'how can I do that?'

'Heavens alive. The boy's all brawn but precious little brain. Just like his dear father. Why, how do you think you show someone how strong you are? By lifting something heavy. That's how.'

'Ooh,' said Dan, thinking hard. 'What'd be heavy then, Mother?'

'Gracious me, was ever so strong a lad so simple? Why! The horse over the road there, that's heavy. And the stall you're standing against. That's heavy.'

'Ah, I see,' said Dan.

'Well then,' said the mother. 'Start lifting.'

'Lifting what?' said Dan.

'Why, the stall at the side of you. Start with that.'

Now the stall was full of vegetables and fruit, and it was the biggest stall in the market and must have been a great weight, but Dan picked up the stall in one hand—without upsetting a single thing on it—and then went over to the horse and picked that up in the other.

'It's a blessing I didn't suggest the church as well, for sure enough he'd have gone and balanced that on his head,' said the mother.

'He's a fine strong lad, and that's true,' said Annie. 'But tell me. Is his dad even stronger?'

'Ten times stronger, if not more,' said the mother.

'Dear me,' said Annie.

'Ay, he's a man among men is his father. And he never tires of telling me so.'

'Dear me,' said Annie again.

'Well it's been a pleasure meeting you,' says she to Annie, 'and now we must be getting along. Come along, Daniel, or your father will be wondering what's happened to us both.'

'And a pleasure meeting you, my dear,' says Annie.

'No, no,' says the mother to Daniel, 'you mustn't bring them with you. Go back and put them down where you found them.' And true enough, Dan was following his mother, with the market stall in one hand and the horse in the other.

'Aye, he's a fine strong lad,' said everyone.

As soon as Annie got home she told her husband what she had seen.

'I don't believe it,' says Tom.

'Believe it or not, it's true,' says Annie.

'I'm going down to the market myself tomorrow, and then we'll see who's the man among men and who isn't.'

'If I were you I'd stay at home and mind my own business. I only told you to teach you a little modesty and cure you of boasting the tongue right out of your mouth. It's like I said, no matter how strong you are, there's always someone who's stronger.'

But even so, Tom went down to the market the next day. And he tried to lift the stall in one hand and a horse in the other, but he failed. And everyone assured him that Annie had been speaking the truth and that Daniel, a mere lad, had performed this fantastic feat only the day before. Tom was so curious to find out for himself whether such a boy existed and whether he could possibly have an even stronger father, that he set out in the direction that Daniel and his mother had gone and kept asking his way of any stranger he might meet until he came to Daniel's home.

The lad's mother greeted him quite pleasantly.

'I've come to see this husband of yours,' he told her. 'They say he's a man among men, and I want to see for myself.'

'He's as strong as they say he is, and that's the truth,' said the good woman, whose name was Mary.

'I don't believe it. I'm a man among men. No one is stronger than I am.'

'Dear me,' said Mary, 'you must be twin brother to my own husband, for he's always saying foolish things like that and I'm warning him not to. But to tell you the honest truth: you're a fine big fellow but you're a midget alongside my husband. Even my little lad is bigger than you. They're both out working at the moment, so why don't you be a sensible fellow and go off home before any mischief befalls you?'

'I'll do no such thing,' said Tom. 'No one makes a fool of a big strong man like me. I don't believe a word you say. I'll wait to see your husband for myself.'

'Well, you have your own way if you must. I only hope you've left your poor wife enough money to pay for the funeral expenses.'

And suddenly Tommy heard a great noise, and turning round he saw the most enormous giant striding up the hill towards the house, with one arm round an enormous young lad—Daniel presumably.

'Is that him?' said Tommy, terrified.

'It is indeed. Now start running, and maybe he'll not bother to chase you.'

'I'll do that,' said Tommy, who immediately ran off in the other direction.

'What's that?' shouted the giant. 'Is that a man I see talking to my wife? No man talks to my wife without my permission.'

And with that the giant started to run off in hot pursuit of Tom, who was running as fast as his legs could carry him. Incredibly enough, as he was running along a country lane he ran smack into an even bigger giant.

'What's this? What's this?' demanded the giant. 'Who dares run into me? I am the man among men. No one dares run into me.'

'Forgive me, forgive me,' said Tom, when at last he got his breath back, and a little of his courage. 'Indeed you are a man among men. I can see that very clearly.'

'As long as you see it, then I don't mind. I'll let you go again.'

And the even bigger giant put him down. And now Tom had a brainwave. 'I do apologise for bumping into you, but it so happens, Sir, that I'm being chased by a much smaller man than you.'

'And why is he chasing you?' asked the giant.

'Because I told him *you* were the man among men. And he says that *he* is.'

'Oh. He does, does he?' said the giant, furious.

'Indeed he does. I told him it was sheer nonsense, and that no man is stronger than you.'

And at that moment the first giant comes running down the lane towards them.

'That's him,' said Tommy.

'Right,' said the second giant.

And with that, the two giants fell upon each other, shouting, 'I am the man among men '—' No, I am.'

And Tommy went off home, to leave them to fight it out for themselves.

'Well, well,' said Annie when she sees him, 'and are we still the man among men?'

'No,' says Tommy, 'not any longer. It's like you always said. No matter how strong a man may be, there's always someone stronger than he is.'

And the last Tommy ever heard of the business, the two giants were fighting still.

Adapted from *Hausa Folk Lore* by R. S. Rattray, Oxford University Press 1913.

22 The Three Princes

A Portuguese Folk Story

There were once three Princes who were the best of friends, and they all fell in love with the same Princess. This was not very surprising for she was the most beautiful Princess for miles and miles around. Each went to her and declared his love.

'My name is Thomas,' said the first. 'I am, as you can see, handsome, of noble birth, and of excellent character. My father rules over a land as big as your own, and my people worship the very ground on which I tread. If you will be mine, I shall love you all the days of my life, and my only thought will be to make you happy.'

'You're most kind,' said the Princess, 'and I shall think carefully of all that you have said. But now I must listen to my other suitors.'

And the second was called to her, and he said, 'My name is Richard. I am, as everyone can see, a splendid-looking fellow and any woman would be delighted to have me for a husband. Indeed many thousands of ladies have already been driven to suicide by the thought that I am seeking another—namely, your fair self. My father is a king like yours. Alone, I am famous for my excellence, but married to you, I would go down in history as the luckiest man who ever wed.'

'Nicely put,' replied the Princess, 'and you can be sure that I shall think carefully over everything you say. But now I must listen to my other suitor.'

And the third Prince was called to her, and he said, 'Dear Princess, I know that my two good friends have already spoken to you, in words so wonderful and in thoughts so noble that only a Prince as noble and wonderful as myself could ever hope to equal them. My name is Harry. I am as splendid in character as I am in appearance. Can I say more? Marry me, and you will never regret it. Reject my suit, and you will never forgive yourself.'

The following day the Princess called the three Princes to her and said, 'Truly I am honoured to receive three such fine Princes as yourselves as my suitors.'

'Truly you are,' they replied.

'And since you are all three equally fine in my eyes, I have decided to set you a little test.'

'Name it,' they said.

'You are all three to go off in opposite directions, and not to return until you have found me a most unusual and marvellous gift. I shall marry the one whose gift I like most.'

And so they each went off to find the Princess a remarkable gift.

And they met again a year and a day later, when Thomas was coming from the North, Richard from the South, and Harry from the East. They were then about a hundred miles from the Princess's palace. After greeting each other in dignified fashion, they asked each other what gift they had brought.

'I have a magic mirror,' said Thomas, 'which I found in a market in the frozen north.'

'I didn't think there were any markets in the frozen north,' said Richard.

'Nor I,' said Harry.

'Well there are,' said Thomas. 'And there I found this magic mirror, and when you look in it, you see the person whom you most want to see.'

'What a splendid gift,' said the other two.

'Mine is rather good also,' added Richard. 'A carpet that I found in a market in Baghdad.'

'Now that's exactly the place where one would expect to find a market,' said Harry.

'Indeed yes,' said Thomas.

'This carpet is a magic one, and it will take you to any place—no matter how near or far—where the person lives whom you most want to be with.'

'A first class gift,' said the other two.

'And mine,' said Harry, 'is equally first class. I have found a candle in an old monastery, and it has the power to bring back to life any person who has died. But it must be a person whom you very much want to bring back to life.'

'But how can we know that our gifts actually work?' said Thomas. 'It would be dreadful if we gave them to the Princess and they turned out to be quite ordinary, and not to have any magical powers whatsoever.'

'Then let us look into your mirror,' said Richard. And they did, and naturally enough all three saw the one person they most wanted to see, the Princess. But she lay dead, and her mother and father were mourning over her.

So, without wasting another second, they climbed on to the magic carpet and almost immediately found themselves at the Princess's palace. Harry took out his magic candle, placed it at her side, and instantly she was restored to life. There was much rejoicing, and then the Princes said to her:

'And now you must choose. Whose gift most pleased you?'

The Princess thought for a moment and said, 'Without the mirror you would not have known I was dead. Without the carpet you could never have come so quickly. Without the candle you could never have brought me back to life. If truth were told, I would like to marry all three of you, for your gifts are as perfect as you are yourselves. So the only honest thing I can do, is to marry none of you.'

And that is exactly what she did.

Adapted from *Portuguese Folk Tales* by Pedroso and Monteiro 1882.

23 How Jiřík won his wife

A Czech Folk Tale

Two apprentices, Borek and Jiřík, were travelling round the country-side one day when they passed the wall of a great castle. They were both curious to see how really rich folk live, so Jiřík lifted Borek on to his shoulders so that he could see over the wall. Borek gasped with admiration. 'There is a beautiful lady walking through the garden,' he said. 'Quick, let me down again, or I'm sure we'll be arrested and shot for our impertinence.' Jiřík was very keen to see the beautiful lady also, and although Borek was anxious to run off immediately for fear of being seen, Jiřík would not go until Borek had lifted him on to his shoulders so that he too could see over the wall. 'Well,' said Borek, 'can you see her? Is she not beautiful?'

'She is the loveliest creature on earth,' replied Jiřík, and at that moment Borek dropped him down and started to run. 'Come,' he called out to Jiřík, 'we mustn't wait here. She's probably a Princess, and commoners like us aren't supposed to look at Princesses—except when they're on official business, like when they get married.'

And very reluctantly, Jiřík ran off with his friend.

Later, when they were resting in a nearby field, Jiřík said. 'You know, I'm sure you're right. I bet she is a Princess. Someone as lovely as that couldn't be anything less than a Princess. And to think of some lucky man actually marrying her.'

'He'll be a Prince, for sure, or perhaps even a King,' said Borek. 'So you can put all thoughts of marrying her out of your mind. Remember—you're a poor young apprentice. No Princess is ever going to marry you.'

'That's what you say, but I would give my soul to the devil if I could marry her,' said Jiřík.

'And that's a foolish thing to say, and you know it,' said Borek.

It was a hot summer's afternoon, and they were both drowsy.

'What is the thing you would most like to have in all the world?' asked Jiřík suddenly.

'That's easy to answer,' replied Borek, '—to finish my apprentice-ship and to have a good business of my own.'

'That's not what I want,' said Jiřík. 'You can keep your apprentice-ship and your good business. I want the hand in marriage of that Princess. Nothing else.'

And then Jiřík saw a gentleman beckoning to him from the other side of the field. 'I think the fellow over there wants to talk to me. I'll just go over and see what he wants,' he said to Borek, who didn't hear him, for he was by now fast asleep.

'It's a fine day,' said the stranger as Jiřík approached him.

'It is indeed,' Jiřík agreed.

'And a beautiful castle over there,' added the stranger.

'And a very beautiful Princess lives inside it,' said Jiřík.

'Very *very* beautiful,' said the stranger.

'You know her?' asked Jiřík.

'A little,' replied the stranger.

'And she really is a Princess?' asked Jiřík.

'Most decidedly.'

'And is she married yet?'

'Not yet. Though every day some new Prince rides over the horizon to come and woo her.'

'But none has yet succeeded?'

'No. She says she has never yet fallen in love, and so cannot marry. But she has promised her father that she will definitely fall in love within the year, and that when she does it will be love at first sight.'

'Love at first sight,' sighed Jiřík. 'Yes, that is how I fell in love with her.'

'Then you must go to the castle, and declare your love for her.'

'Why that is impossible. I'm a mere apprentice. Almost a pauper.'

'If you wish, I will turn you into a Prince. You're certainly handsome enough to be a Prince,' said the stranger.

'Can you do that?'

'Easily. I know I don't look in the least like it, but in actual fact —and I'm not showing off or bragging or anything like that—I'm the devil.'

'The devil?'

'Indeed I am. And if you promise me to give me your soul in return, then I will do anything you wish.'

'But would you want my soul immediately?' asked Jiřík.

'Of course not,' said the devil. 'I wouldn't be so ill-natured. I'll grant you your wish, and come back to collect your soul from you in thirty years' time.'

'Thirty years?' thought Jiřík to himself. 'That's ages and ages.'

'Well, do you accept my proposition?' asked the devil.

'Yes. Willingly,' said Jiřík.

Whereupon the devil disappeared and before you could catch your breath or rub your eyes, there coming across the field towards Jiřík was a magnificent team of horses and a troop of soldiers.

And one of the soldiers came forward to Jiřík and saluted him, saying, ' Your Royal Highness, the Castle is now at hand, just across the other side of the field.'

' Very good,' said Jiřík, without wasting a second, ' tell the men to blow their trumpets to signal my arrival.'

And so it happened that Jiřík made as superb an entrance at the Castle as any Prince could have wished. And after presenting his compliments to the King, and giving him the presents which he found the devil had intelligently provided, Jiřík was taken down into the garden where only an hour or so before he had climbed on to his friend's shoulders and looked with wonder at the Princess's great beauty. And now he saw that the Princess was just as beautiful as she had at first seemed.

Believe it or not, no sooner had the King announced him, with, ' My dear, here is the great Prince Jiřík come to seek your hand in marriage '—than the Princess fell madly in love with him. It really was love at first sight. And within the month they were married, and were extremely happy together. In time the King died and so the Prince and Princess became King and Queen. Jiřík was an excellent king, full of good common sense, and always helpful and considerate to the poor. Not surprisingly, he was extremely popular with his subjects.

The years slipped by. The thirty years that had once seemed so long a time were now almost passed, and as it came to the very last month before Jiřík was due to hand over his soul to the devil, he became ill with worry. The Queen asked him many times to tell her what was troubling him, but he could not bring himself to tell her. Then, one fine summer's afternoon, there was the devil standing before him.

' I recognise you,' said Jiřík. ' I know. My time is up.'

' But it was a good bargain, was it not?' said the devil. ' For you did marry your beautiful Princess, just as you wished to do, and I hear you have been a really good King. So you see there's a good side to everything, even to a bargain with the devil.'

' Yes, we made our bargain, and of course I must keep my side of it,' said Jiřík sadly. ' But could you not possibly let me have just three more days? Please? Then I shall never again ask you for anything.'

' Why, three days is very little to ask for, and very little for me to grant. I'll do more than that for you. You can have your three days and during that time I will grant you anything you may request,' said the devil.

' Anything?' said Jiřík, astonished. ' But is that within your power?'

'Well,' said the devil. 'I'll make another bargain with you: if you are able to think of something which I am unable to grant you, then I shall acquit you of your side of the agreement, and you will not have to give me your soul. You will be free of me for ever.'

'It can't be impossible to think of something that the devil can't grant me,' said Jiřík to himself. 'Very well, then,' he added aloud, 'I'll call you as soon as I've thought of something.'

He decided that the best thing would be to ask his wife what she most wanted in all the world, for women always want quite impossible things.

'My dear,' said Jiřík, 'what would you most like me to give you? —I don't mind what it is, no matter how impossible it may seem to you. Just tell me. I very much want to give you a present, but I want it to be something you have always dreamed of having.'

'Most of all I should like to see you in good health,' said the Queen, 'but I notice you are already looking much better than you have been the last few weeks. So that wish is more or less granted already.'

And certainly the colour had returned to Jiřík's face now that there seemed some chance of not having to give his soul to the devil.

'There must be something else, something more impossible,' said Jiřík.

'Not really,' said the Queen, 'with you for my husband there is nothing else that I need. I am completely happy.'

'But just to please me, try to think of something.'

'It's so difficult.'

'But try,' insisted Jiřík.

'Very good. I should rather like it if the enormous rock at the back of the castle was removed, so that we could have a lovely view of the mountains in the distance. But we all know that would be impossible.'

Jiřík returned at once to his room, called for the devil, and told him the Queen's request. He hoped very much that the devil would find the request beyond his power to grant, but not at all. The following morning the Queen was astonished to see that the vast rock had disappeared and there in its place was a splendid view of the mountains, just as she had requested.

'Now try to think of something else you would like. Something even more impossible,' said Jiřík.

'Now this is really ridiculous,' said the Queen. 'I do believe you are in league with the devil. How else could you have granted such a request?'

'Never mind who I'm in league with,' said Jiřík, 'try to think of another request, even more impossible than the first.'

'Very well—I don't really want it, for like I told you I have everything I need, but how's this for a wish?—I want all the fields around the castle to be turned immediately into beautiful flower gardens.'

Jiřík went off and told the devil, and the wish was granted almost immediately.

This convinced the Queen that Jiřík was in league with the devil, and when she challenged him with the fact, he had to confess that he was, and to tell her the whole story from the very beginning.

'It isn't all that bad,' she said when he had finished, 'it can't be impossible to think of something that the devil can't do.'

And so she arranged with Jiřík that the devil should be sent to her that evening.

'I'm delighted to meet you at last,' said the devil.

'And are you the devil who has made the agreement with my poor husband?'

'I am indeed,' said the devil proudly.

'Good. And will you allow me to make a request in place of my husband?'

'Willingly, and if I cannot grant your wish then your husband will go free.'

'Very good. Then my wish is in two parts. Is that agreeable to you?'

'Certainly.'

'Part one of my wish is that you pull out three hairs from my head —and three hairs only, no more or less—and without hurting me.'

The devil thought this would be easy, but in fact, in pulling out one of the hairs he made the Queen cry out with pain.

'Oh dear,' said the devil, 'did I hurt you?'

'Never mind,' said the Queen. 'I'll forget that. Now for part two of my wish. You are to make each of my three hairs longer than they are, without breaking them and without joining any of them together. Now then: can you do that?'

The devil thought about it a long while, and then he said, 'Will you let me take this back to the other devils to see if they can help me?'

'Of course,' said the Queen.

And so the devil flew off to all the other devils, and they had a great conference to discuss the matter, in the course of which Lucifer himself appeared and said, 'You've lost your bet. You must go back and tell Jiřík that he is free of you for ever.'

And the devil was so upset and ashamed at having been caught out so easily by the Queen that instead of actually going he sent Jiřík

a letter telling him the good news.
   As you can imagine, Jiřík was delighted.
   And so was the Queen.

Adapted from *Tales from Czechoslovakia* by Marie Burg, University of London Press 1967.

In which the question is asked—what would *you* have said?

1   THE DOCTOR'S ONE CURE

A long time ago there was a doctor who spent years and years of his life working to discover a cure for a dreadful illness that killed off many of his patients. He mixed all manner of potions and then at last he found the cure. Now this cure was neither cheap nor easy to produce, and it included herbs from Asia and flowers from the West Indies and lotions from Darkest Africa, and he found that he only had enough of the medicine to cure one patient.

And so, because he was a fair man, he called together all the people of the village and explained the situation to them. ' I have six patients, and they are all suffering from the same illness, but I only have enough of the medicine to cure one of them. You must all help me to decide which of the patients I should cure.'

The villagers asked the patients to come forward, beginning with the lawyer, who said, ' I am the village lawyer, and without me the rest of you would be for ever arguing and fighting among yourselves and living like a pack of savages. I bring the guilty to justice, and I save the innocent when they are wrongly accused. I advise the rich man when he sells his property or when he draws up his will. I help the poor man when his rights and his liberty are threatened. Without me you would none of you be happy. It is I who must be saved by the doctor's cure.'

And the priest spoke, and said, ' I am the one who should be saved —for the laws of heaven are more important than the laws of the earth. In your hour of greatest need you turn to God and it is then you will need me, to guide your prayers, to counsel you and comfort you. The doctor must give me his curing potion, no one else.'

And the teacher spoke, and said, ' Just think where all of you would be if there was no one to teach you and your children. You'd all be ignorant and foolish. I could teach you to do without the lawyer—I could learn about the law myself and then tell you what I learn. And as for the laws of heaven, well I've been teaching them in the school-room for half an hour every morning for as long as I can remember. I'm the one you must save.'

And the farmer spoke and said, ' And a fat lot of good all your priests and your lawyers and your teachers will be to you if you have no food in your stomach. So just think about that, please. I need say no more. I've never been a talking man, and I don't intend to start now.' And with that he sat down.

And the soldier spoke and said, ' As for me, I don't believe in a lot of talking and speech-making either. But I'll say this. Even the food in your stomach is no good to you if there's no one to protect you from your enemies—and heaven knows there's enemies all around you. Let your soldiers die and where would you all be then? Just think of that and I need say no more.'

And the old wise man spoke, and said, ' I've been called the old wise man now for longer than I can remember, and they say I've been right more times than any other man living. So perhaps I've been living too long, and perhaps I'm not as wise as I used to be. But I'll say this. It seems to me that there are six of us when there ought to be only one. So there's five of us too many, so if I sit down and say, " I don't mind dying, you can leave me out of the argument altogether," then there'll only be four too many. That doesn't solve the problem, I know, but it does make it easier.' And with that, the old wise man sat down.

Now the six patients had all spoken, and so it was up to the villagers to argue it out among themselves and then to take the vote to determine which of the patients should be saved . . . and what would you have said?

2   THE BOY WHO WOULDN'T BE GOOD

Mr and Mrs McTavish were ordinary folk like you and me, and they produced three very fine sons. They grew up to be honest, decent, law-abiding and good-natured. They loved their parents and their parents loved them. But their fourth son, who was born after all the others had more or less grown up, was a very different kettle of fish altogether: he never could learn how to behave. He looked nice enough and he was bright enough too. And it wasn't that he was a terrible bully, or that he tried to burn the house down or anything like that. The truth of it was that he kept on stealing things—anything that he reckoned he could steal without anyone spotting him, why, he stole it there and then. Now the strange thing was that he stole lots of things that he had no need of whatsoever—hats that didn't fit him, eggs that he wasn't hungry enough to eat, books that he didn't want to read—and though he was quite clever at not getting caught, eventually he was found out. For he kept all the ridiculous things he had stolen in a hideout of his up on the hill, and one fine day some other children found the hideout and the stolen goods. And Tommy McTavish—for that was his name—was busy at that very moment counting up all the things he had stolen.

He was lucky that time. They let him off with a stern warning. But still he carried on stealing, and when he was caught again a committee was formed to decide what to do with him . . . and what would you have said?

Group III
Older Secondary

N.B.—*In this section there is a small group of folk stories, followed by a group of stories which I have developed and written down from ideas which I have worked on with various classes in improvisation sessions. Several of them are taken from ideas in newspaper stories, others are based simply on broad themes, such as the last one which revolves around the idea of leaving school and going out into the world, or on personal experiences told by students and then discussed around the class and used as a basis for improvisation: into this latter category come the two stories, 'Sam the Scrounger' and 'The Black Moments'.*

25 The Strongest Man in Ireland

An Irish Folk Tale

Mickey O'Shea was the strongest man in Ireland, or he thought he was. He certainly looked as though he could be: he was six feet six in his socks and his shoulders were as wide as the front door of his little cottage in the very little village of Maraughney, which, as far as I know, was somewhere in the middle of Tipperary. Now as you can imagine, O'Shea being such a big man in such a little place, when he decided to tell folks that he was the biggest man in all creation there were very few people in Maraughney—man, woman, or child—who ever dared contradict him. In fact nobody ever did, with the exception of his wife Elizabeth. ' Mickey O'Shea,' she'd say to him, ' you're no more the biggest man in all creation than I am the littlest woman.' In fact Elizabeth was a very little woman indeed, and though she was probably quite right, and she was not, I suppose, the littlest woman in creation, she was most certainly the littlest woman in Maraughney. ' No,' Elizabeth would say, ' you're certainly not the biggest, but you're certainly one of the silliest. What with all the shouting out you do, about how marvellous you are, and how big you are. But you'll regret it, you see if you don't. You'll regret it.' For Elizabeth was never afraid to tell her great big husband what she thought of him, even though she was so small. I really don't know what Mickey O'Shea used to do when his wife told him off, but everyone knew it was Elizabeth who was the master of the house, even though O'Shea would have knocked the brains—or threatened to do so—out of anybody who dared say such a thing in the ' Rose and Crown ' where O'Shea sat drinking with his cronies every evening of his life.

And Elizabeth used to tell him that the Rose and Crown would be the death of him. ' If you had as much sense as muscle, you great big oaf of an O'Shea,' she'd say, without so much as a flicker of nervousness as she looked up at her great big husband, ' why you'd not spend your life and your money in that den of foolishness and iniquity.'

O'Shea would pretend not to hear, and off he'd go, there and then, down the hill to the inn.

But what Elizabeth said came true—or very nearly so.

And this is how it happened.

Every market day O'Shea's pockets were bulging with money and then he loved to go down to the Rose and Crown in his very best

Sunday suit, and with his watch-chain sparkling in his waistcoat and his moustache waxed sprucely into shape. And his cronies in the Rose and Crown were especially fond of him on these days, for he was so pleased with the world and with himself—especially himself—that he would empty his pockets, buy drinks all round, and go home as penniless as a pauper. And his cronies would all urge him on with subtle flattery, saying, ' And who's the strongest man in Ireland, then, Mickey O'Shea?' and O'Shea, daft that he was, would bask in their praise and reply, ' Sure, it's not just Ireland. It's the strongest man in all the world I am, and I'll knock down the first man as ever says to the contrary.'

Now statements like that are the sort of thing you can say once, or twice, or even a few times, but you can't go on and on saying them for ever without somebody eventually telling you you're not the strongest man that's ever been and that he's going to prove it. And so, one market day, Mickey O'Shea had no sooner said he was the strongest man in all the world and he'd knock down the man who said he was not, when a very ordinary-looking man at the other end of the bar, a complete stranger, suddenly spoke up, and said, ' Well now, I'm not the man to be telling you you're not the strongest man in all the world, but I would be telling you this. This here gentleman is a very particular friend of mine—' and with that he pulled out a great big poster. A circus poster it was. And there was this picture of the most enormous man you've ever seen, bending his arm muscles he was, and looking more ferocious than ten lions all cooped up together in a small cage. And underneath the picture was written, in big bold letters:

' GINGER THE GIANT-KILLER '
Stands Seven Foot Two Inches in His Socks
The Biggest Man in the World
Hero of the Zulu Wars
Twice decorated by the Sultan of Zanzibar
Will fight any contestant or group of contestants.

N.B.—THE MANAGEMENT WILL NOT ENTERTAIN CLAIMS FOR COMPENSATION FROM WIDOWS OR CHILDREN OR OTHER DEPENDANTS OF DECEASED CONTESTANTS.

' Now it just so happens,' says the man, putting away the poster, ' that the circus is coming to Maraughney the week after next, on Market Day it will be, and I'll be telling Ginger all about you, Mr O'Shea, and no doubt he'll be wanting to meet you. Good day to you, and keep yourself in good condition till the week after next, won't you now?'

And with that the man was gone, and his cronies were picking poor Mickey O'Shea up from the floor where he'd fallen in a quivering heap. For Ginger the Giant Killer was a famous name in those parts in those times, and in fact he was so famous that some people even doubted whether he really existed. But now there seemed no doubt about it. And Mickey O'Shea was carried up to his little cottage and they put him in his bed where he lay, still shaking like a jelly, and refusing to be comforted by his friends.

'Why for sure,' said one of them, 'you're big and brave enough to lift old Ginger in your two hands and throw him out of the window and out of Ireland itself, and he'll never be heard of again, that's for sure.'

But Mickey O'Shea was not to be comforted.

'Why it's very unlikely he'll be bothered to even make your acquaintance,' said another friend, but nobody believed this, O'Shea least of all, for the most famous of all the many stories that people told, and still do tell, about Ginger the Giant Killer, concerned his exploits with foolish folk like O'Shea who had once, and fatally, boasted that they were stronger than he.

And so it happened that Mickey O'Shea lay shivering in his bed for two whole weeks, and could neither sleep nor eat nor even get the strength enough to pray. And the story went all round the little village of Maraughney, that Ginger the Giant Killer was coming with the circus, and that he was going to track down poor old O'Shea and settle his account with him.

And on the day the circus came, O'Shea shivered so much that Elizabeth was sure he'd break the bed in two. 'Well, well,' she said to him, 'here's a fine thing indeed.' O'Shea wanted to tell her to look after the cottage when he was gone and to pray for the peace of his soul, but the effort was altogether too much for him. Outside he could hear all the children shouting out merrily as they made their way up the hill and towards the circus. And the contrast between the merriment outside and the fear and misery inside himself was almost enough to kill him off there and then.

'So it's come to this,' said Elizabeth. 'And haven't I always told you no good would come of all this showing off and boasting. And now, now who's the biggest and strongest man in the world? Tell me now?'

'Why, Ginger the Giant Killer of course,' said O'Shea, weakly and pathetically from his bed.

'So. And this will be the end of you, I suppose,' said Elizabeth without pity.

'Surely,' said O'Shea, more weakly even than before.

'And what will become of me then?' asked Elizabeth. 'Who'll be looking after me then? And what'll become of me in my old age? You haven't thought of that now, have you, Mickey O'Shea? No of course not. It's yourself and nothing but yourself that you ever give thought for. You and all your boasting.'

'Save me,' said the great big O'Shea to his little wife. 'Save me.'

'Ah, and if I save you,' said Elizabeth, 'if I save you, what'll you be doing for me then?'

O'Shea could not answer.

'Well, I'll tell you what you'll be doing for me. You'll never again go down to that Rose and Crown and be spending all your money, and you'll never again go telling everyone how big and strong and mighty you are. You hear me?'

O'Shea nodded gravely in assent.

'And you promise?'

He nodded again.

'Right you are then.'

And with that she said, 'Now stay where you are. Keep your eyes shut, and don't open them until I tell you. Stop shivering and pretend to be asleep. If you do as I tell you, then I'll try to save you from that Ginger the Giant Killer. But if you don't, Mickey O'Shea, then you're a dead man and not even I can save you.' And, without another word of explanation, Elizabeth walked out of the bedroom and O'Shea closed his eyes, tried to stop trembling, and started, without knowing it, to fall asleep.

It was many hours later, in fact it was almost dusk, when Elizabeth, looking out from the window of the cottage, saw a great figure walking purposefully up the hill. He was taller than anything she had ever seen or imagined, and indeed he made poor O'Shea look quite insignificant in comparison. He had a fine crop of red hair and great wide shoulders. And even Elizabeth had to admit to herself that Ginger was a magnificent-looking fellow.

He paused at the little pathway to the cottage, and Elizabeth was amused to see him walk cautiously round the back of the cottage to make sure that O'Shea was not lying in wait to spring on him. Then he strode up to the door and knocked—just once.

'Good evening to you, Sir, and can I help you?'

The Giant was taken by surprise. No doubt he thought it all a trap.

'No,' he said, without moving from where he stood. 'It's not you as can be helping me, little woman, it's a man by the name of O'Shea as I'm looking for.'

'Well he's not here just right now,' said Elizabeth very civilly, 'but he'll be looking in before the night's set, so you're very welcome to come and sit at my table and wait for him to come.'

'I've heard some interesting things about your Mr O'Shea,' said the Giant, slowly, as he made his way into the cottage and sat himself at Elizabeth's table.

'Why sure,' said Elizabeth, ' he's a highly interesting man.'

'Seems like he reckons he's the biggest and the strongest man in Ireland,' said the Giant with a huge leer.

'Not just in Ireland,' said Elizabeth, quite unconcerned, ' but in the whole world—leastways that's what everyone says.'

With that Ginger almost growled with anger and gripped the table as though he would smash it between his fingers.

'Everyone says that, do they now?' said Ginger. 'Well, that's very interesting, 'cause everyone I know says as how I'm the biggest and the strongest in the world. And when Mr O'Shea comes home, why, him and me will be having a little contest to see which of us really is. Will he be long?'

'Not very long, I shouldn't think,' said Elizabeth, ' he likes to get to sleep about this time.'

'Well, he won't be coming home to sleep tonight, will he?' said Ginger grinning hideously.

'Oh, he never does,' said Elizabeth.

'He never does? What do you mean?' demanded Ginger.

'Lord bless you,' said Elizabeth, ' the poor man can never sleep in his own home, it isn't big enough for him. There's not a house in all Ireland that's big enough for him to stretch his legs in.'

'And where does he sleep then?'

'In the field over the hill. The biggest field in Tipperary it is. That's why we came to live here.'

And while Ginger sat thinking about this, Elizabeth went to the oven and took out three great stones she had found earlier in the garden.

'Well now,' she said, ' while you're waiting for my husband to come home for his supper, why don't you be giving yourself a little nourishment. You'll be needing it if it's a fight with O'Shea you're looking for.'

And with that she placed the hot stones on a plate and placed them in front of him.

'And what are these supposed to be?' said Ginger.

'Why bless you,' said Elizabeth, ' they're his favourite cakes. He always eats a few of those with his supper. Says they're grand for the teeth. 'Course they're too tough for ordinary folk, but O'Shea says he couldn't live without them.'

Ginger put one of the stones into his mouth, and his face assumed a puzzled expression as he took it out again, and put it down on the plate.

'I'm not hungry,' he says, 'not just now.'

'Suit yourself,' says Elizabeth. 'I only wanted you to feel at home.' Ginger continued to look puzzled.

'Well if you've nothing else to do while you're waiting, perhaps you'll do me a good turn. Nothing very much to ask a fine big fellow like you—or O'Shea. You see that house at the top of the hill there?' And she pointed to the big stone house that had been empty since three months back when the old widow died.

'O'Shea uses it as his dining-room. It's not big enough of course for him to sleep in, but it's just big enough for him to sit down in. So when he's out on the farm he always takes it up the hill with him, so he's got somewhere he can sit down in when it starts raining. And when he comes home, he always brings it back down again so he has somewhere to eat his supper. Well he's late, and his supper will be getting cold, so perhaps you could be bringing it down for him and I can get everything ready for when he comes in.'

'It looks a big house,' said Ginger.

'Surely. He's a big fellow.'

'And he lifts it up the hill and down the hill every day?'

'Surely,' said Elizabeth.

And Ginger thought for a moment and then walked out of the cottage and up the hill to the empty house. He leant against the house and tried to heave it up, out of the ground and on to his shoulders. After quite some minutes he abandoned the attempt and walked very slowly back down the hill and into the cottage.

'You're sure he actually lifts it?' said Ginger.

''Course. How else do you think he can get it up and down that hill?'

'He must be a big fellow then, this Mickey O'Shea.'

'Ah, he's big enough.'

'How big?'

'Difficult to say for sure. He's too big for a little body like me to get the tape measure round him. But tell you what, to give you an idea of how big he is, I'll let you have a look at his little boy. Everyone says he's gonna grow up to be almost as big as his father. 'Course, he's only a little fellow as yet. But he's still growing.'

And with that she led Ginger into the bedroom and there, stretched out in all his six feet six, fast asleep and looking as peaceful as a newborn lamb, was O'Shea.

'Isn't he a darling little boy,' said Elizabeth. 'And like I say, they all reckon he'll end up almost as big as his dear father. Almost, mark you. For no one could be quite as big, and no one could ever be bigger.'

Without a word Ginger the Giant Killer turned and walked out of the bedroom and out of the cottage. The following day the circus left the village and so did Ginger. He was never seen or heard of again in Tipperary.

Well, of course, Mickey O'Shea woke up the following morning and could hardly believe he was still alive. Nor could he believe it when all his old cronies, and quite a few total strangers, came to his door, asking to shake his hand, and telling him he really was the strongest man in all the world, for now he had beaten Ginger the Giant Killer. For a long time he could not think how he possibly could have performed this prodigious feat, and for a long time he remained faithful to his promise to Elizabeth, and he did not go down to the Rose and Crown and spend all his money. But all of us are only human, including Mickey O'Shea, and so, after a year or so, Mickey went strolling down to his favourite inn one market day, determined that at last the world should hear how he, Mickey O'Shea, six feet six in his socks, had beaten the invincible Ginger the Giant Killer and proved himself the strongest man in all creation. As time went on, he managed to produce several different versions of how he had performed this great deed, but, interestingly enough, he never made mention in any one of his stories, of his wife Elizabeth, the littlest woman in Maraughney.

Adapted from *Celtic Fairy Tales* by Joseph Jacobs 1892.

26 Muckle-Mou'ed Meg

A Scots Legend

Sir Juden Murray had three daughters and not one of them was pretty. Some folks said they were downright ugly, and all agreed that the oldest daughter, Meg, was the ugliest of the three. Yet Meg Murray married one of the handsomest—as well as the richest—young men in all Scotland, and this is how it happened.

There was no fighting at this time: all the clans and all the country were at peace, and most people liked it that way. But not everyone. Some of the youngsters thought life was rather on the dull side with no wars to go to and no feuds to settle. So they decided to invent a bit of adventure for themselves. And a small band of them, led by the handsome young William Harden, decided to be robbers and highwaymen. Not that they needed to rob anyone of anything, for they were all the sons of rich landowners. William's father was one of the greatest landowners in all Scotland. But they were hot-blooded, and they wanted adventure; and that's how they set out about getting it.

They had no intention of being plain, ordinary robbers. They weren't going to rob plain, ordinary people—that wasn't their idea of adventure at all. Their sights were set on much more ambitious targets, and for their first expedition they decided to rob the great Sir Juden Murray of a fine herd of cattle. Now Sir Juden was as important in his part of Scotland as William Harden's father was in his, and if they were to rob him of his cattle and get away without being caught they would need to be extremely clever, unusually bold, and unbelievably lucky—all of which they very nearly were. Their plans were well laid and were almost a complete success. But while making off with the cattle in the dead of night, a drunken farmhand suddenly appeared from nowhere, ran straight into them, thought he was seeing ghosts, and made such a noise, shouting and crying out, that he woke up the entire neighbourhood, and within minutes Sir Juden's men were out in pursuit. Leaving the cattle behind, the band of robbers fled for dear life, and only one was caught, brought back to Sir Juden's castle, and flung into the dungeon. In the morning he would be executed. And that would be the end of young William Harden.

Later that night, Lady Elizabeth Murray woke up her husband, Sir Juden.

'You're making too much noise,' she said, 'you and your snoring. I can't hear myself thinking.'

Sir Juden continued to snore.

'I said you're making too much noise,' said Elizabeth again, nudging him rather harder this time.

'Oh,' cried out Sir Juden in surprise. 'Who's attacking us? Who's attacking us?'

'Get back into bed, you great silly,' said Elizabeth, 'no one's attacking us.'

'Dear me, it's those youths coming to rob our cattle—they're giving me nightmares,' said Sir Juden.

'No need for that. We've got their leader under lock and key. They won't be coming back for more.'

'Aye—he'll be swinging in the morning, and a good thing too.'

'That's what I've been thinking about,' said Elizabeth.

'It's too late for me to think about anything,' said Sir Juden, yawning.

'What a dreadful shame—a fine young lad like that ending up on the gallows, hanged for a common thief.'

'Mm,' said Sir Juden, almost asleep.

'And the son of rich and noble parents he is, too. It'll break their poor hearts.'

Sir Juden snored in reply.

'He'd make a fine husband for our Meg, don't you think?'

More snores.

'A fine husband. Don't you think so?'

She nudged her husband again. No reply. A more hearty nudge, and he answered, 'What's that you're saying, woman? Why can't you let me get some sleep?'

'You've three daughters to get married off, my man, there's no time to waste on sleeping.'

'Ah,' he said, 'it's no time to be thinking about that now.'

'This is just the time.'

'No one'll be wedding them in the middle of the night, will they?'

'No—but I know someone who may be wedding our Meg, before the next night comes.'

'Our Meg? What—muckle mou'ed Meg?'

'Aye, that's what they call her, just 'cause she's a little on the plain side.'

'No, she's greatly on the plain side, and well we know it. No one'll marry her, my dear, and that's the truth.'

'I've an idea there's someone who may be very willing to marry her. And he's as rich as he is handsome—ah, that makes you wake up

125

and pay attention, doesn't it?'

'What's this you're talking about, Elizabeth?'

'Listen carefully, and I'll tell you.'

Meanwhile, down in the dungeons, young William Harden had not slept at all. It's a sad time when a man's life draws to its close, specially when he's a man as young and as adventurous as William. He was sorry for himself, and also for his poor mother, whose heart would be broken when she heard how and why he had died. Then William could hear men laughing and the sound of nails being hammered into wood. They were building the gallows. So this was the end, and well he knew he deserved what he was going to get: he'd been foolish and reckless, and now he was to pay the penalty. There was no injustice in it. He had nothing to complain of. He had no one to blame but himself.

He expected to be led straight out to the gallows, but when the men came to fetch him they took him instead into the castle and straight to the great banqueting room. 'What's all this about?' thought William. 'Surely they're not going to waste time with some ridiculous trial. Everyone knows I'm guilty. Kill me and have done with it.'

And at the far end of the great banqueting room was Sir Juden Murray with his wife at his side. William thought her a rather formidable-looking woman. And all the servants and all the men and women of the castle were standing down either side of the room. All eyes were on him, except for those of a young woman who stood looking away from the scene, just at the side of Lady Elizabeth. She was not very pretty—or at least she didn't appear to be: it was difficult for William to be sure of this, for she had not yet lifted her face or looked towards him. He was completely puzzled as to what all this ceremony could be about.

'Well sir,' said Sir Juden finally.

'Well sir,' said William in reply.

He might be their prisoner, but he intended to show no sign of cowardice. Nor would he ask for any kind of mercy. He was not William Harden for nothing.

'So, you think you will rob me of my cattle, do you?' said Sir Juden, who seemed to be oddly at a loss for words.

'I thought to do so,' said William, 'and now I hope that you will hang me properly and decently, and not play games with me.'

'I'll do what I like with you, young man, and it's not up to you to start telling me what you want and what you don't want. You can think yourself very lucky that you're still alive,' said Sir Juden, already getting angry.

'I know you'll hang me, so I ask that you hang me now, and get it over with, that is all,' said William.

Lady Elizabeth nudged her husband, as if to say, ' Get on with it,' and he cleared his throat and began again, ' Well now, young Harden, you're a wicked young man and that's the truth, and I'm not sure—'

But William interrupted him before he could get any further with his speech: ' With great respect, my lord, if I wanted a speech I'd go to my father for one. But I don't want a speech. I just want to be hanged. I deserve that. I deserve nothing else.'

' And if you're not careful, young man, that's exactly what you'll get—a hanging and nothing else—'

Elizabeth nudged him again, and this time she leaned forward to whisper in his ear.

' Oh yes—yes. Now then. This will surprise you, young man, but I —that is, I and my wife, I mean my wife and I—we have an offer to make to you.'

' An offer?' said William, astonished.

' Yes—and please don't interrupt me again, or I'll never remember what it is I have to say. Now then. I have three daughters, none of whom is yet married. The oldest is Meg—you see her, standing here beside her mother.'

At that moment Meg turned to look at her father and William thought he'd never seen a plainer-looking girl in all his life.

' By rights I ought to hang you,' continued Sir Juden, ' and I'm still not sure that I won't, but this is the offer I'm prepared to make to you.'

He coughed and cleared his throat with embarrassment before proceeding. Quite suddenly William realised what the offer was going to be, and it was all he could do to stop himself from laughing. As though the youngest and handsomest son of the great Sir John Harden, landowner and nobleman, would ever marry a creature as plain and ugly as Meg Murray!

' My Meg is a good girl. She can cook well, and sew well, and do everything that's fitting in a woman, even though she is not, I must agree, in the least bit pretty. No one, I don't believe, would ever say she's pretty,' said Sir Juden, while his wife looked hard at him, as if to say, ' I'd rather hang you than hang that thief there.'

' Now my offer is this,' said Sir Juden, at last getting in sight of his objective, ' if you agree to marry Meg, then I'll spare you the gallows. In other words, marry my daughter, and I won't hang you.'

At this, Sir Juden was so exhausted that he had to sit down and wipe the sweat from his forehead.

Everyone looked at William, waiting for his answer. Everyone ex-

I   127

cept Meg, who had turned away.

William took less than a second to make up his mind.

'Sir, I'd rather hang than marry a girl I do not love. I've never, never been so much insulted in all my life.'

'What's that you say—insulted? You? It is me you insult, sir, me and my good wife here. Hanging's too good for you, but hang you shall. Take him away this instant.'

And as the men came up to seize him and take him away, William replied, 'No, my lord, it is not you who is insulted. It is your daughter, Meg, and it is not I who insults her—it is you, her own father. What shame for a young woman to have to bear, that her parents offer her to a robber in exchange for his life.'

And there was no telling who was the more angry—the father at hearing the truth so well stated by this upstart young highwayman, or William himself who felt so keenly the injury done to the girl's feelings.

'Take him away. Hang him,' cried Sir Juden.

But at that moment, hearing what William had just said, and hearing him express so clearly the insult she herself felt, Meg turned to look at him for the very first time. It was a look full of humiliation and sorrow. And in that second of time, as the two looked at each other, William suddenly realised that although Meg was indeed as plain as men said she was, possibly even ugly, she was, for all that, a good, honest and sensible woman, and had it not been for her lack of beauty she would have been one of the finest women in all Scotland. And realising this, William felt even more sorry for her. 'My life has been made unbearable by a lack of adventure, and now I'm to die for it,' he thought to himself. 'And her life has been made unbearable because men think her so ugly. And by the look on her face, she too would gladly die for it.' He thought too, of the awful humiliation that he was now inflicting on her: it would be said of her for ever after, 'There goes Meg Murray—a man once hanged rather than have to marry her. Can you blame him?'

'We're ready, my lord,' said one of the men.

'And so is the hangman,' said another.

'Good,' said Sir Juden, 'hang him and have done with it.'

'No! Wait,' said William. 'I have something to say.'

'I'm not sure that we want to hear it,' said Sir Juden.

'Yes we do,' said Elizabeth. 'Speak up and let us hear you.'

'Men will laugh at me for saying this, and you yourselves will never believe me. But I'll say it, for it's true. Your daughter is not pretty. And I'm not a coward. I'd rather be dead than wed to a woman I do not want. But—' and he looked at Meg, 'if Meg will marry me, then I'll be proud to have her for my wife, and if you want to hang me after, then do so.'

And all the men burst out laughing, until Sir Juden said he'd hang them instead if they did not behave themselves.

' But I will not have it be said,' continued William, ' that I married Meg for fear of going to the gallows. I ask her to marry me, because —because—because I like the look of her. And that's God's truth.'

You could see by the looks on their faces that all the men, and most of the women, wanted to roar out laughing—to think of any man wanting to marry Meg because of the look of her!

' Very well,' said Sir Juden, much surprised, ' so be it.'

And the same day, Meg and William mounted their horses, and rode off for the Hardens' castle to tell the news to his mother and father. By now William had had time to think about what he'd done and was beginning to regret it. Meg was even plainer now that he saw her properly than he had previously imagined. His parents would be furious, his brothers and his friends would laugh at him. Could he now undo what he had done? The only honourable thing would be to take Meg back to her parents and ask them to hang him there and then and forget the whole business. He thought of all the pretty girls who would be only too pleased to marry him and then he thought again of Meg. It was impossible. He would have to take her back. And they could hang him, and that would be that. He stopped his horse.

Suddenly Meg spoke to him.

' William,' she said, ' we're a good distance now from my father's home. You will be quite safe now. Ride on and leave me here. I shall find my own way back.'

' But is that the reason why you came with me—to give me the chance to escape?'

She nodded.

' You mean—you didn't expect me to honour my promise?'

' It would be wrong of you to do so, William, for you do not love me. And now you must go. And I shall return to my parents.'

' Meg,' said William, ' my mother once said to me, that if ever I met a beautiful woman I should think twice before I married her. But if ever I met a good woman, then I should marry her without thinking at all. And you're a good woman. Will you marry me?'

And so Meg said she would, and she did. And she made him an excellent wife and they lived happily together for many years, and often they would tell their friends—and their children—how muckle-mou'ed Meg and handsome William would never have got married had William not been so wicked and Meg so plain.

And that's a true story.

Adapted from *Tales from Scottish Ballads* by Elizabeth Grierson 1906.

27 Things aren't what they used to be

An Italian Folk Tale

Two peasants, a husband and his wife, were extremely poor and were for ever grumbling.

' Times are bad,' said the husband.

' They are indeed,' said the wife, ' and they're never going to be any better.'

' Times are even worse than they used to be,' said the husband.

' Even worse,' agreed the wife, ' and they've not been good for years and years.'

' Not for as long as I can remember,' said the husband.

' Nor I,' said the wife.

' Everything's so expensive,' said the husband.

' Don't I know!—why, everything costs twice as much today as it did ten years ago,' said the wife.

' And prices are still going up.'

' All the time.'

' Non-stop.'

' It's terrible.'

' It's awful.'

And then they grumbled about their neighbours.

' There used to be such a nice class of people living around here. Now—well I'd be ashamed to say I know any of them.'

' They're so noisy,' said the wife.

' They're so inconsiderate,' said the husband.

' They're just not nice people. And that's that,' said the wife.

' That's that,' agreed the husband.

And then they grumbled about the weather.

' The sun hasn't shone since I don't know when,' said the wife.

' Never stops raining these days, does it?' said the husband.

' When we were young it was always good weather,' said the wife.

' Aye—when we were young.'

' It's too bad.'

' Aye—it's too bad.'

And then they grumbled about their children.

' They have no manners,' said the wife.

' And no respect for their elders,' said the husband.

'We were quite different when we were young.'

'Very different.'

'No comparison.'

'None whatever.'

And then they grumbled about the government.

And then the husband said, 'Somebody must be to blame for all our troubles.'

'Yes—things must have been better once.'

'Yes—once,' echoed the husband sadly.

'In the Garden of Eden it was perfection. That's whose fault it all is—Adam and Eve. If it hadn't been for them touching the forbidden fruit they would never have been turned out of Paradise, and we'd all have been there still to this very day.'

'You're right,' said the husband, 'it's Adam and Eve we have to curse for all our troubles.'

Now all this time they had been overheard by an extremely rich gentleman, a Duke in fact, who had been fascinated by the way the couple carried on endlessly moaning. So he stepped forward and said, much to their surprise, 'You curse Adam and Eve, do you, for touching the forbidden fruit? Very well. I shall restore you to Paradise—or what you think of as Paradise—and we shall see if you can do any better than Adam and Eve.'

And without waiting to see what they had to say about all this, he ordered his soldiers to take the couple back to his palace. There they were given magnificent apartments and every possible comfort and luxury.

'You will have served at your table exactly the same food and drink as I shall have served at mine. Everything you wish for, you have only to ask and it will be granted.'

'Well, that certainly sounds like Paradise to me,' said the wife. And the husband said the same.

'There is only one restriction I place on your happiness. You will find a beautiful silver bowl, covered, and placed on your table. It will never be taken away. You are never, under any circumstance, to remove the cover or ask what is underneath it.'

'Why that seems a very small restriction indeed,' said the wife, 'why should we worry ourselves about what is inside a little silver bowl when we have everything else in the world that we could wish for?'

And the husband agreed.

With that, the Duke left them to lead their own lives in his fine palace. They had plenty of servants, and plenty of food and drink.

At first, they asked only for a little food, for they had been used to living on even less. Soon they wanted three courses instead of just two. Then four courses, and finally even twelve were not enough.

'Why are there only twelve courses?' demanded the wife one day.

'Yes,' said the husband, 'only a peasant could live on twelve courses.'

'But that is all the Duke himself has,' said the servant.

'Then tell him it isn't good enough, not for us.'

'It's dreadful,' said the husband.

'Things are getting worse and worse,' said the wife. 'Today my bath was not exactly the right temperature.'

'And my manicurist was a minute late,' said the husband.

'And mine was a second early,' said she.

'Oh how irritating,' said he.

'The country's on the decline, that's what it is,' said she.

'We're all going to the dogs,' said he.

'Look at my clothes, look how unfashionable they are,' said she, indicating the most expensive clothes in the land.

'And look at the servants, how little respect they have.'

And then they grumbled about the weather.

And then they grumbled about their children, who had not been to visit them.

And then they grumbled about the government.

And then they grumbled about the Duke.

And then the husband said, 'The only thing that keeps me going is the thought of what might be in that silver bowl.'

'It must be something very valuable,' said she.

'How exciting it would be to find out.'

'Dare we?'

'What do you think?'

'No, what do *you* think?'

'Well—why not?'

'Yes—why not?'

'Ready?'

'Ready.'

'I'll count up to five and then you lift the top of it.'

'No. I'll count and then you lift.'

'Oh, very well.'

And so the wife counted up to five, the husband lifted the top of the bowl to reveal a beautiful white pigeon who immediately flew straight out of the window and into the Duke's chamber. As soon as the Duke saw the pigeon he knew that the two peasants had broken their pledge, so, without more ado, they were turned out of the palace.

'And now,' said the Duke, 'you have tasted Paradise like Adam and Eve once did. Now what will you find to grumble about?'

Adapted from 'A Little Bird' in *The House of Cats and other Italian Folk Tales* by John Hampden, André Deutsch 1966.

28 The marriage of Sir Gawain

An English Folk Tale

It is many years now since King Arthur ruled his kingdom from his palace at Camelot. Some men say they were marvellous days to be alive and that Arthur was a marvellous king and that nothing and no one today could ever be as good. Whether that's true or not we need hardly bother ourselves to so much as wonder, for the most important thing about King Arthur—as far as this story is concerned—is that he was a great one for adventures, and when nothing adventurous was happening he was as bored as can be, and out he would go, riding off in whatever direction the fancy took him, in quest of something exciting to break the monotony. Now as you can imagine his beautiful Queen, Guinevere, herself became bored and irritated by her husband's habit of riding away to no man knew where whenever he felt like it, and she and her friends often tried to persuade him to settle down and to let adventure find him for a change.

This particular Saturday the King was more restless than even he usually was, and nothing of any great note appeared to be happening at court. And so, despite the comments of his Queen, he put on his fine and heavy armour, mounted his noble horse, and charged off into the forest. As he rode along he thought to himself, ' Adventure, adventure, adventure—there must be an adventure somewhere, and I must find it. And tonight, or tomorrow, or next year, or the year after, I shall ride back to Camelot covered in honour and glory, leaving behind yet another legend of my daring exploits for men and women yet unborn to tell their children.' The King scanned the forest carefully for signs of dragons or monsters or ladies in distress, but to his acute irritation there was no sign of anything so interesting. ' Good gracious,' thought the King to himself, ' perhaps those dreary knights of mine have slain all the monsters, and rescued all the distressed ladies, and left nothing for me to do. How awfully boring life will be from now on.' But his spirits rose when, as he came out of the forest, he saw silhouetted against the sunset the figure of a man climbing a hill. Without wasting a second the great King charged forward shouting out, ' Villain, monster, coward, reprobate—' and anything else that came to his lips at that moment, ' here is an end to your wicked ways, for I am no less a person than the great King Arthur himself, and I am come to challenge you. And do not turn away, and do not run, and do not try to deny your wickedness, for as I said, I am King Arthur himself, in person, and I have come to challenge you.' The stranger on the hillside showed no sign of wishing to run away: instead, he stayed precisely where he was, but as the King got nearer and nearer to him, the stranger grew bigger and bigger, until, by the time the King was alongside him, the stranger was as big as any giant that even the adventurous Arthur had ever seen. Naturally enough, the King was a little surprised to discover the magnificence of this creature he had so boldly challenged.

'Well, well,' said the giant, 'so you challenge me, little man, do you?' And he grinned quite hideously.

'Yes I do. Indeed I do,' said the King, trying not to show any trace of nervousness, for he knew from bitter experience that nervousness is the one thing you must never display when confronted with a giant. 'Did I not say I do?'

'Well then, little man,' said the giant, 'I am ready. What are you waiting for?'

'If you don't mind,' said the King, 'I am a King. And no gentleman would ever call a King a little man. Even though I must admit that in comparison with yourself, I am a little man. Or to be more precise, I am a little King.'

'Very well, little king. You challenged me. Now fight me.'

And Arthur moved to take his sword from the scabbard but to his amazement, the sword could not be moved. Then, as he tried to take his hand away to seize his dagger, he found also to his amazement that neither could he move his arm. The giant laughed hideously.

'Aha,' said the giant.

'You wretch,' cried the King. 'So you would stoop to this—denying a King a fair fight, and using some wicked witchery to conquer him. Sir,' said the King, working himself up into a passion, 'you are beneath contempt.'

'So I am,' said the giant, good naturedly, 'and you, my little king, will soon be beneath the ground. For now you are my prisoner and I shall take you back to my castle and throw you into the dungeons and there you shall rot and crumble and decay, alongside all the other rats and vermin that I have captured just as I have captured you.'

'Oh dear,' cried the King, 'you cannot possibly do any such thing.' For the King was thinking how dreadfully the day had gone, first with no adventure at all, and now with too much adventure. 'I am a King, and you cannot throw me in the same dungeon with rats and vermin. If you had a dungeon full of kings and princes and knights, that would be another thing altogether, and I could hardly complain, but really—well, I am speechless with indignation. How could you think of treating me so ungraciously?'

'There's something in that, I suppose,' said the giant. 'You are a king after all, and quite a famous one at that.'

The King began to feel better.

'Tell you what I'll do,' said the giant. 'I'll let you go on one condition. I shall give you a riddle to take away with you. And in a week's time you must come to me at this very place and at this very time, and you will give me the answer to the riddle. And if your answer is the right one, then you shall be free. But if it is the wrong one, then you will be my prisoner for the rest of your miserable days and you will rot away in my dirty dungeons. Agreed?'

'Yes,' said the King. 'I agree. But what is the riddle?'

'The riddle is,' said the giant, 'a very simple one.'

'Well?'

'What is it that every woman always wants?'

'I see,' said the King, 'that sounds very difficult.' In fact he thought it extremely easy, but he did not want to upset the giant. 'I shall see you here then, in a week's time.'

'In a week's time,' called out the giant, as Arthur turned away and galloped off to Camelot.

'What idiots these giants are,' said the King to himself. 'That poor stupid fellow doesn't seem to realise that I have a wife and all the ladies of the court, and they will tell me the answer to the riddle, and then I shall be safe.'

And he was feeling extremely pleased with himself as he charged back through the forest, for he had really had an adventure after all, and there would be plenty to talk about that evening over supper.

And indeed there was. For every lady in Camelot believed she had the answer to the giant's riddle. Queen Guinevere said, 'Why it is the easiest riddle that ever was. What is it that every woman always wants? Every woman knows the answer to that one—she wants a good, strong, loving and faithful husband, one who is not for ever charging off in all directions searching for quite unnecessary adventures. That's what every woman always wants.'

But the Queen's mother disagreed. 'Nothing of the kind,' she said. 'The one thing that every woman always wants is love. Nothing else.'

And the Queen's principal lady-in-waiting said, 'No. The answer isn't that at all. I'll tell you what all women always want: a bold and beautiful young knight, who will rescue her whenever she is in danger.'

At this, a chorus of young ladies-in-waiting called out their agreement. 'How very true,' they all said. 'How very true.'

But then the chief assistant cook came forward. 'Excuse me, Your

Majesty,' said the cook, curtsying to the King, ' I know I'm just the chief assistant cook, but I know what every woman always wants. And it isn't anything to do with romance or love or adventure.'

' It isn't?' said the King. ' Then tell me, what is it?'

' A roof over her head,' said the chief assistant cook. ' And decent food and clothing for the children.'

' Nonsense,' cried someone else. ' Women want gratitude, nothing else.'

' Rubbish,' cried another. ' Women want appreciation. That's all.'

' Balderdash,' cried another. ' Women want fine clothes and beautiful jewels that sparkle and shine around them.'

' Fiddlesticks—'

' Silence—' shouted the King. ' How on earth am I ever to know how to answer the riddle if all of you say completely different things? It's quite impossible. And so are all of you women. All women are impossible.' And the King fell into a great long sulk which cast the whole palace into a deep depression for the rest of the week-end and the whole of the week that followed. One by one the ladies came to him and whispered in his ear the various answers they had offered him earlier, and this merely annoyed the King still further. The thought of the giant and his dismal dungeon and this absurd riddle took all the heart and the life out of him.

' If only,' said the King, ' the riddle had been to say what every *man* always wants. Now that would have been a very different kettle of fish altogether. Men are much more sensible creatures. Every man knows what he wants, doesn't he?'

' Absolutely,' said all the knights together.

' Definitely,' said one.

' Of course,' said another.

' We all want—adventure, don't we?' said another.

' I want romance,' said one of the knights earnestly.

' I want to see all the wonders of the world,' said one exceedingly young knight.

' And I want to see the most beautiful ladies that were ever born,' said another.

' And I—'

' All right,' cried the King in great irritation. ' It doesn't matter what you want. That's not the riddle.'

And there was still more shouting out of advice when the King rode out from Camelot and into the forest the following Saturday at the appointed time. Indeed the King was glad to be rid of everyone, even if it did mean that he would be spending the rest of his days in a dark dungeon in the company of rats and vagabonds.

'Who knows?' said the King sulkily to himself as he rode. 'Perhaps I shall be much better off.'

'You don't really think that, do you?' said a strange voice from among the shadows of the trees.

'I beg your pardon,' said the King, stopping his horse.

'You will be awfully unhappy in the giant's dungeon, and well you know it.'

'Who are you? And where are you? Come forward and let me see you.'

And out into the path stepped the ugliest old woman that the King had ever seen in all his life, and being a highly adventurous king he had seen, as you can imagine, a fairly wide assortment of ugly as well as beautiful women.

'There, now you can see me,' said the old hag, grinning an awful toothless grin. 'And are you not glad to see me?'

'Kings never lie,' replied Arthur solemnly. 'No. I am not glad.'

'Good. I like honest men,' said the hag. 'And since you are an honest man, I'll tell you something that you will be deeply glad to hear.'

'Really,' said the King, without enthusiasm.

'The answer to the riddle,' said the old hag.

'Ah. Then you know about it?'

'Indeed yes,' said she, 'and about the giant and the dungeon. For the giant is my own brother.'

'Well I'm not surprised about that,' said the King, 'for he is quite as ugly as you are. But what about the riddle. Will you tell me the answer?'

'I will,' said she. 'If you will make me a solemn promise.'

'Any promise—you name it, I'll vow to it.'

'The promise is this: when you return to Camelot you will order one of your most handsome knights to marry me.'

'But that is an awful promise to ask of me. Have you seen yourself lately in a mirror? You realise what you are asking of me?'

'Yes,' she said, grinning again her toothless grin. 'I know I am no precious jewel, but I'll make a good wife. You, then, will provide the husband?'

'Well—' and he hesitated.

'It is an awful place, my brother's dungeon. The rats there are the worst in Europe. He imported them specially.'

'Very well then. I promise.'

'Good. I shall look forward to meeting my future husband. But he must be handsome. Don't forget that.'

'All my knights are handsome,' said the King.

'And young,' said the hag.

'All my knights are—fairly young,' said the King.

'Good. Then here is the answer to the giant's riddle. The one thing that all women always want is—'

And she whispered the answer so quietly that even the leaves of the trees could not have heard.

The King smiled, and then he said, 'How right you are.'

And off he rode to the giant, who waited for him at the appointed place. The giant was grinning hideously, just as his sister had done, but his grins turned to rage when he heard the King deliver the correct answer to the riddle.

'Confound you,' he cried, 'you've been talking to that hideous old hag of a sister of mine, haven't you, and she's told you, hasn't she?'

'She has indeed,' replied the King, 'and now I am free of you for ever.'

And with that he turned his horse and rode back to the old hag. She was waiting, her ugly old face wrinkled in smiles. 'Ha, ha,' she cried, 'I'll bet he stamped his great big feet and cursed my name.'

'That he did,' replied the King. 'But that will be nothing to what my knights will say when I tell them you are to marry one of them.'

'I'm ready,' said the hag, gurgling with delight. 'I cannot wait to see my husband.'

You can imagine the surprise in Camelot when the King came home with the old hag at his side, and how the surprise turned to horror when the news of the King's agreement with the hag was made known to the courtiers. Some of the knights were so furious that there was even talk of rebellion, and indeed there might have been a civil war had not the King's young and handsome nephew, Sir Gawain, the noblest knight in Camelot, stepped forward and said, 'I will honour your promise, Your Majesty. I shall marry the—' and he looked for an appropriate word—'the good lady.'

Whereupon the ladies burst into tears, the knights burst into laughter, and the old hag grinned an even more enormous and more toothless grin than before.

'So be it,' she said.

The King was delighted to have the matter so quickly settled, and the royal sewing women were ordered to settle down to work and to prepare the hag a beautiful wedding dress. And when the dress was ready the hag sent for Sir Gawain.

'Ha, ha,' said the hag, 'how do you like my wedding dress?'

'I like it very well,' said Sir Gawain politely.

'And how do you wish to be married, then, with all the court present, or with none present save our two selves and the worthy priest? A quiet wedding or a gay and noisy one?'

'Well I must confess,' said Sir Gawain, 'I rather dread the thought of what all the knights will say when they come to the wedding feast —I think I would rather have a quiet wedding. But then,' and he looked bravely into her face, 'young ladies always seem to prefer a great celebration. It seems unfair to spoil your own enjoyment, so —I think I'll leave it to you. Do whatever you prefer.'

'Ha, ha,' croaked the hag and before Sir Gawain knew what was happening the old hag had transformed into a beautiful young lady with long fair hair.

'Why this is absolutely splendid,' said the Knight. 'I thought I was marrying an old witch, and I am marrying a lovely young maiden.'

'You have yourself to thank,' said the young maiden, 'for you have broken half the spell.'

'I have?' said the Knight, most surprised to hear this.

'Indeed you have,' said the maiden, 'and just as I am now changed back into a young maiden, so my brother, the giant who met the King, will now be changed back into a handsome young gentleman.'

'How delightful,' said Sir Gawain, 'but we must let everyone know at once.'

'But wait. Only half the spell is broken,' said she.

'How do you mean?' said the Knight.

'I cannot be beautiful all the time. For half the day I can be beautiful, as I always used to be before the wicked spell was cast. For the other half of the day I must be ugly. Now you must choose. When do you wish me to be beautiful, and when do you wish me to be ugly?'

'Oh dear,' said Sir Gawain, 'that's a terribly difficult question.'

'I know,' said the maiden, 'but you must make up your mind.'

'Well, if you were beautiful by day, then none of the knights would laugh at me for having such an ugly wife and all the world would envy me for having such a lovely one. And if you were ugly by night then only I would ever know, and no doubt I could learn to put up with that. So as far as I am concerned I think I would prefer—but, well,' and then he hesitated.

'Come now,' she said, 'why do you hesitate?'

'Well, after all,' he replied, 'it's your face that we're talking about, not mine, and you have to wear it. So I think it's for you to decide, not me. Do whatever you will.'

And with that she flung her arms around him and said, 'You are the greatest knight that ever was, and now I shall be beautiful not just for half the day, but for the whole of the day, now and for always.'

'Nothing could be better my dear,' said Sir Gawain, 'but how can this be?'

'You have broken the other half of the spell,' said she. 'For just as the King gave the answer to the riddle in words so you have answered the riddle in action.'

And when the Knight still looked baffled she continued, 'For what is it that every woman always wants? I'll tell you—her own way.'

And Gawain and his beautiful bride lived happily ever after.

From an anonymous dramatisation 1861, based on Bishop Percy's *Reliques of Ancient Poetry*.

29 Sam the Scrounger

A Story from an Improvisation

I never have liked old Samuel, he's always scrounging things. Like one day he leans over to me in the Maths lesson and whispers loud enough for all the school to hear, 'Eh Kevin, lend me your bike tonight will yer?' I pretends I can't hear him so he calls out again to me, even louder than the last time, 'Eh Kevin, lend me your bike tonight will yer?' I give him a dirty look but that don't mean anything to Samuel. He just grins back at me and says, 'You're a pal you are Kevin. You're a real pal.' But I wasn't gonna lend him my bike.

Then he comes running up to me when I'm going out of school but still I wouldn't lend it him.

'Well what's the matter with yer then?' says Sam. 'I thought you was my mate.'

'Then you thought wrong,' I says.

'Nah there's no cause to be unsociable,' says Sam. 'Don't we always share our fags then like a pair of old pals?'

'No,' I says, '*we* don't share our fags, *you* share mine. That's not the same thing.'

'Well someone got out of bed the wrong side this morning and that's a fact. Who's been eating your little bowl of porridge then?'

'No one—and no one's been lending it neither,' I says.

'Nah don't be like that, I gotta go up the Common with old Burkey and the boys, ain't I? And I can't go up there without a bike now, can I?'

'Too bad. 'Fraid I'll be needing it myself tonight. See yer, Sam.'

'But what do you need it for? You'll only be taking the blinkin' dog for a walk.'

'Who says I'm taking the dog for a walk? I'm goin' up the Common myself ain't I, with old Hector.'

'Hector Turnpenny? That weed!'

'Yeah. That weed. He's my best friend, ain't he?'

'Won't need your bike for that. Come on, Kevin, be a pal and lend me your bike.'

'You're a scrounger you are, you're always lending things off people and they don't get them back very often neither.'

'You watch what you're saying young Kevin.'

'Scrounger. Sam the Scrounger.'

'Yeah—wanna punch-up?'

'Yeah—who by?'

' Me, that's who.'

' Yeah—you and 'ose army?'

' Hah, hah, very funny—well I'll get a bike off one o' my mates. Better bike than yours it'll be—you see.'

' And he'll be bloomin' lucky if 'e gets it back, this mate o' yours, won't he?'

' You watch it,' calls out Samuel.

' Scrounger,' I call back at him. ' Sam the Scrounger.'

And he really is a scrounger too. One day he lent Hector's transistor radio—straight off he did—and it ain't never worked since. 'Course, old Hector was a big idiot to let him have it, but that's the sort of person Old Samuel is . . . a real scrounger.

Believe it or not, half an hour later, I was doing some shopping for my mum when suddenly this fellah bumps his bike into mine, and he roars out laughing and it's Samuel again.

' Watcha Kevin—I got the bike yer see. Off one of my mates.'

' Yeah,' I said, not very friendly. ' Whose is it?'

' Old Tommy Tuffin's ain't it.'

' Old Tommy Tuffin's grandpa's more like it.'

' Ha ha. Very funny. It's good enough to get me up the Common ain't it?'

' Reckon it'll get that far? Well let's 'ope there ain't no breeze up there, for your sake, or it'll fall to blinking bits.'

' Eh Kevin, before yer go. Lend me a fag.'

' No.'

' Ah come on Kevin. Be a pal. Lend us a fag.'

' No. Don't have no fags. I'm too young to smoke, you know that.'

' Come off it Kevin. I ain't never known you when you ain't had a packet of fives on you. You've had smoker's cough since you failed that eleven plus and that's a fact.'

' Well you can start buying your own cigarettes Samuel Ferguson. You're big enough and ugly enough.'

' But Kevin, I gotta go up the Common with old Burkey and the boys, ain't I?'

' You're a miserable scrounger, that's what you are.'

' All right, all right, keep your hair on. I only asked for a blinkin' fag didn't I? Didn't ask for no Buckingham Palace did I?'

' You'll be asking for that before long. Dear Queen Elizabeth: please can Burkey an' me borrow your old palace for a week or two 'cause we're fed up with bein' on the Common and its gets so cold in the winter. Thanking you, R.S.V.P. Samuel the Scrounger Ferguson.'

' You're asking for something you are.'

'Yeah?'
'You just watch it. That's what I say.'
'I'm watching.'
'Yeah.'
'Yeah.'
So Sam didn't get his fag.

Later that evening I was up the Common with Hector, and a crowd of hard nuts come up and start bullying Hector, but the keeper comes along and so the hard nuts go away. Then Hector remembered something.
'Heh, did you hear about Sam Ferguson?' he says.
'What about him?' I says.
'Well he got run over by a steamroller, didn't he?'
'You're joking,' I says, and I really thought he was.
'No, straight off,' says Hector, 'he borrowed someone's old bike and went smack into a steamroller down the High Street.'
'What—Samuel Ferguson?'
'Yeah—Samuel Ferguson.'
'But is he dead then?'
'I reckon he could be now.'
'How d'yer mean?'
'Well they took him in the hospital, didn't they?'
I felt really sick and awful, 'cause if I'd lent him my bike like he asked me to, then the accident would never have happened 'cause my bike's a new one and a good one too, and Tommy Tuffin's is such an old one that no one ought to ride on it, it ain't safe. And then I thought how I'd always hated poor Sam, and how he'd never really done anything bad to me. He was always scrounging, that's true enough, but then we've all of us got our faults—like my Mum is always saying. And to think of Sam lying dead in that hospital, all because of me who'd always hated him. And he'd always been so friendly to me.
So me and Hector went straight off to Sam's house to ask his mum, but there weren't no need to ask his mum anything, 'cause there in the front garden was the old bike that Tommy Tuffin had lent him, and it was all smashed up, flat as a pancake. That was that. The only hope left for me was that old Sam wasn't quite dead yet, so Hector and me went back to his house and we picked a lovely bunch of flowers from his front garden and took them up to the hospital. And I said to the nurse there, 'These are for Sam Ferguson—is he dead yet?' And the nurse laughed and said, 'Not quite dead yet. Here. Come and see for yourselves.' And she took us up to the ward, and there was Sam in bed with one leg in plaster and the nurses mak-

ing a fuss of him and him having the time of his life, laughing and talking and enjoying himself. ' Watcha Kevin,' he calls out to me, large as life, ' be a pal, Kevin, lend us a fag.'

30 The Black Moments

A Story from an Improvisation

We often talked about our days at school and the things we had done there. One time, Dave asked all of us about our blackest experiences.

'How d'yer mean, " blackest " experiences?' I asked.

'Well you know: the worst things that ever happened to you as school-kids.'

'What—being bullied, you mean, things like that?'

'Maybe. Just any experience that was so awful you'll never forget it.'

Some of us told about times we'd been in trouble. Or when great gangs of kids had picked on us and made life hell. But it didn't get really interesting—or at least I didn't think so—till Martin told us about himself and old Rawlins.

This is the story.

Mr Rawlins was our history teacher, and he was something of a character. Some kids liked him—well they thought he was an amusing chap to have around. Others loathed his guts. We never called him Rawlins, except to his face of course—we had a nickname for him, but it's not the sort of nice jolly nickname that teachers have in all those jolly story-books about boarding schools. His nickname's unprintable, and that's that. For the purposes of this story we'll have to do without it. He was extremely strict and he ruled over the classroom like the Fuehrer ruled over Germany. There was never any doubt about who was in power and who wasn't. And like the Fuehrer, most of his ' subjects ' went the way of all flesh rather earlier than he did himself.

Perhaps he was a good teacher. He certainly had a ' system ' and all of us knew precisely what was happening, what was expected of us.

' Little boys may not be able to learn, for most little boys have no brains. Little boys may not be able to concentrate, for most little boys have no will power. But all little boys can look at the teacher, for all little boys have eyes.'

This was one of his many sayings—he had a whole anthology of wisdom such as this, most of which was quoted at us at least once a week. Another one was: ' Little boys may not be able to remember the notes they write down from the blackboard, but all little boys will write down their notes neatly: for although all little boys do not have memories, all little boys have hands.'

Now all this may sound pretty childish to you, especially when you remember that he was speaking to great big lads of fifteen and sixteen, who, a generation before, would by this age have been out at work. But when Rawlins quoted from his collection of wisdom in that awful condescending tone of his which implied that we were all a pack of overgrown babies, there was never so much as a titter in the classroom. Incredibly enough, we were all dead scared of him. We were even scared to sneer at him: our very faces had to register respect and humility. Nothing less would satisfy him.

As I have said, all his lessons followed the same routine. The door monitor would warn us when he was coming. We would all stand. He would enter. He would put his books on the master's desk, and look at the blackboard. If the blackboard was clear, then he would tell the blackboard monitor—who would have taken up his position at the side of the blackboard—to return to his place. If the blackboard was not clear he would either give the monitor a ' detention ' or else cane him. The caning would not take place there and then: the monitor's name would be entered in a small book which Mr Rawlins kept in his brief-case, and he would be caned either at the very end of the lesson or else at a much later date. This ' suspension ' of punishment created, as you can well imagine, an even more dramatic impact than any form of immediate and informal punishment can ever hope to create. After the blackboard had been inspected, then Mr Rawlins would inspect the class. This meant that we had to be in the correct positions around the room: their Majesties in the front row, the Lords in the second, the Commoners in the third, and the Serfs in the back row. You will no doubt wonder what all that meant. It was very simple. Their Majesties were the group of boys who, in Mr Rawlins' opinion, were of excellent moral character. They were the really good boys. To become one of their ' Majesties ' it was not necessary to be good at History. But it was necessary to play at least one sport really well, preferably by playing for a school team. It was also necessary that you should never display any sign of moral flabbiness, such as appearing to have a sense of humour, or not liking Mr Rawlins, or not belonging to some organisation such as the Scouts. The Lords were the boys who were the best all-round scholars in the class. The Commoners were the boys who, without being especially good at History, were, in Mr Rawlins' opinion, boys who were clearly trying hard in their school-work generally. The Serfs were the rest.

I need only add that it was Mr Rawlins who decided which category you should be placed in, and that he decided it very quickly after first meeting you, and very seldom changed his mind, no matter how long he might know you.

148

He was extremely proud of his system of ' Majesties, Lords, Commoners and Serfs,' and said that it not only gave us a sense of the ordering of our ' society '—meaning presumably the country as a whole, but also told us much about English History—' for,' he said, ' the history of this country, and its decline from a great world power, can be traced in the movement of power and authority away from the monarchy and down eventually to the serfs.'

He not only checked that we were in our right places, he also checked that we were of smart appearance, that our hands were clean, and that our ties were straight. Any boy who failed to meet his standards in such matters was at once given a ' detention '.

Then he would tell us to be seated. And the lesson began.

His lessons usually started in a very deceptive manner: he would tell some personal anecdote, always involving himself and always proving his own superiority over all of us and of our generation. It might for instance concern his adventures of the previous week-end when he went into a shop to buy the groceries, and found himself served by a youngster of about our own age. This youngster would turn out to be lacking in elementary arithmetic, good manners and cleanliness, and the story would end with Mr Rawlins complaining to the manager of the shop and the manager saying, ' Well, Sir, we don't get good youngsters these days. We just don't get them. Not like the good old days. Not like the good old days.'

He might tell this story in a very pleasant way, perhaps even smiling at us. But then the tone would change, and he would work himself into an Old Testament rage as he plunged from the end of the story into the moral of the tale: the youth of the country are leading us to the dogs, and only he and one or two others were trying to do anything about it. This would bring us to the subject of history.

We would copy down from the blackboard the heading for the next section of our studies while Rawlins would walk round the room inspecting our handwriting. Then he would seat himself at the desk and speak to us on a particular subject—it might be, say, the causes of the Seven Years War. Then he would dictate notes. In the middle of these notes he would always stop and tell us a joke. The joke was never funny but all of us always laughed. Not too loud and not too long, but we laughed. We had to. If we did not, we had no idea what might happen to us. Whatever it was, it would be something awful.

The joke finished, we then completed the notes, and then he appointed the new monitors for the next lesson. The boy who had displayed the greatest ' integrity ' during the lesson would be appointed door monitor. The ' runner-up ' would be appointed books monitor. The boy who had displayed the least ' integrity ' would be appointed blackboard monitor. The books monitor would then collect our exercise books, the door monitor would stand by the door, the class would stand, and Rawlins would fill in the two or three minutes to the sounding of the bell with a few odd quotes from his book of wisdom. Then he would leave.

All his lessons were the same.

When Martin came into our class he'd never been taught before by Mr Rawlins: he was suddenly promoted, in the middle of term, from his old class into ours, and he was quite unprepared for the way Rawlins conducted his lessons. Nor did Rawlins in any way make him feel at ease.

'What's this?' he said, after he'd inspected the blackboard. 'A foreign thing?'

'The name's Hawley, Sir. Martin Hawley.'

'Speak when I tell you to. Not before. Well, boys, what do we make of this foreign thing? What primitive country does he come from?'

'I've been moved up from 4c, Sir.'

'Silence. I have already told you: speak only when I tell you to. Do you understand that?'

'Yes Sir.'

'Well, let me remind you that little boys who are moved up can also be moved out and moved down. Remember that.'

'Yes Sir.'

'Now, look me straight in the eyes.'

'I beg your pardon Sir.'

'I said, Look me straight in the eyes.'

'Yes Sir.'

'Mm. You don't look the shifty sort, I'll say that for you. But not much leadership, I'd say. Nervous type. Probably a fidget. May make a good clerk in a little office somewhere. But you'll be a reliable little employee. You won't steal or lie or cheat. Good. You're a serf.'

'I beg your pardon Sir.'

'You're in the back row. Move.'

'Yes Sir.'

'And now you will tell me and also the rest of the class, what you have been learning in history in 4c.'

'Well Sir—I've been learning about Napoleon, Sir, and the French Revolution.'

'Describe briefly and simply the events leading up to the fall of the French Republic and its transition into an empire under the leadership of Napoleon.'

'I beg your pardon Sir.'

'Did you not hear me?'

'Yes Sir.'

'Then answer the question.'

'Well, Sir, I don't think I can, quite, Sir.'

'Does that mean you cannot answer at all, or that you cannot quite answer?'

'Well, Sir, I've been away the past two weeks with a bad cold in the head, Sir, and I've lost the track, sort of, in the history lessons. Never was my best subject Sir.'

'You will notice, boys, that I classified this boy as a serf *before*, not *after* I had interrogated him. Now you can see how right I was. I am never wrong in such matters. My instinct is infallible. The boy is clearly a serf, and always will be. Tell us, by the way, whether you play any sports on behalf of the school?'

'None Sir.'

'There you are boys,' and he beamed, 'right again. I'm never wrong in such matters. Never wrong.'

Later in the lesson, we came to the interval for jokes.

'Today I'm going to tell you an exceedingly funny story, boys, about the time when I was a Petty Officer in the Navy. The most exciting and remarkable days of my life.'

I won't bother you with the story. It was a poor one. I have forgotten it. We all laughed. Except Martin.

'Boy. Serf. Do you not find it funny? My anecdote?'

'No Sir.'

'I see.'

Silence, and then he went on with the notes. He patrolled the room, looking at our exercise books. The usual comments until he came to Martin.

'What's this?'

'What's what Sir?'

'This—disgrace. I have never in my life seen such handwriting. A bear could not have done worse. It is an insult to me. Can you not read what I have written on the board?'

'Of course I can, Sir.'

'Do you have a muscular disease in the right hand?'

'No Sir.'

'Has any other master ever had cause to comment on your handwriting?'

'Not that I remember Sir.'

'Ah—then I am the first master with whom you have had the cheek and the confounded impudence to produce work of this calibre. Is that not so?'

'No Sir.'

'Then others have complained?'

'No Sir.'

'Then it is as I have said. You are impudent. You take advantage of me.'

'No Sir. I meant, I always write like this. But no other teacher has ever commented on it. Not that I can remember.'

'Then what you are saying is that the teachers at this school are thoroughly and hopelessly incompetent.'

'No Sir.'

'Oh yes you are.'

'No I'm not Sir.'

'Don't answer me back, boy. I say you are.'

Silence.

'Do you hear me? I say you are.'

'Yes Sir.'

'Ah—you admit it. You were insolent.'

'No Sir.'

'Yes Sir, yes Sir. One minute you say the other teachers are incompetent. Now you admit that you were simply trying to play me up, to test me, to see how far you can go. This will not end as simply as it has begun, be assured of that my good boy. It will go much farther. Much. Much.'

And he turned to the class and said, 'This reminds me, boys, of a little incident that happened in the navy once. When I was a Petty Officer.'

He narrated this quite pointless tale in great detail, and ended it with a few random quotes from his 'collection'. The class stood. The door monitor held the door open. Rawlins got to the door and turned and said to Martin, 'You will be hearing again from me, later in the day.'

And later, Martin was sent for by the Deputy Head, who wasted no time asking for any kind of explanation. 'If I have any further complaints from Mr Rawlins, the consequences will be extremely serious my boy. That is all I shall say.'

'But I did nothing,' said Martin. 'I only—'

'I am not interested in what you did or did not do. Mr Rawlins is a teacher who never once has been to me to complain about any boy. Now he comes to complain about you. That fact speaks for itself. I may add that Mr Rawlins is a teacher of great distinction in the school—his examination successes are quite remarkable, quite remarkable. What I would suggest to you, my boy, is that you learn to control your tongue, to accept criticism and to have respect. You may go.'

And that was the end of it.

'After that,' said Martin, 'I just sat at the back of the room. And I never said another word. And he never said another word to me. I suppose it was all of no importance, really. I carried on at school. It didn't kill me. I never even talked about it. And it was such a little thing at any rate. And I suppose it's a silly thing to say this now, but I used to sit in that classroom every lesson after that, thinking how much I hated him. And I never could do anything about it—except for one thing. I never once laughed at his jokes.'

31 Masked Raider

A Story from an Improvisation

Mr and Mrs McPherson arrived home earlier than they had expected. Their weekly visit to their son and daughter-in-law had not been a success. Tempers had been roused. Unpleasant words had been exchanged—some of them very unpleasant—and in a flurry of hurt feelings and injured pride, the McPhersons had made a brisk departure.

'What does he mean, saying things like that to us? Our own son?' asked Mrs McPherson.

'It's her as puts him up to it. You can see that,' said the husband.

'I don't think she's as bad as you say she is. She seemed such a nice girl when they were courting.'

'They all are, when they're courting,' replied the husband.

'And I used to look forward so to seeing them,' said the wife.

'It'll be a time before we see them again. I'll tell you that for nothing. He'll have to apologise, that's what he'll have to do.'

Mrs McPherson thought about this all the way home on the bus. 'He'll never apologise, not our Wally. He's not the type. Never has been. He's like you. Never could bear to be wrong.'

Her husband ignored this.

'But fancy them getting so angry, just 'cause we wouldn't give them the money,' she continued.

'Called us misers, that's what he did. Misers,' said the husband.

'Ssh,' said his wife, 'we don't have to tell all the bus about it do we?'

'Just 'cause we've gone careful. That's all. Can't see him going careful. The way he spends his money he'll have nothing left when he's an old man and his kids have grown up.'

'And to think,' said Mrs McPherson, 'we gave him £300 when he got married. That's a lot of money you know.'

'More than anyone ever gave us when we got married.'

'Aye. Times were bad then. Times were really bad.'

'Yer know—I just can't get over it. I can't straight. My own son asking me for my house like that. Cool as cucumber about it too. "Come on, Dad," he says, "what about you two doing a swap with us two?" That's how he said it. Cool as you like. As if he was asking to borrow your bicycle for a couple of days. "After all," he says, "there's only two of you, and you don't want a great big house like that just for the two of you. I mean, in a few years' time you won't be able to get up and down it, will you, to keep it clean?" The cheek of it. The confounded cheek of it.'

'There's some truth in it though. The house is too big for us. And that flat of theirs is too small for 'em, specially with another kid on the way,' said Mrs McPherson.

'Maybe. Maybe. I'm not saying there ain't some truth in it, and I'm not saying there is. But what I am saying is you don't just go up to your father like that and say, " Come on Dad, let's do a swap." And then just 'cause we didn't jump up and down and say " Of course, son, walk all over us. Take everything we have. Turn us out on the street." Just 'cause we didn't do that, then he goes and starts insulting us. You heard what he called our house, didn't you? You heard what he called it?'

'I heard,' said Mrs McPherson with some sadness, ' a museum. That's what he called it.'

'Just 'cause I like to collect nice things around me. Some of the nicest bits of antique in the town, I've got. They're worth something my antiques are. They're really worth something. Old Jawmedead up the road was saying so only the other week. You've got a small fortune in that house of yours, make no mistake about it, he says.'

'It'll be miserable if we don't see them again for a month or two. I'll miss seeing them. I really will,' said Mrs McPherson.

And she was still thinking how sad life would be without the weekly visits to her son and his family, when they reached their house. In Mrs McPherson's present state of mind it looked big, and dark, and lonely.

Mr McPherson slipped the key into the lock and was about to open the door when he stopped quite still and said, in a whisper, ' What's that noise?'

'I don't hear no—'

'Ssh, not so loud. There's a noise in there.'

'There is?' said Mrs McPherson, her voice now subdued to a terrified murmur.

'Don't fidget, woman,' demanded Mr McPherson.

They both stood, dead still, listening.

There was silence for a while, and then Mrs McPherson's face assumed an extremely puzzled expression.

'It's music,' she said at last.

'I think it is,' agreed her husband.

'Did we leave the radio on?'

''Course not.'

'I don't understand it.'

'Must be burglars,' said Mrs McPherson.

'Mm,' said her husband. 'Why are they playing music then?'

'Shall we get the police?'

They both waited a second before deciding on their next move.

'Did you close the door properly when we went out?'

''Course I did,' said the wife.

All this time the husband had kept his hand on the key in the lock, and now, without his quite intending it, the door slipped silently open. The music was now perfectly audible.

'It's from upstairs,' he said.

'But the radio's downstairs, and so's the telly,' said the wife. The whole thing was becoming so incomprehensible that she was almost forgetting to whisper. And then, with a sudden flash of understanding, she said, right out loud, 'I know what it is. It's the old phonograph.'

The husband gripped her arm, as if to tell her to be quiet, murmured, 'You're right. That's what it is all right. It's the old phonograph. Someone's upstairs playing it.' And this was such a total mystery to both of them that they forgot all about fetching the police to solve the business for them. Burglars who broke into the house simply in order to go upstairs and play the old phonograph were not really burglars at all. They were more like ghosts or some other even more supernatural beings whom the normal forces of the law were hopelessly unsuited to deal with. Indeed, through Mrs McPherson's mind there raced confused pictures of her two grandchildren, who when they visited the house, loved to go upstairs to grandad's room and listen to the crumbling sounds of music from nearly a century ago, played on grandad's pride and joy—one of the first phonographs ever made, with the date boldly imprinted on its base: 1866. Was it possible that, by some act of magic, the grandchildren were up there now, listening to the music? Who knows, it might be some delightful gesture, devised by her son and his wife, for undoing all the unpleasantness that had been created earlier in the evening. And then her mind considered another more remote possibility, that her other son, the older one, who had gone to Australia years before and never returned, had suddenly come back and was enjoying again one of the pleasures of his childhood—listening to the music of the phonograph.

Some such thoughts must have been passing through Mr McPherson's mind also, for he now said, with a combination of foolishness and courage that was not typical of him, 'You wait here. I'm going upstairs.' She closed the front door behind her and watched him as he slowly moved up the staircase. There was a sudden silence as he turned the corner of the stairs and moved up and out of sight, for the cylinder on the phonograph had presumably played itself out. Now very nervous again, she walked over to the stairs and thought about following her husband, decided not to, heard a slight movement somewhere behind her, turned, looked, and would have let forth the most piercing scream that anyone has ever heard had she not been too utterly terrified to make any sound whatsoever. Instead the knees gave way beneath her and she sank down, still gaping at the object of terror, and found herself seated on the bottom rung of the stairs.

The object was not a ghost. It was something more hideous than a ghost, for it had some kind of a body and also some kind of face. She remained still and speechless with fright, and the object just stood there, looking back at her. It seemed that a century passed before anything else happened, and still Mrs McPherson was too weak to call out to her husband. Then the music of the phonograph started up again and she found the courage to clutch at her own throat, as if to assure herself that she was still there, and to take a deep breath to revive herself.

And then, quite incredibly, the object spoke: 'Eh missus, you all right then?'

It was altogether too much to expect her to reply at once.

The object put out one hand to touch her gently on the shoulder, and said again, 'Eh missus, you all right? You ain't gonna faint are you?'

'Oh my God,' said Mrs McPherson, 'it isn't a ghost, it's a boy.'

'Don't you say nothing, or I'll kill you,' said the boy.

It wasn't quite clear what he would kill her with. He had no lethal weapons in his hands, nor was his stance a specially murderous one.

'Aye—I daresay you will,' said Mrs McPherson quietly. She was now much more interested in the boy who stood before her than in the mystery of the phonograph. He seemed quite small, no more probably than twelve or thirteen. More than that was difficult to tell. Not only was the house so dark, but he had covered his face, rather comically she now felt, in an old silk stocking.

The boy was at a loss as to what to do next.

'Don't move,' he said, in a menacing whisper.

'I won't,' she assured him quietly.

'You on your own then?' he asked.

'Yes,' she lied.

'You keep quiet and you won't come to no harm. You understand?'

'I think so.'

'Thought you was gonna faint just now.'

'I thought I was too.'

'We ain't gonna hurt you.'

'Good.'

'Yeah.'

Another pause. The boy was clearly no expert in matters like this. There was no further sound from McPherson upstairs, and the phonograph could still be heard playing merrily.

'How many of you are there?' she asked.

'Just the two of us. Just Jerry 'n' me,' said the boy.

'Just you and Jerry eh?'

And she could almost see him curse himself for having released this vital piece of information with such casual unconcern.

'And what's your name then?' said Mrs McPherson, pressing home the advantage.

'Not telling you,' said the boy. 'And his name ain't Jerry neither. I said that to fool you.'

'Yes,' she replied, 'I'm easily fooled. Always have been.'

The boy coughed and pulled slightly at the stocking.

'I bet that's a bit uncomfortable isn't it?' said Mrs McPherson, now beginning to enjoy the adventure.

'You bet. Too tight.'

Any moment now her husband would burst in on young Jerry upstairs, and that would be the end of it. He'd have the two boys off to the police station and that would be that. A pity. Then she had a less pleasant thought. This boy was young and harmless, a complete amateur at this kind of thing. She could have done it better herself. But supposing the other one, Jerry, was a great big thug, leading this one around like a stooge. Jerry might be dangerous, and her husband at this very moment might be walking straight into him. Should she call out to him? Or would that perhaps create more problems than it would solve? She thought of an alternative solution.

'You're a bit young, the two of you, aren't you, to be breaking into people's houses?'

'We're thirteen, ain't we?' said the boy, obligingly.

'I'm glad to hear it,' replied Mrs McPherson with honesty. 'I only hope you don't do silly things like this very often. It'll get you into a great deal of trouble one day, my boy.'

'Yeah,' said the boy, almost in agreement, 'but we don't do much harm, not really.'

Absurdly enough, the boy seemed decidedly pleasant, almost good-natured.

'But don't you have better things to do with your time?'

'Nah, not really. Besides, this is exciting, this is.'

The phonograph stopped. The light went on at the top of the stairs. Mr McPherson called out, 'Mother, get to the phone. Call the police. I've got a thief up here. Caught him red-handed. Call the police.' And then he was running down the stairs towards her. 'Come on woman, be quick about it. It's only a kid. I'll stop him getting out while you—'

'I can't move,' said Mrs McPherson. 'There's another gangster down here, and he's threatened to kill me.'

Mr McPherson stopped dead in his tracks and stared at the boy. 'Another one?'

The boy looked back at him, completely confused by this unexpected development.

'But you said you were on your own,' he said to Mrs McPherson. She made no reply.

'You said there was no one with you,' he insisted.

'Get out of my way,' said Mr McPherson, who had now sized up the situation and decided that neither this boy nor the one upstairs constituted any real threat to his safety. And he pushed the boy aside, saying, 'We'll see what the police have to say about this pair. I've never known such a thing. I swear I haven't.'

But before he could get to the phone another voice called out from the top of the stairs, 'I wouldn't do that if I were you, Mr McPherson. Not if you like your old phonograph.'

This presumably was Jerry. He had come down and round the corner of the stairs. Mrs McPherson stood up and turned to face him.

'If you so much as touch that telephone, I'll smash this phonograph to smithereens.'

He held the precious instrument in both hands. 'I'm sure it's worth a lot of money. Be a pity to see it all smashed up.'

He stood in the bend of the staircase, looking down on them. He too had covered his face in a silk stocking. He seemed slightly bigger than his friend.

'So this is Jerry,' said Mrs McPherson, 'I'm pleased to meet you.'

She was enjoying the situation so much that she was tempted to make everyone a cup of tea. Had her husband not been there she would certainly have done so.

'You bloomin' fool,' said Jerry to the other boy, 'what d'yer think you're doing, telling her my name?'

'It slipped out,' said the other boy simply.

'You bet it did. Your blinkin' brains slipped out too, if you ask me, a long time ago.'

'Yeah,' said the other one, without attempting to defend himself.

'I said I'm phoning the police,' Mr McPherson repeated.

'And I said that if you touch the phone I'll throw your dear old phonograph to the floor, and it'll smash to bits.'

'We gotta go,' said the other boy, coughing again and pulling at

L   159

the stocking that covered his face. 'This blooming thing's killing me. Can't breathe prop'ly.'

'You're a dead loss you are,' said Jerry.

'I know,' came the hopeless reply.

'Why don't you take the silly thing off?' said Mrs McPherson.

'I can't do that,' said the boy, 'it's my disguise, ain't it? You'd give my description to the police if I took it off.'

'We'll be in no need of any descriptions my boy, 'cause the police'll be here any minute now,' said Mr McPherson.

'No they won't,' said Jerry.

'Now you listen to me—'

'No. You listen to me.'

Mr McPherson moved as if to go up the stairs towards him.

'Come any nearer and I'll smash this thing to the floor. Don't you doubt it, old man, I will.' And he lifted the phonograph above his head to indicate how ready he was to execute his threat.

'And what good would that do you?' asked Mr McPherson.

'It'll teach you a lesson, that's what it'll do. Show you some people mean what they say.'

'You're the one to be learning a few lessons my boy. Not me.'

'That's as may be. All I know is I want to get out of this house, and I'm not gonna have you phoning no police. Understand?'

'Jerry, I'm suffocating,' said the friend. 'I've gotta take this thing off.'

'Yer blinkin' fool, you'll do no such thing. Take it off and they'll have got you. Then we've both had it.'

'I think we've got you already,' said Mr McPherson calmly, 'we can't describe your faces, that's true, but we've got the build of you, and we know the name of one of you, too. Jerry. We'll remember that.'

'Won't do you much good neither. 'Snot my real name. 'Sonly what some o' the fellahs call me.'

'You've got an answer for everything you have, but we'll see what good it does you. We'll see.'

The other boy, however, was now choking in real earnest.

'I can't breathe, Jerry, honest I can't. I'm choking to bloomin' death I am.'

'Shut up,' commanded Jerry. 'Now then, mister, you let my young friend there out of the house. Go on, open the door, and let him go.'

'And what happens then, if I may be allowed to inquire?'

'You leave the door open after my friend's gone. You go and stand over there, both of you. Then I walk out too. And if you ever tell the police about this, you'll never get this phonograph back. Understand?'

'You mean—you're taking it with you?'

''Course we are. That's what we came for. Not that we meant to take it with us, we didn't. We just wanted to study it. See how it's made. We weren't going to interfere with anything, or steal anything. But you interrupted us. Now we'll have to take the thing with us, and bring it back to you when we've finished with it. Provided you don't tell the police.'

'You came to—study it? Did you say, study?' demanded Mr McPherson.

'That's it. We're not thieves. But that's all we're gonna say. Go on. Open the door for my friend before he chokes hisself to bloomin' death.'

'I shall do no such thing,' said Mr McPherson.

'I would if I were you.'

'I'm gonna phone the police.'

In reply, Jerry again lifted the phonograph above his head.

'I've never heard the likes of this, that's the truth I haven't.'

'It doesn't matter,' said Mrs McPherson, 'the boys have done no harm. They shouldn't have broken in, that's for sure. But they've not damaged anything, and they've not stolen anything. I've never heard anything so daft as two kids turning into housebreakers in order to " study " an old phonograph, but let's leave it at that, with no harm done to person or thing. Let them go.'

'I'm half dead,' said the other boy. 'I've gotta take this thing off, I've got to.'

And he did, half-fainting with exhaustion.

'You fool, you fool,' cried Jerry.

'Well if you're as worried as all that about it, I'll go and get you another to wear in its place,' said Mrs McPherson, partly in jest and partly in all seriousness.

'It'll be too late,' said Jerry sulkily, 'now you've both seen him, and you can describe him to the police.'

'That we can,' cried Mr McPherson triumphantly. And he switched on the light in the hall. 'We can see you now, you little devil.'

But the little devil looked remarkably pale.

'He's gonna be sick,' said Mrs McPherson.

'I think I recognise him. I've seen him before. I'm sure I have. He doesn't live far from here,' said Mr McPherson.

'Here, lad, come and sit down. You're looking a dreadful colour, you really are.'

'It was that stocking, it nearly killed me,' said the boy. He was feeling as awful as he looked.

'It don't make no difference,' said Jerry defiantly, 'you let us go, and I'll let you have your phonograph back in a month's time. But you mustn't bring the law into it. That clear?'

'I've had enough of this,' said Mr McPherson. 'Two kids come breaking into my house and start laying the law down to me, telling me what I can do and what I can't do. I've had enough. More than enough.'

He moved towards the phone.

'Don't,' shouted Jerry. 'Don't.'

'And don't you shout at me, my boy,' said Mr McPherson.

He lifted up the telephone, and proceeded to dial. As he did so, Jerry lifted the phonograph above his head and hurled it down the stairs on to the wooden floor where it exploded instantly into a thousand pieces. A moment later Jerry himself rushed down the stairs, calling to the other boy, 'Come on—what you waiting for?' and threw open the front door and charged out.

The other boy replied quietly, 'I can't. I'm not well.'

Mr McPherson almost vibrated with fury, then finished dialling and said, 'Is that the police? Mr McPherson here, 29 Fontain Avenue. Couple of juvenile delinquents just broken into my house. One of them's run out, but we've got the other one. Keep him till you get here.'

He replaced the receiver, and said briskly to his wife, 'You hold tight to that one, I'm gonna try and catch the other one.' And he ran out in pursuit of Jerry.

'It's not necessary,' said Mrs McPherson sadly, 'all this business of calling the police. It's not necessary.' But her husband had already gone.

'I'll be all right now,' said the boy quietly, without attempting to move.

'You sure?'

'It was the stocking over my face. Nearly killed me it did.'

'You still look pale, I must say.'

'I'll be all right. Police'll be here in a minute.'

'I'm afraid so.'

'I'm sorry about the old phonograph. We didn't plan on doing anything like that.'

'No, I don't think you did.'

'We make things yer see, we're good at making things. Jerry 'n' me. 'Bout the only thing we are good at.'

'What sort of things?'

'You know, technical things. Made a telephone we did once. Straight off we did. We had our own private telephone we did. You know, like the "hot line" to the Kremlin from the White House.

We pinched the telephone from down the street that time.'

'But it's wrong to steal things. Surely you know that? Hasn't your mum ever told you?'

'We didn't steal it. We just took it and studied it. Then we put it back again. Was harder putting it back than it was taking it in the first place. Took us all night it did.'

'And how did you find out about the old phonograph upstairs?'

'Heard some bloke telling me dad about all the antiques your old man has. Heard 'em talking about the old phonograph, and we thought we could make one just like it, only we'd have to come and study your old man's one first. So we watched you for weeks and weeks. Saw when you went out and how long you stayed out. Then we broke in. It was easy. You always leave the kitchen window open.'

'But it's wrong to break into people's houses, surely you know that. Couldn't you have come and asked us if you could look at our phonograph? Couldn't you? We'd have been pleased to let you borrow it. Didn't you ever think of that?'

'No, never.'

Mrs McPherson was almost overwhelmed by the difficulty of making the boy understand.

'Has no one ever taught you the difference between right and wrong?' she asked.

'Oh—we read the Bible at school and all that.'

'Oh dear. Oh dear. You'll break your poor mother's heart when she hears this. What's your name?'

'Dudley Jones. They call me Dud. I am a bit of a dud too, I'm not much good at anything, and that's the truth, 'cept making things.'

'And what'll yer dad say?'

'Not much. He'll shout a bit, and knock me about a bit. That's all.'

There was a silence between them both.

Mr McPherson had not yet come back when the police car was heard coming down the road.

'It'll be them,' said Mrs McPherson. 'Why didn't you run away with the other one, Dudley, with that friend of yours?'

'What's the sense? They'll get yer sooner or later. Besides, you had my description, and you had Jerry's name. The police would have got us at any rate before the night was out.'

They heard the car come to a stop and the doors opened.

'Oh Dudley,' said Mrs McPherson, 'I am sorry.'

The boy looked at her in surprise.

'Oh no, missus,' he said simply, 'it's me as should be sorry.'

32 The Senator

A Story from an Improvisation

The Senator could still hear the applause as the chauffeur opened the door for him to get into the car.

' Another fine speech, sir,' said the chauffeur politely.

' Yes, I believe it was,' said the Senator.

' Do you think the Bill will be defeated?' asked the chauffeur.

' Yes—if I have anything to do with it.'

And very clearly the Senator would have a great deal to do with it.

That day the Senate had debated a new law which aimed to provide emergency funds for all the out-of-work plantation workers. The Senator had opposed it. In all probability the law would be defeated.

' I do not believe, nor have I ever believed, in giving something to somebody for doing nothing,' the Senator had said. ' If this law is passed, then all the men who are already working hard for their living will say to themselves, " Why should I waste my time, when I can earn money for doing nothing?" Gentlemen, if you pass this law you will destroy the country.'

This statement had been greeted with rapturous applause. One or two other senators had got to their feet to say that many thousands of those who had been thrown out of work on the plantations had no chance of finding other work, but these had been contradicted: ' Any man who wants to work will find it somewhere,' said the Senator, to even more applause.

The car swept over the hill and on towards the City's most expensive residential district. It was late. The Senator had had a tiring and difficult day.

Suddenly the chauffeur called to him: ' Do you mind if I take a short cut, sir? Just discovered a new and quicker way of getting back.'

' By all means,' murmured the Senator.

At once the car moved forward at fantastic speed and the city flashed past. In the sheer darkness the Senator had no idea where he was. He called out to the chauffeur to stop, but there was no response; the car swept on at such reckless speed that the Senator was convinced that any moment now the car would be smashed up in some fatal collision. Then, just as unexpectedly, with a great screeching of brakes, the car came to a stop.

' Get out,' called the chauffeur.

' I beg your pardon.'

' Get out.'

And the voice was so commanding that the Senator astonished himself by doing just as he was told. And no sooner had he stepped out of the car than the door was closed behind him, and the car moved swiftly and silently out into the night, leaving him standing there.

Just ahead of him was a great queue of hungry-looking men and women.

' You in this queue or you just sightseeing?' asked one man.

' What is this?' asked the Senator.

' We're queueing for work,' said another.

' But where am I?'

' Easton's Plantation. The biggest in the country. And the whole lot of us have been laid off. They're closing it down.'

' There must be other jobs for you to do.'

' Where?'

' Somewhere. It's a big country.'

' And where do we get the money to go all over the country looking for it?'

' I'll give you some money,' said the Senator, feeling inside his jacket pocket for his wallet. But he had only five dollars with him.

' That won't get us far,' said someone.

' I'll go home and get some more,' said the Senator.

' Yeah,' they laughed, ' and phone us when you get there.'

' Don't phone us, we'll phone you,' said another.

' You can all go home,' called out a voice from the head of the queue. ' There's no more jobs today. Tomorrow we may be needing a couple of road-sweepers. We'll let you know.'

' And what do we do tonight?' called out one of them. ' What do we take home to the wife and kids?'

' That's your business, friend,' replied the voice.

' They're starving as it is. I've been out of work now for nine months,' said the man at the side of the Senator. ' Still, no sense in grumbling.'

' What you gonna do?' asked the Senator.

' Go down to the City Hall and get in the queue for the road-sweeping job.'

' But what about going home?'

' What's the sense in going home, if I've no money to take with me? I'd be more nuisance than anything else. What are you doing?'

' Me—well, I don't know. I'm not worried really. I'm a rich man as a matter of fact.'

The other grinned, as if to say, ' Ah well, we all like to deceive ourselves.'

'You better come with me, then maybe you'll get the road-sweeping job too.'

But even now, in the middle of the night, there was already a large queue outside the City Hall.

'We're too late,' said the man, 'but we might as well just stick around. You never know. The whole country may send down for more road-sweepers. Then we'll be laughing.'

There was pushing at the head of the queue, where a group of men were arguing about who was the first in the line. Tempers flared and almost at once the police were on the scene.

'May I remind you,' shouted the police to jeers from the crowd, 'that it is a criminal offence to be out on the streets without visible means of support.'

This caused a great deal of laughter.

'The only visible support that I have,' said one, 'is the wall I'm leaning on.'

'Then I'm afraid we must arrest you,' said the police.

'Then you'll have to arrest all of us,' said someone.

And that is precisely what the police did. This involved quite a bit of crowding in the police cells, but that did not seem to bother the police.

'You'll be better off where you are: at least we can give you some breakfast in the morning.'

And so the Senator spent the night in prison and in the morning was brought before the magistrate.

'This man is charged with loitering on the street after midnight, and with having no visible means of support. Unfortunately we have not been able to discover his real name,' said the policeman. 'He insists on telling us he is a Senator.'

Much laughter in court.

'Silence in court,' demanded the magistrate.

'I am a Senator,' said the Senator. 'The whole thing is a ghastly mistake.'

'Apart from playing the fool, and wasting our time, what have you to say in your defence?' asked the Magistrate.

'I told you. I am a—'

But the policeman interrupted him.

'The accused has no defence, sir; he does not deny loitering outside the City Hall, and when we searched him he had no money.'

'I had five dollars,' said the Senator.'

'Really. Where are the five dollars now?' asked the magistrate.

'Here in my—' but the money had gone.

'I had five dollars in my pocket—someone must have—'

This was greeted with more laughter.

'It is men like you,' said the Magistrate, 'who are dragging down the high tone and standards of this city. You are a disgrace to the decent law-abiding men and women who have made this city and this country into the fine places they are. Just because the plantation closes down, that doesn't mean you can't find yourself some other job. It is up to you to find work—walk from one end of the country to another if need be. Do you hear me?'

'Yes sir, but—'

'There's no buts about it. No one's going to give you something for doing nothing, you know. You must work for your living like anybody else.'

'Yes sir, but—'

'And stop interrupting me. Now. The police tell me that this is your first offence, so I am going to be very fair and just. I'm going to give you another chance. I find you guilty as charged, but I am not going to send you to prison. I shall fine you fifty dollars and I don't expect to see you here ever again. Do you understand that?'

'But I don't have fifty dollars,' said the Senator.

'Then it is up to you to go out to work and make enough money to pay your fine. Now then. Off you go. Next case.'

The Senator went straight over to the City Hall and asked for the road-sweeper job.

'The position is still vacant,' said one of the clerks, looking down his nose at the Senator.

'Then can I apply for it?'

'You'll have to fill in the forms first.'

'Good. Can I have the forms?'

'Ask at that desk over there.'

He went over to the desk.

'I want an application form for the road-sweeper's job.'

'Are you under the age of sixty?'

'Yes.'

'Do you have your birth certificate, marriage certificate, labour card, identity card, reference from a clergyman, and reference from your previous employer?'

'No I don't—'

'Then I'm afraid you can't apply for the post.'

'Well—well, all right, I'll write off now and get all those. It'll take a couple of days though.'

'We don't mind. We'll still be here.'

'But I need a job right now.'

'We never give jobs immediately. We have to make a thorough

search of the applicant's record before we employ anyone.'

'But I'm starving,' said the Senator. 'I've had nothing to eat for hours and hours.'

'Too bad,' said the clerk.

'But don't you see, all I've had to eat in the past twelve hours was a lousy breakfast in prison this morning.'

'Prison? You've been to prison?'

'Well—yes. I must admit I have.'

'Then I'm afraid no one in this town will ever give you any job of any description. Don't bother to write off for your various certificates. They won't be any use to you.'

'But—'

'Good day to you.'

'But you don't seem to understand, I—'

'I beg your pardon sir.'

'You don't seem to understand—'

'Understand what sir?' asked the chauffeur.

'Where the devil am I?' asked the Senator.

'You're home, sir.'

'Why, so I am. I must have fallen to sleep.'

'Very probably, sir. It's been a hard day. And that was such a fine speech you made. Must have worn you out.'

'Yes, it must have done,' said the Senator, and he stepped out of the car, still thinking over his dream.

'Tell me, George,' he said to the chauffeur, 'tell me honestly what you think.'

'Gladly sir.'

'Do you think there's anything in dreams? I mean, do you ever believe in them?'

'Oh no sir. They're just a lot of silly notions that come into your head when you're asleep. There's nothing in them. I never take any notice of them.'

'I'm glad to hear it,' said the Senator, 'and neither shall I.'

And off went the Senator, whistling, and looking forward to a good beefsteak supper.

33 Today's Arrangements

A Story from an Improvisation

For many years now, life had been exceptionally quiet in the pleasant state of Ruritania. Too quiet for the Prime Minister. He called a cabinet meeting. Not only did he call a cabinet meeting, but he demanded that it meet that very minute, without a moment's delay. This was not as difficult as it might sound, for the cabinet consisted only of himself, the Rt Hon. A. B. Browne (Prime Minister, Foreign Secretary, Chancellor of the Exchequer and Home Secretary), his wife, the Rt Hon. Mrs A. B. Browne (Minister of Education, Minister for Colonial Affairs, Minister of War, and Minister of Justice) and his son, the Rt Hon. C. D. Browne (Minister of Culture, Minister of Sport, and President of the Board of Trade).

In fact, calling an instantaneous meeting of the cabinet was even easier than that, for his son still lived at home, and so all the Prime Minister had to do was to announce over breakfast, ' The Cabinet is assembled. The Prime Minister in the chair.'

' Let's finish breakfast first,' said his wife.

' It's a crisis. The meeting can't be postponed,' said the Prime Minister.

' There's always a crisis,' said the son. ' It gets monotonous.'

' Of course there's always a crisis,' said the Prime Minister, ' that's what politics is about. Without crises there couldn't be any politics.'

' What is it this time?' asked his wife.

' Nothing,' said the Prime Minister ominously.

' Well how can that be a crisis for heaven's sake?' asked his wife.

' Aha,' said the P.M. mysteriously.

' And what does that mean—aha?' asked the wife.

' It means,' said the P.M. solemnly, ' that the situation is extremely serious and could easily get out of hand.'

' Is that all?' said the son.

' Although,' said the P.M., ' I remain as loyal a servant of the Ship of State as I have ever been, and none will dispute that I am and always have been a loyal servant of the Ship of State—will they?'

' None,' said his wife.

' None,' said his son.

' And although I keep at the helm like a good old captain guiding his ship as it slips over the waves, even so, things can go wrong. Crises can occur. And now my friends, we are in the middle of the worst crisis that has ever been.'

' We are?' asked the wife, slightly interested.

' Father, is this crisis a good one or a bad one?' asked the son, who had learnt that some problems were invented by his father especially that he might himself solve them and hence add to his reputation.

' This, my son, is a bad one.'

That meant the situation was quite out of hand and that the Prime Minister had no responsibility for its creation.

' It could mean that we all three of us lose our jobs.'

Silence.

His wife stopped eating her cereal.

' Would that mean we would lose our wages as well? That you, in your capacity as Chancellor of the Exchequer, would have to stop paying us?' she asked.

' I would no longer be the Chancellor of the Exchequer,' he replied.

The son too stopped eating his cereal.

' What shall we do?' asked the wife.

' Yes, what shall we do?' asked the son.

' I propose,' said the P.M. and the other two leaned forward in expectancy, ' I propose a motion. The motion is—'

' Yes?'

' That in the opinion of this cabinet, the country faces a crisis of unparalleled magnitude.'

' Hear, hear.'

' Those in favour say " Aye ".'

' Aye.'

' Aye.'

' Aye.'

' The motion is carried unanimously.'

' And now,' said the wife, ' perhaps you will tell us what the crisis is all about.'

' The problem is this,' said the P.M. ' Nothing is happening.'

' Nothing?'

' Absolutely. Tell me, my dear, in your capacity as Minister of Education, Minister for Colonial Affairs, Minister of War and Minister of Justice, is anything happening?'

' Nothing to speak of,' said the wife.

' And you, my son, in your capacity as Minister of Culture, Minister of Sport, and President of the Board of Trade, is anything happening?'

' Nothing to speak of,' said the son.

' And there we are. If there is nothing happening, then the people will get bored and restless, and before we know where we are they'll demand a change of government and that will be the end of us.'

'The end?' asked the mother.

'The very end,' said the P.M.

'Something,' said the son, after a long pause, 'must be made to happen.'

All three went off to delve deeply into their various government departments to check if something, however small and insignificant, was happening. They kept their various departments upstairs, so they didn't have far to go. Nor did it take them long to report back to each other that indeed nothing was happening, just as they had thought.

Then the son had an idea. For a long time he had been greatly interested in the stars. Culture, Sport and Trade bored him to excess, but the stars fascinated him. The movement of the earth and planets around the sun, and the movement of the stars across the universe, were marvellously interesting, and he could read about them all day and all night. And now he remembered.

'It occurs to me, father, that in a month's time, at twelve noon approximately, the sun will be eclipsed by the moon. I remember reading it in one of my books.'

'That, my son, is most interesting.'

'Most interesting,' repeated the mother, who thought it was only moderately interesting and of no use whatsoever in the present crisis.

'The question is—does anybody else in the country, other than yourself, also know about this proposed eclipse?'

'I don't know,' said the son. 'It depends how well educated other people are.'

'You should know the answer to that,' said the P.M., turning to his wife, 'you're the Minister of Education.'

'As you know, because of the recent economy cuts, there is at the moment no education in the country whatsoever. Therefore I think it safe to say that nobody else will have the remotest idea of the existence of such a phenomenon as an eclipse, let alone know when the next one will occur.'

'Excellent.' And he rubbed his hands with glee. 'My son, I think you have saved the day. The crisis can be circumvented. The Ship of State will not after all be crushed in the cruel winds through which we now pass. We shall sail on. And we shall triumph against adversity.'

'Bravo,' said the son.

'Thank you,' said the P.M.

'I propose a vote of confidence in the Prime Minister,' said the wife.

'Those in favour say aye.'

'Aye.'
'Aye.'
'Aye.'
'Carried unanimously.'

And so, to give the people something to think about, the P.M. had it announced that his son, the brilliant President of the Board of Trade, etc., etc., had arranged for a total eclipse of the sun to take place at twelve noon on Wednesday, 15th April. Such an event had never before occurred. Ruritania, said the Prime Minister, would now occupy first place among the technological nations of the world. This was an achievement which would probably win for his son half a dozen Nobel prizes, and other prizes beside.

The Leader of the Opposition suspected a trick, but then he always did, and nobody ever listened to him. Everyone was delighted with the news. The P.M. was the toast of the country, and had never been more popular.

Notices were put up everywhere.

'By special arrangement with the Rt Hon. C. D. Browne, President of the Board of Trade, etc., etc., at twelve noon on Wednesday, 15th April, total eclipse of the sun. God Save the Government. Long Live the Prime Minister and his Wife and his Son. God Bless Ruritania.'

And when the great day came, the P.M. and his wife and son dressed up in their Sunday best and put on all their medals and ribbons and took up their positions on the steps of Parliament House.

At eleven o'clock the son made a speech, and the crowd cheered.

At eleven-twenty the wife made a speech, and the crowd cheered.

At eleven-forty the P.M. made a speech and the crowd went mad with enthusiasm and sang the National Anthem three times.

At one minute before noon, the army band played a salute. Then the trumpets sounded and the drums rolled. Then there was silence. The Parliament clock sounded twelve, and all eyes were turned upwards where the sun was just coming out of a dark cloud and seemed to smile on them. There was no indication of an eclipse.

Two hours later, the people started to go home, seething with disappointment.

Three hours later news came through that the eclipse of the sun had taken place, but had been visible only from the top of a mountain in Tibet.

The Leader of the Opposition demanded a full inquiry. A Royal Commission was set up, consisting of the P.M. and his wife and his son. The Commission completely cleared the government of all responsibility for the sun's failure to perform its eclipse as arranged. But you can't fool all of the people all of the time, and when the next general election was held the government was soundly defeated and the Leader of the Opposition formed a new government in its place. There was widespread rejoicing.

Apart from that, nothing has happened in Ruritania for years and years.

34 Freedom—At Last

A Story from an Improvisation

We all left school the same day—Sid, Roger and me. To be absolutely honest we left the same morning, 'cause we'd handed in all our books and things by lunchtime and we didn't go back for the afternoon. We thought it only right and proper that we should mark our last day at school by playing truant.

That afternoon we'd planned on having a party round at Sid's house and we'd somehow hoped that it would be one of those parties where everybody gets so merry they don't ever want to go home. Then the party would have lasted into the evening, the night, and maybe even the next day. As I remember it, we had the idea that if we started in the afternoon, we'd all have been so far gone by the time Sid's father got home there'd have been no getting rid of us. Needless to say this did not work at all. The party never even started. Nobody came, except for Sid and Roger and me. And none of the girls came either, 'cause they were either at work or at school, and unlike us, they were not the type who play truant.

So the three of us sat looking at each other.

'It's marvellous,' said Roger. 'All those poor kids sitting in that lousy school, and us sitting here.'

'Yeah. Ain't it marvellous,' said Sid, moodily.

'Well it is. We're free, don't you realise that? After years of imprisonment, they've pulled back the prison doors. The bars have disappeared. We're free at last.'

'That's true,' I said. 'It's unbelievable to be free. We've never known freedom before.'

'Yeah,' said Sid. 'I hated school.'

'Oh, I didn't hate it,' I said. 'Wasn't too bad.'

'I was so bored,' said Sid, 'all the time I was bored. Those boring teachers, talking, talking, talking all day long.'

'That didn't bother me much,' I said. 'It was the games I hated most. Freezing to death on that blinking sports field. I really hated that. Marvellous to think we'll never have to play games again.'

'Now we can do what we like,' said Roger.

'Don't be so daft,' said Sid, 'we've gotta work, ain't we? Unless we spend our lives on the National Assistance. But one thing about it, won't be so bad as the school was. No teachers. No one to boss you around like they do.'

'Well, what about the boss himself? Won't he " boss " you around?'

'Give my cards in if he does,' said Sid.

'No, he won't boss you around,' said Roger. 'He wouldn't dare. He'd have the union after him if he did. Have a strike on his hands, just like that.'

'They've got things organised these days.'

'Yeah.'

A pause.

'I hated school,' said Sid.

Another pause.

'Weren't too bad,' said Roger.

Another pause, and then Roger broached the subject that we were all unconsciously, perhaps, trying to avoid.

'My dad reckons he can get me a job at the railway,' said Roger.

'Yeah? What sort of job?'

'Office job, I think.'

'Good money?'

'So so.'

'What does that mean, so so?' asked Sid.

'Well, not too bad.'

'My cousin Jo works on the railways,' I said. 'He said they only start at four pounds or something like that!'

'But I'd be in an office, so I'd probably be earning more.'

'Don't think so,' I said, 'my cousin Jo's in some office, but that's what he said the boys earn there.'

'Four pounds?' asked Sid angrily. 'What for—cleaning out the office on Saturday morning?'

'No, no fooling,' I said. 'That's what boys get in the offices with the railways. You know. Boys like us, straight out of school.'

'I think I'd be getting more than four pounds,' said Roger.

'You think so? I don't,' said Sid. 'And I'll tell you this, you won't catch me working in no office for four pounds a week. No, not for five pounds neither, nor for six or seven. Eight pounds a week, that's the least I'll take. And if they can't pay me that, I'll live on the dole instead.'

'Oh, things'll work out,' I said, hoping that we wouldn't pursue this particular conversation any further.

But Sid asked, 'What are you gonna do then?'

'See what turns up. Something'll turn up. There's plenty of jobs for youngsters these days. It's the old ones who can't get work.'

'My dad says there's too many unqualified young men on the market these days. He says the country only wants qualified youngsters. He says we're not much use,' said Roger.

'Nice of your dad to say so,' said Sid.

'So he says we should take whatever we can get, and be satisfied, and then see how we can work ourselves up.'

'Yeah, I'll work my way up all right,' said Sid.

'Only trouble is, my dad says, kids like us can never hope to keep up with people with qualifications.'

'Maybe,' I said.

We were now quite depressed.

What a party.

'Your dad must be a real tonic for you all,' said Sid.

'Well it's only common sense, isn't it?' said Roger.

'Dunno about that,' said Sid. 'My brother didn't have any qualifications, but when he left school he went straight into the Merchant Navy. Been there for six years, and do you know how much money he's saved? Take a guess. In six years. Just an ordinary fellow, with no qualifications. Steward on a ship. Take a guess.'

'Five hundred?' I suggested.

'Way out. No. Four thousand pounds.'

'I don't believe it,' said Roger.

'No, and probably your old man wouldn't believe it either, but it's true.'

'Four thousand?' I asked.

'That's it my friends. He's gonna do another four years then he's coming home for good and buying a business of some kind. And he'll still only be in his mid-twenties. Good going eh?'

'Is that what you're going to do then?' asked Roger.

'No. Not on your life. Spending the best years of your blinking life sailing round the world on some crummy ocean liner? Not for me. I don't see myself bowing and scraping on everyone and being nice to them for a good fat tip. I had enough of being a little goody when I was at school. Those days are over, thank heaven.'

'Yeah, thank heaven,' I said.

'So what're you going to do then, Sid?' persisted Roger.

'Do? I don't know what I'm gonna do. I'm gonna have a look around, aren't I? See where the openings are. Enjoy myself.'

'What sort of openings do you reckon there are for a kid of sixteen, who's just left school, never done anything, never passed no exams, who doesn't want to go to sea, but who does want to enjoy himself?'

'You think you're very sarcastic,' said Sid, 'but you wait and see. I'll do as well as anyone else. You wait and see. I bet you this: say what you like about qualifications, I will be as rich when I'm twenty-five as the bloke who sits at home all night doing his homework and goes off to university and gets himself a great big beautiful university degree. You wait and see.'

' All right,' said Roger. ' I believe you. I'm not arguing.'

' Not much you aren't,' said Sid.

Then Sid's mother came home. She was a pleasant woman. We got on well with her.

' You're home early the three of you,' she said.

' They let us out on parole,' I said.

' That's right,' said Roger, ' we're free. Free at last.'

' Free? What are you talking about?'

' We're free of school,' Roger explained. ' It's marvellous.'

' I liked school,' she replied. ' I always did.'

' Schools were different in those days,' said Sid, ' with all the girls in crinolines. Schools aren't as nice as they used to be.'

' Make fun of me if you like,' she said, ' school is a good place. There's lots of variety, there's lots of opportunities, and there's no responsibilities. You wait, just a few years, and you'll all be saying how you miss your old school. You see if you don't.'

' By then,' said Roger, ' Sid will be earning so much money he won't have time to remember anything. He'll be so busy spending his fortune.'

' Very funny,' said Sid.

' It's no laughing matter,' said his mother. ' You've got to settle down to work. Earn yourself a bit of money. Make something of yourselves. It won't be easy. Still, you're not bad lads, you could be a lot worse. Things won't turn out too badly.'

' Mum, this is supposed to be a celebration. Not a funeral.'

' But you've got to face up to things, haven't you? So you've finished at school now. So you've got to settle down to a job—that's true isn't it?' And she turned to me and said, ' And what are you going to do then? Have you anything in mind?'

' Not much,' I said. ' I'm going to look around. I may take a proper job with Wyndhams. I've been working there Saturday mornings. They said they could fix me up with a proper position. I don't know.'

' Lousy money that'd be,' said Sid.

' Never you mind about lousy money,' said his mother. ' It'd get the boy started, that's the main thing.'

' And what about you?' she said to Roger.

' Oh, for goodness' sake, Mum, we've been into that once already. Look, Mum, can you—er—can you let me have a pound? Let you have it back on Saturday.'

' Heard that before. How will I get it back?'

' Well, I'll go and work down the market again, won't I?'

'But you haven't been there for weeks and weeks.'

'Doesn't matter. I can always go down there when I want to earn a pound or two.'

'I'm hard up,' said his mother.

'Oh come on Mum. It's like Roger said. It's our first day of freedom. We want to celebrate.'

'Well—'

'Good old Mum. Just a pound. Or thirty shillings if you like.'

'No, I don't like.'

'Then just a pound.'

'Here you are. And that's the last time I give you any money, my son. You're a free man now, so you can start supporting yourself. Other people do.'

'Good old Mum.'

And while he was upstairs changing his clothes, Sid's mother said, 'He never did much good at school did he? Funny though. He seems bright enough at home.'

'None of us has done much good at school,' I said, trying to be sympathetic.

'I don't understand it, you have plenty of opportunities these days. Not like when I was young.'

'But we can't all be great scholars, and go to university, can we?'

'That's true,' she said. 'It takes all sorts to make a world. And like I said, you're good lads, we've that to be thankful for.'

For a moment I wondered how she would feel if she knew one half of the various antics that Sid got up to—would she still regard him as such a 'good' lad? Possibly.

'Right we are,' said Sid, looking spruce and sounding cheerful. 'Now let's go and get drunk.'

'To celebrate our freedom,' said Roger.

'You'll do no such thing,' said Sid's mother. 'Besides, you're too young to go into pubs.'

''Course we are,' said Sid, 'we're too young to do anything that's naughty. Trust us, Mother.'

'I'd be a blinking fool if I did,' she replied.

And as we were going out into the street, she called to Sid, 'And be back here by eleven o'clock at the very latest. You hear me? Eleven at the latest.'

'Freedom,' said Sid, 'wonderful thing, isn't it!'

Notes for Improvisation

Group I Older Infant and Younger Junior

1 Johnny the Giant-Catcher

There are three good scenes here:

1. Johnny telling his mother that he wants to give up tailoring, and his mother trying to dissuade him.
2. Johnny meeting the King and Princess, who are clearly not much impressed by him.
3. The scene between the two giants, neatly divided into three parts by Johnny's throwing of the stones.

All three of these lend themselves to quite varied treatment in improvisation. Mother might bring other people in to dissuade Johnny from quitting. (Grandparents? Neighbours?) He might actually be dissuaded. Can other methods be devised for bringing the two giants to heel? A good follow-up scene could perhaps be improvised around Johnny's triumphant return home, with those congratulating him who had earlier tried to stop him going.

2 Leah and the Tiger

Interesting changes can be made in the characters of Leah and the tiger—he can be made a more attractive character, for instance, than she. The various scenes are:

Leah and her parents deciding that she should have her own house.
The tiger's various trips to the blacksmith.
The parents' various trips to their daughter.
Possibly an earlier scene depicting the queue of suitors, the complaints of the neighbours, and the way in which Leah disposes of the suitors.

3 The Tiger, the Brahman and the Jackal

Best worked on in groups of five, so that the whole story can be handled by each group. Vary the characters—and their responses.

4 The Boy who had everything

A marvellous story, with four excellent scenes:

1. The game of tennis, with the Prince sulking.
2. The council meeting, and the Prince's first interruption.
3. The resumed game, with the Prince sulking again.

4 The meeting, with the second interruption, and the friend's plan for reaching the moon.

5 *The Death of Abu Nowas and his Wife*

This story is probably best handled in one consecutive sequence. Afterwards, perhaps ask the Sultan to be less than amused by the joke that is played on him.

6 *The Nun's Priest's Tale*

Can be divided up into four sections, each of which can be adapted and extended:
Chanticleer tells his wife his dream.
The fox persuades him to come nearer.
The chase, and Chanticleer's plan of escape.
The fox again tries to persuade Chanticleer to trust him.
The first two scenes in particular lend themselves to variation. The wife could be more nervous of the dream's prophetic accuracy than he is himself. They could have quite an argument about it. He could be much more difficult for the fox to persuade. The wife could join in this argument, and so could the other hens.

7 *The Twilight of the Gods*

A good contrast to the series that have gone before. There are some good moments here—between Loki and Frigg, between Loki and the blind man, and between Hel and Hermod. The whole story is perhaps best treated initially as one sequence, with quite large groups. It is not an easy story to handle, but can help to extend the range of the work that is being done.

8 *The Husband of Rhiannon*

Improvise Rhiannon's successful attempt to persuade her father to let her marry the man she really loves. Vary the scenes in the two banquets: in the second, especially, the husband-to-be could prove much more difficult to catch out than he is in the story.

9 *The Foolish Weaver*

The best scene is the quintet in search of their missing number. See how many explanations can be devised for the sudden diminution of five into four.

10 How Finn was Married

The sequence from the arrival of the Prince to Finn's successful leap is probably best treated as one unit. See how many variations can be devised for the Prince's splendid preparations for the leap.

11 Sana, the Cowardly Prince

There is a good scene here between Sana and his father—the means that the son employs to save himself from having to travel through foreign lands, can be much extended and varied. Very persuasive arguments could be devised, and the Queen and the Government could be brought into the consultation. Advisers might be employed to discover why Sana is a coward and to suggest ways of curing him. The two scenes where the Princess tries to persuade Sana to go to war are also good ones. She also might bring others into the argument.

Group II Older Junior and Younger Secondary

12 The Peasant and his Mother-in-Law

Can be divided up into:
The peasant at home, about to go off to get his mother-in-law's supper.
Meeting the crane.
His first trip to the mother-in-law's.
Return home.
Second trip to mother-in-law's.
Second trip home.
See how many changes and variations can be made in the characters—and the styles of grumbling—of the wife and her mother.

13 Urashima

An attractive but difficult story—try handling it as a piece of group story-telling—i.e. with the group both narrating the story and also acting out parts of it.

14 Jack Frost and the Sisters

Three good scenes here:
1. The breakfast scene before Mara's departure.
2. The same scene the following morning, plus the arrival of the gossipy neighbour.
3. The sisters' meeting with their two boy-friends.

15 Robin Hood and the King

Try it as one sequence with large groups.

16 The Prince who lost at Cards

Extend the scene where David insists on going off on his travels. Both the card-playing scenes are good ones.

17 The silliest thing you can think of

Four scenes:
1. Mother and son.
2. Mother, son, and teacher.
3. Son and witch.
4. Son and Betsy, and final visit to the witch.

18 The Ghost who was afraid of being bagged

The 'nagging wife and exhausted husband about to leave home' situation is full of scope, and makes a nice contrast with the next sequence in the forest.

19 The Farmer's Pot of Gold

Could other means be devised to make the wife part with the gold? or the husband part with his horse?

The four scenes are clearly marked out:
1. Husband and wife, husband urges wife to take care of their property, wife urges husband to take care by not leaving her in charge.
2. Wife and knave.
3. Wife and husband.
4. Husband and knave, and final reconciliation of husband and wife.

20 Emrys and the Ghost

Two interesting scenes—between the farmer and Emrys, and between Emrys and the Ghost. Emrys and the Ghost can tell each other much more about their reasons for leaving home.

21 A Man Among Men

This is an African variation on the marvellous Irish Story, ' The Strongest Man in Ireland '—Number 25. Try the whole story as one sequence, and then experiment, especially with the opening scene between husband and wife, and with the first market scene. Afterwards, try Number 25.

22 The Three Princes

The opening and the closing scenes are the best—between the Princess and the Princes as they come to propose, and between the same characters after the Princess has been restored to life. The Princess could of course dispute her decision to marry none of them.

23 How Jiřík won his Wife

Three main scenes:
1 Borek and Jiřík looking over the wall.
2 Jiřík and the devil, first meeting.
3 Jiřík explaining the situation to his wife and the two of them considering various ways of defeating the devil.

There is also interesting scope in the scene with the devils discussing together.

24 Two Dilemma Tales

Ask the groups to improvise the patients' petitions to the villagers, and then ask the groups to repeat their improvisations to the whole class, with the whole class refuting, disputing or agreeing with the claims of each character and eventually voting which one should in fact be saved.

In the second tale, ask each group to improvise, say, a committee meeting of magistrates to decide what should be done, perhaps interviewing the boy and his parents in the course of it. Then ask the whole class to improvise the ' great committee ' at which the boy is again interrogated, and possibly the parents also. A chairman will be needed, and eventually some sort of solution should be reached by majority vote.

Ask the class to devise other dilemmas.

Group III   Older Secondary

25 *The Strongest Man in Ireland*

Several excellent scenes here:
O'Shea and his wife.
O'Shea at the pub, culminating in the stranger's threat.
O'Shea prior to Ginger's arrival.
Ginger and Elizabeth.
A year later—O'Shea's account of his victory, as given in the Rose and Crown.

26 *Muckle-Mou'ed Meg*

A more difficult story, but a very good one. The sequence in the banqueting hall, leading up to the offer of the daughter's hand in marriage, and ending in William's own proposal, is clear and dramatic.

27 *Things aren't what they used to be*

Two delightful scenes:
1. The first scene, with husband and wife grumbling about everything from the weather to the government to Adam and Eve.
2. The complement to the first scene, from the point where they start grumbling again when surrounded by all the luxuries of the palace.

28 *The Marriage of Sir Gawain*

This is a delightful story, and could be developed into a full-length play:
Arthur at the court, his restlessness, his Queen's dissatisfaction.
Arthur meets the giant, challenges him for no reason.

Arthur is trapped; pleads for mercy; is given the riddle.
He returns to Camelot, and is confused by all the various answers given him by the ladies.
He prepares to return to the giant.
He meets the old hag—accepts her offer—goes off to the giant.
He brings the hag back to the palace; Gawain offers his hand.
Gawain and the hag, and the two-stage resolution of the dilemma.

A Group of Stories from Improvisations

29 Sam the Scrounger

Full of scope, probably best handled in pairs, with pupils changing characters as they go along. Vary the characters as much as you choose —they could be girls just as plausibly as they are boys.

30 The Black Moments

After some initial group work, this can be an improvisation for the whole class. The details of the lesson are included in the story so that there is a whole framework in which to work. Ask the class to suggest their own versions of such ' black moments '.

31 Masked Raiders

Consists of two well divided scenes. This improvisation grew out of a newspaper account of a masked raid on a post office in the course of which the supervisor of the post office gave one of the raiders a stocking to put over his face, because the one the raider was wearing was choking him to death. Notice how far this improvisation has travelled from this simple basic idea. Newspapers are full of useful stories. Collect them.

32 The Senator

This also is taken from an idea suggested by a newspaper report—of an American senator who vetoed legislation designed to bring relief to masses of the unemployed, while himself receiving vast ' support ' from government funds for *not* keeping his plantation in operation. Notice again how far an improvisation can develop from the idea on which it is based.

33 Today's Arrangements

This improvisation was suggested by a famous item in *The Times* some fifteen years ago, when, under the heading of 'Today's Arrangements' was listed: the day's programme of royal visits, a luncheon party given by the Foreign Secretary, and an eclipse of the sun!

34 Freedom—At Last

A story taken from an improvisation on the theme of leaving school. Many different improvisations can be woven round this theme—it is a very fertile one. Note in this story how the conversation between the boys develops, how the subject of 'what are we going to do?' eventually arises and how it is taken up by the mother when she arrives.

North-East Asian regional security

Note to the reader from the UNU

The UNU Project on North-East Asian Regional Security and the Role of International Institutions was initiated in 1994 in order to explore the prospects for North-East Asian regional security in the twenty-first century. More specifically, the project has analysed North-East Asian security and regional organizations and arrangements to encourage collective security and confidence-building measures, with particular emphasis on the current problems of nuclear proliferation on the Korean peninsula, long-term Chinese strategies and concerns about integration, and disputed territorial claims in the South China Sea. The project also contributed to one of the University's ultimate goals of bringing together persons and countries of different perspectives in an effort to devise proposals aimed at conflict resolution.

The present volume, which emanated from the initial workshop of the project, is unique in the sense that it represents views from "indigenous" academics residing in the region. They reveal in this volume their own original and stimulating thinking on the international security issues that were monopolized by North American and West European specialists during the Cold War period.

North-East Asian regional security: The role of international institutions

Edited by Takashi Inoguchi and Grant B. Stillman

United Nations University Press

TOKYO · NEW YORK · PARIS

United Nations University Press
The United Nations University, 53-70, Jingumae 5-chome, Shibuya-ku, Tokyo 150, Japan
Tel: (03) 3499-2811   Fax: (03) 3406-7345
Telex: J25442   Cable: UNATUNIV TOKYO

UNU Office in North America
2 United Nations Plaza, Room DC2-1462-70, New York, NY 10017
Tel: (212) 963-6387   Fax: (212) 371-9454
Telex: 422311 UN UI

United Nations University Press is the publishing division of the United Nations University.

Cover design by Kerkhoven Associates, London

UNUP-954
ISBN 92-808-0954-7
02495 P

Contents

v

Preface

The United Nations University, in cooperation with the Singapore Institute of International Affairs, held a two-day workshop on the topic treated in this volume at Singapore in October 1994. The authors presented the first drafts of their chapters, which have been substantially revised and updated for this publication.

Given the absence of strong multilateral regional security institutions, and the perceived urgent need to construct some security-related arrangements in North-East Asia, the initial aim of the workshop was to assess the merits of international institutions as actors, with more or less autonomous will and authority, and as arenas where more traditional state actors interact with each other to co-ordinate their differences. The major research emphasis concerned the encouragement of collective security and confidence-building measures, in connection with the current problems of nuclear proliferation on the Korean Peninsula, long-term Chinese strategies and concerns about integration, and the disputed claims in the South China Sea.

The editors would like to express their gratitude to all the authors who participated in the workshop and the preparation of this volume. We would especially like to thank Professor Lau Teik Soon and his staff at the Singapore Institute of International Affairs for their generous hospitality.

We trust that the ideas advanced in this volume may contribute to the continuing debate on regional cooperation in North–East Asia and the general Asia-Pacific community.

Introduction

Takashi Inoguchi and Grant B. Stillman

Overview

The basic purpose of this collection of essays is an investigation of the role that international institutions can or might play in certain enduring and developing security problems in North-East Asia. Generally, the majority view is cautious and, while not rejecting a northern analogue of the Association of South-East Asian Nations (ASEAN) or a wider ASEAN Regional Forum (ARF), there is a scepticism as to whether international or regional institutions can or should replace traditional bilateral and closed-door negotiations on stubborn and sensitive security issues. The current confusions on the future of the Korean Peninsula and Taiwan, with contradictory developments occurring simultaneously, has made it harder to reach any firm conclusions on these basic questions.

Nevertheless, the recurrent theme seems to be that international institutions in either the economic, development finance, or technical regulatory areas are playing – and will continue to play – a useful role in the comprehensive security of North-East Asia. At this stage the utility of formal and independent security organizations (apart from existing self-defence alliances) is still questioned and these proposals must compete with traditional bilateral or second-track dialogue

1

methods like the Council for Security Cooperation in Asia-Pacific (CSCAP). This is not to say that such international institutions will never fully develop to stages similar to those in Europe or North America, for instance, but the process will definitely be different and the ultimate form probably uniquely Asian in character. In the meantime, the postwar network of US security alliances and the overarching security apparatus of the United Nations will continue to suffice.

For working purposes we have used the term North-East Asia fairly loosely, but it may be broadly understood to include the Russian Far East, the Korean Peninsula, Japan, Taiwan, and Hong Kong, as well as China's pivotal position in the Spratly Islands dispute, but which involves mainly South-East Asian countries.[1] (Although strictly within our mandate, we are not covering the Northern Territories dispute between Russia and Japan here.)

In this volume, Song Yimin, Cheng-yi Lin, and James Tang deal with the Spratlys and South China Sea issue. Lau Teik Soon touches on it from the angle of the possible mediating role that ASEAN, AFR, or other entities might play in the dispute. China's unification issues are tackled by Song Yimin, Lin, and Tang, while the chapters by Byung-joon Ahn and, to a lesser extent, Peter Hayes deal with the Korean counterpart problem. Ahn and Hayes also cover the nuclear non-proliferation issues on the Korean Peninsula. Alexei Zagorsky and Atsuyuki Suzuki survey the current strategic nuclear thinking in Russia and the commercial justification in Japan for plutonium reliance, respectively. Suzuki also considers the need for a regional nuclear energy agency similar to the one established in Europe.

Apart from these issue-specific chapters on regional pressure points, Kevin Clements and Lau Teik Soon generally explore, in the first part, the possibility, feasibility, and desirability of institution building in North-East Asia, drawing upon the mixed experiences of other regions, notably South-East Asia and occasionally Europe. In the concluding chapter, Takashi Inoguchi develops and investigates the utility of certain security models in explaining the current and future direction of North-East Asian security and then summarizes the major themes. The Conclusion also tries to generalize somewhat about the relationship between the nature of security problems and the kind of role that international institutions could play, and to draw out some implications about confidence- and institution-building efforts through international institutions.

ASEAN Regional Forum and beyond

By the early 1990s the regional environment was conducive for security developments to match the progress in economic cooperation. ASEAN had the experience, structure, clout, and willingness to nurture a new security forum rather than the fledgling Asia-Pacific Economic Cooperation (APEC) forum. Moreover, ASEAN strengths on consensus building, sensitivities to national priorities, and cooperation on common goals were well suited to the start-up phase of ARF where friction and missteps had to be minimized.

The achievement of ARF in mid-1994 was a milestone as it brought together for the first time all the major powers in the region for an explicit security dialogue. Nevertheless, ARF will remain fragile in the short term and will face various growing pains. Most importantly, China should continue to be engaged in the process, even at the risk of slow progress on the most important issues like the South China Sea disputes.

For Lau Teik Soon, one of the best aspects of the forum is that it will allow the other members (generally responsible middle powers) to keep a watchful eye over the ambitions of the four major powers in Asia-Pacific. This is a prime example of the utility of *institutionalism* for middle powers. In this respect, ARF is expected to become the key mechanism for maintaining peace and security in the region.

As long as confrontational negotiations, lack of subregional cooperation and edgy security stand-offs persist in North-East Asia, the chances of an ARF being replicated there on a local basis are slim (and possibly even superfluous). A number of our writers wonder whether it might not be better to bring North Korea somehow into the ARF or a related process at an appropriate time (most probably after the United States has suitably stabilized this situation).

According to Kevin Clements, the basic question we should ask is how it will be possible to design some subregional security architecture to enable conflicting forces to be confined within agreed institutional arrangements and resolved peacefully. Furthermore, can a genuine North-East Asian cooperative security community evolve out of any pragmatic institutional frameworks initially set up? Disjunction at any level of regional or global relations is likely to have flow-on effects and negative impacts on the other levels. In this way, regional advances are keyed to national-level developments only when cooperation is used to meet basic human needs rather than dissipated through unnecessary competition.

Modern economic and political relationships, communications, and transport and, particularly, other technical and scientific areas, require some diminution of state-centric nationalism and a parallel expression of regional and global multilateralism. Clements believes that middle powers are well placed to act as go-betweens with the hegemonic and subordinate states, especially in proposing new ways of approaching security problems.

The ASEAN experience resulted in heightened levels of interdependence. Organizations like ARF respect the interests of middle powers in seeking to develop institutional mechanisms that might handle potential or actual disputes in a non-violent fashion. But the PRC generally would prefer contentious issues like the Spratlys to be handled bilaterally rather than in open multilateral settings. North-East Asian players may see merit in the ARF processes if they offer appropriate venues or mechanisms, possibly such as conflict prevention centres or structured dialogue/mediation in private. Finally, any blatant mismatch between ARF rhetoric and the military modernization programmes of many participants will need to be called quickly to task lest the credibility of the process begins to suffer. In the meantime, second-track dialogues will build bridges to tie in North-East Asian outsiders to a growing AFR family. Eventually, ARF should be an important politico-security counterpart to all Asia-Pacific economic interdependence institutions.

Asia's undoubted concentration on economic growth has also had a positive impact on the region's security as growth and rising living standards are generally conducive to politico-social stability. And realignment in power balances has accelerated a multipolarization process that is also sympathetic to regional peace and stability. Song Yimin notes that the stubborn persistence of hegemonism means that unhelpful interference in other countries' internal affairs, both political and economic, continues unabated by the end of the Cold War. In the view from Beijing, as China has decreed Taiwan to be an internal affair, it is by definition off the agenda of international concern (Indonesia uses a similar argument in relation to East Timor).

But as long as all regional states can follow an approach of cultural respect, enhancing mutual understanding, increasing dialogue, and promoting cooperation, relative stability in North-East Asia should be maintained. As Asia differs from Europe, the security set-up cannot slavishly follow the European pattern. The best system would appear to be a gradual, loose, and open regime not infringing too much on sovereignty or internal affairs and eschewing pressure and enforcement. It is also clear that any institutional mechanism for North-East Asia must offer a choice of flexible dispute resolution channels (i.e. bilateral, multilateral, all-hands, etc.).

China Circle

The People's Republic of China (PRC), according to Song Yimin, has consistently pursued an independent and peaceful foreign policy. But it will vigorously oppose interference, bullying, and any efforts perceived as encouraging a partitioning of China (from Taiwan). China must remain strong, and that will have to mean an upgrading of its military capabilities.

In Beijing's view, the democracy movements in Taiwan and Hong Kong are perceived to be cloaks for foiling the smooth transfer of power to the PRC. Moreover, attempts to refer the South China Sea question to institutions or mediation are seen as unhelpful internationalization of the issues and exertion of pressure by the formation of alliances against China's legitimate interests. Yet, in theory, the PRC has called for the joint exploration of natural resources in the South China Sea ahead of resolving niggling territorial disputes.

Broadly, for our purposes, the incorporation of Hong Kong in the PRC could either intensify China's economic interdependence with the rest of the world and facilitate the emergence of a more benign regional state or encourage the more menacing aspects of Beijing's lingering hegemonic ambitions. Tang wonders whether the regional institutions really have any meaningful role to play in shaping the political and economic changes in China's transformation. Or is this something for the interplay of bilateral *realpolitik* yet again?

The waning regional influence of the United States, if it continues, could lead to an intensification of East Asian state rivalries. A harsher treatment of Hong Kong after hand-over could signal a greater possibility of force being used to incorporate Taiwan. China's economy and strategic interests are becoming more maritime based, witness its increasing the stakes over the South China Sea. But in the case of China, Tang considers that there is the chance that greater interdependence may also heighten rather than defuse political tensions. The last-minute Patten democratization package is seen by Beijing as a throwback to the old Western world's anti-China mentality.

In the end, attempts to evaluate a China threat are not particularly meaningful. Unless the PRC runs into great turmoil (which will benefit no one in Asia-Pacific), Asian countries will have to learn to live with a more powerful neighbour and to adjust to new realities. In the coming decades, economic concerns will probably dominate international relations (if they do not already) and this will only be strengthened by the growth of institutions for regional economic cooperation. Other states and international institutions – especially the economic, developmental, and financial – can assist in these developments by recognizing Hong Kong's special status internationally and continuing to encourage it to play an active part in these regional affairs.

Similarly, it is unclear if the Taiwan factor will in the end play a stabilizing or destabilizing role in the region's security equation. Though, in Cheng-yi Lin's assessment, the PRC seems unlikely to incorporate Taiwan forcibly, it has consistently refused to rule out the option of resorting to armed force to settle the Taiwan issue. Moreover, the United States and the international community's commitment to defend the island is rightly in question.

The much-vaunted change of emphasis of the United States at the APEC Seattle meeting, from strategic to trade priorities, mirrors the greater shared regional concentration on economics and the benefits of interdependence. Here, Taiwan's economic strength becomes a very useful way in which to expand its international relations (witness its rare membership in APEC and the Asian Development Bank, simultaneously with that of the PRC). And a genuine democracy movement in Taiwan has won it grudging respect overseas.

Although not a member of the United Nations now, Taiwan wistfully supports all forms of existing UN and potential regional collective security measures as insurance to supplement its own military strength. Tourism, trade, investment, culture, and sports linkages are growing across the Taiwan Strait, aided by informal technical foundations that have learned to cooperate on functional issues. Future developments can be expected in the areas of crime prevention, illegal immigrants, fishing disputes, judicial cooperation, extradition, and even cross-strait exploitation of natural resources. Cheng-yi Lin considers that Taiwan will continue to play the South China Sea game, but in reality it just does not have the current force projection capabilities to be credible. Yet funnily enough, compared with ASEAN claimants to the Spratlys, Taiwan has sided more with the PRC.

NPT regime and IAEA monitoring

Political and economic uncertainty, coupled with armaments transformation delays, continue to dog Russian efforts at rationalizing and/or modernizing its nuclear weapons potential. Nevertheless, more modest post-Cold War strategies are starting to be proposed and apparently sincere efforts are being made to abide by the Strategic Arms Reduction Treaty (START)-2 targets and requirements. Zagorsky points out that Russia continues to perceive herself as encircled by suspect nuclear-capable neighbours. To the extent that it can influence them, Russia is committed to encouraging their denuclearization, particularly in the Ukraine.

As in the case of the old Cold War protagonists, a well-established bilateral nuclear reduction and elimination treaty regime is already in place and will continue, as it is clearly in the interests of both parties. Indeed, a START-3 can also be anticipated presently. But the overwhelming interests and dominance of the bilateral parties in this still highly sensitive area leave very little space for the independent action of international institutions. This is clearly the undisputed realm of *balancing realism*.

The Non-proliferation of Nuclear Weapons Treaty (NPT) regime has proved useful in dealing with the slippery multilateral aspects of the non-proliferation problem and that was why it was indefinitely extended, despite some criticisms. As Zagorsky observes, this regime may be fairly characterized as a successful institutionalization paradigm according to our security model.

Suzuki believes that Japan, as an Asian country, will have to extend its nuclear cooperation to other parts of Asia. Perhaps the time has come for Asians to discuss how they can promote the peaceful uses of nuclear energy in such a way as to reassure each other. Given rapid expansion of nuclear generation, it will be important for a framework for cooperation on peaceful uses of nuclear energy to be set up, as was the case with the European Atomic Energy Community (EURATOM) (although it will probably be difficult to replicate the same sort of mechanism in Asia).

In dealing with the North Korean dilemma, some of the old Cold War alliance methods are still useful. The North-East Asian allies of America, together with China and Russia, must show a steady and consistent policy to accomplish peace and stability by taking quiet, effective, and credible action (something that sadly escaped the European allies during the Bosnian war). Ahn suggests that if North Korea ever evolves into a reformist regime, it might be possible to see more engagement and even, at the right time, the integration of North Korea into the existing economic, developmental, and political regional institutions.

By bringing North Korea completely and unambiguously back into the NPT regime and the International Atomic Energy Agency (IAEA) monitoring system, the international community should be able to hold together this important international institution and mechanism. Of course, ultimately, reunification must be for the Koreans to decide themselves with the support and guarantees from concerned powers. Ahn posits the merits of a two-plus-four regional forum with China, Japan, Russia, the United States, and the two Koreas, or some other version of a limited North-East Asian security forum. In this way it might be possible to complement and reconcile the "Koreanization" of the unification question with the globalization approach for the denuclearization of the peninsula.

Finally, Hayes agrees that the North Korea nuclear matter is best thought of as an American hegemonic power application (primarily in the areas of economic and technological might) in the post-Cold War era. The major thrust behind the US negotiating position has been to convince the new North Korean regime that cooperation rather than confrontation with the international system would be in their best interests.

Even so, buying the compliance of hard-core proliferating states may not be the neatest or most politically correct way to maintain and extend the global NPT regime. But Hayes persuasively argues that, from a *realpolitik* perspective, it may be the cheapest and only way to do so. The phased easing of North Korea's entrance into international financial institutions might be very helpful as well.

Summary

It seems clear that steady progress will continue to be made by regional organizations as state-actors recognize their utility in tackling common problems, particularly in the technical and non-controversial areas. The need for regional preventive action and/or human rights centres, with their potential to interfere in domestic questions, will continue to prove harder to justify. Finally, the substance of the most sensitive issues of national security, incorporation, nuclear containment, and border demarcation will remain to be handled by traditional back-room diplomacy. Although that is not to say that, in certain situations, some confidence-building and dialogue channels may not be usefully opened up on a multilateral plane.

Note

1. The names of countries mentioned in this volume were chosen by the chapter authors. The UNU and UNU Press wish to respect their academic freedom and are in no way responsible for the usage.

Part 1
Institution building

1

North-East Asian regional security and the role of international institutions: An Australasian perspective

Kevin P. Clements

Introduction

The Asia-Pacific region consists of four distinct but interconnected subregions: North-East Asia, consisting of China, Japan, North and South Korea, Hong Kong, and Taiwan; South-East Asia, which includes the six nations of the Association of South-East Asian Nations (ASEAN), Indo-China, and Burma; the South-West Pacific, which consists of Australia, New Zealand, Papua New Guinea, and the diverse states and territories of Micronesia, Melanesia, and Polynesia; and South Asia, consisting of India, Pakistan, Bangladesh, and Sri Lanka.

Of these four subregions, the one that excites most global interest, and which is the subject of this volume, is North-East Asia. This region is a convergence point for some of the most powerful economic, political, and military forces in the world. Despite surface calm, North-East Asia is an area of considerable competition and rivalry, a point reinforced recently by US Deputy Assistant Secretary of State for East Asia and Pacific Affairs, Thomas Hubbard, when he stated:

There are still threats to stability in East Asia. The most visible reminder of this is North Korea's efforts to acquire nuclear weapons ... Pyongyang's

13

refusal to accept its obligations under the Nuclear Non-Proliferation Treaty ... [which it was claimed] threatens the security of key U.S. allies, dramatically increases the likelihood of a destabilising nuclear arms race in Asia; and it raises the spectre of the spread of nuclear materials to rogue regimes like Iran.[1]

The critical question for those interested in peace and security in North-East Asia, therefore, is how to develop a subregional security framework that will enable conflicting forces to be confined within agreed institutional arrangements and dealt with non-violently. Lying behind this question is an additional concern about whether it is possible to move beyond pragmatic institutional arrangements towards a genuine cooperative "security community"[2] in North-East Asia. This sort of community, if it were to evolve, would be expected to nourish cooperative relations between states and peoples in the region and assist the players to solve their problems collaboratively rather than in competition with each other.[3]

Since each Asia-Pacific subregion is porous, with profound interconnections to the others through multiple economic, political, cultural, and military exchanges, the promotion of cooperative security and the development of a recognizable security community will have a very important effect on the economic and political direction of the region as a whole. If no such community evolves – if there are important discontinuities, unresolved contradictions, and tensions without any mechanisms for resolving them – the result is likely to be a reassertion of competitive rather than cooperative politics and an assertion of national rather than regional interests. Because of the economic and political significance of the Asia-Pacific region, economic rivalry, political uncertainty, and a revival of historic antagonism are likely to have a very negative impact globally.

Political stability and economic growth in North-East Asia is critical to the economic development and buoyancy of the rest of the region and, arguably, to the world economy as well. (It is a paradox that, in this context, economic growth that degrades or destroys the environment, or that brings about economic inequalities within or between states in the region, will also have negative effects regionally and globally.)

There is a very complex security dynamic linking national, subregional, regional, and global levels of activity. Disjunction at any level is likely to result in negative impacts at others. It is not possible, therefore, to discuss regional (or, for that matter, national or global) security in a vacuum. The security of states and peoples in North-East

Asia rests, in the final analysis, on the extent to which basic human needs are being met and on whether there is a disposition on the parts of states and governments to pursue their national interests competitively or cooperatively. As Thucydides noted, "strong and powerful countries do as they will while the weak will do as they must." There is a concentration of nations in North-East Asia that are currently or potentially rich and powerful. What incentive is there for these countries to think in terms of cooperative rather than competitive security systems?

While economic and political differentials have a powerful effect on whether national security will be pursued through competitive or cooperative means, there is nothing inevitable about the fact that large and powerful countries will always pursue coercive means to achieve national objectives, or that small and relatively weak states will always eschew such means. Thus, it is important when viewing North-East Asian security issues from other subregional perspectives (in this instance from an Australasian perspective) that the analyses do not prejudge what is possible, in order that the strong and powerful states in the region might contemplate a variety of different options.

One of the important and positive consequences of the post-Cold War era has been an expansion in the numbers of options available to states and non-state actors in determining new ways of doing business.

In Asia this is particularly exciting. Not only is there a recognition of greater fluidity in terms of political options but this recognition is coupled with serious discussions about the nature and meaning of "Asia" and about the diverse conceptions of Asian identity (or, more appropriately, Asian identities). How are these connected with each other? Is there sufficient commonality of political, economic, geographic, and cultural interest to bind one-and-a-half billion[4] people – divided into multiple ethnic, cultural, and linguistic groupings – together?

This new articulation of Asian identity is proceeding at the same time as new and more inclusive concepts of security are being articulated and developed. The community-building processes in Europe that culminated in the establishment of the European Community took many years to evolve. While there is some concern to avoid the development of such a close-knit community in the Asia-Pacific region in the immediate future, there is, however, also a sense that the logic and dynamic of global interdependence make the emergence of such a community inevitable at some stage. Despite official reluctance to bind Asian states and peoples into institutional arrangements that will result in the emergence of supranational regional authorities, there is, nevertheless, a quiet movement in this direction. This is because states and peoples within Asia acknowledge that modern economic and political relationships, communications, transportation, and many other facets of present-day life require some diminution of state-centric nationalism and a parallel expansion of regional and global multilateralism.

This trend can be seen in a number of different areas. It started with minimalist cooperation within ASEAN 25 years ago, which provided the basis for the development of much more dense and durable links over a variety of sectors. In the past decade this basic cooperation has established a base for closer collaboration on political and security issues. These new forms of collaboration have resulted in explicit commitments to structured dialogue, confidence, and trust building, and the development of a security architecture capable of giving some stability and predictability to exchanges between states and peoples in the region.

It is interesting that the initiatives for these new developments have come, by and large, not from the strong and economically powerful countries of the North Pacific but from states and peoples representing what could be called democratic middle powers.[5] It is these states, among which Australia would count itself, that can see a need for a new orientation to security and that are promoting new ways of guaranteeing peace and security. The reason that middle powers are willing to move in this direction is that they realize they cannot hope to achieve their political, economic, or military objectives by force and coercion. They can achieve their own objectives, solve their own problems, only in collaboration with like-minded countries sharing similar sorts of problems. They have little choice about being regional or global multilateralists: their future well-being hinges on having forums where their deepest political and security concerns can be taken seriously.

Middle powers (like middle classes) are well placed to be innovative and creative, politically and economically. By definition they stand between the rich and powerful and the poor and weak (or, in international relations terms, the hegemonic and the subordinate) and can appreciate the interests of both groups. Their position in the middle gives them a manoeuvrability denied to those that stand above or below them. They can see in both directions and have neither to defend entrenched power, privilege, or status, as do hegemons, nor to resist the powerful or struggle in the same way as the poor and dispossessed. Being in the middle is stabilizing, as long as there is a disposition to ensure equality of opportunity, democratic participation, and the fair distribution of economic, political, and social benefits. This is so within different societies, and there is no reason why it should not be the case between states and societies.

If middle powers are to assume this stabilizing role internationally, however, there has to be an acknowledgement on the part of the larger powers of the importance of middle powers in this regard. Similarly, states and peoples that are in a poor and vulnerable position need to know (by actions as well as rhetoric) that middle powers acknowledge their interests and needs and will seek to improve their plight to the best of those powers' ability.

It is interesting that, in the Asia-Pacific region, the countries that have been the strongest advocates of regional and international institutions – that see the point of multilateral, collaborative problem solving – are, indeed, middle powers. It is no accident that Australia, New Zealand, Canada, Indonesia, Malaysia, and Singapore, for example, have committed themselves to enhancing regional and global processes. Each one of these countries is unable to exert a determinant effect on global politics while acting alone. But acting in collaboration with others on a range of issues, these countries, and others like them, can begin to have a very important impact on a range of political and economic outcomes.

In the past, many middle powers did not realize this collaborative power because they were trapped by the realist proposition that the power of states or nations rests solely on the mobilization of national resources for national purposes. Now, there is a recognition (even on the part of the most powerful autarchic state) that mobilizing national economic, political, and cultural resources is an important prerequisite for political influence, but that it is not sufficient on its own and cannot always be relied upon (witness the relative powerlessness of the European Union, the West – or any other state, for that matter – to have any obvious political or military impact on the warring protagonists in the former Yugoslavia).

On the contrary, if peace and security are essentially sociopolitical processes, then political influence (authoritative influence) in relation to these issues rests as much on the quality of relationship negotiated with other states and peoples as it does on control of economic or political resources.[6] Of course, it is easier to forge positive relationships with other states when you have resources to share or allocate; nevertheless, increasingly, even foreign ministries are beginning to acknowledge that it is the overall quality of a nation's bilateral, trilateral, or multilateral relationships, or its "good name," that will be the crucial determinant of political influence. This is why so much attention is directed to ensuring that the personal chemistry between political leaders is good and why so much effort is directed towards enhancing cultural, linguistic, and other ties between states and peoples.

In addition to acknowledging the importance of relationship and the need to view relationships as intrinsically important rather than as a means to an end, middle powers in the Asia-Pacific region have been encouraged to think innovatively about security by a significant diminution of the threat of international armed conflict. For the first time in many years, defence and foreign-policy planners have to develop new defence doctrines in the absence of realistic or probable enemies. In addition, policy makers now acknowledge the expanding number of problems for which there are no national solutions. There can be no unilateral solutions, for example, to global pandemics, environmental degradation, global inequality, or population pressures. This has had the result that middle and smaller powers, in particular, are grudgingly beginning to acknowledge the definite limits of state power and sovereignty. They understand that many problems can be solved only within the context of multilateral regional or global institutions, and are beginning to cede some sovereignty to these institutions. This has always been the case, as smaller and middle powers have generally been prepared to cede sovereignty when necessary, whereas the powerful are reluctant to do so.

Nations are also being forced to acknowledge the relative ineffectiveness of military force, both domestically and internationally. Clubs are not trumps any more: they are being seen for what they always were – namely, blunt instruments that are inappropriate for solving complex problems.

In the Australian context, Foreign Minister Gareth Evans argues that the best way for Australia to guarantee its security is by Australia being a "good international citizen" and assuming its share of international responsibility in the social, economic, and humanitarian spheres. This has been given very specific focus in his "Blue Book," *Cooperating for Peace*, which focused on reform of the United Nations, and Australia has followed through with a heightened commitment to regional organizations.[7]

In recognition of many of these factors, Evans and his advisors have been studying new ideas about security, suggesting concepts that highlight the dimensions of process and relationships. There has been a definite shift in Australia, for example, from concepts of national, collective, and comprehensive security to what Evans chooses to think of as "cooperative security," a concept that embodies elements of all of the former understandings of security. "Cooperative security" is described as:

a broad approach to security which is multi-dimensional in scope and gradualist in temperament; emphasises reassurance rather than deterrence; is inclusive rather than exclusive; is not restrictive in membership; favours multilateralism over bilateralism; does not privilege military solutions over non-military ones; assumes that states are the principal actors in the security system, but accepts that non-state actors may have an important role to play; does not require the creation of formal security institutions, but does not reject them either; and which, above all, stresses the value of creating 'habits of dialogue' on a multilateral basis.[8]

It is salutary to see how this positive and collaborative understanding of security meshes with political and economic reality in the Asia-Pacific region, particularly in North-East Asia.

As mentioned above, in the past the large and powerful countries of North-East Asia have demonstrated a resistance to moving in the direction of cooperative security, because they saw little political or economic advantage in constraining their independent spheres of activity. When, for example, Senator Evans and his Canadian counterpart, Joe Clark, suggested independently the idea of developing a Conference on Security and Cooperation in Asia (CSCA), an Asian equivalent of the Conference on Security and Cooperation in Europe (CSCE or now OSCE), the most powerful countries of North-East Asia, Japan, the United States, and China, expressed (in 1990) grave reservations about its necessity or utility. In 1995, conditions are more propitious, and these countries can now see the manifest national demand for such initiatives. Because of this they have been willing to participate in the functional equivalent of such an institution, the newly formed ASEAN Regional Forum (ARF).

By and large, however, it has to be said that the major impetus for the development of regional economic, political, and security institutions in Asia has been from "middle powers" in the South-West Pacific or South-East Asian regions. This is because the North-East Asia players believe that it is possible to resolve their security prob-

19

lems bilaterally, whereas the ASEAN nations acknowledged the necessity of regional integration 25 years ago. These initiatives have resulted in heightened levels of economic, social, and political interdependence, and the evolution of "regimes" to help govern international economic and political behaviour, although with considerable resistance on the part of some states to processes that might constrain internal domestic behaviour. There have been a variety of international initiatives that have had this effect. The establishment of the South Pacific Nuclear Weapon Free Zone in 1985, for example, represented a desire on the part of states in the South-West Pacific to develop a subregional regime against nuclear proliferation. This has been reinforced by initiatives flowing out of the South Pacific Forum, a similar regime.

Similarly, the ARF, which held its inaugural meeting in Bangkok in July 1994, is an important new institutional contribution towards the maintenance of stable peace and security in the Asia-Pacific region, and is the emerging equivalent in Asia of the European OSCE. The formation of a Regional Forum was proposed at the 1993 ASEAN Ministerial Meeting held in Singapore and marks a significant step for ASEAN, which has normally eschewed explicit political defence and security discussions for fear of splitting the Association. Of this recent development, the ASEAN Secretary-General, Datuk Ajit Singh, has expressed the hope that it will generate its own momentum and become the focus of all matters relating to political and security issues.

In the absence of any such institutions in the North Pacific or, for that matter, in the South-West Pacific, this new ASEAN forum is the only vehicle for "official" peace and security discussions for the whole of the Asia-Pacific region. But this initiative owed little or nothing to the actions of the big powers of the North Pacific, even though they found the inaugural meeting very useful: the initiative flowed from "middle powers" seeking to generate institutional arrangements that would facilitate the habits of dialogue that Evans and others consider a prerequisite for cooperative security.

There are two parallel but complementary integrative processes that reflect the desires of "middle powers" for more security, stability, and fairness in the Asia-Pacific region: these are the economic discussions occurring within the Asia-Pacific Economic Cooperation (APEC) forum, and the political and security discussions being fostered by ASEAN. Both are important in the determination of a stable security community, and Australia and New Zealand have been active advocates of both. They emphasize ASEAN as the subregion's most important multilateral forum, and underline its central importance in providing links between the subregions of the Asia-Pacific region as a whole. These developments have generated dense and durable relationships that have significantly lowered (but not eliminated) the probability of armed hostilities between states in South-East Asia.

ASEAN appears to have been working constructively in two directions, seeking to deepen the relationships between the original ASEAN partners and, at the same time, reaching out to other nations in the region to create a wider security network. The deepening and enlarging processes have generated three concentric circles within the ASEAN framework.

1. The first and most intimate circle involves the six original ASEAN members: Indonesia, Thailand, Singapore, the Philippines, Malaysia, and Brunei. They meet at official and ministerial levels and share the results of their deliberations with their dialogue partners.
2. The second, somewhat larger, circle represents ASEAN and those nations designated ASEAN dialogue partners, which includes the United States, Canada, Japan, South Korea, New Zealand, Australia, and the European Union.
3. The third and largest circle includes ASEAN members, dialogue partners, and observers. This grouping brings in Russia, China, Viet Nam, Laos, and Papua New Guinea. Viet Nam and Laos have formally applied to become members of ASEAN, while the other three nations wish to forge the closest possible relationships with the Association. It was this largest circle that ASEAN invited to form the ASEAN Regional Forum, the first non-alliance forum dedicated to discussing Asia-Pacific security issues. Cambodia and Burma are likely to be invited to join ASEAN at some stage in the future, as observers initially and then possibly as fully fledged members.

These concentric circles represent degrees of perceived closeness and trustworthiness. In terms of organizational arrangements, for example, observers are allowed to observe the openings of the ASEAN Ministerial Meetings, but are then excluded from the substantive discussions. They can, if they wish, take advantage of this time to conduct bilateral meetings with each other and with ASEAN foreign ministers. Observers are not invited to the ASEAN Post-

Ministerial Conference, but are able to observe the opening session along with the media. The Regional Forum, therefore, provides an important new opportunity for observer nations to make a substantive contribution to regional peace and security discussions.

What is important about the ARF is that it includes erstwhile enemies – China, Russia, and Viet Nam – in discussions about regional peace and security issues. It also links North-East Asia (which is arguably the most unstable subregion within the Pacific rim) with South-East Asia and the South-West Pacific.

From a structural perspective it is interesting that those countries that are developing a pluralistic security community are extending invitations to those, arguably more volatile, countries in North-East Asia to join a multilateral forum for discussing threats to security and how to deal with them peacefully. There is a recognition in ASEAN, for example (as there is in Australia), of the necessity for restraints on China, Japan, Taiwan, and the two Koreas, so that none of these countries choose military options to advance their national interests. There is an acknowledgement that the new "enrichment" or "empowerment" of the Asia-Pacific region would be profoundly jeopardized by any military action within the wider region.

The United Nations is not in a position to exercise these ongoing informal constraints, so the responsibility passes to regional organizations. Organizations such as the ARF represent the interests of "middle powers" in seeking to develop institutional mechanisms that might deal with potential or actual disputes in a non-violent fashion.

Although there is some concern within ASEAN about imitating European security models, there is also an acknowledgement now that the ARF is the functional equivalent in Asia of the OSCE in Europe, although its agenda and structure are nowhere near as clearly defined. It is important that it should not be driven too hard or too fast in the initial stages. Diplomatic participants at the inaugural meeting of the Forum in Bangkok on 25 July 1994 (which included the foreign ministers of all the ARF members) compared it to the 1975 Helsinki Accords in Europe, because of its potential for becoming the major venue for Asia-Pacific security discussions at an official and ministerial level, thereby supplementing the well-established "second track" processes that have emerged from the ASEAN Institutes of Strategic and International Studies (ASEAN-ISIS) discussions.

In a major turnaround from 1990, Strobe Talbott, the US Deputy Secretary of State who led the United States delegation to the ARF, stated:

In the years to come, we believe that this Regional Forum can play a historic role in conveying intentions, easing suspicions, building confidence, and, ultimately, averting conflicts.[9]

It was never intended that the first session of the ARF would result in substantive negotiations on issues. On the contrary, much stress was placed on developing a process that would make possible substantive discussions at subsequent meetings. Thai Foreign Minister Prasong Soonsiri, who chaired the ARF, said afterwards, "It was a very good meeting, it went very well." Singapore Foreign Minister S. Jayakumar reiterated these sentiments and stated that "the meeting went off better than most people had expected." The Australian Minister for Foreign Affairs and Trade, who had taken an important lead role in framing a number of the discussions at the meeting, urged cooperation in "guaranteeing security with others rather than in guaranteeing security against others" and announced after the meeting that "Prospects for cooperation are good."[10]

In the final communiqué it was agreed that the Forum had enabled countries within the region to engage in dialogue and consult with each other on "political and security issues of common interest and concern" and that participants saw the ARF as a body capable of making "significant contributions to efforts towards confidence-building and preventive diplomacy in the Asia-Pacific region."

In relation to the non-proliferation of nuclear weapons in the region, the ARF expressed concern about nuclear developments on the Korean Peninsula, welcomed the continuation of US–Democratic People's Republic of Korea (US–DPRK) negotiations and "endorsed the early resumption of inter-Korean dialogue."

The meeting agreed to convene the ARF on an annual basis and to hold the second meeting in Brunei Darussalam in 1995. It also endorsed the purposes and principles of ASEAN's Treaty of Amity and Cooperation in South-East Asia "as a code of conduct governing relations between states and a unique diplomatic instrument for regional confidence-building, preventive diplomacy, and political and security cooperation." It entrusted the next chairman of the ARF at Brunei Darussalam to work in consultation with ARF participants to develop a more substantive agenda for the 1995 discussions. ARF senior officials would determine the contour of these discussions prior to the Ministerial Meeting.[11]

Ideas which might be the subjects of such further study include confidence and security-building, nuclear non-proliferation, peacekeeping cooperation including a regional peacekeeping training centre, exchanges of non-classified military information, maritime security issues and preventive diplomacy.[12]

The Forum also urged a detailed analysis of the "comprehensive concept of security, including its economic and social aspects, as it pertains to the Asia-Pacific region" and "other relevant internationally recognised norms and principles pertaining to international and regional political and security cooperation," in order to determine what might apply to the Asia-Pacific region specifically. It agreed to promote "the eventual participation of all ARF countries in the UN Conventional Arms Register" and foreshadowed the possibility of convening informal sessions of officials in between annual meetings in order to advance the ARF process.[13]

It is too early for final or definitive evaluations of the utility and success of the ARF. The first meeting, however, did establish some important new processes for facilitating peace and security discussions in the Asia-Pacific region and placed a number of important substantive items on the regional agenda as well. States within the region view these substantive areas with differing degrees of enthusiasm. In the light of arguments about the divergent interests of large (potentially hegemonic) powers and those with no such pretensions, it is interesting how size and political pretension influence perceptions of what was achieved at the Regional Forum's inaugural meeting.

China is deeply suspicious of processes that generate transparency in regard to its military affairs, is sceptical about the benefits of a regional arms register, and stated quite clearly at the Forum that the entire South China Sea (including areas of contention such as the Spratly and Paracel Islands) was under Chinese sovereignty. The Chinese Foreign Minister also suggested that the ARF Forum should not rush into specific cooperative arrangements. Somewhat ironically, given the new willingness of Japan and the United States to promote regimes advancing international and multilateral norms and procedures for dealing with disputes, the Chinese Foreign Minister underlined that China preferred bilateral to multilateral negotiations on contentious issues such as the Spratlys. The cautiousness of the Chinese position contrasted strongly with the enthusiastic responses of Thailand, Australia, and New Zealand, all of whom saw the ARF as a new and important part of the security architecture for the region.[14]

The ASEAN Regional Forum will have to address a number of problems in the next year or so but, if it is able to deal with them succesfully, then it is highly likely that this new initiative, willed into existence by ASEAN middle powers with the enthusiastic support of Australia and New Zealand, will have a very important effect on North-East as well as South-East Asian security and international relationships. If the major players in North-East Asia, for example, know that there is a forum in which they can air some of their major security concerns, then the ARF may provide a venue for resolving disputes while they are still tractable and negotiable, before they degenerate into intractable or potentially violent conflicts.

To do this effectively, however, will require the conscious development of mechanisms such as conflict prevention centres, and of structured and focused dialogue whereby the ARF can begin addressing some of the outstanding security problems in the region. For example, how can the ARF help Cambodia generate internal peace and stability? What role should the ARF play in relation to the South China Seas initiative in order to ensure a just and fair outcome for all claimants to the Spratly Islands? How can the ARF help prevent nuclear proliferation in Korea, or promote speedier internal reform in Burma (all these issues figured in the informal discussions). What role could the ARF play in relation to regional anxieties about future Japanese military postures and intentions, or Sino-Japanese relations? What is the connection between the ARF and the United Nations in relation to the maintenance of international peace and security? These are difficult questions that will require both intensive analysis and political will if effective responses are to be made.

Another question is whether there is any desire to invite Cambodia, Burma, North Korea, and Taiwan (which is a Spratly claimant) to join the ARF at some stage in the future. While there is a strong possibility that Cambodia will be invited to next year's Forum, the other countries remain somewhat problematic. Genuine cooperative security, including processes aimed at collaborative problem solving, has to be inclusive rather than exclusive if new forms of enmification and new regional divisions are to be avoided.

Whether the ARF, like ASEAN itself, can address these issues on an informal basis or whether there may be a need to develop some more formal mechanisms to advance preventive diplomacy, early warning, and timely intervention in response to threatening trends, will have to be considered at future meetings. Evans's proposal, for regional peace and security resource centres that would generate timely intelligence of impending problems and have some capacity for early conflict prevention, might fit neatly into such developments.[15]

A major concern is the contradiction that exists between the declaratory purposes of the Forum and the fact that many states within the Asia-Pacific region are engaged in ambitious military modernization programmes, some of which are destabilizing. The patterns of rising military expenditure in the region seem to undercut the desire for greater transparency and openness in relation to peace and security issues, to undermine rather than build confidence, and to raise questions about the commitment to preventive as opposed to coercive diplomacy. It will be a major issue for the Brunei conference, of most importance to those countries in the region that are active players in the regional and global arms trade and that see no inconsistency between trafficking in arms while engaging in dialogue and rhetoric aimed at developing more positive peaceful relationships within the region.

Future meetings of the ARF will have to address all these issues. In the meantime, this initiative should be nurtured by member states and peoples, since there is no equivalent forum anywhere else in the region.

The ARF will be supplemented by slightly less "official" second-track dialogues on the major peace and security issues confronting the region. These second-track initiatives will tie North-East Asia into ASEAN and South-West Pacific frameworks, and the Council on Security Cooperation in the Asia-Pacific Region (CSCAP) will act as the vehicle for them. CSCAP consists of a series of national committees comprising government and military officials in their private capacities as well as scholars and business leaders from countries within the region. Using the Pacific Economic Cooperation Council (PECC) as its model, these national committees will feed into a series of regional discussions and will commission regional task forces to concentrate on issues such as defence modernization in the Asia-Pacific region, maritime cooperation in South-East Asia, North-East Asian security dialogue, comprehensive security in the Asia-Pacific, and human rights in the region. The issue of human rights is one that may in the future generate considerable tension, since there is substantial Asian resentment towards the universal application of human rights instruments. It may be one area in which regional institutions will need to be guided to some degree by the activities of the United Nations, especially those of its social, economic, and human rights agencies.

CSCAP, the ASEAN Ministerial and Post-Ministerial Meetings, the ARF, plus whatever continues to happen under the auspices of the ASEAN-ISIS groups will, for the foreseeable future, be the elements shaping regional security architecture. The impact of these different elements on North-East Asia will be profound, since each one of these initiatives suggests the need for countries within that subregion to link their national security concerns much more directly to regional and multilateral dialogue processes. These institutional arrangements, although flexible and mainly for encouraging dialogue, are nevertheless the beginning of regimes that may generate patterns of compliant behaviour that will reduce the necessity for armed conflict in support of national interests and will, it is to be hoped, result in diminished emphasis on military force. The issue of how to generate genuine compliance with an international regime is in itself interesting. At the moment, it would have to be said that the ARF is nowhere near being an international security regime, but it has the potential for becoming such, and it is important that the process is not pushed too hard at this stage so that effective compliance mechanisms can be built into future arrangements.[16]

Security regimes in North-East or South-East Asia do not exist in a vacuum, and a primary motivation for the development of dialogue on security matters has been the parallel efforts to enhance economic integration in the Asia-Pacific region as a whole.

There has been a proliferation of groups dedicated to this sort of economic integration. Movements towards an ASEAN Free Trade Area (AFTA), closer economic relations between Australia and New Zealand, APEC, and the East Asian Economic Caucus (EAEC) proposed by Malaysia, all suggest that the Asia-Pacific region is highly interdependent. Of these, APEC is undoubtedly the most important. APEC brings together the three largest national economies in the world – the United States, China, and Japan – alongside some of the most robust smaller economies, and represents a combined population of nearly two billion. This means that APEC is well placed to become the motor for the world economy in the twenty-first century.

While a number of questions remain about how APEC will link to PECC, to ASEAN (and the EAEC), to the ASEAN Free Trade Area (AFTA) and the North American Free Trade Association (NAFTA), the Asian Development Bank, and other multilateral financial bodies, there is no doubt that the institutional and organizational logic of all of these developments is to stimulate and consolidate a regional economic framework that will ensure free trade, growth, development, and an equitable sharing of resources to satisfy the immense human needs of the region. The ARF, therefore, is an important political and security counterpoint to these economic developments. Appropriate modalities for generating functional co-operation between and across the different organizations and between the state parties that constitute these entities will have to be established jointly.

There is no denying the central significance of these institutions. They are creating frameworks for complex multidimensional exchanges throughout the region. They are critical to North-East Asian development but benefit all the other subregions as well. The crucial security question that relates to this, however, is not whether interdependence will continue: there seems little doubt that it will. What is crucial is how widely or narrowly the boundaries of the Asia-Pacific should be drawn. Already India and other countries in South Asia feel excluded from some of the developments in the Pacific rim. Similarly, Latin American countries bordering the Pacific feel that they should be included in these processes. It would be a pity if the positive developments within the Asia-Pacific region were to be contradicted externally by the development of competitive rivalries between this region and others less well endowed. These and many other problems will be on the regional agenda in the foreseeable future. The most recent developments, however, are important elements in ensuring that the others will be resolved amicably.

What is clear from this brief *tour d'horizon* of Asia-Pacific economic and political integration is that North-East Asia cannot afford to cut itself off from cooperative security thinking, a commitment to collaborative problem solving, and the evolution of new regional institutions aimed at facilitating and promoting creative dialogue within the region.

Australian official views on these matters are very close to those of other middle powers in the region and in other parts of the world. The Australian government and people acknowledge that regional and global mutilateralism are not optional extras in the area of peace and security, whether in North-East or South-East Asia or in the South-West Pacific. Multilateralism is absolutely vital to the development of cooperative, collaborative relations and provides the most likely means of generating resilient relationships, building a durable consensus, and generating the transformations necessary to take the region and the world into the twenty-first century.

It is important in this regard that there should be close and collaborative links between these new regional institutions and the United Nations if regional peace and security are to be achieved and maintained. This means that those countries setting the economic and political agenda in North-East Asia should take the time to respond to the concerns of subregional organizations, should see the advantages to be gained from full participation in the emerging security framework, and should ensure that synergies generated regionally are transferred into support for an enhanced and more effective United Nations. It would be helpful for states in North-East Asia to give their wholehearted support to the United Nations' "Guidelines and Recommendations for Regional Approaches to Disarmament within the Context of Global Security."[17] Only in this way will the major security problems of the region, nuclear proliferation, conventional arms transfers, and the pursuit of political interests through military means be engaged creatively.

Notes and references

1. See State Department Report, reproduced in *North-East Asia Peace and Security Network Daily Report*, Monday 26 September 1994.
2. See Deutsch, K.W. and others (1957) *Political Community and the North Atlantic Area* (Princeton, New Jersey: Princeton University Press) for an elaboration of this idea.
3. For an interesting discussion of what a stable security could look like, see J. Martin Rochester (1994) *Waiting for the Millenium: The United Nations and the Future of World Order* (Columbia: University of South Carolina Press). This book considers what might happen if international relations were conducted within a community relying on "habits of compliance" and "fair and reasonable societal norms" rather than on deterrence and threats of punishment. An ideological shift in this direction is an important circuit breaker in terms of encouraging new ways of thinking about international relations.
4. Thoughout this volume, the term "billion" means a thousand millions (10^9).
5. See Yoshikazu Sakamoto (1994) "The role of Japan in the future international system," unpublished manuscript, p. 7, for an elaboration of the idea of "post-hegemonic democratic middle powers."
6. For an analysis of security as a process see Kevin P. Clements (1990) "Transcending national security: Towards a more inclusive conceptualisation of national and global security," *New Views of International Security*, Occasional Paper Series No. 1 (Syracuse, New York: PARC, Syracuse University).
7. See G. Evans (1993) *Cooperating for Peace: The Global Agenda for the 1990s and Beyond* (St Leonards (NSW): Allen and Unwin) and also Kevin Clements and Robin Ward (eds) (1994) *Building International Community: Cooperating for Peace Case Studies* (St Leonards (NSW): Allen and Unwin in association with the Peace Research Centre, Australian National University).
8. See Evans, p. 16.
9. "Talbott explains US policy goals for region to ASEAN," USIS, *Wireless File*, EPF303, 07/27/94, 28 July 1994.
10. Yang Razali Kassim (1994) "ASEAN: ARF ends on surprisingly upbeat note," Reuter News Service, Article Ref: 000491795703; Peter Eng, "ASEAN emerges from Cold War era in cooperation," *Canberra Times*, 29 July.
11. ASEAN Regional Forum, Press Release, "Chairman's Statement, The First Meeting of the ASEAN Regional Forum (ARF), 25 July 1994, Bangkok," reproduced in full at appendix 2.

12. Ibid.
13. Ibid.
14. The New Zealand Foreign Minister, Don McKinnon, stated that he thought the 1994 ASEAN Ministerial Meetings and the ARF were the best that he had ever attended and that he felt the informal atmosphere of the forum's sessions was extremely conducive to discussions and to establishing good working relationships between states in the region and their leaders. "ASEAN: How effective is the ASEAN Regional Forum?," Reuter News Service, Article Ref: 000494411485, 31 July 1994.
15. See Evans, pp. 75 and 79.
16. See Ronald B. Mitchell (1994) "Regime design matters: International oil pollution and treaty compliance," *International Organisations* 48(3): 425–459 for an interesting discussion on these matters.
17. The Guidelines are a set of 52 principles adopted in a consensus resolution of the General Assembly on 16 December 1993 (see UN Resolution 48/77). This document maps out diverse ways and means of enhancing confidence and security-building measures in different regions of the world. It has particular application to North-East Asia, since this is one part of the Asia-Pacific region that has not made significant progress in regional arms control, zones of peace, nuclear weapon-free zones, and other areas. This contrasts strongly with the South-West Pacific and South-East Asia, where progress has been made in all of these areas and where, as mentioned above, energy has been put into developing regional security institutions. The Guidelines are being analysed and promoted by the Asia-Pacific Regional Office for Disarmament Affairs.

2

ASEAN Regional Forum as a model for North-East Asian security?

Lau Teik Soon

Introduction

In recent years, the governments, officials, academics, research institutes, and the mass media in the Asia-Pacific region have been making statements on the need for the states to cooperate on security matters. In South-East Asia, an intergovernmental organization, the Association of South-East Asian Nations (ASEAN), has played an active and long-standing role in regional security. The United States has maintained its key role through formal and informal security arrangements with many states in Asia-Pacific, for example the ANZUS security treaty with Australia and New Zealand and the bilateral defence treaties with Japan, South Korea, the Philippines, and Thailand.

But in the North-East Asian region there is an absence of a subregional organization like ASEAN and there has not been the experience of bilateral security relations between the states there. The question arises as to whether the North-East Asian region should look to the ASEAN experience and the associated relationship between ASEAN and its dialogue partners in the ASEAN Post-Ministerial Conference (ASEAN-PMC) for inspiration in order to organize a regional forum. The issue, however, may have to be discussed against the backdrop of the newly formed Asia-Pacific-wide regional security forum called the ASEAN Regional Forum (ARF).

In June 1991, non-governmental regional research institutes, namely the ASEAN Institutes of Strategic and International Studies (ASEAN-ISIS), put forward to their governments the proposal that the ASEAN-PMC could be the foundation of a regional security dialogue and that China, Russia, Viet Nam, Laos, and Papua New Guinea should also be invited to join the ASEAN-PMC members.[1] Unfortunately, before the ASEAN governments had reached a consensus, Japanese Foreign Minister Nakayama decided to jump the gun and, in July 1991, made the public proposal that the ASEAN-PMC should be elevated to a regional security forum. Understandably, the ASEAN governments responded coolly to the Japanese Foreign Minister, who it was felt had pre-empted the ASEAN initiative.

The ASEAN initiative was finalized at the Fourth ASEAN Summit in January 1992 in Singapore, when the Heads of Government agreed that ASEAN should consider regional security issues and suggested that the ASEAN-PMC could be the forum for the discussion of regional security cooperation. From then on, the momentum gathered for the eventual formation of the ASEAN Regional Forum.

This chapter deals with the background to the ASEAN initiative, the place of the ASEAN-PMC, and the formation of the ARF. It concludes by addressing the issue of whether the North-East Asian region should consider the ARF as the most appropriate model for a possible resolution of the regional security problems in North-East Asia.

The security environment

Since the mid-1980s, the security environment in the Asia-Pacific region has been relatively stable in the sense that there has not been any serious outbreak of military conflict between states. The United States eventually lost interest in its huge naval and air bases in the Philippines, the Vietnamese withdrew from their military occupation of Cambodia, and there was a gradual *rapprochement* between former adversaries on both sides of the ideological divide.

But several old security issues remain unresolved and new ones emerged. Together they pose serious challenges to the peace and security of the Asia-Pacific region. These issues include the nuclear weapon development stand-off in North Korea, the future of Taiwan either as part of China or as independent state, the rival claims over the Spratly Islands, overlapping territorial waters and economic zones under the Law of the Sea regime, the military expansion and modernization of China and Japan, and intra-ASEAN issues such as arms build-up, territorial disputes, ethnic irredentism, and rebellious or insurgency movements. Consequently, there are numerous security issues of various levels of seriousness, all of which require careful management and (it is hoped) compromise solutions so that the relative peace and security of the Asia-Pacific region can be maintained.

In the early 1990s, a number of developments created an environment conducive to the consideration of a regional security arrangement that could manage these security issues and eventually seek a solution to some of them. These developments include the following.

First, there was the United States review of its security role in Asia-Pacific: the need for burden sharing besides self-sufficiency, and supplementing unilateralism and bilateralism with multilateralism. Second, there was the review of Japan's role in regional security and the need to accommodate Tokyo's ambitions. Third, there was the reassertion of power by China and the need to restrain Beijing's growing strength. Fourth, there was the end of the Cambodian conflict, which ushered in a period of *rapprochement* between the ASEAN and Indo-Chinese states. Finally, there was the general rise in economic development of all the East Asian and South-East Asian states. All these factors generated a desire on the part of the Asia-Pacific states that there should be a mechanism to discuss and manage the troublesome security issues of the region.

Role of ASEAN and ASEAN-PMC

In ASEAN, the Asia-Pacific region found an organization willing and able to initiate a proposal for the formation of a regional security arrangement. ASEAN has the experience and the organization structure to undertake the task. It has been said that ASEAN was founded primarily on security considerations. At the time of its formation in August 1967, the ASEAN states had just emerged from a period of confrontation. Indonesia between the years 1962 to 1966 opposed the formation of Malaysia and had used diplomatic and military means to undermine the new federation. Malaysia and the Philippines had tense relations as a result of their dispute over Sabah. Singapore and Malaysia had serious political differences and bloodshed was averted only with the separation of the former from Malaysia. These bilateral frictions were carried over during the first few years after ASEAN's formation. In 1968, Malaysia and the Philippines suspended their diplomatic relations over the Corregidor incident, and Indonesia and Singapore nearly broke off diplomatic relations over the execution of Indonesian marines. Hence the periods prior to and immediately after the formation of ASEAN were very tense and they could have seriously ruptured the newly formed regional grouping.

The formation of ASEAN in August 1967 was the first initiative of South-East Asian states to build trust and confidence among themselves. The Bangkok Declaration stated that the main objective of ASEAN would be cooperation in the social, economic, and cultural fields. But the preamble maintained that ASEAN would strive for peace and security in South-East Asia, a region free from the military entanglements of the Cold War.

A major factor that held ASEAN together was the need on their part to face new challenges in the regional security environment brought about by the British decision to withdraw its military bases east of Suez; by the American decision to halt the military offensive against the North Vietnamese and seek a negotiated settlement; by the increased influence of the Soviet Union and China in Indo-China; and by the expansion of North Viet Nam into South Viet Nam and the neighbouring territories. The fear that the threat from the north might spread southward with the replacement of friendly Western powers by communist giants gave rise to the Declaration on the Neutralisation of Southeast Asia in August 1971. Essentially, it called for the creation in South-East Asia of a zone of peace, freedom, and neutrality. This was a significant initiative of ASEAN concerning security in the Asia-Pacific region (apart from the formation of ASEAN itself).

Following the reunification of Viet Nam in 1975, ASEAN advocated normalization of relations and the reconstruction of Indo-China. It formulated in February 1976 the Treaty of Amity and Cooperation (appendix 1), which attempted to lay down the basis and principles for the peaceful settlement of disputes in the region.[2] In fact, it was not until 24 years later that Viet Nam and Laos were finally admitted to the Treaty.

Between the years 1979 and 1990, ASEAN took the lead in opposing the Vietnamese occupation of Cambodia. In the United Nations and other international forums, ASEAN states condemned the aggression and occupation by Viet Nam against a smaller neighbour. The active diplomacy and peace overtures by ASEAN, particularly on the part of Indonesia, contributed greatly to the final peace settlement accords signed in Paris in 1990.

ASEAN seeks to create a strong, cohesive, and united South-East Asia in all fields – diplomacy, economics, and security. The way that ASEAN handled its own security problems and its active role in regard to the Cambodian settlement reflected the success of ASEAN's diplomacy. The characteristic style of ASEAN diplomacy has certain attributes: these are consultation and consensus building, sensitivity to national priorities, and cooperation on the basis of common interests and benefits. In the economic field, ASEAN has come a long way from its first tentative suggestions, such as the preferential tariff arrangement and industrial joint ventures, to a more concrete project such as the ASEAN Free Trade Area or AFTA.

In the security field, ASEAN has long experience in security cooperation on both a bilateral and a multilateral basis. On a bilateral basis, military exercises have been conducted among the army, navy, and air force units of the various ASEAN armed forces. On a multilateral basis, ASEAN has undertaken measures including the conducting of exchanges of visits among military personnel, the exchange of intelligence information, and the training of senior officers in each other's defence academies. In fact, since the early 1980s ASEAN has begun to implement confidence-building measures, long before that term came into vogue among the strategists of today.

ASEAN has had discussions on economic and security matters not only among the constituent nations but also with their dialogue partners, namely the United States, Canada, Japan, South Korea, Australia, New Zealand, and the European Union. These so-called ASEAN Post-Ministerial meetings (ASEAN-PMC) in fact became the foundation of the ARF. As stated earlier, this was first suggested by the ASEAN-ISIS in their memorandum to the ASEAN governments in June 1991.

The ASEAN initiative to play a more active role in security cooperation in Asia-Pacific was based on a decision reached at the Singapore Summit in January 1992. The political leaders expressed the need for ASEAN to begin discussion of security matters in view of the changes in the strategic environment. In Manila in July 1992, the ASEAN foreign ministers adopted the Declaration on the South China Sea, which called for the peaceful settlement of the dispute over the Spratly Islands.

The occasion for the launching of the ARF proposal came at an informal meeting of foreign ministers from all the ASEAN-PMC countries, as well as ASEAN's consultative partners (China and Russia) and ASEAN's observers (Viet Nam, Laos, and Papua New Guinea), in Singapore in July 1993.

The ASEAN Regional Forum

The formation of the ARF in Bangkok in July 1994 is rightly recognized as the most significant development contributing to the peace and security of Asia-Pacific. For the first time, all the major powers in Asia-Pacific – including the United States, China, Japan, and Russia – are involved in a security dialogue.

The United States remains the most vital actor for maintaining regional security. The defence treaties that it has with Japan, South Korea, the Philippines, and Thailand, and the defence arrangements with the other ASEAN states, are likely to continue as the major assets of the American security presence in Asia-Pacific. But increasingly, because of domestic and external constraints, the United States has to share more openly the burden of its defence commitments with other states. Further, its participation in a multilateral dialogue within the ARF may also serve to contribute to the reduction of tensions and conflicts in the region.

China and Japan are the two emerging global actors and their security roles may be better defined in a multilateral forum. This could also be more acceptable to the other Asian states, which fear the expansionist ambitions of these two Asian giants. As for Russia, despite its domestic economic and political turmoil it remains a significant player because of its military strength, and it can provide the role of balancer *vis-à-vis* China and Japan.

Decisions were taken to continue the ARF dialogue on an annual basis. ASEAN will continue to host the ARF meeting in conjunction with the annual ASEAN Ministerial Meeting and ASEAN-PMC meetings. Between the annual meetings, there will be the inter-sessional meetings at the official level to deal with issues set out in the ARF Statement of July 1994.

The ARF made the decision to conduct studies on various issues. The subjects of these studies include the following: confidence and security building; nuclear non-proliferation; peace-keeping cooperation including regional peace-keeping training centres; exchanges of non-classified military information; maritime security issues; preventive diplomacy; comprehensive concepts of security; and norms and principles pertaining to political and security cooperation.[3]

It should be noted that the issues that the ARF meeting decided on have been taken up by the non-governmental organizations, ASEAN-ISIS and the recently formed Conference for Security Cooperation in the Asia-Pacific (CSCAP). CSCAP had submitted its Memorandum No. 1 on "The Security of the Asia-Pacific Region" dated April 1994 to the ARF officials for their consideration. Many of the issues included in the ARF Chairman's Statement of July 1994 were mentioned in the CSCAP memorandum, including confidence-building measures, preventive diplomacy, regional peace-keeping centres, information exchanges including intelligence exchange, information about military exercises, security of sea lanes, and comprehensive security. More specifically, CSCAP has embarked on four projects, namely comprehensive security, maritime cooperation, enhancement of security cooperation in the North Pacific, and confidence- and security-building measures.[4]

The ARF is a new and fragile organization and faces certain problems. The central problem seems to be whether other members are prepared to accept and follow ASEAN's leadership in the development of the ARF – at least for the next five years or until the end of the ASEAN round of meetings. Officials from Australia and Japan, for example, have expressed reluctance to accept that ASEAN should not only chair the ARF meetings but also set the agenda and programme of the meeting. But on the other hand, the ASEAN officials do consult the other ARF members when they draw up the final agenda.

Another problem concerns the consultative nature of the ARF. It is hoped that the Western members (e.g. the United States, Canada, and Australia), as well as Japan, will not impose their various decision-making styles upon the ARF process. Instead, they should display patience and understanding and not undermine the coherence of ARF with hasty decisions.

Due regard for the sensitivities of various member states such as China, concerning certain security issues, must also be taken into account. Under no circumstances should China be "frightened off" by the demand to arrive at concrete or substantive results on the part of ARF members.

However, there is the recognition that progress should be made in the ARF process; otherwise, it will become redundant, or overtaken by contentious events. ASEAN has adopted a consensual approach with caution, patience, and sensitivity. In the ASEAN way, progress can be made only on the basis of the lowest common denominator. If this approach is adopted, the ARF will make progress, albeit slowly.

Finally, and most importantly, member states should not come with any grand design to institutionalize the ARF process too soon with a view to making it into a collective security arrangement, whether on the proposed CSCAP model or on other more formal arrangements. The shape, structure, and other characteristics of such a regional security arrangement must be left to evolve with time and patience.

It is envisaged that eventually ARF will be enlarged to include other states in Asia-Pacific, such as North Korea, Mongolia, and Myanmar, so that it will truly be an Asia-Pacific and encompassing organization; it is also envisaged that the ARF might become an Asia-Pacific Regional Forum (APRF).

From a strategic point of view, the ARF may have captured the major forces that are vital to the peace and security of the region. It may even have contained the potential of the threat from China and provided a deterrent against the possible future emergence of militarism from Japan. It has usefully engaged the participation of both the United States and Russia in a multilateral forum on security matters in Asia-Pacific. Finally, within the ARF, all the other member states can keep a watchful eye on the development and ambitions of the four major powers in the Asia-Pacific. In this respect, the ARF constitutes the key mechanism for maintaining peace and security in Asia-Pacific.

A model for North-East Asia?

From the foregoing discussion it is obvious that certain conditions must be present for the meaningful consideration of a regional security dialogue in North-East Asia.

First, there should be a conducive security environment. As noted, the general security environment in Asia-Pacific was conducive to the formation of the ARF in July 1994. Such a condition might have applied to the issue of North-East Asian security, except that the North Korean nuclear development programme has become a major obstacle. The US–North Korean talks on the need to curb nuclear weapons development and the inter-Korean discussion have made irregular headway. Whether these issues can be overcome on a permanent and lasting basis remains to be seen.

Second, there should be a regional organization willing and able to initiate the implementation of the proposal for a serious and sustained regional security dialogue. In South-East Asia, only ASEAN is an organization with both the experience and capability to embark on such a precarious exercise; in North-East Asia there is no such subregional organization. Various suggestions have been floated in the past, for example that by Canadian Foreign Minister Joe Clark to have a North-East Asian security forum, but all efforts to form it have failed. Again, the main stumbling-block seems to be the participation of North Korea.

Third, there should be a move toward the adoption of a consensual approach for problem solving. The ARF adopted this approach when its members entrusted the development and progress of the regional security organization to ASEAN. For the next few years or more, ASEAN states in turn will host the ARF and, thereby, ASEAN will set the agenda, albeit in consultation with other members. But clearly, the consensual approach of ASEAN will be the guiding principle concerning problem solving. In North-East Asia, the dominant negotiating style has been one of confrontation as each side, whether it be the United States or North Korea, attempts to force the issue out into the open and to take a firm decision on it. Such an approach is not really suitable for a multilateral dialogue.

Conclusion

The formation of the ASEAN Regional Forum may pre-empt the need for a North-East Asian security dialogue. ASEAN was formed long before the ARF came into being. The formation of a new subregional forum for North-East Asia now may be superfluous. The issues affecting the Korea Peninsula are international in nature and they have international repercussions; hence, they may be more suitable for a multilateral forum that also includes North Korea.

In security matters, ASEAN and the ASEAN-PMC processes may have been replaced by the ARF. It may prove to be that North-East Asian states will look to the ARF as the more appropriate mechanism to deal with the security issues of the region.

Notes and references

1. The ASEAN-ISIS submitted a memorandum to the ASEAN government prior to the Fourth ASEAN Summit in Singapore. The memorandum was entitled *A Time for Initiative, Pro-*

posal for the Consideration of the Fourth ASEAN Summit: ASEAN-ISIS Memorandum No. 1, June 1991, Jakarta.

2. See the *Treaty of Amity Cooperation in Southeast Asia*, 24 February 1976, Bali, reproduced in full at appendix 1. In July 1994, the first meeting of the ARF endorsed the principles of this treaty as, among other things, a code of conduct governing relations among states in the wider region.

3. See para 7 (a–c) of the Chairman's Statement: *The First Meeting of the ASEAN Regional Forum (ARF), 25 July 1994, Bangkok*, reproduced in full at appendix 2.

4. See *The Security of the Asia Pacific Region, CSCAP Memorandum No. 1*, April 1994.

3

China and North-East Asia's regional security

Song Yimin

Introduction

North-East Asia is an important part of the Asia-Pacific region, and the converging place where the interactions among the four major powers – China, Japan, Russia, and the United States – are given full play. North-East Asia's regional security is thus closely related to the security of the whole Asia-Pacific, especially to that of East Asian security. This chapter focuses on three aspects: the security of the Asia-Pacific region and North-East Asia; China's policy considerations toward regional security; and several specific issues, namely the Korean Peninsula situation and its nuclear dimension, the Taiwan issue, the Hong Kong issue, and the issue of Nansha Archipelago and the South China Sea.

A cautiously optimistic view of North-East Asia's security environment

Peace and stability, and development and cooperation have become the twin mainstreams in the Asia-Pacific region. The security of North-East Asia and the Asia-Pacific region as a whole is, at the time of writing (October 1994), in its most favourable state since the end of World War II.

During the Cold War years, owing to the direct military confrontation between the United States and the Soviet Union, the situation in the region was tense and the danger of major wars erupting in the Asia-Pacific region always existed. The regional hot spots had either the direct or indirect involvement of the two superpowers. After the end of the Cold War, the danger of major wars in the Asia-Pacific region was basically removed and relations among countries of the region were greatly improved. But generally, the situation in the region has been comparatively stable all along. This could be due in part to the rapid and continued economic growth in Asia, which has rightly attracted world attention.

The possibility of armed conflicts among various regional countries has also been greatly reduced as the relationship among the major powers went through an evolution of historic significance. All of these countries are at a stage of policy readjustment but, significantly, none of them takes any other powers as actual or imminent threats to its own national security. The existing contradictions and conflicts among the countries other than the major powers are, on the whole, not likely to get out of control, still less likely to lead to large-scale wars; the civil wars left over from the Cold War days, although nationally and neighbourly destabilizing, are not likely to escalate into international conflicts either. The rapid end of the Cold War has shocked the world, but its impact on Europe is far greater than that on East Asia. It has not unleashed simmering fierce ethnic or religious conflicts in this region. Internally, most Asian countries are, generally speaking, relatively stable.

All the Asian countries give economic growth the highest priority in their national strategy for development and in their foreign relations. This has had a positive impact on the region's security. As economic growth and the rising standard of people's living are always conducive to political and social stability, a favourable and mutually enhancing interaction between economic development and political stability has come into being. This provides countries in the region with more common ground. For example, in order to foster economic growth they need to maintain regional stability, to take part in economic cooperation among themselves, and to improve their mutual relations.

The rise of Asia constitutes an important feature of the international situation after the Cold War. Asia has become an economic zone with relative independence, less reliant on the United States and Western Europe. Owing to its rapid economic growth and comparative stability, Asia's international status has been unprecedentedly elevated. Many countries in other parts of the world have readjusted their foreign policies and accorded Asia higher priority in the past year or two.

More importantly, the balance of power in the region has experienced tremendous change and realignment. Russia is not likely to play any conspicuous role for some time to come. The influence of the United States has somewhat declined and Japan's standing is on the rise. The developing countries such as China, ASEAN countries, and South Korea are playing an increasingly bigger role in both economic and security affairs. The acceleration of the multipolarization process is conducive to regional peace and stability.

In the foreseeable future, the above-mentioned factors will surely become even more powerful. Therefore, the prospects for the security of Asia are quite good. However, it must also be borne in mind that the following uncertain and destabilizing factors still exist.

The biggest destabilizing factor is the persistence of power politics and hegemonism, most commonly manifested in interference in other countries' internal affairs, and the imposition of one's own will and values on the others, bringing pressure to bear everywhere or carrying out sanctions at every turn. This indicates that in certain countries the way of thinking and the policies that took shape in the Cold War years still linger on.

Relations among the relevant major powers and power centres are neither well defined nor stable. The regional balance of power and the alignment of forces in the region are undergoing both dramatic and subtle changes. Some powers are contending for the dominating position in certain fields and their long-term policy orientations are not yet clear.

The hot spots left over from the Cold War period have either not completely cooled down or are still unsettled. The perennial situation on the Korean Peninsula and the new nuclear issue there, which caused great concern around the world, is a case in point.

Among a number of countries there are disputes on territories and territorial waters that are historical remnants or subsequently have been artificially created.

Ethnic contradictions and religious conflicts exist within or among various countries. Some countries have grave social problems, and foreign involvement in a number of these issues has made matters even more complicated.

Some international forces interfere in the internal affairs of China on the Taiwan issue. They support and encourage the separationist forces in Taiwan, making the Taiwan issue a continual destabilizing factor in the Asia-Pacific region. If such activities continue further and become more rampant, the consequences could be very serious.

Beside the positive effect of giving priority to the economic growth, as described above, there is also a negative by-product. Economic competition and contention for natural resources among various countries certainly will intensify. Protectionism in some countries and economic groupings will probably increase. In particular, some major powers will, more often than not, resort to economic means to interfere in the others' internal affairs and exert pressure on them.

The above-mentioned uncertain and destabilizing factors are having a negative effect on regional security. Regional peace and stability will be seriously damaged if certain issues are mishandled or some unforeseeable accidents take place. But peace and development are the main theme of the contemporary world. The general trends, in the world as a whole and in this region in particular, are directed toward the easing of tensions. Comparatively speaking, all the destabilizing factors are of a secondary nature: they cannot prevail over the mainstream of regional stability. As long as all the countries in the region follow the approach of mutually respecting each other, enhancing mutual understanding, increasing dialogue, and promoting cooperation, a relative stability in North-East Asia and the Asia-Pacific region will surely be maintained and improved. All the existing issues mentioned so far should not get out of control; on the contrary, some of them will probably be alleviated or resolved step by step. Therefore, one can be reasonably optimistic on the prospects for regional security and peace.

China's foreign policy: A major element of regional peace and stability

Since the end of the Cold War, the security of the Asia-Pacific region in general, and that of North-East Asia in particular, have increasingly been in the spotlight and have become an object of world attention. The question of establishing a mechanism for dialogue on regional security has been the order of the day, with various proposals and suggestions being put forward. We can find a lot of similarities as well as areas of disagreement among them. In this regard, it is of great importance to seek common ground while laying aside differences.

The viewpoints that are more or less in common include the following:
– that since economic development is the highest priority, countries in this region all want to maintain peace and stability;
– that all hope to achieve relaxation and denuclearization on the Korean Peninsula;
– that all seek to mitigate or resolve the existing issues related to regional security through dialogue, and to prevent them from slipping into confrontation and conflicts;
– that all are aware that the Asia-Pacific region, including North-East Asia, differs from Europe; thus, the security set-up in this region cannot follow the European pattern;
– that all believe that the security cooperation cannot take the form of any bloc building and the only desirable form will be a relatively loose and open regime; and
– that the building of the Asia-Pacific security regime cannot be accomplished overnight but should proceed in a gradual manner.

On the other hand, the starting points and the ways to solutions put forward in the proposals and suggestions by various countries are markedly diverse. There are different opinions in regard to the sources of threats to regional security, and certain countries take one another as the sources of uncertainty and instability. The United States, has, all along, wanted to establish a security regime that would be dominated by itself, and to make the issue of security an excuse for interfering in the other countries' internal affairs. With regard to the ways of solution, many countries advocate peaceful dialogue, whereas some others agree to dialogue but put emphasis on exerting pressure and resorting to threats or enforcement. Regarding security cooperation, as with economic integration, there are different views on the degree and speed of institutionalization, as well as on the relationship between multilateralism and bilateralism. It is only natural that such different opinions and suggestions exist. What is important is that these differences should not be allowed to become obstacles to security cooperation. Therefore, it is desirable to take an approach of mutual respect, with consultation on the basis of equality and seeking common ground on major issues while laying aside differences on minor ones. Moreover, it should be realized that some of these differences originate from a lack of understanding and trust. This very fact shows how important it is to enhance official consultation and non-governmental exchanges.

Dialogue on security issues in North-East Asia is becoming increasingly active. Bilateral dialogues are being held everywhere and trilateral and multilateral seminars are more frequently convened on a non-governmental or semi-official basis. However, the precise mechanism of security dialogue has not yet crystallized: it is still an object of exploration. At present, the conditions for establishing an intergovernmental multilateral security dialogue regime have not matured. The crux lies in the issue of the Korean Peninsula left over from the Cold War period. Once the nuclear issue of North Korea has been satisfactorily and (it is hoped) finally resolved through dialogue, the relations between North Korea, the United States, and Japan have been normalized, and the framework of the relations between North and South Korea has been shaped, the security regime for North-East Asia will come into being step by step.

The following are some of my personal views on China's policy considerations on regional security, starting with a brief description of the cardinal course of China's foreign policy.

China has consistently pursued an independent and peaceful foreign policy. This basic line of peaceful diplomacy has never been (and will not be) changed, even though China also makes important policy readjustments according to the changing situation and its own assessment of the situation. Since the late seventies, China's judgements on the international situation have undergone some major re-evaluations. These include the viewpoint that a new world war can probably be avoided, with the hope that peace will be maintained; that peace and development are the two main themes of the world; and that the economic factor has become the focus of both international relations and each country's national strategy. With these new elements in its assessment, China has readjusted its foreign policy correspondingly. In order to concentrate its efforts on economic construction, it has pursued a policy of all-dimensional opening to the outside, has led its economy into the world economic system, and has dovetailed its economic practice with the majority of international norms; state-to-state relationships should not be allowed to be affected by ideological factors. In short, the general goal of China's foreign policy is to maintain world peace, promote mutual development, and create a favourable international environment for China's reform and opening-up policy and modernization. Economic development will remain the central task of China for another 100 years, and its foreign policy, which serves its economic construction, will inevitably be unchanged for a very long time to come.

Promoting friendly cooperation with other Asia-Pacific countries constitutes a particularly important factor in China's foreign policy. China's policy toward the Asia-Pacific region, North-East Asia included, can be summalized as set out below.

China aims to preserve lasting peace, stability, and prosperity in the region. Maintaining the political stability and economic growth in China will be an important contribution to the stability and development of Asia-Pacific and the world. Meanwhile, the stability and prosperity of the countries surrounding China are the crucial outside imperatives for China's continued economic construction.

China faithfully pursues a policy of good neighbourliness. It is the foremost task of China's diplomacy to maintain and enhance the relationship of peaceful coexistence and friendly cooperation with its surrounding countries. In fact, after the Cold War, China has been enjoying the best relations with those countries since the founding of the People's Republic.

China pushes forward economic internationalization and participates in international economic cooperation. In recent years, China has actively expanded economic links with the outside world and is seeking membership in GATT and the new World Trade Organization. It is taking an active part in international economic cooperation in various forms and on different levels, on the basis of equality and mutual benefit. Importantly, China does not stand for establishing any trade bloc in confrontation with other economic groupings.

China advocates establishing and developing friendly cooperation with all countries on the basis of the Five Principles of Peaceful Coexistence first advanced by China, India, and Burma in 1954: these are mutual respect for territorial integrity and sovereignty, mutual non-aggression, non-interference in each other's internal affairs, equality and mutual benefit, and peaceful coexistence. While taking the strengthening of the unity and cooperation with the other developing countries as the foundation of its foreign policy, China also attaches great importance to improving relations with the developed countries. China regards the development of friendly cooperation with Japan as an important component of its foreign policy, pays special attention to maintaining and improving relations with the United States, and greatly cherishes the good neighbourliness that has already been established with Russia. The nature of the relationship among the major powers in the Asia-Pacific region has under-gone fundamental changes in this new situation. There is no strategic basis for any two or three powers being allied against the other one or two. On the contrary, their relations are now characterized by interdependence and competition, and mutual restraint and promotion. Normal relations among major powers are the essential guarantee of peace and security in North-East Asia and the Asia-Pacific region as a whole.

China maintains that a new political and economic order should be established in the Asia-Pacific region in accordance with the UN Charter and the Five Principles of Peaceful Coexistence while opposing hegemonism and power politics. China advocates resolving international disputes through peaceful dialogue and consultation on the basis of equality. One should not take the approach of exerting pressure or carrying out sanctions at every turn, not to mention the use or threat of force.

China is determined to preserve its independence, sovereignty, and territorial integrity. Having suffered the full bitterness of aggression and bullying, the Chinese people cherish their independence, which was achieved through great difficulties. They will spare no effort to oppose interference from outside and any activities directed to the partition of China.

All the above-mentioned demonstrates that China is an important force in preserving peace and security. A flourishing and strong China will only benefit peace and the development, stability, and prosperity of the Asia-Pacific region, and will never constitute a threat to any country.

It should be pointed out that in recent years on the international arena, but mainly in certain Western countries, some people have been spreading the fallacy of the so-called China threat, and the alleged building up of China's armed forces. Some such people, owing to a lack of understanding, are only echoing the views of others; some are even doing so through an unscientific interpretation of statistics; yet others do so out of their intention to make money through arms sales. But the main reason underlying these assertions is that they do not want to see a stronger China, so they deliberately play up and exaggerate the strength of China to create unfavourable opinion about China, and attempt to drive a wedge between China and its neighbouring countries.

As a matter of fact, many people in the United States and some other Western countries looked down upon and underestimated China's strength not long ago. They even believed that, with the dramatic changes in the Soviet Union and the Eastern European countries, plus the pressure from the West, China would very soon collapse, so that they would be able to announce "the end of history." But, as always, things developed in an opposite direction to their expectations. Then these people made a dramatic U-turn and began to overestimate China's power all of a sudden, raising China's position to the third-biggest economy in the world. Undeniably, since its reform and opening up, China has certainly achieved rapid growth, but it is still a developing country at a low level. It has as many as 80 million people who go short of many necessities. It still needs 30–50 years to catch up with the medium-developed countries, without even mentioning the really developed countries.

China has, indeed, spent somewhat more in real terms on defence in recent years, but that is primarily to offset the effects of inflation. Commodity prices went up 1.3 times from 1980 to 1993 and military expenditures 1.16 times. Consequently, the real purchasing power of the military expenditure in 1993 was lower than that of 1980. Moreover, quite a large share of the increase has been spent on improving the well-being of the troops, because the living standards of the Chinese people as a whole have been raised notably. Of course, China will have to accomplish the modernization of its national defence step by step and in a moderate way on the basis of its economic development, as China is quite backward in its military technology and equipment compared with the developed countries. This is imperative for China in order to preserve its national independence and uphold its economic construction. But China has not taken, and will never take, part in arms races. China's defence expenditures are modest, only about US$6 billion annually, which is lower than those of its neighbours, such as Japan, South Korea, and India, and lower than that of Taiwan as well.

As for China's policy considerations on a regional security regime, it is my understanding that they consist of the following main points:
1. China advocates the following principles in efforts to establish any dialogue regime on regional security: mutual respect, equality, and mutual benefit; peaceful dialogue; friendly cooperation; non-alignment; and no control by any specific country.
2. China actively supports and participates in regional security cooperation, as well as bilateral and multilateral dialogues on security.

China has already engaged in bilateral dialogues with most Asia-Pacific countries, and has worked out some security guarantee measures with some of its neighbouring countries.

3. China actively supports and participates in regional security forums that serve to exchange views and enhance mutual understanding and mutual confidence. China opposes any practice to make decisions or take common action against a particular country or subregion, or on specific issues, and opposes the formation of military blocs.

4. China stands for building up a regional security regime suited to the unique regional features. It is undesirable simply to copy the security regime patterns from other regions. It is preferable to establish a regime of security dialogue with multi-forms, multi-levels and multi-channels.

The specific issues unlikely to become out of control

In this part, I would like to address various specific issues.

The Korean Peninsula situation and its nuclear dimension

The nuclear issue of North Korea has been a major problem for the security in North-East Asia, and has attracted widespread attention, particularly in the region, for more than a year. In the first half of 1994, tensions on the Korean Peninsula were once again greatly heightened. A critical juncture came when the former US President Carter paid a visit to both North and South Korea, and then the situation eased and a feeling of relaxation emerged. Since President Kim Il Sung's passing away, people have closely watched the trends in the Korea–US dialogues, which culminated in the agreement of October 1994.

The nuclear issue of North Korea is not only a military one: to a great extent it is a political and diplomatic problem. Whether North Korea already possesses or is trying to make nuclear weapons is an open question. North Korea has, all along, flatly denied any intention to acquire nuclear weapons. It made a new commitment in the North Korea–US agreement to abandon its nuclear development project, so the question is somewhat moot now. In the meantime, North Korea persistently emphasized that there should be a package solution through North Korea–US negotiations. North Korea probably considers that it has already made great efforts to ease tension on the

Korean Peninsula and improve its relations with the United States, Japan, and the other countries. For instance, it has carried on the North–South dialogues and reached a number of agreements with South Korea, and agreed to enter the United Nations with South Korea at the same time. But it feels that it has not received the response it deserved. The United States has not conferred the cross-recognition upon North Korea that it promised previously. The North Korea–Japan talks also broke down because of the nuclear issue raised by the United States, when Japan postponed the eighth round of relation-normalization talks with North Korea in November 1992. Under these circumstances, North Korea places even higher hopes on the negotiations on the nuclear issue, looking forward to a diplomatic breakthrough through these negotiations. In order to get rid of its economic difficulties and gain more space for manoeuvring in the international arena, North Korea is serious in seeking a package solution and the normalization of its relations with the United States. The terms of the agreement reached recently between North Korea and the United States have confirmed this.

Since North Korea's nuclear issue is mainly a political one, seeking a political solution for it through peaceful dialogue is the only feasible way. Exerting pressure, or threatening to use force, does not help matters; on the contrary, that may make things worse, with countries in North-East Asia the first to be harmed. That is why China consistently stands for dialogue and is against the imposition of sanctions. North Korea is a close neighbour and so China's concern with the nuclear issue on the Korean Peninsula is no less than that of the United States. The aim of the policy that China pursues is to bring about relaxation of the situation and ultimately the denuclearization of the Korean Peninsula. It is undeniably beneficial to the security and stability of North-East Asia to help North Korea to become more involved in international affairs, to develop its economy, and to improve the living conditions of its people.

China is now glad to see that, after repeated and tense negotiations, the dialogues between North Korea and the United States have at last produced an agreement that is the result of the positive approaches taken by both parties and the efforts made by other parties concerned who have helped the situation to take a turn for the better. This important breakthrough not only indicates that the situation regarding the Korean Peninsula and the nuclear issue will tend to relax from now on, but is also persuasive evidence of the new positive changes in the relationship among the countries in North-

East Asia. This is once again a favourable development for security in North-East Asia. Patience and continued efforts are certainly still required from all the parties concerned to implement the agreement, as there might still be some unexpected zigzags in the path ahead. But as long as the momentum for dialogue is focused on settling North Korea's nuclear issue, as well as on solving the issues of establishing and improving the relations between North Korea and the Asia-Pacific counties, the Korean Peninsula situation should continuously move forward in the right direction. At the time of writing it already seems quite improbable that the situation will have a major reverse: it will continuously improve. China will, as always, make its own contribution to the promotion of relaxation of the situation on the peninsula and the realization of its denuclearization.

The Taiwan issue

The Taiwan issue has been a destabilizing factor in the Asia-Pacific region for a long time. This issue was, in the first place, the outcome of China's civil war, so it is purely a Chinese internal affair. It is completely distinguishable from the division of Germany and Korea. After World War II, Taiwan returned to its motherland from the hands of the Japanese according to the Cairo Declaration and the Potsdam Proclamation. It is only because the Kuomintang clique (relying upon support from foreign forces) launched the civil war after the end of World War II, was defeated, and then retreated to Taiwan, that the long confrontation between the two sides of the Taiwan Straits came into being. The division of Germany and Korea was entirely different: each was divided into two nations with full sovereignty according to related international agreements. The existing Taiwan issue is also the result of foreign intervention, especially the involvement by the United States. Therefore, it is also an issue of intervention and counter-intervention. Taiwan is an inalienable part of the Chinese territory. The Chinese people are resolutely determined to preserve their sovereignty, independence, and territorial integrity. On this point they will never give in on any account. This is a prerequisite for any discussion of the Taiwan issue.

In the long run, the prospect for the reunification of China is bright. Since China readjusted its policy toward Taiwan and put forward the basic line of "peaceful reunification and one country, two systems," the relations across the Taiwan Straits have been eased, and ties between the two sides have increased. These developments have made the Taiwan authorities take flexible measures. People-to-people contacts are continuously increasing. Economic and trade relations, in particular, have been growing rapidly. However, a considerable adverse current has appeared within the island of Taiwan recently. The activities for "an independent Taiwan" have run increasingly rampant. On the surface, the Taiwan authorities are advocating two "political entities on an equal footing." In substance, they are pursuing the idea of "two Chinas" or "one China one Taiwan" and "dual recognition" from foreign countries, and have even vainly attempted to "return to the UN." The seriousness of the question also lies in the fact that certain foreign powers, particularly the United States, have never abandoned their efforts to interfere in China's internal affairs. Overtly or covertly, they are supporting the forces of separatism on the island, and do not want to see China become reunified. Recent signs show that certain foreign powers are further enhancing their relations with the Taiwan authorities, and supporting them to become a "political entity" and expand its space for international activities. It will be dangerous if the countries concerned insist on breaking the promise that they made when they established diplomatic relations with China, and take serious steps or go too far. This certainly will undermine their relations with China and be harmful to Asia-Pacific security.

China perseveres in its policy of "peaceful reunification, and one country, two systems." It will continuously work hard to ease the situation on the Taiwan issue and to increase contact and communication between the two sides. As long as the Taiwan authorities neither take provocative action nor seek "independence," and as long as foreign powers do not intervene, there will be no crisis on Taiwan issues and the situation there will relax further. The ultimate reunification of China will only benefit peace and development in the Asia-Pacific region. If foreign powers put obstacles in the way of China's reunification and interfere in China's internal affairs, tension will be created, and security and prosperity in the Asia-Pacific region will be jeopardized. The crux of the impact of the Taiwan issue on Asia-Pacific security lies in the behaviour of these foreign powers. However, in any event, Taiwan and the mainland ultimately will be reunified. This is the common aspiration and resolute determination of the 1.2 billion or more Chinese people, including the people in Taiwan. No force on earth can stop them.

The Hong Kong issue

The relationship between the Hong Kong issue and East Asian security is manifested by the fact that Hong Kong's smooth transition and lasting prosperity will be further beneficial to regional peace and development and are in the interest of the Asia-Pacific countries, in particular, and of the world as a whole. This is especially relevant at a time when increasingly greater importance is being attached to economic security.

It is the long-cherished wish of the Chinese people to regain their exercise of sovereignty over Hong Kong and to end British colonial rule. According to the Joint Declaration between China and Britain, Hong Kong will be returned to China on 1 July 1997. This will not only correct a historical mistake but also remove an obstacle on the road to developing stronger relations between China and Britain.

On the Hong Kong issue, cooperation between China and Britain was fairly good in the first few years after the signing of the Sino-British Joint Declaration. But in recent years the British government has changed its Hong Kong policy and played the same old trick that it used to play whenever the British Empire was forced to withdraw from its colonies: it went back on the pledges it had made, violating the Joint Declaration, the Basic Law, and the agreements that the two parties had reached, and it covered the so-called reform of political institution with the cloak of democracy. It appears that the British government wishes to keep some of its influence in Hong Kong after 1 July 1997, effecting a sort of indirect control instead of the direct rule, thus maintaining its vested interests and creating difficulties for the normal operation of the Hong Kong Special Administrative Region of the People's Republic. It has thus set impediments and created trouble for the handover of the Hong Kong regime and the smooth transition. Under British colonial rule, which lasted for as long as 150 years, there was never any democracy in Hong Kong. Britain has indulged in unbridled propaganda for democracy in the last two or three years of its colonial rule. Its aim is no more than to foster pro-British forces there and to continue its control over Hong Kong in the future. The Chinese government and people will certainly never agree to this. That is the crux of the disagreement between China and Britain, and obviously it is in no way a question of whether democracy is practised. China put forward its basic policy toward Hong Kong long ago: that policy is one country, two systems; Hong Kong governed by Hong Kong people; a high degree of autonomy; and no change to the capitalist system and way of life for 50 years. This policy will not only guarantee Hong Kong's further prosperity but also lay a firm foundation for developing democracy in Hong Kong.

It should be noted that other foreign powers are also attempting to interfere in Hong Kong's affairs under various pretexts, especially under the banner of democracy. This would only add fuel to the flames of the Hong Kong issue, cause chaos, and jeopardize regional security. The Chinese government has repeatedly made it clear that the Hong Kong issue is a matter between China and Britain before 1 July 1997 and thereafter a matter of China's internal affairs, in which no foreign intervention will be allowed. This is not only in order to preserve China's sovereignty but also to maintain regional security and stability.

The rise of Hong Kong depends mainly on the diligence and wisdom of the Chinese and on the economic growth and reform and opening-up of China's mainland. The Chinese government and people have the full capability and confidence to overcome all foreign intervention, to implement Hong Kong's smooth transition, and to maintain its long-term stability and prosperity. This is where China's fundamental interest lies. The international community is also generally optimistic regarding Hong Kong's prospects. Therefore, in spite of the obstacles and troubles instigated by the British government, Hong Kong's economy is still flourishing and the momentum in expanding economic and trade relations with Hong Kong by foreign countries is increasing. In view of the current trends, neither impediments from Britain nor involvement by certain foreign countries will succeed: the smooth transition and continued prosperity of Hong Kong are guaranteed, and will only serve to help regional security and development. Consequently, there is little cause for concern over the Hong Kong issue.

The issue of Nansha Archipelago and the South China Sea

The issue of Nansha Archipelago and the South China Sea is regarded by quite a few people as a major destabilizing factor for security in the Asia-Pacific region. Indeed, there are territorial and sea area disputes. If all the related parties in the disputes restrain themselves and make efforts to promote mutual understanding, engage in dialogues and consultations, carry on cooperation, and do away with intervention from outside, the issue will not affect regional security and stability. However, if one party tries to join hands with other parties concerned or to internationalize the issue with support from outside forces, in order to exert pressure on another party; or if certain outside forces also want to meddle with the issue and seize the chance to intervene; the issue will be made more complicated, the situation will be more tense, and regional security and stability will be badly affected. Taking all these into account, for the benefit of peace and development in the Asia-Pacific region and out of its basic policy of good neighbourliness, China actively advocates the former trends and makes efforts to avoid the latter scenario.

Nansha Archipelago has belonged to China since ancient times. This is a fact solidly established on history and international law. The littoral countries of the South China Sea did not raise major challenges to this as recently as 20 years ago. Some countries confirmed their acknowledgement of China's sovereignty over Nansha Archipelago in their government statements. It was only in the second half of the seventies, when the countries in question began to invade and occupy various islands and reefs of Nansha Archipelago along with the discovery of oil and gas there, that the so-called South China Sea issue arose. Even so, China has still persisted in giving consideration to the regional peace and stability, and has suggested "putting aside the disputes and jointly exploiting the area." China opposes any action that would create tensions, encourage a resort to force, and provoke conflicts. China maintains that all the countries concerned should do their best to prevent the disputes from affecting the normal relationship among them. The practice of putting aside the disputes and jointly exploiting the South China Sea area will promote the regional and subregional economic cooperation that is increasingly dynamic in the Asia-Pacific region. This will also be conducive to maintaining and enhancing the relaxation of the situation in the subregion. It is groundless to exaggerate China's military activities in the South China Sea and to assert that China poses a threat to South-East Asia.

China is relatively optimistic about the prospect of the South China Sea issue, and believes that a tense situation that would become out of control will not develop. First, China's policy and proposition reflect largely the other related parties' wishes and demands. Secondly, the determination and capabilities of the East Asian countries to resolve independently their own issues and the regional issues have been increasingly strengthened in recent years. This will effectively restrain intervention by outside forces and its negative influence. It is hoped that all the parties involved in the territorial dispute of the Nansha Archipelago and South China Sea area will constantly uphold the spirit of cooperation and resolve the disputes in an appropriate way, with the inherent farsightedness and wisdom of the Asians.

Conclusions

The following conclusions can be drawn.

China believes that establishment of the security mechanism, either in the Asia-Pacific region or worldwide, is inseparable from the fundamental features of the world pattern in the post-Cold War era, which include the acceleration of the trends of multipolarization and the ever-increasing dominant role of the economic factor in international relations. These two major features have promoted – and will continue to promote – equalization and democratization of international relations. Those days in which one or two superpowers (or several major powers) could manipulate world affairs and pursue the so-called balance of power are over. Now, the major powers have only an unshirkable duty to make greater and more important contributions to the healthy development of international relations; they should not enjoy any privileges in handling international affairs, not to mention hegemonism. The new changes in international relations call for all the countries in the world to foster and strengthen cooperation in various fields. Their increasingly high degree of economic interdependence provides favourable conditions and a guarantee for their cooperation.

The goal of establishing security institutions in the Asia-Pacific region is to achieve a relationship of mutual confidence through enhancing mutual understanding among various countries. First, such a mechanism should embody the principle of equality and democratic consultations among all the countries in the region, without regard to their size. Such a mechanism should also correspond to the characteristics of Asia, as follows:

1. No country should intend to seize dominance of the mechanism, nor should any country pursue their own selfish interests while sacrificing those of other countries.
2. The principle of non-interference in the internal affairs of any country should be adhered to.
3. Depending on the issues involved and the opinions of the parties concerned, the forms of the mechanism should be diversified and

dialogues – bilateral, multilateral, or covering the whole region – should be carried out so that solutions to the issues can be advanced without making the issues more complicated.

4. Such a mechanism should be shaped in an orderly and gradual manner, starting with the setting up of a dialogue regime with multi-forms and multi-channels.

5. The practice of imposing a decision about a certain problem on a certain country should be avoided, the only desirable way being to exchange views and to seek common ground.

China believes that to enhance peace and security in the Asia-Pacific region it is necessary to establish and improve various security institutions in the region step by step; it is, therefore, actively promoting and participating in the establishment of such a regime. China has made great efforts to solve the existing issues with its neighbouring countries properly and believes that such efforts themselves contribute to the further improvement of the security situation in the Asia-Pacific region. In the meantime, China has taken an active part in the multilateral efforts to resolve the regional issues. It did its part responsibly in the political solution of the Kampuchea issue and now it is actively involving itself in the ASEAN Regional Forum. China advocates pragmatism, and never seeks spectacular face values. It would work perseveringly to promote substantial progress towards the solution to any issue in dispute.

4

A Japanese perspective with special reference to the international nuclear management regime

Atsuyuki Suzuki

Prospects on nuclear power generation in East Asia

In Japan, nuclear power reactors as well as oil-fired plants are the largest source of energy for electricity generation.[1] Nearly 30 per cent of all electricity is now provided by 47 nuclear power plants, totalling about 38,500 MW in generating capacity. While seven plants are still under construction, the number of reactors being planned is limited, mainly because of difficulty in procuring new sites. To meet both the future demands for electricity, which are projected to increase continuously, and the requirements for protecting the global environment, Japanese utilities will have to rely more upon nuclear power, and it is anticipated that a plan to build some additional plants will be finalized in the near future.

South Korea has one of the most active nuclear programmes in the world. With nine plants now operating with about 7,600 MW capacity, an additional nine units are planned to be added by the year 2001, and then another nine by 2006. Approximately 50 per cent of the total electricity of South Korea is now nuclear sourced. The suspected nuclear programme in North Korea was recently disclosed by an International Atomic Energy Agency (IAEA) special inspection. In addition to a 5 MW reactor now under operation in North Korea, two power reactors of capacity 50 and 200 MW are under construction, and three more reactors are planned. All the reactors may be based on Russian conventional reactor technology. In the course of the recent US–North Korean negotiations, however, the prospect of the alternative creation of safer light-water reactors emerged.

The nuclear share in generating electricity is also high in Taiwan, where about 40 per cent of total electricity is now supplied by six nuclear power plant units of about 5,100 MW capacity. Two more plants are now ready to order and four more are being planned, subject to public agreement.

China has started its nuclear power production programme. The first nuclear power plant, a 300 MW light-water reactor, which was built with indigenous technology, is now under test and is expected to go into full-power operation in the near future. Two more reactors have been constructed, both of 950 MW capacity and based on French technology; these started to generate electricity in 1994. Of the power produced in China, 80 per cent is thermal and 20 per cent is hydraulic; 87 per cent of the thermal power is from coal. Although China has abundant resources they are unevenly distributed: the coal-producing regions are in the north, while power is produced mainly in the west. However, it is the eastern coastal region where the demand for electric power is highest. China is making efforts to develop nuclear power in order to close this gap. The projection shown at the Ninth Pacific Basin Nuclear Conference held in Sydney in May 1994 was so ambitious that nuclear power plants will provide 3,500 MW by the year 2000, 135,000–170,000 MW by 2030, and 300,000–350,000 MW by 2050.

Indonesia has been following a policy of diversifying its energy sources, including hydroelectric power, geothermal, and coal, in an effort to spare a greater amount of oil, which is an important export product for the country. But recently, as a result of considering technological and environmental factors, it has become more compelling for the government to select nuclear power as an alternative energy source in the future. Feasibility studies and site surveys at three proposed sites in Java are now under way. The government has been considering the possibility of operating the first nuclear power plant in 2003/04 and constructing plants continuously from that time on. If all goes according to plan, the total nuclear capacity will be increased to a share of about 10 per cent of the total electricity output in 2019.

The Philippines had almost completed the construction of its first nuclear power plant (620 MW) under a turnkey contract with the

US Westinghouse Company in 1985. Owing to safety and economic problems, however, it has been mothballed since then, and the government has been looking into the possibility of converting it into a combined-cycle power plant. On the other hand, spurred by perennial power shortages, the government is now considering a comprehensive nuclear development plan, including an option of reactivation of the nuclear power plant, under which nearly half of the national electricity consumption will be covered by nuclear power by 2020.

Thailand's total capacity for the generation of electric power stands at 8,500 MW. As its economy grows, so does its demand for electric power, which is now increasing by more than 10 per cent per year. The view that both fossil-fuel fired thermal power and nuclear power will be important sources of electricity by the year 2000 is gaining ground, and feasibility studies for the introduction of nuclear power are under way. Malaysia, too, is making progress with its plan to introduce a medium-to-small reactor by 2005.

In short, nuclear power generation plants in Japan, South Korea, Taiwan, and China currently stand at a total of 53,000 MW, but if each country's plans are advanced and the many related difficulties are overcome, nuclear power generation in the East Asian region will probably exceed 100,000 MW by the year 2010; by the year 2030, even 300,000 MW might be reached.

There are several reasons why the Asian countries are so positive about nuclear power. First, there is insufficient electric power. Electricity is an elementary basis for industrial development and for people's daily lives. A lack of sufficient electrical power sometimes exerts a negative influence on foreign investment. In the region's newly industrialized countries (NICs), the living standards of the people, together with economic development, have markedly improved. The rate of those in absolute poverty – those without clean drinking water, food, and adequate housing – has decreased from 58 to 17 per cent in Indonesia from 1960 to 1990 and, over the same period, from 37 to 5 per cent in Malaysia. If the lifestyles of people are advanced, this in itself increases the demand for electricity. For the Asian countries, electrification is an important development policy issue.

Second is the likely prospect that oil reserves will be reduced and oil prices increase in the long run. Between 1986 and 1991, the annual rate of increase in the world demand for oil was 1.5 per cent per year, but for all of East Asia it was 5.2 per cent per year. In the future, demand will be likely to increase further. There is the prospect that

Indonesia and Malaysia will exceed their oil production peaks in the latter half of the 1990s and shift to becoming simple oil-importing countries. Moreover, there is a high degree of possibility that China will also become an importer of oil. The nations of East Asia will probably depend largely on the Middle East for their imports of oil, but there is anxiety concerning the steady supply of oil and it is expected that prices will rise in the future.

The third reason has to do with environmental problems. The Framework for Climate Change treaty, adopted at the Rio Earth Summit in June 1992, set as its objective the return to 1990 levels of carbon dioxide emissions by the end of the 1990s. According to the International Energy Agency (IEA), however, the emissions of carbon dioxide will increase from the 1990 level of 5.5 billion tons to 8.6 billion tons in 2010 – an increase of 50 per cent. As we enter the twenty-first century, the increasing level of carbon dioxide emissions is becoming more evident. As pointed out in the report of the International Panel on Climate Change (IPCC) on global warming, when rising sea levels and unusual weather become more pronounced, global reliance on nuclear power will have to increase. Developing countries, in particular, can be expected to feel the worst effects of unusual weather.

It appears that East Asian countries will inevitably rely more and more on nuclear power. For the sake of safe and secure introduction of nuclear power, however, advanced technologies are required for quality control of parts and materials employed in equipment, and operator training needs to be reinforced. A long-term plan must be worked out and preparation for promoting the public awareness of the people living in the area is also necessary. International co-operation among the countries is more or less indispensable in these matters.

Japan's nuclear policy: Nuclear fuel recycling

Recently, the Japan Atomic Energy Commission (AEC) released a new long-term programme; previously, such programmes have been revised every 5–6 years. The following is the AEC's official explanation of why Japan has adopted a nuclear fuel recycling policy.

Japan's nuclear energy development and utilization programme, since its initial stages, has consistently called for recycling of nuclear fuel. This involves reprocessing spent fuels and recycling the recovered plutonium and uranium as nuclear fuels. This policy is based on the reasoning that Japan, being scarce in natural resources, must efficiently utilize uranium resources to enhance the stability of nuclear energy as a domestic energy source. In view of recent domestic and international circumstances, the necessity and significance of nuclear fuel recycling have been re-emphasized and can be summarized as set out below.

First, in recent years, warnings about the destruction of the global environment and deterioration of our living environment through wasteful consumption of scarce natural resources have been increasing. The response has been to accelerate efforts to recycle and conserve natural resources and to save energy. Efficient utilization of natural resources is of vital importance in preserving the global environment. The necessity and significance of nuclear energy, especially nuclear fuel recycling, must be defined in this context.

Nuclear energy has several highly attractive features. It produces a massive return of energy from an extremely small amount of resources; the amount of waste generated, therefore, is also extremely small. It does not generate carbon dioxide (which is regarded as one of the main causes of global warming) as fossil resources do. It has been consistently confirmed at various international meetings, including the IPCC and the G7 Summit, that utilization of nuclear energy under strict safety measures can contribute to the protection of the global environment while playing an important role in energy supply.

Nuclear fuel recycling is intended to make better use of the features of nuclear energy referred to above, and to contribute to the formation of a so-called recycling society, where people routinely recycle used objects. Nuclear fuel recycling reuses useful materials, all of which would otherwise be wasted, as an energy resource. In addition, reducing the consumption of natural uranium resources by recycling could eventually also reduce the impact of nuclear energy itself on the environment. Therefore, nuclear fuel recycling could be very significant in both resource conservation and environmental protection. For a nation such as Japan that consumes a large amount of resources, it is an important policy matter to play a leading role in efforts to save and recycle resources.

Second, as in the recycling of other resources, the economy of nuclear fuel recycling depends to a large extent on the market price of its basic resources. The price of uranium has been stable at a relatively low level in recent years. Consequently, worldwide interest in the necessity and significance of nuclear fuel recycling in securing an economic and stable long-term supply of uranium has tended to fade. In longer-range perspectives, though, future supply uncertainty, similar to that in the oil market, may also plague the uranium market. Accordingly, nuclear fuel recycling is necessary for Japan from the viewpoint of the efficient use of uranium and energy security. It should be noted that nuclear fuel recycling could also stabilize demand and supply in the uranium market, which could encourage stable and affordable uranium prices in the future.

Another important point in the economic value of nuclear fuel recycling is that nuclear energy is considered to be a technology-intensive source of energy because there is a very high return of energy produced by means of technology from a small amount of natural resources. Therefore, the economy of nuclear energy is determined largely by the effectiveness of technology, rather than natural resource costs. Thus, as technology matures, the cost–performance ratio of nuclear energy improves and it becomes a more reliable energy source. It is expected that the economy of nuclear fuel recycling will continue to improve as further progress is made in research and development, more experience is gained, and the scale of the recycling is expanded step by step. It is considered significant that Japan is committed to taking a lead in this technological development, from the viewpoint of making nuclear energy a more economic and stable energy source that can be safely used worldwide for a long time to come.

The final point concerns aspects of radioactive waste management. Although much less waste is generated by nuclear power generation than by thermal generation firing fossil fuels, the waste is dangerously radioactive and must be managed with the utmost care. Spent nuclear fuel includes high-level radioactive matter and must be very carefully managed, while its radioactivity decreases rapidly according to the half-lives of its radioactive materials. Currently, some nations are trying to dispose of spent fuel as waste without recycling.

If spent fuel is reprocessed, however, large amounts of useful resources can be recovered, and high-level radioactive waste can be separated and managed more easily. The uranium fuel spent from a current light-water-moderated nuclear power reactor still contains a proportion of useful uranium amounting to more than 95 per cent of the total weight of used fuel. This material can be reused with plutonium after reprocessing. On the other hand, the high-level radioactive waste contained in the used fuel is only a few per cent of total weight of the (used) fuel. In fact, the volume of the high-level radioactive waste after reprocessing, which can then be easily solidified into a stable form suitable for disposal storage, is much smaller than that of unreprocessed spent fuel. In addition, the period of radio-activity of the high-level radioactive waste becomes relatively shorter. Such a radioactive-waste-management method is particularly appropriate in Japan, where land space available for disposing of waste is extremely limited.

Japan's commitment to nuclear non-proliferation

Japan has followed a policy compatible with the nuclear non-proliferation regime. Again, the following are the official views of Japan's AEC.

Japan has demonstrated a firm commitment to peaceful uses of nuclear energy. Domestically, this is set forth as a national commitment in Japan's Atomic Energy Basic Law, where the development and utilization of nuclear energy is limited solely to peaceful purposes. Internationally, the nation adheres to the Treaty on the Non-Proliferation of Nuclear Weapons (NPT) and accepts the full safeguards of the IAEA for all nuclear materials related to any of its nuclear programmes. Japan also adheres to the Convention on Physical Protection, and has whole-heartedly fulfilled the obligations and responsibilities set out in these international agreements.

While Japan's commitment to nuclear non-proliferation has been consistently reaffirmed as national policy, Japan must fully take into account the fact that recycling is based on the utilization of plutonium recovered from spent fuel, and that plutonium is a militarily sensitive material. Accordingly, it is most important for Japan to maintain stringent measures with regard to nuclear non-proliferation and to give as much transparency as possible to its nuclear fuel recycling programmes so that concerns regarding nuclear proliferation in relation to Japan's programmes will not be raised internationally in any case.

Therefore, it is a national principle that, in addition to continuing to maintain stringent controls over plutonium, Japan will not possess plutonium beyond the amount required to implement its nuclear fuel recycling programmes. To that end, Japan will make steady use of plutonium in accordance with appropriate recycling programmes, considering that it makes sense, from a nuclear non-proliferation viewpoint, actively to utilize and consume plutonium as a nuclear fuel by means of recycling. The government publicly announced, at the end of 1994, that it currently held approximately 10,900 kg pluto-nium: about 6,200 kg are being stored in reprocessing plants in the United Kingdom and France (and Japanese electric power compa-nies, who are owners of that plutonium, plan to have them fabricated into nuclear fuels in some of the European fuel fabricators as soon as possible); about 3,300 kg are located in the domestic fuel fabrica-tion facility, about 2,300 kg of this being stored temporarily (there is a definite plan to consume them in some Japanese specific nuclear reactors in the near future) while the remainder is actually in the fabrication process; about 1,100 kg are being used in the nuclear reactors; and about 300 kg are located in the domestic reprocessing plant, where most is currently undergoing reprocessing.

At the 1990 and 1995 NPT Review Conference, it was confirmed that the NPT is the fundamental framework for nuclear non-pro-liferation and that the IAEA system of safeguards plays the central role in ensuring non-proliferation. It was also confirmed that the effectiveness of the IAEA safeguards should be maintained, particu-larly for reprocessing and plutonium utilization, responding to the expanded peaceful use of plutonium.

Japan has been of the view that it is important to facilitate effective and efficient application of IAEA safeguards to nuclear facilities, and has actively contributed to maintaining and strengthening the IAEA system: for example, the IAEA's international joint study on safe-guarding large-scale commercial reprocessing plants has been spe-cially funded by Japan.

With regard to the international, long-distance transportation of plutonium, Japan has been whole-heartedly fulfilling all obligations and responsibilities laid down in bilateral nuclear energy agreements and the Convention on Physical Protection, and has been working closely with the countries concerned to get more understanding and cooperation in this field, recognizing that it is Japan's international responsibility fully to apply stringent physical protection measures to transportation.

The measures outlined above comprise Japan's efforts to fulfil its international responsibilities concerning non-proliferation aspects associated with its nuclear programmes. In particular, Japan has made every effort to cooperate with the IAEA safeguard system and, indeed, is the country that has most utilized that system. In fact, if the system were not in place, Japan's use of nuclear power could not have been developed so smoothly.

On the other hand, there have been notable cases when the safeguard regime was not able to prevent the proliferation of nuclear weapons: South Africa, which was not a signatory to the NPT until 1991, produced nuclear weapons but then renounced them; a number of reports indicate that Israel may possess nuclear weapons; Iraq, a member of the NPT, proceeded with nuclear development through secret activities and undeclared facilities until it came under the control of the United Nations in the aftermath of the Gulf War.

Japan, West Germany, Sweden, and other such developed states with technological capabilities for using nuclear power to generate electricity, were the main countries for which the NPT was designed initially. However, the cases where doubt arose or where nuclear weapons were actually being produced were not really cases of diversion of technologies from the peaceful use of nuclear power but were, in fact, the development of technologies that are specifically intended to produce nuclear weapons. The IAEA's security measures did not foresee this kind of nuclear development. Although the IAEA can make a special or ad hoc inspection, there are limitations concerning its effectiveness in relation to safeguards.

Henceforth, as established earlier, the amount of nuclear material circulating in the Asian region will probably increase markedly. There is, however, also the danger of hindering the peaceful usage of nuclear power when trying to prevent nuclear proliferation through the strengthening of security measures. Consequently, it is important to create a security system, side by side with the NPT, that will restrain the use of nuclear weapons and will foster trusting international relationships on many fronts, discouraging the proliferation of nuclear weapons.

Japan's possible contributions to a new international regime

Now, one interesting question concerns what Japanese technologies for the peaceful uses of nuclear energy can do in the way of cooperation for nuclear disarmament. It seems there are two sides to this.

On one side, it might be significant and timely that Japanese technologies for the peaceful uses of plutonium, which are considerably advanced, are offered positively for application in finding an effective use for plutonium released from dismantled nuclear weapons. For example, the Japanese could help to change plutonium from dismantled nuclear weapons into fuel for nuclear reactors. It would be desirable if the Japanese government could make a positive step in this direction.

Plutonium from dismantled nuclear weapons will go a long way toward nuclear disarmament if it has some value added. For example, a relatively easy solution has been found for the release of highly enriched uranium from dismantled nuclear weapons. For the release of plutonium as well, reassuring and reliable Japanese technologies and methods could be offered to the extent of a possible international agreement, or on international requests for a positive Japanese contribution. These techniques produce some added value.

In April 1994, the Japanese prototype fast-breeder/consumer reactor Monju achieved initial nuclear chain reaction. There was an article in one widely read American newspaper, which stated:

Environmental groups – particularly foreign ones – have taken issue with Japan's nuclear power program, both for its development of breeder reactors that would increase the world's plutonium glut and for shipping a ton of plutonium by sea from France to Japan in late 1992 and early '93 for use as fuel in the breeder reactor. Mindful of such criticism, Japanese officials are stressing another aspect of the breeder reactor concept: with some design changes, a reactor like the Monju can be made to consume rather than breed plutonium. If that is possible, breeder reactors might be beneficial to the United States and other countries saddled with plutonium supplies that nobody has found a good way to dispose of.[2]

Indeed, it is true that a fast reactor can become either a breeder or burner of plutonium. As a burner, the Monju can possibly help to deal with an excess of plutonium arising from dismantled nuclear weapons.

Looking at the other side of the question, the intentions of Japan may be in doubt if it does not take its positive share of this burden at a time when there are active international efforts going on toward nuclear non-proliferation and the elimination of nuclear weapons. Actually, if one were on an inspection trip, for example, it would be apparent that there is a very real need for a technology that would enable us to find out whether certain solutions or wastes contain plutonium. The precision measurement devices and equipment that might meet these requirements can be developed only under advanced technologies. Such technologies will also be needed to enable computer programs to devise future strategies to prevent nuclear proliferation.

If Japan has the technologies to find economic and safe uses for plutonium, they could be used in advance to prevent nuclear proliferation from occurring in other countries. As a sort of by-product of Japan's programme for the peaceful use of nuclear energy, such technologies quite possibly could become a reality.

Another important point is the responsibility that Japan, as an Asian country, will have to extend its nuclear cooperation to other parts of Asia. The time has come for Asians to discuss how they can promote the peaceful uses of nuclear energy in such a way as to reassure each other.

As mentioned earlier, the exploitation of nuclear energy has begun in China, is making steady progress in South Korea, and is far more advanced in Taiwan. Japan is Asia's most advanced nuclear-energy state. Similarly, conditions are growing for the introduction of nuclear power in Indonesia and the Philippines, and eventually in Thailand. So it is important that a framework for cooperation in the peaceful uses of nuclear energy is set up, as was the case with the European Atomic Energy Community (EURATOM). Although it will probably prove difficult to replicate the same sort of mechanism as EURATOM, an "AsianATOM" would enable researchers in regional countries to keep in contact with each other and to establish reliable rules within which they can feel free to go ahead with their development projects.

It would be, however, most inadvisable to keep some specific countries in isolation. Ideas should be developed for setting up something like EURATOM to promote organic and steady development of international cooperation in East Asia. Such a framework might be extended to include other Pacific Basin countries, such as the United States, Canada, and Australasia.

Answers to frequent criticisms of Japan's plan

Japan's plan to use plutonium mixed with uranium to generate electricity has caused much misunderstanding and created many misconceptions. Many criticize the plan in the belief that plutonium is a deadly substance, but this view is scientifically unfounded. Radium emits more alpha radiation than does plutonium, but hot springs that contain radium in their water pose no hazard to guests who frequent such spas. Plutonium, like radium, is quite safe in small amounts and at low density. Utmost care must, naturally, be taken to ensure safety at nuclear facilities and scientific laboratories where radium or plutonium is in a concentrated form. The dangers of handling high concentrations of these substances are well known: Marie Curie, the chemist who discovered radium, is assumed to have died from overexposure to it. But in view of the stringent safety standards that have now been established, and based on all the experience accumulated on the use of uranium and plutonium worldwide, these risks do not warrant unnecessary concern.

If we consider the annual limit of intake, for instance, the ingestion hazard of radium is about 300 times more than that of plutonium. At the turn of the century, the ingestion of radium posed a bizarre risk:

The Curies' discovery of radium, for example, kicked off the Milk Radium Therapy movement among American socialites, and precipitated a lucrative trade in radium-based belts, hearing aids, toothpaste, face cream, and hair tonic. Most lucrative of all was Radiothor, a glow-in-the-dark mineral water that promised a cure for more than 150 maladies. The Federal Trade Commission, ever vigilant, cracked down on competing potions that lacked advertised levels of radioactivity. The steel mogul, socialite, and amateur golf champion MacBurney Byers faithfully drank Radiothor every day from 1926 to 1931. By the latter year he had developed cancer of the jaw, a presumed but unproved consequence of the radiation. He died miserably in 1932. This well publicized incident alerted the public to the dangers of ionizing radiation, and helped spur much-needed government action.[3]

Some people may wonder why Japan is proceeding with a plan to use plutonium at a time when other countries are abandoning similar policies as being economically unattractive. One of the main reasons lies in the difficulty of directly disposing of highly radioactive spent fuel from nuclear power generation. For instance, the United States, which is endowed with a vast land area and many geologically stable zones, has attempted to eliminate spent fuel directly by burying it deep in the ground. However, this direct disposal method is not always possible for a small, earthquake-prone country like Japan. Another concern centres on the adverse effects of buried waste on the environment. In this regard, the Japanese plan, under which plutonium is recovered from spent fuel, would contribute substantially to mitigating the burden on the environment.

Turning to the cost-effectiveness of the Japanese plan, while it is true that the world prices of uranium are declining and it would seem of no economic benefit to use plutonium, which is more expensive, the cost difference between the use of the two kinds of fuel for nuclear power generation in Japan, as illustrated already, amounts to less than 10 per cent. This should be justifiable from the public viewpoint, since the use of plutonium is more conducive to environmental preservation. To cite a comparison, almost all present thermoelectric plants in Japan have had to install de-SO_x and de-NO_x devices to reduce environmental pollution, and the cost of these devices accounts for about 10–20 per cent of the total cost of power generation.

Japanese plans to begin operating a prototype fast reactor and to construct a "demonstration plant" to prove the commercial feasibility have also been questioned on the grounds of economic efficiency and safety. Yet the suspicious are often unaware of the realities of nuclear power generation. At present, nuclear power supplies about one-third of the electrical energy generated by the member countries of the Organisation for Economic Co-operation and Development (OECD). Nuclear energy has also allowed the world today to prise itself away from its excessive dependence on oil, which invited the oil crises in the 1970s. Light-water reactor technology has matured in terms of both economic efficiency and safety, and the same progress can be achieved in the realm of fast-reactor technology if projects are steadily carried out. Innovation, on the other hand, cannot be attained without initiatives.

Some may also question why Japan is trying to increase its capacity to supply plutonium when the world already has a surplus. First, plutonium for military use should be distinguished from that for civilian use. Second, the surplus plutonium around the world is not necessarily available internationally, since its trade is restricted. What is more significant is the amount of plutonium held by individual countries. In this respect, the former Soviet Union has by far the greatest amount of plutonium in the world where, in addition to tons of surplus of civilian-use plutonium, an approximately 100 ton surplus of military-use plutonium is being created as a by-product of disarmament agreements between the United States and Russia. This being the case, the civilian-use plutonium to be used under the Japanese plan cannot be compared with the military-use plutonium remaining in the former Soviet Union. Japan is promoting the use of plutonium as part of the management of its own spent fuel. Even so, Japan should feel obligated to extend as much assistance as it can to the former Soviet Union in order to give further impetus to its nuclear disarmament.

Finally, some argue that further use of plutonium by Japan will increase the risk of nuclear proliferation by encouraging other nations to advance similar plans. The risk of nuclear proliferation does exist, but it is hardly affected or influenced by Japanese plans to use plutonium for peaceful purposes. Civilian use of plutonium is not of industrial value unless it generates a substantial amount of electricity, as is intended for use in Japan. It would make no economic sense for countries with few nuclear power plants to utilize plutonium for their energy needs. However, to ensure better understanding on the use of plutonium, it is important for Japan to make every effort to enhance the transparency of its nuclear energy plans, so as to dispel any global or regional concern over nuclear proliferation.

In fact, in 1993 the Science and Technology Agency in Japan first disclosed the amount of plutonium stockpiled, either domestically or overseas. Japan is the first and only country to disclose, on its own initiative, information concerning the long-term programme of plutonium use and its own current stockpiles of plutonium.

Lessons learned from the past

A Pulitzer prize laureate, Richard Rhodes, has offered a very interesting view on what we can learn from the past nuclear arms race.[4]

First, he recalled that, immediately after the discovery of how to release nuclear energy, the great Danish physicist Niels Bohr used his utmost endeavours to stop the creation of "a weapon of unparalleled power." In particular, Bohr emphasized that common security against nuclear threat requires transparency: a nuclear-free world will have to be completely transparent where nuclear technology is concerned. Rhodes cited the famous Bohr lecture given at the United Nations in 1950:

An open world, where each nation can assert itself solely by the extent to which it can contribute to the common culture and is able to help others with experience and resources must be the goal to put above everything else.... The very fact that knowledge is itself the basis for civilization points directly to openness as the way to overcome the present crisis.

Then, Rhodes touched upon the goal of science, referring to Bohr's idea that it is "the gradual removal of prejudices." As a matter of fact, science has gradually removed the "prejudice" that there is a limited amount of energy available in the world to concentrate into explosives, and that it is possible to accumulate more of such energy than one's enemies and thereby militarily to prevail. Rhodes also said that science has revealed at least world-scale war to be historical, not universal, and a manifestation of destructive technologies of limited scale.

In this context, Rhodes mentioned that today we seem to have come to a turning point in the history of the application of nuclear energy – the levelling-off of the first step of the learning curve. One of today's vital concerns with nuclear proliferation is what is happening in North Korea. Rhodes, however, argues that the diminished third wave of nuclear-weapons development that is now proceeding, particularly in this region of the world (East Asia), is not likely to rise as steeply nor to continue for as long as the first superpower arms race. The world knows more now than it knew then, including the economic waste and the ultimate futility of piling up nuclear arms. What we have learned from the past is that the first great historical consequence of the discovery of how to release nuclear energy, then, has been to put limits to national sovereignty and to forestall world war. The next great consequence, already ongoing, will be to add significantly to human welfare by increasing sustainable energy resources and decreasing pollution.

Then, Rhodes decisively elucidated the role of nuclear energy from a global view, with which I am in total agreement:

Satisfying human aspirations is what our species invents technology to do. Some people, secure in comfortable affluence, may dream of a simpler and smaller world. However noble such a dream appears to be, its hidden agenda is élitist, selfish and violent. Millions of children die every year in the world for lack of adequate resources – clean water, food, medical care – and the development of those resources is directly dependent on energy supplies. The real world of real human beings needs more energy, not less. As oil and coal continue their historic decline, that energy across the next half-century will necessarily come from nuclear power and natural gas.

There are a number of people who fear the diversion of plutonium in a nuclear power economy. In this connection, Rhodes places emphasis on the necessity of more objective and careful discussion, noting that people should look more carefully at the historical patterns of horizontal proliferation and the behaviour of terrorists. What is suggested from the fact that Iraq had returned to electromagnetic separation of uranium – a technique the United States had abandoned at the end of World War II – is that nations who choose to develop a nuclear-weapons capability inevitably find a way to do so, whether it may be being used for peaceful purposes in other countries or has been abandoned for the sake of nuclear non-proliferation. In other words, nuclear proliferation is far less a technical than a political problem. In addition, it is Rhodes' view that terrorists have shown little inclination or ability to add nuclear engineers and metallurgists to their ranks. An example he cited is that the weapon of choice in

New York's World Trade Center bombing was nitrate fertilizer and fuel oil, common ingredients that the terrorists found easy to purchase in a foreign county and were confident they knew how to ignite.

In considering the impact of the end of the Cold War on the peaceful use of nuclear power in the future, it is very important for Japan to be aware of international trends regarding nuclear disarmament. Again, Rhodes mentioned that adjusting across the last five decades to the new knowledge of how to release nuclear energy has put us at no little risk. And his observation on the impact of the end of the Cold War is that, with the demise of the former Soviet Union and its replacement by a volatile but resourceful collective of new states, we are already moving to a new level of world security with reduced numbers of nuclear weapons and – what is equally valuable – extended response times for the arsenals that remain. Certainly, we will not easily find our way to a world free of nuclear weapons and it will also be necessary to pursue major reductions in conventional armaments. But I want to associate myself with Rhode's opinion that the evident uselessness of nuclear weapons may bring that millennium about sooner than expected. He concluded his talk by saying that the end of the Cold War surely counts as the new morning of the world.

Concluding remarks

The region of East Asia is showing remarkable economic growth and its energy demands are growing rapidly, as is indicated in the symbolic expression "East Asian Miracle." The end of the Cold War produced conditions for the further development of this region. Each country is proceeding with affirmative plans for the use of nuclear energy. When one considers the scarcity of indigenous oil resources and the worsening of global and regional environments, the smooth development of the use of nuclear energy would seem to be a key element to the continued economic growth of the region.

There is no doubt that the NPT has been playing, and will continue to play, an important role in controlling the proliferation of nuclear weapons. This alone, however, is not always sufficient. The complete prevention of nuclear proliferation is difficult, even with a strict management regime for nuclear technologies and nuclear substances. Together with the NPT and with the IAEA safeguard system, it is also necessary to bring about an international environment that seeks to avoid nuclear proliferation or to give a disincentive to possessing nuclear weapons.

The conclusion of the Cold War brought not only the end of East–West confrontation but also a change where mutually interdependent relations in the international arena have become a more important element. As a regionally collaborative organization to support the NPT, it seems worth trying to create an Asian Atomic Energy Community or Pacific-Basin Atomic Energy Community. The Asian countries could jointly develop technologies to make peaceful use of nuclear energy and thereby to enhance safety and to implement security measures. All of these aims are worth pursuing for a more secure promotion of nuclear energy.

Notes and references

1. The views expressed herein are entirely those of the author and do not necessarily represent those of the Japanese government.
2. Reid, T.R. "Reactor start-up fuels Japan's energy plans," *Washington Post*, 6 April 1993.
3. Foster, K.R., D.E. Bernstein, and P.W. Huber (eds) 1993. *Phantom Risks: Scientific Inference and the Law*. Cambridge: MIT Press, pp. 23–24.
4. Rhodes, R. "The new morning of the world," presented at the 27th Annual Conference of the Japan Atomic Industrial Forum, Hiroshima, 13 April 1994.

Part 2
Pressure points: Threats
to peace and stability
in North-East Asia

5

China incorporates Hong Kong: Implications for international security in the Asia-Pacific region

James T.H. Tang

Introduction

While uncertainties about Hong Kong's future have not been entirely clarified, the territory's new status as a Special Administrative Region (SAR) of China will be a reality at midnight on 30 June 1997. The Chinese leader Deng Xiaoping has remarked that the constitutional arrangements for the Hong Kong SAR are of historic and international significance. None the less, the transfer of Hong Kong's sovereignty is largely seen as a bilateral issue between Britain and China before 1997 and a domestic question thereafter. The international dimension of China's resumption of sovereignty over Hong Kong is almost unexplored, along with the impact of Hong Kong's changing status on regional affairs.[1]

Since the territory has never been an independent political entity, the shortage of academic analysis on the external implications for Hong Kong's transition to and beyond 1997 is, perhaps, not too difficult to understand.[2] The transfer of Hong Kong from British colonial rule to Chinese Communist rule may be highly significant for the six million inhabitants of the territory, but neighbouring states do not appear to be too concerned about its ramifications for regional development (cf. more active interest of US Congress). Many observers seemed to have concluded that, as the scope of the territory's international activities will be very much limited, there is little point in analysing the international implications of the transfer of sovereignty.[3] The conflict between Britain and China over arrangements for Hong Kong's return to China is widely seen as a short-lived phenomenon that will not last beyond 1997, and clearly is not expected to generate a serious problem for regional security.

At a time when the post-Cold War international security structure of the Asia-Pacific region is undergoing transformation, the implications of Hong Kong's transition for regional security may prove to be more far-reaching than is commonly perceived in the region. China's rise as an economic power has already become a focus of regional attention, with neighbouring states expressing concern about the international security implications. Will the incorporation of Hong Kong in China create a menacing regional force? Or will the process intensify China's economic interdependence with the rest of the world and facilitate the emergence of a more benign regional power? Do regional institutions have any role to play in shaping the political and economic changes in China's transformation?

This chapter attempts to examine the implications of Hong Kong's changing political status for international security in the East Asian region. The impact of Hong Kong's transition from a British colonial territory to an SAR on international and regional affairs can be examined from two perspectives – (1) Hong Kong's formal and informal international capacities as a non-sovereign entity, and (2) Hong Kong's role in China's international interactions with the rest of the world. These two perspectives are clearly interrelated. The extent to which Hong Kong can adopt a more proactive approach in regional affairs obviously depends very much on China's Hong Kong policy. China's attitude towards Hong Kong, however, may in turn be determined by the results of the 1997 reunion.

The territory's separate entity as an international actor is still a matter of much discussion, and the degree of autonomy the territory can really enjoy will be clarified only sometime after 1997. Nevertheless, China does seem to have committed itself to maintaining Hong Kong's separate status for some time to come. In fact under the Basic Law, which governs post-1997 Hong Kong, the scope of the territory's international presence in the economic, cultural, and sports arena will be widened. Since the importance of Hong Kong's interactions with the international community has been discussed elsewhere,[4] this chapter concentrates on the impact of Hong Kong's transition on China's international position.

The Hong Kong–China union will probably boost China's stature as an ascending power in the world and change the strategic picture in the region. The further integration of the Hong Kong–China economy will also strengthen China's role as a rising economic force. China's incorporation of an efficient capitalist and dynamic economy will clearly benefit the country, but the consequent deepening of interdependence with the outside world may also shape the nature of China's regional role. Although the territory is strictly a colonial territory, it has enjoyed in practice a high degree of political openness and plurality. A politically stable SAR may provide useful lessons in the management not only of a successful market economy but also of a more dynamic and pluralistic society for China.

In the realms of both economics and politics, the territory's changing status is clearly significant for China's position in the region. In economic terms, China's incorporation of Hong Kong (even as a separate entity) will mean an even higher degree of economic integration and closer political cooperation between the world's eighth and eleventh largest traders. Their combined share of world export in merchandise trade for 1993 was 6.2 per cent, or the world's fourth largest trade power after the United States, Germany, and Japan.[5]

In political and strategic terms, China's resumption of sovereignty over Hong Kong is clearly also important. The People's Liberation Army (PLA) is to take over key military facilities from the British in Hong Kong. On 30 June 1994 the British and Chinese governments reached agreement for transferring British military sites in the territory. Under this agreement, the Chinese military will obtain almost three thousand hectares of land, including a naval base with modern facilities. The Hong Kong government is to provide almost HK$4 billion for the reprovisioning of military facilities that the PLA is to take over in 1997. If China's emergence as a economic power is presenting security challenges to the region, the China–Hong Kong presence may have major consequences.

The China threat?

The emergence of China as a major economic power in the Asia-Pacific region is now a fact rather than a projection. Since the early 1990s several reports have presented a highly positive picture of the Chinese economy, suggesting that it would become the world's largest in the next century. The *Economist*, for example, suggested in October 1992 that China's economy could surpass even that of the United States in one generation. In March 1993 the International Monetary Fund, using purchasing power parity, ranked China as the world's third-largest economy. Such optimistic calculations have since been questioned by more cautious analysis, but there is little doubt that China's economic performance in the past two decades has been truly spectacular. The average annual growth rate of the Chinese economy between 1953 and 1990 at 7 per cent was the third highest in the world. It is also generally regarded as the engine of growth in the Asia-Pacific region.

What will be the impact of China's new economic status on regional security? Whether China becomes a threat or offers new opportunities for prosperity and peace in the region has become a major theme for academic analysis about regional security in recent years.[6] China's economic development clearly would offer benefits in terms of trade and investment opportunities, but a more powerful China (with greater military capability)[7] may also give rise to a set of uncertain factors for international security. China's clashes with Western powers, particularly the United States, over issues such as human rights and arms sales have been well covered.[8] More recently, however, the focus of attention has shifted from bilateral difficulties between China and other countries, to the possible impact of China on the structures of international security in East Asia. In effect, is there a China threat to regional security?

Arguments supporting the China threat thesis usually centre on two themes: first, China is not a status quo power, and therefore it may seek regional domination, with profound implications for international security; second, even if China does not seek regional domination, its ascendancy may upset the existing power configuration, leading to regional instability and possible military conflict.[9] With the waning of external influence in the region, especially that of the United States, regional rivalry between East Asian states may be intensified. A powerful China, for example, could threaten Japan's status in the region, not to say other potential powers such as a united Korea or Indonesia.

China's historical willingness to use force in border disputes and involvement in external military conflicts have given support to the China threat argument. More specifically, an assertive China or a harsher treatment of Hong Kong may indicate that it could be more ready to resort to force against Taiwan in its bitter bid for reunification. Taiwan's attempt to raise its international profile and the popularity of the independence movement on the island have become a source of confrontation. Moreover, with a more open economy, China's strategic interests have also shifted to being maritime based rather than continental based.[10] Such a shift, manifested in China's assertiveness in the maritime arena, particularly over the South China Sea, is an area of major difficulties between China and South-East Asian countries.

Those who argue that the emergence of China as an economic power will not threaten regional peace, usually make reference to the deepening of China's involvement in the global economy, and the increasing interdependence that developed between China and other states in the Pacific rim area. Since the late 1970s China has developed an outward-looking market-oriented economy. China's share of total world trade almost quadrupled from a mere 0.6 per cent in 1977 to 2 per cent in 1992. China is also the world's leading destination for foreign investment, and borrows rather intensively from international capital markets and major official agencies such as the World Bank.[11] Indeed, sceptics of the interdependence argument maintained that economic interdependence may "heighten rather than defuse political tensions" and that liberal capitalist pressures on China over issues such as human rights had not been effective.[12]

In many other spheres (including science and technology, culture, and even national security and politics) there is little doubt that China's interdependence with the outside world will develop further. But it may seek to manipulate "the balance of dependence" in its favour for political objectives, and "try to reap the benefits of interdependence but avoid its costs."[13] The phenomenon of China's rise as an economic power and its implications for regional international relations are further complicated by the emergence of the so-called "Greater China," comprising the integrating economies of mainland China, Taiwan, and Hong Kong.[14] China's economic prowess would be even more impressive with the addition of Taiwan and Hong Kong's economic strength. Politically, however, the three are still separate entities. In fact, relations between mainland China and Taiwan have become rather strained recently, partly as a result of Taiwan's attempt to raise its international profile and improve political relations with other countries through "flexi-diplomacy" and "holiday" or "class reunion diplomacy." Internal political change in Taiwan and the possibility that the Taiwan independence movement may gain ground has also become a matter of serious concern for the leadership in Beijing. Although the Taiwan question can be a regional security problem, which may involve outside powers such as the United States, Chinese leaders have naturally always regarded it as an internal matter and are determined to keep it off the regional agenda.

If the emergence of a Greater China or a China Circle in the form of a China–Taiwan–Hong Kong bloc is problematic, the incorporation of Hong Kong into China appears to be more straightforward. The Hong Kong question is not usually seen as a regional security problem. After the conclusion of the 1984 Sino-British Joint Declaration, the Chinese and British governments agreed that China would resume sovereignty over the territory in 1997 under the "one country; two systems" formula.

The Joint Declaration has not, however, fully resolved British and Chinese differences about political arrangements in Hong Kong. The 1989 Tiananmen incident, and the subsequent shift of British policy towards Hong Kong, following the arrival of Governor Chris Patten in 1991, created major difficulties in Sino-British relations. The Patten constitutional reform package led to serious confrontation between the two sides. It is almost certain that the political arrangements that are being put in place by the British administration in Hong Kong will be dismantled in one way or another after 1997: another set of arrangements that the Chinese consider to be more consistent with the Joint Declaration and the Basic Law will replace the Patten package.

This Sino-British confrontation since 1991 has attracted much international attention, and the Chinese government accused Governor Patten of playing the international card when a number of Western governments supported his proposal to introduce a greater degree of representation in the Legislative Council. But the process of Hong Kong's incorporation into China is unlikely to be a source of serious conflict in the regional context. Most countries in the region do not have difficulties with China's resumption of sovereignty over the territory. In fact, most of them acknowledged the "one country; two systems" formula, and welcome the continuation of Hong Kong's existence as a separate customs territory.

Hong Kong's strategic role as a British territory

If Hong Kong's changing status may not pose a direct threat to regional security, it certainly represents a major shift in the East

Asian strategic equation. Hong Kong's glittering economic performance, and China's toleration of its colonial status even during the Cold War, have created an impression that the territory has not been important in strategic terms. Economics clearly have been the foundation of the territory's colonial existence. It has been a major trading centre since the British occupation in 1841. But as a British colonial territory, Hong Kong was also seen as a symbol of British influence in East Asia.[15]

After the end of the Second World War, London's desire to keep Hong Kong was also partly driven by the British aspiration to remain a major world power for as long as possible.[16] The territory was also embroiled, if reluctantly, in the Cold War and was sometimes referred to as the Berlin of the East. British forces from the territory were sent to Korea during the 1950–1953 Korean conflict. Although the British government clearly realized that Hong Kong's survival as a British colony depended on China's continuing acquiescence, the territory has served as a port of call for Western naval ships stationed in the region, and an important port for the transshipment of strategic goods. During the Viet Nam War, Hong Kong was a useful destination for American soldiers for rest and recreation. The territory is still offering facilities for Western naval forces passing through the region.

The strategic role of Hong Kong in the Cold War conflict rapidly declined when the global interests of China and Britain shifted in the early 1970s. The Sino-American *rapprochement* dramatically altered the global strategic equation. China formed a tacit alliance with the United States against the Soviet Union. The policy of containment was no longer relevant. By that time Britain also no longer sought to maintain its position as a global power, and had already withdrawn from Asia militarily.

In recent years, the British military presence in Hong Kong has been limited but it has nevertheless been fairly active; furthermore, Western warships in the region often found the deep-water port of Hong Kong, as a British territory, ideal for docking, without charges as part of NATO arrangements. After the transfer of sovereignty in 1997, such facilities will no longer be available automatically to NATO or other Commonwealth forces.

British naval presence in the region is relatively minimal and is usually linked to arms sales. In recent years the major tours included HMAS *Orient* (in 1992), *Outbreak* (1988), and *Global* (1986). There were no restrictions on the ports they called upon in the region, and British naval vessels have also visited Chinese ports as part of their tours. But the general pattern of British naval activities may have to be altered, with the focal point being shifted to Singapore.[17]

In fact, the British military presence in Hong Kong has been scaled down considerably in the past five years to less than ten thousand, with seven thousand-odd military personnel. In 1992 the British garrisons in the territory numbered 9,800, with 7,500 military and 2,300 civilian support staff. The British army was reduced from four battalions in 1991 to three in 1992, consisting of one UK battalion, and two Gurkha battalions (following the amalgamation of two other Gurkha battalions). The Peacock class patrol craft of the Royal Navy has been reduced from five to three since 1988. The Royal Air Force employed one squadron of Wessex helicopters, and there was an Army Air Corps equipped with Scott helicopters.[18]

The British forces in Hong Kong, including Gurkha soldiers and locally recruited Chinese soldiers, have been regularly involved in the long-standing Five Power Defence Agreement (Britain, Singapore, Malaysia, Australia, and New Zealand) military exercises. They have also paid host to military detachments from other Commonwealth countries and have supported British military efforts elsewhere. British forces in Hong Kong were deployed throughout the region, involved in overseas exercises in Malaysia, Brunei, New Zealand, Australia, Singapore, and other countries. Royal Navy tours often visited the territory when they were in the region, and warships from Australia, New Zealand, Singapore, the Netherlands, Sweden, France, and the United States often visited the Hong Kong port. In 1991 more than 250 members of the Gurkha Transport Regiment served in the Gulf conflict in an ambulance squadron. A 130-strong transport squadron also undertook a six-month tour of duty with the UN forces in Cyprus.[19]

Under NATO arrangements the US Navy is able to make use of facilities in Hong Kong and dock in the harbour. At present about 70–80 US naval vessels visit the territory annually. After 1997 China may deny the continuation of Western use of military facilities in Hong Kong. The US Navy seems keen to continue visiting the territory, because Hong Kong's deep-water port is a convenient location for visiting US Navy ships, the presence of which is important for regional security. There are reports suggesting that the United States has been reluctant to force the issue, fearing that China might refuse the visits after 1997. Admiral Charles Larson, a former Commander-in-Chief of US forces in the Pacific, has suggested that improving Sino–US military cooperation may help to resolve this question.[20]

Hong Kong in Chinese strategic planning

China's attitude towards Hong Kong has usually been thought to be associated solely with the territory's ability to produce wealth. In fact, Hong Kong's strategic position has been a crucial factor for its existence, even after the establishment of the People's Republic of China in 1949. The Communist government's tolerance of the territory's colonial status was, contrary to popular belief, not entirely based on economic calculations. Senior Communist officials have recently revealed that the territory forms a vital part of the Beijing leadership's global strategy against Western containment.

In addition to economic considerations, the Chinese leadership's decision not to take over Hong Kong was also based on a belief that the existence of a British colonial territory dependent on Chinese tolerance might help to exploit any divisions within the Western alliance. The Chinese leadership believed that Britain might have to protect its interests in Hong Kong, which was a symbol of British influence in the Far East, even at the displeasure of the United States. A British Hong Kong, vulnerable to pressure from China, could therefore hinder Anglo-American solidarity.[21] In fact, it is widely known that the British government was the first major Western government to accord diplomatic recognition to the People's Republic soon after its establishment.[22]

Hong Kong's peculiar strategic role in Chinese security calculations became less important as China's security environment improved in the 1970s. Western military presence in Hong Kong was therefore of limited significance for the Chinese. The collapse of the Soviet bloc and the end of the Cold War has, at the same time, reduced the importance of China's role in the global strategic equation, and created a favourable security environment for China. The two major global powers that have dominated world politics ever since 1945 are no longer threats to China: the Soviet Union has disintegrated, and the United States is unlikely to adopt a policy of confrontation against China, except in the fair trade arena and occasionally over human rights. The Chinese military has, in fact, become more powerful in regional terms: it is the world's third-largest nuclear power and the size of its armed forces outranks that of all its neighbours.[23]

For the Chinese leadership the security challenge in the post-Cold War world comes from a different direction in the form of a "peaceful evolution," mainly as a result of post-Tiananmen Western attitude towards the Beijing government. While the Chinese leaders' concern for a Western-inspired conspiracy against China is no longer a central issue on China's foreign policy agenda, their perception about peaceful evolution has not completely disappeared. The Beijing government's unwillingness to yield to Chris Patten's attempt for more democratic constitutional change in the last years of British colonial rule is, in part, a reflection of China's concern about the Western world's anti-China strategy. The increasing assertiveness of China was, therefore, partly a reflection of China's growing economic strength, and partly a defensive response to the post-Cold War security agenda.

China's resumption of sovereignty over a prosperous Hong Kong, and its unchallenged authority to take care of Hong Kong's defence, should not be seen as an alarming development. But it does present a security challenge for the region. The Sino-British agreement on the transfer of military sites in June 1994 has been discussed primarily with reference to Sino-British relations and its impact on confidence in Hong Kong, and to PLA discipline and the commercial dimensions of PLA activities in the territory. Most people in Hong Kong were apprehensive about the stationing of armed troops in the territory, suggesting that such a presence might undermine local confidence. Many argued that the Chinese garrison in Shenzhen would be more than adequate in meeting the territory's defence needs. The Chinese leadership, after wavering on the issue, decided that the stationing of PLA troops was a necessary step in "realizing China's sovereignty over Hong Kong." During a meeting with Hong Kong journalists, Deng Xiaoping rebuked former Defence Minister Geng Biao for saying that China may not send the PLA to Hong Kong after 1997. Since the Chinese government's decision at the highest level was made known, the debate in Hong Kong shifted to what form the Chinese military presence would take, rather than whether or not the PLA would be in Hong Kong.

Interestingly, the agreement on military sites in Hong Kong was concluded at a time when Sino-British relations were at one of their lowest points. In the assessment of former British ambassador to China and one of the chief architects of the Joint Declaration, Sir Percy Craddock, Sino-British cooperation was replaced by confrontation.[24] The appointment of a senior Tory power-broker, Chris Patten, as the last Governor of Hong Kong, and the reform package that he presented, were seen by the Chinese as a conspiracy to continue British influence in the colony and to resist Chinese involvement in its political development. Subsequent Sino-British negotiations over Hong Kong's future eventually collapsed. The unexpected deal on military sites transfer was hailed as a breakthrough locally and as an example of Sino-British cooperation at a very difficult time in the two countries' bilateral relationship. There were some concerns about the financial commitment for reprovisioning the military facilities for the PLA, and lingering fears about the presence of PLA on Hong Kong territory. But the funding was approved by the Legislative Council, and apprehension about PLA presence was replaced by a collective sigh of relief that progress had been made over substantive issues in the vexed Sino-British Joint Liaison Group.

This agreement has been widely welcomed as a breakthrough, which may pave the way for Sino-British cooperation over practical matters affecting the territory's future.[25] The presence of PLA troops in Hong Kong, as many observers have suggested, will also have implications beyond the defence of the territory. The PLA has already become an economic player with enormous commercial interests. Acquiring a foothold in one of the region's most dynamic economies will certainly facilitate their economic activities. Equally important is the fact that PLA presence in Hong Kong and the availability to the Chinese government of a deep-water port with modern military facilities may change the strategic equation in the region. While references have been made to the new naval base on Stonecutters Island, the event received little notice outside the territory[26] (see table 5.1).

The international security significance of the agreement, however, escaped the majority of the media.[27] In strategic terms, the naval base on Stonecutters Island, which replaces the former Tamar base, will provide modern facilities for the Chinese Navy. Some military analysts believe that the Chinese will use the base as the headquarters for nearby port facilities. The base, with a berthing capacity of 400 m by 400 m, would provide easy access for the larger frigates of the Chinese fleet, and it could be the monitoring base for maritime territorial disputes. Stonecutters Island will be too shallow for submarine operations, but it will certainly be a convenient coordinating point between the Shanghai-based East China Sea Fleet and the Zhanjiang-based South China Sea Fleet.

While there is little information on how the Chinese intend to use the port facilities in Hong Kong, they clearly attach importance to the construction of the base. Their demand for building a larger naval base was reportedly one major reason that delayed the conclusion of the agreement at the latest stage of the Sino-British negotiations over the military sites.[28] The Chinese government has refused to disclose

Table 5.1 **The PLA garrison in Hong Kong**

Hong Kong Island		Kowloon		New Territories	
Site	Area (ha)	Site	Area (ha)	Site	Area (ha)
Prince of Wales Barracks (excluding East Tamar)	2.8	Gun Club Barracks	11.0	Shek Kong Camp and Shek Kong Village	159.0
Stanley Barracks	122.3	Osborn Barracks	10.0	Casino Lines and Tam Mi Camp	57.0
Headquarter House	0.5	Stonecutters Island	75.7	Castle Peak	2263.0
Queens Lines	1.4	1A Cornwall Street	0.1	Coastal Watching Station (Tai O)	0.3
Bonham Towers	0.1				

Source: Hong Kong government.

formally the number of PLA troops who will be stationed in the territory. Reports have suggested that about ten thousand PLA soldiers have been undergoing special training in nearby Zhangmoutou for Hong Kong duties. Chinese officials have indicated that the number of military personnel will be fewer than the existing British strength, which is about seven thousand at the moment.[29] Another important development is the construction of a new military base in Shenzhen, which reportedly will serve as command headquarters for the entire East and South China Sea region, including Hong Kong, Macau, and Taiwan.[30]

Although the intention of the Chinese government regarding Hong Kong's role in China's defence planning still remains unclear, the acquisition of the Stonecutters Island naval base, and the presence of the PLA in Hong Kong, coupled with the development of a regional army base in Shenzhen, will strengthen Chinese coastal defence and possibly facilitate China's military projection in the region. This will undoubtedly have implications for the South China Sea territorial conflict and cross-strait difficulties between mainland China and Taiwan. It is also up to the Chinese government to make decisions about warships from other countries seeking to dock in the port of Hong Kong. The strategic balance in East Asia will therefore shift in favour of China after 1997.

But Hong Kong's status as an SAR might also serve as a constraint on Chinese military power. If the territory is to be embroiled directly in China's dispute with South-East Asian countries over the Spratly Islands, or other similar disputes, its trade links might suffer. Thus, China may find it important to isolate Hong Kong from such conflicts. The incorporation of Hong Kong in China, if not smoothly accomplished, may also create economic and political problems for the Beijing government and become yet another source of tensions between China and Taiwan and, indeed, the Western world.

The other dimension of China's resumption of sovereignty over Hong Kong is economic. Will China become more powerful and in turn more assertive in the region? China should definitely benefit from a closer economic association with Hong Kong. But the Chinese leadership will also have to accommodate the deepening of interdependence with the outside world that such economic links are bringing about. The transnational nature of economic activities and the need for closer international cooperation in conflict resolution have emerged as critical issues on the regional agenda. One broader question for regional security is therefore whether China will be able to accommodate its own changing power status at a time when the international environment is undergoing dramatic transformation.[31]

The role of international and regional institutions

While the 1984 agreement on Hong Kong's future was primarily bilateral, and the creation of the Hong Kong SAR is based on a set of domestic arrangements, the transition of the territory should have a significant impact on international relations in East Asia. Hong Kong's transition, as discussed in this chapter, suggests that, while China's position will be strengthened as the twenty-first century approaches, the incorporation of Hong Kong will also deepen China's interdependence with the world.

The implications that a powerful China will have for international relations within the Asia-Pacific region are highly complex: there are factors that may point to great benefits for peace and prosperity, but there are also other potentially destabilizing factors that may come into play, generating tensions and upsetting the regional order. Attempts to evaluate the China threat are, perhaps, not particularly meaningful. Unless China runs into great turmoil (which will benefit no one in East Asia), Asian countries will have to learn to live with a more powerful neighbour and to adjust to the new realities in the region.

The China threat thesis also ignores critical domestic developments that are changing the nature of the Chinese polity. While the Chinese Communist Party has remained firmly in power, the Chinese polity has undergone significant changes, leading to a more defused political decision-making process, and the balance of the state–society power relationship has changed in significant ways. China's rise as a major power is clearly a challenge to East Asian international security but not necessarily a threat. The country's growing involvement with regional affairs and mutual dependence therefore calls for a new approach to international relations in East Asia.

The security implications of the rise of a more powerful China, and the issues concerning territorial disputes as well as China's unification, have to be seen in the context of the emergence of a new strategic environment in East Asia. Yet the transformation of the post-Cold War international security framework in the Asia-Pacific region still remains incomplete at the mid-point of the 1990s. So far, what form the post-Cold War regional security structure will take is not entirely clear. It has been correctly observed that "debate about the direction of change, let alone the reality of the transformation, has been much slower to develop in this region than in Europe."[32]

It is true that the outlook for regional security still remains a matter of speculation. The end of the Cold War did not bring down the East Asian communist states, and peace in the region is still threatened by an undercurrent of historical and ethnic tensions. Nevertheless, amidst the confusion and uncertainty, five broad trends that will probably lay the foundations of a lasting security relationship in the future can be identified: they are (1) a gradual scaling-down of a permanent American military presence, (2) the emergence of multilateral dialogues, (3) the domination of economic concerns in international relations, (4) the emergence of institutions of regional economic cooperation, and (5) the growing assertiveness of Asian countries in international affairs, including trade.

The problem is that, while the direction of the general trends may be identifiable, the implications of such developments have remained unclear. The decline of US power, for example, clearly does not signal a general American retreat from Asia similar to the departure of the British "East of the Suez" in the early 1970s. The United States remains the world's leading power, with substantial political and economic interests in the Asia-Pacific region. In fact, the actual extent of American decline is itself a matter of considerable scholarly debate.[33] The fact that US interests in this region have been shifted from security to economics driven means that the United States will probably have to stay engaged in the world's most dynamic economic region, but its involvement may take different forms (cf. engaged balancer, multilateralist, distant balancer).[34]

Since the end of the Cold War, multilateral dialogue on regional security in the Asia-Pacific has become a growing enterprise. The regional multilateral process, concentrated more on so-called "track two" or "back channels" – which involve meetings of academics, journalists, off-duty government officials, and, occasionally, politicians – has been rightly highlighted as a significant novel feature of the security landscape in the 1990s. One review of such meetings calculated that there were at least four per month in 1993.[35] The development of the multilateral process in the region has prompted one optimistic observer to remark that "a new era of confidence-building and security cooperation has begun in the Asia/Pacific region."[36] Multilateral efforts have been given further impetus at the intergovernmental level with the recent setting-up of the Association of South-East Asian Nations (ASEAN) Regional Forum. The estab-

93

lishment and proliferation of multilateral security dialogue channels may have become a permanent fixture in the regional security framework, but the effectiveness of such channels, and whether they can play a more concrete role in resolving security problems, is still open to question.

The spectacular success of the East Asian economies has attracted global attention. The World Bank estimated that key East Asian economies in the region have consistently out-performed the rest of the world.[37] The importance of maintaining economic growth appears to be at the top of the agenda for most governments in the region. The optimistic view, that a desire for greater economic achievement and growing interdependence between Asian economies and the global economies will greatly reduce the threat of any military conflict in the region, has been dubbed "econophoria."[38] Although economic concerns have become a major preoccupation of most Asian states, the level and nature of interdependence in East Asia are less substantial than those in Europe, for instance. Mutual suspicion and uneven economic development may in the end be just another source of regional conflict.

The establishment of institutions of economic cooperation such as the Asia-Pacific Economic Cooperation (APEC) forum may, of course, provide the foundations for resolving regional conflicts. The 1993 Seattle APEC meeting, for example, paved the way for an improvement in the much-troubled post-Tiananmen Sino-US relationship. The development of APEC as an effective institution for conflict management, however, has a long way to go. In fact, there are growing concerns that APEC may yet become another unwieldy gathering of government officials without meaningful functions.

Finally, the growing assertiveness of East Asian states offers both opportunities and dangers. For years, regional security has been determined largely by global politics in the form of the Cold War. Economic success and the end of the Cold War provided an opportunity for Asian states to develop their own new framework of security arrangements without external influences. The rise of Asian powers, particularly China, however, has also created new tensions requiring readjustments in regional international relations. If Asian states want to prevent the return of a balance of power future,[39] they will have to manage the forces of change more effectively by building on the positive aspects of the emerging trends (for example strengthening multilateralism, fostering closer economic cooperation), and steering away from those with negative implications (such as pursuit for regional domination, or a policy of isolation).

As a new agenda in world politics emerges in the post-Cold War world, international and regional institutions should have a more important role to play in regional affairs and conflict resolution. While states remain the central elements of the evolving international system, East Asian states will also have to confront the complex transnational problems arising from the globalization of the world economy, and worldwide issues such as environment and human rights as well as the rise of non-governmental international organizations and other non-state actors. The development of regional and international institutions in East Asia has suggested that the concept of sovereignty is not incompatible with regional cooperation.[40] International security will be better safeguarded if regional economic activities continue to be integrated and region-wide mechanisms can be developed to resolve political conflicts. In spite of the limitations of international and regional regimes, the development of international standards and norms plays a part in shaping state behaviour and creating a more secure international environment.[41]

The preservation of an economically dynamic and politically open Hong Kong as an integral but autonomous part of China should be seen as a positive development for international security and stability in the region. The existence of such an SAR is a unique phenomenon. If it works it will deepen China's growing economic interaction with Taiwan, the region, and the world, and encourage China to accommodate diversity and plurality in managing political affairs. Other states and international institutions can contribute to the process by recognizing the territory's special status internationally and encouraging it to play an active part in regional affairs.

Notes and references

1. One exception is Lee Ngok, "Interdependence or conflict? China, Taiwan and Hong Kong and security issues in the Asia-Pacific region," paper presented to the Fourth Soka University Pacific Basin Symposium, 22–24 August 1994, Macau. A large part of this paper focuses on the mainland China–Taiwan problem, but there are some discussions on Hong Kong too: see pp. 17–19. Another is Donald Hugh McMillen (1994) "The PLA and regionalism in Hong Kong", *The Pacific Review* 7(1).
2. Deng Xiaoping's impromptu remarks to members of the Drafting Committee for the Basic Law of the Hong Kong Special Administrative Region on 17 February 1990. (*Deng Xiaoping on the Question of Hong Kong*. Hong Kong: New Horizon Press, 1993, p. 63).
3. A counter-argument is provided in James T.H. Tang (1993) "Hong Kong's international status." *The Pacific Review* 6(3).

4. James T.H. Tang (1993) "Hong Kong's International Status." *The Pacific Review* 6(3).
5. See report in *GATT Focus*, No. 108, June 1994.
6. See, for example, Vincent Cable and Peter Ferdinand (1994) "China as an economic giant: Threat or opportunity?" *International Affairs* 70(2): 243–261.
7. See recent issues of the *Military Balance* produced by the International Institute of Strategic Studies, London.
8. See, for example, the discussions on Sino-American relations during 1993 by James T.H. Tang (1994) "From Tiananmen to Blake Island: 'Renormalizing' Sino-American relations in the post-Cold War era." In: Maurice Brosseau and Lo Chi-kin, eds. *China Review 1994*. Hong Kong: Chinese University Press, pp. 6.1–6.19.
9. See, for example, Denny Roy (1994) "Hegemon on the horizon? China's threat to East Asian security." *International Security* 19(1): 149–168.
10. See discussions in Larry M. Wortzel (1994) "China pursues traditional Great-Power status." *Orbis* 38(2): 157–175.
11. See discussions in Vincent Cable and Peter Ferdinand (1994) "China as an economic giant: Threat or opportunity?" *International Affairs* 70(2): 244–246.
12. See discussions in Denny Roy (1994) "Hegemon on the horizon? China's threat to East Asian security." *International Security* 19(1): 158.
13. Thomas W. Robinson (1994) "Interdependence in China's foreign relations." In: Samuel Kim, ed. *China and the World: Chinese Foreign Relations in the Post-Cold War Era*. Boulder: Westview, pp. 187, 199.
14. See the *China Quarterly*'s special issue on Greater China, January 1993. The notion is controversial, but the integration of the economies on mainland China, Taiwan, and Hong Kong has clearly made an impact on economic development in East Asia, as well as on political, social, and economic developments in the three areas.
15. See James T.H. Tang (1994) "From Empire defence to imperial retreat: Britain's post-war China policy and the decolonization of Hong Kong." *Modern Asian Studies* 28(2), May.
16. Ibid.
17. "Navy set to raise anchor in 1997," *South China Morning Post*, 10 October 1994.
18. See *Hong Kong 1993* (Hong Kong: Government Printer, 1993), chapter on Armed Services.
19. Ibid.
20. "Admiral warns on end to US ship visits," *South China Morning Post*, 10 October 1994.
21. See Jin Yaoru's recollection of briefings on the subject in *Dangdai*, No. 15, 15 June 1992, pp. 32–35, and Xu Jiatun, *Xu Jiatun Xianggang Huiyilu* [The Hong Kong Memoirs of Xu Jiatun] Vol. 2 (Hong Kong: United Daily News Publications, 1993), pp. 473–474. More detailed discussions on this issue can be found in James T.H. Tang (1995) "The international dimension of Mainland China's unification policy: The case of Hong Kong," in Jaushieh Joseph Wu, ed. *Divided Nations: The Experience of Germany, Korea, and China*. Taipei: Institute of International Relations, National Chengchi University, pp. 149–169.
22. For a detailed account of Britain's recognition of the Beijing government see James T.H. Tang (1992) *Britain's Encounter with Revolutionary China, 1949–54* (London: Macmillan).
23. See *The Military Balance, 1993–94* (London: International Institute of Strategic Studies, 1993).
24. Craddock's assessment of the change in British policy is in Percy Craddock (1994) *Experiences of China* (London: John Murray), chapter 24: The End of Cooperation, pp. 247–258.
25. See, for example, the editorial in *Ming Pao* (a widely respected independent Chinese-language newspaper) on 5 July 1994, which criticized reservations about government funding for building facilities for the Chinese military as myopic.
26. The *Far Eastern Economic Review* did not cover the agreement, focusing instead on Legislative Council's debates on Hong Kong Governor Chris Patten's constitutional reform package which was passed on 1 July 1994.
27. One exception is "Stonecutters to boost Chinese navy," *South China Morning Post*, 1 July 1994.

28. "Britain firm on naval base," *Eastern Express*, 27 June 1994.
29. See, for example, reports in *South China Morning Post*, 25 June 1994 and *Hong Kong Standard*, 11 October 1994.
30. *Eastern Express*, 22 July 1994.
31. One useful discussion of the evolving international order is James N. Rosenau and Ernst-Otto Czempiel, eds (1992) *Governance without Government: Order and Change in World Politics* (Cambridge: Cambridge University Press).
32. One recent effort in understanding the transformation of East Asian security relations is Barry Buzan and Gerald Segal (1994) "Rethinking East Asian security," *Survival* 36(2): 3.
33. Paul Kennedy (1987) *The Rise and Decline of Great Powers: Economic Change and Military Conflict from 1500 to 2000*. New York: Random House; Joseph Nye (1990) *Bound to Lead: The Changing Nature of American Power*. New York: Basic Books.
34. See discussions in Edward A. Olsen (1992) *US Security Perceptions in the Asia Pacific Region*. North Pacific Co-operative Security Dialogue Working Paper, Number 21. Toronto: Centre for International and Strategic Studies, York University.
35. Paul Evans (1994) "Building security: The Council for Security Cooperation in the Asia Pacific (CSCAP)," *The Pacific Review* 7(2): 125, 127. See also the inventory of dialogue channels, pp. 133–136.
36. Desmond Ball (1994) "A new era in confidence building: The second-track process in the Asia/Pacific region." *Security Dialogue* 25(2), June.
37. See *The East Asian Miracle: Economic Growth and Public Policy*, a World Bank policy research report (New York: Oxford University Press, 1993).
38. Barry Buzan and Gerald Segal (1994) "Rethinking East Asian security," *Survival* 36(2): 11.
39. Barry Buzan and Gerald Segal suggest that there is a distinct possibility for a balance of power future for the region. See "Rethinking East Asian security," *Survival* 36(2): 18.
40. One useful discussion of the challenge for international institutions in the post-Cold War world is Paul Taylor (1993) *International Organization in the Modern World: The Regional and the Global Process* (London: Pinter Publishers). For a discussion of the development of regional cooperation up to the 1980s, see Michael Haas (1989) *The Asian Way to Peace: A Story of Regional Cooperation* (New York: Praeger).
41. A useful discussion about this is Oran Young (1992) "The effectiveness of international institutions: hard cases and critical variables," in James N. Rosenau and Ernst-Otto Czempiel, eds, *Governance without Government: Order and Change in World Politics* (Cambridge: Cambridge University Press), pp. 160–194.

6

The Taiwan factor in Asia-Pacific regional security

Cheng-yi Lin

Introduction

The Kuomintang (KMT) government on Taiwan greatly benefited from Washington's containment policy towards Communist China in the years prior to the Nixon administration's *rapprochement* with Beijing. Considering the size of the territory and population that it actually controlled, Taiwan was granted an unmatched international status, including permanent membership of the United Nations Security Council from 1949 to 1971. Taiwan was so economically, politically, and militarily dependent on the United States that it hardly bothered to formulate any long-term foreign policies. But Taiwan, the faithful anticommunist ally of the United States, became a mere pawn in the great game when Washington decided to normalize its relations with the People's Republic of China (PRC). As its diplomatic standing deteriorated, Taiwan downplayed the ideological element in its foreign policy and adopted a more flexible posture, developing substantive but unofficial relations with countries that recognized the PRC.

After Sino-US relations were fully normalized in 1979, Beijing initiated a peace offensive directed at Taiwan and based on the "one country, two systems" formula, which offers Taiwan a high degree of autonomy as a "special administrative region" (SAR) of the PRC. Taipei has rejected these overtures, however, as it is loath to give up its present de facto independence. But the KMT's "one China," anti-independence stance, which it basically shares with Beijing, makes it difficult for Taipei to reject reunification as a long-term goal. In 1987, Taiwan President Chiang Ching-kuo decided to open up relations with China to a limited extent, though the government's "three-nos" policy (no contacts, no negotiations, no compromise) was maintained. Since then, Taipei has proven its willingness to be flexible by stating its preconditions for talks with Beijing in answer to Beijing's peace overture. In the meantime, the government has importantly relaxed restrictions on investment in mainland China as a result of pressure from Taiwan's business community.

Tension has been gradually reduced through limited but growing interaction between the two sides of the Taiwan Strait. Whether the Taiwan factor will play a stabilizing or a destabilizing role in the region remains to be seen. The Taiwan government claims sovereignty over Hong Kong and the various islands in the South China Sea, and these claims are challenged by other parties in the region. But if one takes into account Taiwan's overseas aid and investment flows, its rapid democratization, and growing defence capability, the role of Taiwan in the security of the Asia-Pacific region cannot be disregarded.

Taiwan's perception of the "new world order"

George Bush has summarized the principles of the "new world order" as follows: "Peaceful settlement of disputes, solidarity against aggression, reduced and controlled arsenals, and just treatment of all people." He also called for "a partnership based on consultation, cooperation, and collective action, especially through international and regional organizations. A partnership united by principle and the rule of law and supported by an equitable sharing of both cost and commitment. A partnership whose goals are to increase democracy, increase prosperity, increase the peace, and reduce arms."[1] However, despite the expulsion of Iraqi forces from Kuwait, the world seems to be no safer than it was before the end of the Cold War. Civil wars in the former Yugoslavia and Rwanda have cost the lives of thousands of innocent civilians. Waves of uncontrolled illegal immigrants from Cuba and Haiti have flooded into the United States. In Asia, particularly, communist regimes are still resisting the global tide of democratization, and military build-ups have intensified. Since the world remains a dangerous place and the United States is implementing a policy of selective global commitment, some critics are dismissing the "new world order" as merely a delusion. As Lawrence Freedman has put it, "the persistence of old political vices is highlighted by reference to the virtue promised by 'new'; selectivity when taking decisive action in support of international law is shown up by the universalist promise of 'world'; while the prevalent disorder in so many regions contrasts neatly with the hopes for stability implied by 'order'."[2]

From Taipei's perspective, the end of the Cold War has not brought peace and stability to East Asia. Though wars of independence and civil wars derived from emerging nationalism have been absent in the region, the phasing out of the US military presence has encouraged a regional military build-up. Moreover, four out of the five remaining socialist or communist countries (North Korea, the PRC, Viet Nam, and Laos) are in East Asia. Two anachronistic regimes in particular present a potential threat to regional peace.[3] North Korea's supposedly secret nuclear programme, the number one threat to stability in the Asia-Pacific region, has the potential to trigger a chain of nuclear proliferation in Japan, Taiwan, and South Korea. And though the PRC is unlikely to invade Taiwan, Beijing has consistently refused to give up the option of using force to settle the Taiwan issue. Finally, there are the nagging territorial disputes – such as that between Russia and Japan over the Northern Territories; the little-known dispute between Japan, Taiwan, and the PRC over the Senkaku Islands; and the growing problem of the Spratly Islands, which involves claims by Taiwan, the PRC, Viet Nam, Malaysia, Brunei, and the Philippines – all reasons behind the regional military build-up. This is why Taiwan's foreign minister, Fredrick Chien, has observed that "the Cold War structure remains largely intact in East Asia."[4]

President Lee Teng-hui of Taiwan seems even more pessimistic about the new world order and, particularly, about the order in East Asia. Again and again, Lee has pointed out that the gradual US military pull-out from Asia may have a strong impact on the region's stability and he has urged Washington to maintain a military presence in the region. Lee has warned of the implications of Beijing's new Law on Territorial Waters and Their Contiguous Areas and the PRC's moves to build up its naval strength, which he says could pose a threat to peace and stability in the Asia-Pacific region. In answer to this, Lee has proposed the establishment of "a system for protecting the collective security of the region." In particular, Lee has called upon Japan and the United States to provide leadership in economic cooperation and regional security in East Asia.[5]

Even though Taipei is pessimistic about Asia's power structure in the post-Cold War period, the new international environment does have some advantages for Taiwan's security. At least four factors are making a positive contribution to Taiwan's security in the post-Cold War era. First, as interdependence among nations intensifies, economic issues are becoming more important than military and political issues. In these circumstances, Taiwan's economic strength becomes a useful instrument for expanding its international relations. Second, Taiwan was able to break out of a long-term deadlock and upgrade its weapons systems when President Bush decided to sell 150 F16 A/Bs to Taiwan in 1992, thereby modifying the US position as expressed in the August 1982 communiqué with the PRC. Third, democratization in Taiwan has improved KMT's overseas image and won much public sympathy abroad.[6] Taiwan's democratization has also enhanced its ability to resist the infiltration of Chinese Communist ideology. Fourth, with the collapse of communism in the Soviet Union, China is far less valuable as an ally to the United States and Taiwan is no longer a pawn in the US–PRC power game.

Of course, the end of the Cold War has also had a negative impact on Taiwan's security outlook. First, the PRC and Japan are stepping in to fill the role previously played by the United States in the Asia-Pacific region. Instead of being a deterrent or protector, the United States has assumed the role of a balancer. Second, no longer preoccupied with the threat from the Soviet Union to the north, the Chinese military can now concentrate deployments in the south where it poses a more serious threat to Taiwan. Third, the general resurgence of nationalism in the post-Cold War era and, in particular, the entry of the newly independent Baltic states into the United Nations has encouraged the opposition Democratic Progressive Party (DPP) and people in general in Taiwan to pursue *de jure* independence for the island (see table 6.1). It is difficult to predict what kind of coercive action Beijing could use against an independent Taiwan, but a declaration of independence would certainly heighten tensions between Taiwan and China while the response of the United States and the rest of the international community, in light of recent security threats around the globe, would be uncertain at best.

In the post-Cold War era, the Taiwan government no longer

Table 6.1　**Public opinion on Taiwanese independence**

Date	Survey conductors	Approval ratio (%)
September 1989	PORF[a]	15.8
December 1989	PORF	8.2
March 1990	PORF	15.8
June 1990	PORF	12.5
October 1990	*Lianhebao*[b]	21.0
December 1990	PORF	12.0
June 1991	PORF	12.7
September 1991	*Lianhebao*[b]	18.0
October 1991	*Lianhebao*[b]	14.0
October 1992	Gallup Poll (Taiwan)	15.1
October 1992	*Lianhebao*	16.0
March 1993	*Lianhebao*	17.0
May 1993	Gallup Poll	23.7
April 1994	Gallup Poll	27.0
May 1994	Gallup Poll	27.3

Sources: Mainland Policy: *Selected Opinion Polls Conducted in Taiwan, 1988–1992*, Mainland Affairs Council, the Executive Yuan, Taipei, August 1992, p. 6; *Zhongyang ribao* (Central Daily News), 1 November 1992, p. 1; 11 May 1993, p. 1; *Lianhebao*, 18 April 1994, p. 2; 3 June 1994, p. 6.
a. PORF: Public Opinion Research Foundation, a private and independent poll organization based in Taipei which later became Gallup Poll, Taiwan Branch.
b. *Lianhebao* (United Daily News), an influential conservative newspaper.

depends on US support to legitimize its rule over Taiwan. However, Taiwan's changing international role can be only partially explained by the development of democracy and a new generation of well-educated decision makers: the new world order also plays a part. Taiwan is now more eager to demonstrate its national power and to pursue a policy of acquiring international prestige in the Asia-Pacific region. The role of Taiwan has shifted from that of an anticommunist agent and a faithful ally of the United States to that of a seeker of a balance of power, a supporter of collective security, and the practitioner of a functionalist approach in its relations with mainland China.

Taiwan and peace across the Taiwan Strait

After 40 years of confrontation with the PRC, Taiwan has developed a new national security strategy. First, by means of military build-up, Taipei seeks to maintain a balance of power with Beijing. Taiwan closely monitors the PRC's military modernization programme to evaluate its potential impact on Taiwan's security. Second, Taiwan is eager to place itself under the protection of an effective United Nations or regional collective security system. Third, Taiwan has adopted a functionalist approach in its cultivation of cooperative interaction with the PRC and its attempt to alleviate tension between the two sides. Furthermore, the current KMT leadership believes that a declaration of *de jure* independence would almost definitely result in a strong response from Beijing, including possibly even the use of force against Taiwan. For that reason, it believes it is necessary to restrain the movement in favour of self-determination for the people of Taiwan. Some members of the opposition DPP, however, regard Beijing's warnings to be no more than bluff.

The post-Cold War slump in arms sales gave Taiwan an opportunity to negotiate many new contracts with Western defence manufacturers and implement a military modernization programme. For example, in 1992 Taiwan negotiated contracts for 150 F16 A/Bs from the United States and 60 Mirage-2000-5s from France. Paris reversed its decision not to sell frigates to Taiwan in 1991, and agreed to sell six, with a possible total of 16, Lafayette-class frigates. In the short term these arms purchases have greatly aided Taiwan in its effort to maintain a military balance with the PRC, though it would be impossible for Taiwan to compete with China in every aspect of military capability. Taiwan does hope to make up in quality what it lacks in the quantity of military hardware. Because Taiwan no longer publicly aspires to unite China by means of military force, its arms purchases are for defensive purposes only, but it does hope to deter Beijing by raising the potential cost of any attack on the island to an untenable level.

Taiwan stands no chance of establishing an alliance with any countries in the Asia-Pacific region, but realists in Taiwan are quick to explore the possibility of creating a buffer zone between China and Taiwan. In May 1990, President Lee called for Beijing's leaders to withdraw their troops to a position at least 300 kilometres from the coast of Fujian Province opposite Kinmen (Quemoy) and Matsu.[7] The DPP, in its party platforms and action plans, has publicly endorsed the idea that Kinmen and Matsu be demilitarized. In May 1992, Cheyne Chiu, President Lee's close aide and presidential spokesman, even suggested a non-aggression treaty between China and Taiwan.[8] Beijing has rejected all these proposals from Taiwan.

Taipei believes that its military capability is not sufficient to resist an attack by the PRC, and for that reason is looking to collective security measures to supplement its military strength. As part of its effort on behalf of existing collective security systems, Taiwan, though not a UN member, supported the 12 UN resolutions condemning and imposing sanctions on Iraq for its invasion of Kuwait. In addition, in September 1990, Taipei announced that it would contribute US$30 million to three frontline states – Jordan, Turkey, and Egypt – whose economies were directly affected by the Gulf War and embargoes. It was reported that Taipei also offered US$100 million to the United States to help foot the bill for Desert Shield and Desert Storm, though this was turned down by the Americans. The KMT newspaper *Zhongyang ribao* (*Central Daily News*) suggested in an editorial at the time that the Taiwan government should make available non-military and military assistance. Had this been implemented, it would supposedly have included a medical team, a minesweeping naval unit, and frigates for use in the Persian Gulf operation.[9]

Taipei's support for UN actions against Iraq was aimed at encouraging the development of a collective security system that would someday protect Taiwan from the PRC, and Taipei's recent bid to join the United Nations should also be regarded as a part of the same grand strategy. In the meantime, Taipei has declared that it will no longer compete with Beijing for the right to represent China in the international arena.[10] Even so, Beijing has condemned President Lee and the countries that support Taipei's UN bid, and the Chinese claim that Taipei's efforts in this direction are hampering reunification. But both Foreign Minister Chien and Jason Hu, the Taiwan government spokesman, argue that allowing Taipei to enter the United Nations and other intergovernmental organizations (IGOs) would actually promote the unification of China. Chien argues that obstruction of Taipei's UN bid or its other international activities, such as President Lee's attendance at the Asian Games in Hiroshima or his participation in Asia-Pacific Economic Cooperation (APEC) summits, not only impairs relations between people on the two sides of the Taiwan Strait but also "aid[s] and abet[s] agitation for Taiwan's independence."[11]

In addition to UN membership, Lee Teng-hui has been trying to enlist US support for the establishment of a collective security system in South-East Asia that could later be expanded to include the entire Asia-Pacific region. President Lee also proposed the establishment of a collective security fund, general arms reduction in Asia, and joint exploration of the natural resources of the South China Sea, in order to avoid potential conflicts arising from territorial disputes.[12]

One school of opinion in Taiwan holds that the development of economic and social cooperation between states is a prerequisite for the ultimate solution of political conflicts without resort to war. In other words, the spillover from social and economic cooperation can aid the settlement of security issues. This form of the functionalist approach has been used by Taiwan in its dealings with the PRC. Functionalists in Taiwan firmly believe that, as economic, social, and cultural differences between the two sides of the Taiwan Strait diminish, the prospects for peaceful reunification will improve. That is why the Taiwan government suggests that the two sides set aside their dispute over sovereignty and conduct cross-strait relations according to the principles of rationality, peace, parity, and reciprocity.[13] In February 1991, the Taiwan government adopted the "Guidelines for National Unification," a three-phase programme according to which a period of exchanges and reciprocity will, it is hoped, lead to a phase of increased mutual trust and cooperation, leading finally to consultation and unification.[14] Rejecting Beijing's proposal for party-to-party talks between the KMT and the Chinese Communist Party (CCP), Taipei insists that cultural exchanges must come first, followed by bilateral trade, and only then direct political contacts. It is clear from the "Guidelines" that Taiwan's policy is not to have official contacts with the PRC unless and until Beijing renounces the use of force as a means for unification and gives up its efforts to isolate Taiwan in the international arena.

Despite their lack of official contacts, relations between Taiwan and China have developed considerably since 1987. Tourism, trade, investment, and cultural and sports exchanges are increasing rapidly. For example, residents of Taiwan are reported to have made over five million visits to the mainland between 1987 and 1993. Bilateral trade through Hong Kong was worth US$1.5 billion in 1987, US$5.8 billion in 1991, US$7.4 billion in 1992, and US$8.6 billion in 1993. While Taipei rejects two-way investment, Taiwan's investment on the mainland is estimated at over US$10 billion.[15] A private but government-endorsed Straits Exchange Foundation (SEF) has been established in Taiwan to handle bilateral issues in conjunction with its PRC counterpart, the Association for Relations Across the Taiwan Straits (ARATS).

The first high-level, semi-official meeting between Koo Chen-fu,

Chairman of Taiwan's SEF, and Wang Daohan, his ARATS counterpart, was held in Singapore in April 1993. The Koo–Wang talks were described by Taipei as "non-governmental, administrative, economic, and functional in nature." Three agreements were signed between the SEF and ARATS on that occasion, covering the delivery of registered mail, verification of official documents, and the establishment of a regular channel of communication between the two organizations. The two sides also issued a joint statement listing topics to be addressed in future meetings, including crime, illegal immigrants, fishing disputes, copyright protection, and judicial cooperation and cross-Strait joint exploitation of natural resources.[16]

Since the historic Koo–Wang talks, at least seven rounds of negotiations have been conducted between the SEF and ARATS, and two joint statements have been issued. In the August joint statement, the SEF and ARATS announced a preliminary consensus regarding the return of air hijackers and illegal entrants, and the resolution of fishing disputes.[17] Tang Shubei, the Vice-Chairman of ARATS, who came to Taipei in August 1994, is the highest-ranking mainland official to set foot on the island and his visit signalled a recovery in cross-Strait relations after a group of 24 Taiwanese tourists were murdered at Qiandao Lake in Zhejiang in March 1994. However, the prospects for relations are far from rosy, and they will depend on Taipei's foreign relations and domestic political developments. Whenever Beijing tries to limit Taiwan's international activities, Taipei becomes more resistant to cross-Strait relations and reunification. As Taiwan becomes more democratic and pluralistic, the PRC adopts more measures to forestall the trend toward Taiwan independence and then finds it more difficult to persuade Taipei to expand cross-Strait interaction.

Taiwan and the power transition in Hong Kong

Beijing has promised that under the "one country, two systems" formula, Hong Kong and Taiwan would be able to keep their existing political, economic, and social systems for the time being. But the PRC has made it plain that both territories are expected to adopt socialism eventually. The future status envisaged for Taiwan, according to Article 31 of China's 1982 Constitution, is similar to that planned for Hong Kong: both are to be SARs under the central government in Beijing. According to Beijing's white paper, "On the Taiwan Question and the Reunification of China," Taiwan would not be allowed to establish diplomatic relations or negotiate air traffic agreements with other countries, nor would it be permitted to participate in intergovernmental organizations or acquire its own defensive weapons from the West.[18] If Taiwan were to become an SAR, its future fate would be purely an internal Chinese affair and Beijing would not tolerate any intervention from either the United States or the United Nations. Any form of conflict between China and Taiwan would then be regarded as being essentially within the PRC's domestic jurisdiction. This is why Taipei opposes the application of the Hong Kong formula to the settlement of the Taiwan issue.

Taipei feels secure in its defence for the time being because the PRC is likely to be preoccupied with consolidating its power base in the Hong Kong SAR in the period before and after 1997. But there will be a period of vulnerability in Taiwan's security before the F-16s, Mirage-2000-5s, and second-generation frigates come into operation, as Taiwan's obsolete F-5Es and destroyers hardly constitute a deterrent to Beijing. Once Hong Kong is settled, Beijing will probably pay more attention to Taiwan. But by then, Taiwan will have a complete new fighter force and a sophisticated navy, so its power projection will be much better than it is now in the mid-1990s. But one may also argue that Beijing will try to dispatch Taiwan before 1997 without waiting for Taipei to complete its defence modernization.

The real impact of the Hong Kong issue on Taiwan is not military but political, economic, and even psychological. The return of Hong Kong to the PRC exposes the fictitious nature of the Taiwanese claim to sovereignty over the territory. Even though Taipei issued statements denouncing the Sino-British Joint Declaration on Hong Kong in 1984 and the Basic Law of 1990, the KMT government applauded the end of British rule in Hong Kong, which was regarded as an inalienable part of the greater China. The KMT government was excluded from any negotiations for the return of Hong Kong, and therefore Taipei could hardly develop a creative Hong Kong policy. High-ranking Taiwanese officials are often barred from visiting Hong Kong, and only a few members of the Hong Kong Legislative Council have ever visited Taiwan. There is only occasional "passive collusion" between Taiwan and Hong Kong and they are unable to counterbalance PRC pressure. As Lowell Dittmer put it, the PRC developed a relationship of patronage and assimilation with Taiwan and Hong Kong, respectively, and Beijing played a dominant role in this hegemonic triangle.[19]

The Taiwan government would like to see democracy, freedom,

Table 6.2   **Taiwan's representative agencies in Hong Kong**

Agency	Supervising body in Taiwan
Chung Hwa Travel Service	Ministry of Foreign Affairs
Chinese Overseas Travel and Transport Service	Overseas Chinese Affairs Commission
Far East Trade Service, Inc., Hong Kong Branch Office	Ministry of Economic Affairs
Taipei Trade Office in Hong Kong	China External Trade Development Council
Hong Kong Kwang Hwa Information and Culture Center	Government Information Office
Chinese Cultural Association	KMT

Source: Author.

and prosperity in Hong Kong after 1997, but it rejects the "one country, two systems" formula as a solution to the Taiwan question. Of most concern for Taipei is the future status of its representative agencies in Hong Kong (see table 6.2). Deng Xiaoping has promised that these offices will be allowed to stay in Hong Kong after 1997 as long as Taipei guarantees not to create turmoil in the territory or implement a "two-Chinas" policy.[20] Taipei has said that its Hong Kong offices will fall under the jurisdiction of the Mainland Affairs Council after 1997, though Taipei has attempted to register them as "private judicial persons" to ensure their legal protection after 1997.

Bilateral trade between Taiwan and Hong Kong surged more than 10-fold between 1983 and 1993, from US$1.9 billion to US$20 billion (see table 6.3). Hong Kong is Taiwan's second most important export market, with about half of the exports being transshipped to the mainland. Hong Kong is also the major transit port for China-bound Taiwanese, an average of 1.5 million annually between 1990 and 1993. Taiwan and Hong Kong are connected by some 195 flights a week.[21] Owing to the lack of direct trade and transportation links between Taiwan and China, Hong Kong is regarded by Taipei as a bridge to the mainland. The PRC's takeover of Hong Kong in 1997 will deprive Taiwan of this buffer zone, so Taipei is looking into the possibility of using Singapore instead. The draft Statute Governing Relations between the People of Taiwan and Hong Kong and Macao, drawn up by the Taiwan government's Mainland Affairs Council, regards Hong Kong as a special region different from the mainland, allowing Taiwan to maintain direct trade and transportation links

Table 6.3 **Taiwanese trade with Hong Kong**[a]

Year	Exports	Imports	Total amount
1983	1,643.3	298.9	1,942.2
1984	2,087.1	370.4	2,457.5
1985	2,539.2	319.7	2,858.9
1986	2,915.1	379.3	3,294.4
1987	4,112.9	706.7	4,819.6
1988	5,588.5	1,922.0	7,510.5
1989	7,029.1	2,197.2	9,226.3
1990	8,557.0	1,446.0	10,003.0
1991	12,430.5	1,944.5	14,375.0
1992	15,416.0	1,780.9	17,196.9
1993	18,454.9	1,728.1	20,183.0

Source: Ministry of Finance, Taiwan, cited from *Gang'ao yuebao* (Hong Kong and Macao Monthly), No. 34 (15 August 1994), p. 22.
a. Values are millions of US dollars.

with Hong Kong after 1997.[22] Taipei also does not preclude the possibility of conducting negotiations (through the SEF) with Beijing when Taiwan's bilateral air-rights agreement with Hong Kong expires in 1995.

In its short-, medium-, and long-term policies toward Hong Kong and Macao, Taiwan has developed a three-stage plan for relations with Hong Kong based upon the following principles: (1) safeguarding democracy, freedom, prosperity, and progress in Hong Kong; (2) maintaining [Taiwan's] strongholds in Hong Kong, and disseminating the ideas of freedom and democracy throughout the mainland; and (3) countering the use of Hong Kong by the Chinese communists in their schemes to reduce Taiwan's status to that of a local government by promoting their "one country, two systems" model.[23] Without setting a quota, the Taiwan government reviews applications from staunch KMT followers to resettle in Taiwan after 1997. From 1984 to July 1994, Taipei granted permits for at least 21,000 Hong Kong residents, though it is hoped that they will return to Hong Kong to help preserve democracy and prosperity there.[24] If Hong Kong stays prosperous but not democratic after 1997, Taiwan will still be justified in rejecting "one country, two systems." But for the KMT to try to use Hong Kong as a base to promote "peaceful evolution" on the mainland would risk provoking Beijing. Taipei knows very well that it can do little on its own to protect the well-being of Hong Kong, so it encourages the internationalization of the Hong Kong issue and has called on the international community to be concerned about the future of Hong Kong in its Current Agenda for Hong Kong and Macao. Taipei's welcoming of the US–Hong Kong Policy Act of 1992 is only one example of this passive policy.

While the PRC is occupied with the takeover of Hong Kong, Taipei is beginning to adjust its policy to the power transition in 1997. The government has focused its attention on developing trade and financial and cultural exchanges with Hong Kong, and also has plans to replace Hong Kong as a regional operations centre for multinational corporations. Even at this late stage, Taiwan has begun to adopt other more assertive policies toward Hong Kong, including the following:

1. Pressing for the establishment of a quasi-official Hong Kong office with a branch in Taipei;
2. Inviting Hong Kong officials to visit Taiwan;
3. Promoting exchanges between non-governmental organizations and cultural exchanges;
4. Calling upon those 20 or so countries that recognize Taiwan to issue visas in the name of their representative offices in Taiwan rather than their consulates in Hong Kong;
5. Allowing Taiwan banks to establish branches in Hong Kong and promoting the establishment of a Taiwan Businessmen's Association in Hong Kong and a Trade Cooperation Commission set up jointly by the Taiwan Industrial Association and the Hong Kong General Chamber of Commerce;
6. Increasing contacts with the Hong Kong government through APEC channels.[25]

Taipei's greatest concern regarding 1997 is its impact on Taiwan's future, rather than what it can do for the people of Hong Kong. From this perspective, Taipei has been passive rather than creative in its policy toward Hong Kong. Taipei is also anxious to safeguard the status of Taiwan's representatives in Hong Kong and protect Taiwan from infiltration by a fifth column from PRC-controlled Hong Kong. Taipei keeps a close watch on political developments in the territory and its future status in international organizations and investigates their implications for Taiwan. The Taiwan government is careful to avoid any public expression of support for particular politicians or parties in Hong Kong's elections. Even so, Taiwan remaining independent from PRC jurisdiction could force Beijing to adopt a magnanimous assimilation policy toward Hong Kong.

Table 6.4 **Countries that occupy the Spratly Islands**

Country	Islands occupied	No. of troops
PRC	Yungshu Chiao (Fiery Cross Reef) and 6 others	260
Philippines	Peitzu Tao (N.E. Cay) and 7 others. Airstrip on Pagasa (Thitu)	480
Viet Nam	Nanwei Tao (Spratly Island) and 24 others. Runway on Nanwei Tao	600
Malaysia	Tanwan Chiao (Swallow Reef) and 3 others. Runway on Tanwan Chiao	70
Taiwan	Taiping (Itu Aba Island)	100

Source: *1993–1994 National Defense Report, Republic of China* (Taipei: Li Ming Books, 1994), p. 31; Allan Shephard (1994) "Maritime tensions in the South China Sea and the neighborhood: Some solutions." *Studies in Conflict and Terrorism* 17 (2; April–June), 209–211.

Taiwan and peace in the South China Sea

While Taipei lays claim to a U-shaped area of the South China Sea, including the Spratly Islands, the Paracels, Macclesfield Bank, and the Pratas Islands, it has effective control of only Tungsha (the Pratas Islands) and Taiping (Itu Aba Island in the Spratly Archipelago). The Paracels have been occupied by the PRC since its naval clash with Viet Nam in January 1974. The Spratlys, which consist of 104 islands, reefs, cays, and banks, are also claimed wholly or in part by the PRC, Viet Nam, Malaysia, and the Philippines. Viet Nam, Malaysia, and the Philippines have even built airstrips on the islands they occupy (see table 6.4). Taiwan maintains marine corps troops (approximately 100 soldiers, down from 500 in the late 1980s), a radar station, a meteorological centre, and a power plant on Itu Aba, the largest of the Spratlys. Taiwan is also completing construction of communications facilities on the island and an airstrip is under consideration.[26]

Even though the Spratly Islands are the traditional fishing grounds for small Taiwanese vessels and are potentially rich in oil and gas deposits, they are some 800 miles south-west of Taiwan and beyond Taipei's power projection. Nevertheless, Taipei has given the South China Sea issue quite high priority in the post-Cold War era. In 1990, Taiwan Executive Yuan approved placing the Pratas Islands and Itu Aba under the temporary jurisdiction of the municipal government of Kaohsiung, Taiwan's southernmost city. In 1992, an inter-ministerial South China Sea Task Force was established to review and revise

Taiwan's South China Sea policy, and a new section on the situation in the South China Sea was added to the 1993–1994 edition of the *ROC National Defense Report*. However, the draft Territorial Sea and Contiguous Zone Law and the Exclusive Economic Zone and Continental Shelf Law do not contain any specific references to the Spratlys. In October 1992, the Taiwan Ministry of National Defense declared a 24-nautical-mile restricted sea zone and a 30-nautical-mile restricted air zone surrounding Taiwan and the Pescadores, within which foreign aircraft and ships are prohibited. However, for the Pratas Islands and Itu Aba, a 4,000-metre restricted sea zone and 6,000-metre restricted air zone were announced.[27] This is a sign that Taipei has adopted a policy of self-restraint with regard to the South China Sea, and it has done this simply because it does not have the military capability to support its historical claim.

In 1993, the Taiwan government adopted a South China Sea Policy Guideline that included (1) safeguarding Taiwan's sovereignty over the islands in the South China Sea, (2) strengthening development and management of the South China Sea, (3) promoting cooperation among the littoral states of the South China Sea, (4) resolving disputes peacefully, and (5) protecting the area's ecological environment.[28] Overall, Taipei's policy is to seek the peaceful resolution of territorial disputes in the South China Sea, particularly in the Spratly Islands. Taiwan has indicated a willingness to cooperate in technical areas such as navigation safety, pollution control, natural disasters, seaborne rescue, oceanographic research, and ecological conservation, and has proposed that the countries concerned develop resources jointly, thereby eliminating potential causes of conflict. Such a position follows the principles contained in the 1992 Association of South-East Asian Nations (ASEAN) Declaration on the South China Sea, which called on all claimants to settle disputes by peaceful means and resolved to "explore the possibility of cooperation in the South China Sea relating to the safety of maritime navigation and communication, protection against pollution of the marine environment, coordination of search and rescue operations, efforts towards combatting piracy and armed robbery as well as collaboration in the campaign against illicit trafficking in drugs."[29]

Even though Taipei has adopted a policy of self-restraint, other claimants to the South China Sea are suspicious of a tacit understanding, and even military cooperation, between Taiwan and China. Such suspicion is not groundless: Taipei is sometimes ambivalent in its attitude toward the settlement of territorial disputes in the area.

For nationalistic reasons, some people in Taiwan would rather see the Spratlys occupied by the PRC than by members of ASEAN. Some Taiwan scholars have even urged the government to form an alliance with the PRC to counterbalance other claimants. At the Workshop Series on Managing Potential Conflicts in the South China Sea, initiated by Indonesia, the representatives of both Taiwan and the PRC have put forward identical claims to most of the South China Sea on historical grounds. After the Chinese and Vietnamese navies clashed in March 1988 in the Spratlys, Taipei's Defence Minister at the time, Cheng Wei-yuan, indicated that, if asked by Beijing, Taiwan would help defend the island group from a third party.[30] In a *Jane's Defense Weekly* interview in 1993, Defence Minister Sun Chen said that Taiwan "does not preclude and does not eliminate the possibility of exchanging views on these issues [peaceful development and administration of the archipelago] with the Chinese mainland."[31] It was also reported in March 1994 that the Chinese Petroleum Corporation of Taiwan, the PRC's China National Offshore Oil Corporation, and Chevron would form a joint venture for oil exploration in the East China or South China Sea.[32] In June 1994 an unprecedented academic conference on the South China Sea, sponsored by the Chinese Society of International Law (Taipei) and with paper presenters from Taiwan and the PRC, was held in Taipei. At the conference, Chang King-yuh, a Minister without Portfolio from Taiwan, even proposed that Taiwan and China jointly map the waters for the four island groups and exercise jurisdiction accordingly.[33]

There are others in the government who would prefer cooperation with the PRC to take place within a multilateral context. Foreign Minister Fredrick Chien, for instance, has hinted that it was most unlikely for Taipei and Beijing officially to conduct joint exploitation of natural resources in the South China Sea, and that Taipei might actually side with other Asia-Pacific countries to counterbalance the PRC's assertive posture in the region.[34] It is well known that the United States has adopted a neutral stand on the merits of the territorial claims, and that Washington asserts freedom of navigation in the South China Sea and is opposed to the use of force in settling the disputes.[35] But President Lee Teng-hui has suggested that Japan and the United States could help to stabilize the South China Sea:

The one destabilizing element in South East Asia is the growth of Communist Chinese military might. The Chinese Communists want access to the South China Sea, since the amount of petroleum there could exceed that under the North Sea. Communist China and other neighboring countries have economic interests in the South China Sea. But if the United States and Japan can prevent Communist China from continuing to expand its military might in the South, there should not be any major problems.[36]

It is apparent that the Taiwan government itself is divided as to the strategy it should adopt regarding the South China Sea. Generally speaking, those sections of opinion in Taiwan that heartily endorse China's reunification believe that Taiwan should stand side by side with the PRC in refuting other claimants. Those that favour either independence or maintenance of the status quo would prefer Taiwan to ally itself with other claimants to counterbalance the PRC. If the PRC continues to isolate Taiwan in the international arena and Taiwan continues to improve its relations with South-East Asian countries, one can be sure that Taiwan would adopt a less ambiguous but more neutral stand between the PRC and other claimants to the South China Sea.

Conclusions

In the years ahead, diplomatic isolation and lack of international status could continue to trouble the government and the people of Taiwan despite the island's emerging international role as a collaborator in the regional community. The rising importance of economic indicators of national power has made Taiwan more influential on the international stage. However, Taiwan, whose population of 21 million is greater than that of two-thirds of all UN members, is still excluded from the UN and its specialized organizations. Beijing may claim that it can represent Taiwan's interests in the international arena, but the PRC has never exercised real sovereignty over Taiwan.

Agreements on the designation "Taipei, China" for Taiwan in the Asian Development Bank (ADB) signified the wisdom of compromise to untie the complicated dispute over Taiwan's representation in IGOs that had haunted Taipei and Beijing since 1949. The participation of Taipei and Beijing in the same IGOs, as in the ADB and APEC cases, doubtless helps to ease tensions between the two rival regimes. As democratization, development, and *détente* become global trends in the post-Cold War period, Taipei is looking forward to making a greater contribution to the new world order, either by acting as an economic and political development model or by helping the United Nations and other IGOs to alleviate their serious financial crises.

Beijing believes that "one country, two systems" is too generous an offer for Taipei to refuse, but what Taiwan has at present is better than anything on offer from Beijing. Though the PRC claims to want peaceful reunification, it declines to give up the option of using military force against Taiwan. The lack of such a guarantee justifies Taipei's ongoing military modernization programme and its resistance to any meaningful reunification talks, despite the reduction in tension between Taiwan and the mainland. Although the immediate impact of politics upon functionalism often becomes a problem before functionalism takes effect, Taipei believes that if both sides of the Taiwan Strait pursue common interests in non-political fields, it could eventually lead to political changes conducive to peace.

Taiwan has said that it will regard Hong Kong as a special region different from mainland China after 1997, thus justifying the continuation of direct links with the territory. Though Taipei has drafted bills regarding its future relations with Hong Kong, Taipei knows very well that it is up to Beijing to set the rules of the game. Now that talks on functional matters between the SEF and ARATS have become routine, Taipei might explore the possibility of including the implications of the Hong Kong transition on the agenda. Taiwan's high cost of living and uncertain future make it unattractive as a bolt-hole, but it might provide a refuge for some KMT followers from Hong Kong after 1997.

Taipei has adopted a low profile in the South China Sea dispute, proposing that all countries concerned settle disputes peacefully and exploring the possibility of joint exploitation of the area's natural resources. It is believed that Taipei will formulate a more comprehensive strategy regarding the South China Sea as Taiwan's southward policy begins to take root. While its power projection remains limited, Taipei will continue to favour confidence-building measures as a way of avoiding military conflict.

Taiwan has sustained two serious diplomatic setbacks – expulsion from the United Nations and loss of US recognition. Taiwan still faces a hard battle to turn its economic strength into political capital and to break out of diplomatic isolation. However, as democratization and growing self-defence capability take root in Taiwan, the people of the island are not likely to stand by as passively as residents of Hong Kong while their future is determined for them.

Notes and references

1. *Public Papers of the Presidents of the United States, George Bush, 1990, II* (Washington, DC: Government Printing Office, 1991), p. 1332; see also *Public Papers of the Presidents of the United States, George Bush, 1991, I* (Washington, DC: Government Printing Office, 1992), p. 366.
2. Lawrence Freedman (1992) "Order and disorder in the new world." *Foreign Affairs* 71(1): 21.
3. Lien Chan, "The ROC's role in a multilateral world order," *The Free China Journal*, 15 July 1994, p. 7; Jason Chih-chian Hu, "The prospects for a changing Asia: A case for open-regionalism," Government Information Office, Taipei, 18 February 1994, pp. 2–4.
4. Fredrick F. Chien (1991/92) "A view from Taipei." *Foreign Affairs* 70(5; Winter): 94.
5. Lee Teng-hui (1993) "Asia-Pacific and America." *Sino-American Relations* (Taipei) 19(3; Autumn): 13; Lee Teng-hui, "A New Asian-Pacific Order and Open Regionalism," Government Information Office, Taipei, 19 November 1993, p. 6.
6. "Snubbing Mr. Lee," *Asian Wall Street Journal*, 9 May 1994, p. 10; "Taiwan deserves respect," *International Herald Tribune*, 18 July 1994, p. 6; "Do better by Taiwan," *International Herald Tribune*, 16 August 1994, p. 6.
7. Lee Teng-hui (1993) *Creating the Future Towards a New Era for the Chinese People*. Taipei: Government Information Office, p. 29.
8. For details on Chiu's proposal and Beijing's response, see *Voice of Free China*, 19 May 1992, in *FBIS-China*, 21 May 1992, p. 54.
9. *Zhongyang ribao* (Central Daily News), 3 February 1991, p. 3.
10. *Relations Across the Taiwan Straits* (abstract), Mainland Affairs Council, The Executive Yuan, Republic of China, July 1994, p. 5; Lien Chan (1993) "The Republic of China on Taiwan belongs in the United Nations." *Orbis* 37(4; Fall): 633–641; Lien Chan (1994) "The Republic of China and the United Nations." *Strategic Review* 22(3; Summer): 7–14.
11. Fredrick F. Chien, "UN Should Welcome Taiwan," *Far Eastern Economic Review*, 5 August 1993, p. 23; "Gov't: Beijing Fuels Independence," *The China Post (Taipei)*, 18 September 1994, p. 12.
12. *Zhongyang ribao*, 18 September 1992, p. 4; 9 November 1992, p. 2; 1 April 1993, p. 2.
13. *Relations Across the Taiwan Straits* (abstract), Mainland Affairs Council, The Executive Yuan, Republic of China, July 1994, p. 8.
14. For details on the "Guidelines for National Unification," see *Lianhebao*, 21 February 1991, p. 2, in *FBIS-China*, 25 February 1991, p. 62.
15. *Gang'ao yuebao* (Hong Kong and Macau Monthly), Taipei, No. 34 (15 August 1994), p. 24; Li Rongxia, "Taiwan Investment on the Mainland," *Beijing Review*, 20–26 June 1994, p. 26.
16. For text of agreements, see *International Legal Materials*, 32(5; September 1993): 1221–1227.
17. Virginia Sheng (1994) "Talks break deadlock on hijacking, other issues." *The Free China Journal*, 12 August, p. 1.
18. "The Taiwan question and reunification of China," *Beijing Review* 36(36; 6–12 September 1993): VII–VIII.
19. Lowell Dittmer (1986) "Hong Kong and China's modernization." *Orbis* 30(3; Fall): 541.
20. *Deng Xiaoping Wenxuan* (Collection of Essays of Deng Xiaoping), vol. 3 (Beijing: People's Publishers, 1993), p. 75.
21. *Gang'ao yuebao* (Hong Kong and Macao Monthly), No. 34 (15 August 1994), p. 31; *The China Post* (Taipei), 18 February 1994, p. 4.
22. *The Free China Journal* (Taipei), 28 May 1993, p. 1.
23. *ROC Yearbook 1990–91* (Taipei: Kwang Hwa Publishing Company, 1991), p. 143.
24. *Gang'ao yuebao*, No. 34 (15 August 1994), p. 31; *Gang'ao shiwu shouce* (A Handbook of Hong Kong and Macao Affairs) (Taipei: Mainland Affairs Council, 1993), p. 95.

25. *Dalu zhengce wenda shouce* (A Question and Answer Handbook of Mainland Policy), (Taipei: Mainland Affairs Council, 1993), part 5-5.
26. Shim Jae Hoon, "Blood thicker than politics," *Far Eastern Economic Review*, 5 May 1988, p. 26; *The Free China Journal*, 22 March 1994, p. 1; *Zhongguo shibao* (The China Times), 4 February 1994, p. 4.
27. Tammy C. Peng, "ROC will protect its air and sea zones," *The Free China Journal*, 16 October 1992, p. 1.
28. Tammy C. Peng, "ROC sovereign over Spratlys," *The Free China Journal*, 8 December 1992, p. 1; see also *Free China Review*, August 1994, p. 47.
29. *ASEAN Documents Series*, 1992–1994, Supplementary Edition (Jakarta: The ASEAN Secretariat, 1994), p. 90.
30. Shim Jae Hoon, "Blood thicker than politics," *Far Eastern Economic Review*, 5 May 1988, p. 26.
31. *Jane's Defense Weekly*, 17 July 1993, p. 32.
32. *Shijie ribao* (World Journal), 12 March 1994, p. 8.
33. *Lianhebao*, 29 June 1994, p. 4.
34. *Lianhebao*, 9 December 1993, p. 4; *Zhongguo shibao*, 9 December 1993, p. 6.
35. Susumu Awanohara, "Washington's priorities," *Far Eastern Economic Review*, 13 August 1992, p. 18; Keith B. Richburg and Steven Mufson, "Saber-rattling on Spratlys raises risk of Asian conflict," *International Herald Tribune*, 6 June 1995, p. 4.
36. Lee Teng-hui, "Asia-Pacific and America," *Sino-American Relations* (Taipei) 19(3; Autumn): 12.

7

The NPT regime and denuclearization of the Korean Peninsula

Byung-joon Ahn

A test case for the NPT regime in the Korean Peninsula

Resolving the nuclear issue on the Korean Peninsula will be a test case as to whether the Non-proliferation of Nuclear Weapons (NPT) regime can be effective and denuclearization realized, especially after the United States and North Korea reached their first basic framework agreement on 21 October 1994.[1] With the death of Kim Il Sung on 8 July 1994 the Korean Peninsula is facing a period of uncertainty and challenge. In all probability it is entering a most dangerous transitional time, leading to a reunited Korea. The uncertainty boils down to what will occur in North Korea and the main challenge is how to resolve the North Korean nuclear question. The world's attention is being focused on how these issues will be played out in a strategic place where the interests of all major powers – China, Japan, Russia, and the United States – are intersecting and where the United States in particular continues to maintain up to 37,000 troops to deter another war. It is important, therefore, to examine how the future of the nuclear issue will be resolved on the Korean Peninsula for the viability of the NPT regime, along with overall peace and stability not only in the peninsula but also throughout East Asia generally.

We can raise a host of questions about the current state of, and future prospects for, the Korean Peninsula after Kim Il Sung. Can it be nuclear free? What change will occur in North Korea under Kim Jong Il, the anointed successor to Kim Il Sung? How is the nuclear issue going to be resolved? Is the "package deal" that the United States and North Korea struck in Geneva, and later renegotiated, going to produce the desired results? How will North–South Korean relations and the moves toward reunification develop? What should South Korea, the United States, Japan, China, and Russia be doing to ensure peace, cooperation, reconciliation, and orderly unification? These are but some of the questions that this chapter addresses.

The Geneva agreement on the nuclear issue came at a critical moment just when Kim Jong Il assumed power shortly after the sudden death of his father, who had been nationally revered as a demigod. Therefore, the future of the peninsula will largely depend on how North Korea under Kim Jong Il tackles change to meet the requirements of domestic and international challenges. More starkly, it will depend on whether Pyongyang transparently gives up the political imperatives of developing nuclear weapons as the last means for survival and security and chooses instead the economic imperatives of carrying out reforms and open-door policies. Whichever choice it will make is up to the North Korean people. But it is vitally important for South Korea, the United States, and Japan to contain any external provocation by sustaining their partnership for denuclearization, security, and unification on the peninsula with important support from China, Russia, and other concerned parties.

Several more observations on the future of Korea are in order. First, Kim Jong Il's rule will be a transitional one from that of Kim Il Sung to a new type yet to emerge. Initially, Kim Jong Il will try to continue his father's legacy by defending the "revolutionary" regime and the Democratic People's Republic of Korea (DPRK) in the name of *juch'e* (self-reliance) and the thought or memory of Kim Il Sung. As he is facing various economic difficulties, however, the son will be forced to accommodate some limited reforms and open policies in practice, not unlike Castro's newly reformed Cuba. If Kim Jong Il fails in this endeavour, either a military–bureaucratic coalition or a messy collapse may well be the result.

Second, since North Korea has regarded the nuclear option as the most important means for regime survival and national security, like his father Kim Jong Il will also try to ensure these core interests by normalizing relations with the United States. If he does implement freezing of the present and future nuclear programmes, as he promised in the Geneva agreement, and also fully accounts for the past nuclear record, he will be able to normalize relations and obtain economic cooperation, including light-water reactors and power grid infrastructure from South Korea. But it will be difficult for him to abandon the nuclear card once and for all, as long as he relies on the military and party seniors for his legitimacy. Hence, it is likely that the nuclear issue will remain unsettled along with the fate of the North Korean regime itself. This will be more so if the United States lets North Korea get away with a *fait accompli* of apparent nuclear capability by permanently acquiescing to its ambiguity, in keeping with America's basically meek and reactive foreign policy displayed in other regional conflicts arising in the aftermath of the Cold War.

Third, the state of North–South Korean relations is subject to the turn of domestic politics in the North and to the implementation of the US–North Korean agreement reached in Geneva. Nuclear weapons in the North not only will disrupt the balance of power and deterrence between the two Koreas but also will probably trigger nuclear proliferation in North-East Asia by prompting South Korea, Japan, and even Taiwan to develop their own countervailing nuclear capabilities. South Korea has an acute sense of being left out of the normalization process between the United States and North Korea, when the latter was willing to tackle the nuclear issue only with the United States while refusing to have any meaningful dialogue with South Korea.

It is a matter of course that, should a reformist regime emerge in the North and take the economic imperatives of survival instead of relying on the political imperatives of developing nuclear weapons, a truly new era of reconciliation and cooperation will get under way. This is the best scenario for change and reunification by mutual consent. But, sadly, we cannot also rule out other scenarios for violent change and reunification by default, depending on how such change plays out in the North and how the South might respond.

Fourth, South Korea, the United States, and Japan need to sustain their common goals, not merely on containing North Korea's current and future programmes but also on preventing the deployment of the few nuclear weapons it may have produced in the past; they should promote reunification through peaceful means by maintaining their steady partnership and by facilitating a regional approach to a nuclear-free Korea with China, Russia, and North Korea. At the same time they must be prepared for other contingencies, such as a nuclearized North Korea or even its messy break-up, by strengthening their joint deterrence and defence capabilities to meet the North's war scare and other possible provocation in case a negotiated settlement should falter. More than anything else, they must show a steady and consistent policy to accomplish peace and stability by taking quiet but effective and credible action.[2]

North Korea under Kim Jong Il: Political or economic imperatives?

North Korea under Kim Jong Il has entered an uncertain transition. He can survive by relying either on political imperatives for advocating the *juch'e* ideology at home and the one-Korea policy stemming from it in dealing with South Korea, or on economic imperatives for introducing reforms and open policies as China, Viet Nam, and even Cuba are doing. Since he was designated as the successor, and has been groomed as such since 1973 by Kim Il Sung, and since he has justified his claims to power as the most qualified successor by inheriting his father's ideology and policy in its entirety, Kim Jong Il has no choice but to try to build his legitimacy, too, by continuing the political imperatives that his father and he himself had defined. The more he tries to do so, however, the more economic difficulties and diplomatic isolation he will face. As a result, he is facing an acute dilemma of maintaining the "Old Thinking" of revolutionary and nationalist rhetoric or of exploring the "New Thinking" of reform and open policies in order to tackle the worsening shortages of food, energy, foreign exchange, and information.

How well and for how long he will be able to sustain power depends on his health and ability; on the extent to which he can preserve unity and stability among the military, the party, and his "revolutionary small groups"; on the degree to which he can feed his people; and, most importantly, on how he handles the nuclear issue. His shaky formal succession to head of state and party suggests the existence of some dissension on power-sharing within the current hierarchy. However, as long as he "adheres to and brightens our style of socialism," as Foreign Minister Kim Yong Nam said in his eulogy for the late Kim,[3] the son has to seek the following two contrasting goals.

His first goal is to guard the regime's survival in the name of the *juch'e* ideology and the unification policy of one Korea or "the Koryo Confederal Democratic Republic" as defined by Kim Il Sung. Like his father, Kim Jong Il's legitimacy rests almost entirely on this thesis of exclusive nationalism, which has been upheld under the principles of independence, peace, and a grand national unity. Now that he cannot build his legitimacy by raising the standard of living for his people, as Deng Xiaoping did in China, or by liberalizing the political system, as Boris Yeltsin and other leaders are doing in Russia and East European countries, Kim Jong Il has to rely on the unification rhetoric of "one nation, one country, and two systems, two governments," still denying the legitimacy of the Republic of Korea.

Since the very legitimacy of his regime and the first communist dynastic succession are based on this rationale, it becomes extremely difficult for Kim Jong Il to abandon it and at the same time keep his power and legitimacy in the eyes of the North Korean people. Much more difficult will be the attainment by the DPRK of genuine political reconciliation with the Republic of Korea (ROK). Hence, the DPRK is still seeking to conclude "a peace agreement" with the United States ostensibly to replace the armistice, while refusing to consider the same with the ROK. This aspect of the united-front strategy that Kim has been pursuing for his domestic interests is not well understood by Western observers.

His second goal is to defend national security and development by obtaining political recognition and economic cooperation from the United States, Japan, and other Western countries. This goal is not so different from the national interests that other states are seeking in international relations. Unlike the unification and domestic policy of one Korea, in its foreign policy, therefore, North Korea is practising a two-Korea policy in order to protect the core national interests of the DPRK as a state. This is why we call the former "political imperatives," reflecting Kim's domestic interests, and the latter "economic imperatives," reflecting his national interests. As long as Kim Jong Il tries to consolidate his power in the mantle of his father, political imperatives will remain dominant.

North Korea has used the nuclear weapons option as the best means to promote these domestic and national interests simultaneously, especially since the end of the Cold War. Faced with almost total international isolation after the Soviet Union (and later Russia) and China normalized relations with South Korea, and the severe economic disruption that resulted from both this isolation and the failure of collective and autarkic management, the North has found the nuclear card very useful in securing the survival of the regime and the state, especially when the United States has been willing to accommodate its political demands and diplomatic style of brink-manship. (A not dissimilar American accommodation or "buy-out" of certain former Soviet republics' nuclear potential has also encouraged this approach.)

It is not easy for us to delineate in precise terms the scenarios that North Korea might follow after the demise of Kim Il Sung. At the risk of oversimplification we can, nevertheless, conceive of three likely scenarios – a transitional regime under Kim Jong Il, a military–bureaucratic regime, and a violent collapse of the regime. Whichever can last the longest will depend on the quality of leadership, the cohesion of the élite, the capabilities to cope with economic problems, and the management of nuclear issues. But one thing seems clear: the regime under the Kim family is unlikely to survive for very long; North Korea is, therefore, bound to undergo structural transformations, with and without reforms.

A transitional regime under Kim Jong Il: Limited reform and engagement

Without the charisma and cult of the Kim Il Sung personality, the Kim Jong Il regime is most likely to become a transitional one before either a reformist coalition or a messy break-up takes place. For the time being, however, there is no alternative for the North Korean Labor Party, the People's Army, and the state bureaucracy other than to rally behind Kim Jong Il as their supreme leader, so that he can completely succeed to his father's legacy and unite a demoralized people. While Kim assumes power, though, he can institute only limited reforms and opening and, as long as he keeps to this slow pace, North Korea will enjoy only limited engagement with the West, such as the exchange of liaison offices with the United States without fully normalizing diplomatic relations.

Kim Jong Il has been hand-picked and groomed as the "party center" and "Dear Leader" by the "Great Leader" since the 1970s. He has cultivated his own support force of "revolutionary small groups" since the 1980s and has come to control the military as the supreme commander from the 1990s. As long as his health and competence are sufficiently good to command these groups with the support of such top leaders as Marshal O Jin U, Prime Minister Kang Song San, and Kim Il Sung's younger brother Kim Yong Ju (who returned to the Politburo in December 1993 after a long absence),

Kim Jong Il's power will be relatively safe. But there may be some doubt among these senior leaders about Kim's ability to rule without relying on his father's historical mantle and authority.

But we know very little about his real character and abilities. He has been variously connected with the kidnapping of a South Korean actress in 1978, the Rangoon bombing in 1983, and even the explosion of the Korean airliner in 1987. There has been a rumour that he was also behind Pyongyang's move to withdraw from the NPT in March 1993 and from the International Atomic Energy Agency (IAEA) in June 1994. With the exception of Jiang Zemin, Yang Shangkon, and Norodom Shihanouk, he rarely met with foreign dignitaries. Thus, he remains an unknown entity and his reported behaviour appears erratic.

In principle, Kim Jong Il has no other choice than to continue his father's line and policy; in practice, however, he needs to introduce reforms and open policies to cope with shortages of food, energy, and foreign exchange. The North's gross national product was estimated to be US$20.5 billion in 1993,[4] which was roughly one-sixteenth of the South's $328.7 billion and dropped 20 per cent from 1989 to 1993. Its foreign trade declined 1.1 per cent to $2.4 billion in 1993.[5] People are urged to have only two meals a day and factories are reported to be operating at 30 per cent capacity. The North Korean Treasury is short of foreign exchange and has been in default. For the first time in history, the regime acknowledged in December 1993 that its third 7-Year Plan had failed to accomplish the production targets. Thus, in many ways, North Korea is a sinking ship.

Kim Jong Il must try to reverse this trend. To do so, he will be forced by economic imperatives to take tentative steps toward integrating his country with the outside world, possibly with some help from China. China remains the only major power that lends support to North Korea by supplying roughly one million tons of oil and half a million tons of food every year. The entire Chinese leadership sent wreaths to the North Korean embassy in Beijing after Kim Il Sung died. Top People's Republic of China (PRC) leaders such as President Jiang Zemin and Premier Li Peng went in person to the North Korean embassy to pay their respects to the late Kim Il Sung in July 1994.

Whether Kim Jong Il can succeed with mild reform measures will depend on his decisions on abandoning the nuclear weapons aspirations by putting plutonium reprocessing on hold and by allowing transparent international inspection to verify that fact. The Geneva deal indicates that he seems to be continuing his father's policy. If he refuses to do so by implementing the contents of this agreement, however, he will inevitably face unbearable pressures and sanctions that may seriously threaten his ability to weather the economic crises.

Faced with these divisive issues, intense debates will occur in the élite circle. Subsequently, they may split into contending factions, or mass rebellions could rise up to challenge the regime when forced to face deprivation and possibly starvation. If the corruption and other immoral aspects of Kim's life are fully exposed to the public, they will probably undermine the basis of his regime, especially because its crisis-management capabilities are yet to be tested. For example, he can fall by default when he makes his own mistakes or provokes external crises to divert internal attention.

A reformist military–bureaucratic coalition regime: Extended reform and full engagement

The fall of Kim Jong Il could lead to a military–bureaucratic regime that will distance itself from the Kim dynasty by following the Chinese example of reforms and opening from above. As of now, we do not find reformers like Deng or Yeltsin, but as the real needs of the North Korean people and the outside world grow to question the viability of the Kim dynasty, their equivalents may gradually emerge in North Korea, too. The new coalition will probably be led by a collective leadership, to reflect a consensus-building process among the reformers. To maintain law and order, this leadership will try to preserve the one-party system but to carry out economic reforms and open policies along the paths taken by China and Viet Nam. Under this kind of regime, North Korea will enjoy full engagement with the United States, Japan, and South Korea by normalizing diplomatic relations and even by joining such regional organizations as the Asian Development Bank, Asia-Pacific Economic Cooperation (APEC) forum, and the Association of South-East Asian Nations (ASEAN) Regional Forum (ARF).

It is hoped that such a regime will be more conducive to accommodating the South's quest for undertaking reconciliation and the American demands for giving up the nuclear weapons programme. Hence, this is the most desirable scenario that could open a new era of smooth North–South Korean relations and North Korean integration into the world community of civilized norms and economic interdependence.

There is no guarantee, however, that such a benign evolution can be realized. For one thing, as the expectations of people rise it will become increasingly difficult to satisfy their escalating demands, given the limited availability of resources and management capabilities. Moreover, reforms can succeed only when further reforms are being carried out. But, unlike China, there has not been any agricultural reform in the North as the degree of collective farming is perhaps the highest in the world. Once the practice of "seeking truth from facts" is fully allowed, as Deng has called for, it can also accelerate a "peaceful evolution" toward capitalism and democracy. A rising revolution of frustration could topple even the reformist regime, too, as the Tiananmen incident almost did in China in June 1989.

A violent collapse: Chaos and reunification

A violent collapse could result from failure of either the Kim Jong Il regime or the military bureaucratic regime if it were challenged by an internal power struggle or civil strife. As has happened in Romania, Albania, and Bulgaria, a messy break-up of the regime can occur and result in a highly anarchic situation. It is unlikely that civil society and pluralism will develop in North Korea as it did in the other East European countries. Millions of refugees would cross the Tuman and Yalu rivers and the demilitarized zone, taking to the sea as "boat-people." This scenario is the worst, and one that South Korea, China, Japan, and the United States are trying to avoid at all costs. However, should such a chaotic situation occur, the South would have no choice but to absorb the North and achieve reunification, even if this involved enormous costs and sacrifices in terms of material and human resources. The international community would be forced to recognize this and to provide assistance.

It is against this background that one really hopes that North Korea can achieve a "soft landing" by taking the path of gradual and slow economic reform. Only when economic imperatives prevail over political imperatives can such a soft landing materialize. But, given the rigid nature of the regime and the erratic quality of Kim Jong Il's leadership, it is more likely to end with a "crash" than a soft landing. Out of such a crash will emerge another attempt to construct a reformist regime or a possibility of being reunited with the South.

North Korea's nuclear programmes and US policy

There is little doubt that North Korea has relied on the threatened nuclear weapons programme to save the regime and state in the face of enormous adversities. The United States under President Clinton tried to stop it from becoming a nuclear power by negotiation. Adroitly playing a brinkmanship game, Pyongyang had tried to get away with a *fait accompli* of nuclear weapons, while allowing only limited inspection to IAEA. Only when former President Jimmy Carter made his "private" journey to Pyongyang while Washington was considering UN sanctions against North Korea did Kim Il Sung agree to freeze his ongoing nuclear programmes in return for high-level talks with the United States. It remains to be seen whether Kim Jong Il can fully implement the framework agreement with the United States, not only by freezing the North's present and future programmes but also by dismantling the one or two bombs that it may already have in its arsenal in return for the US normalization, security guarantee, and economic cooperation, including light-water reactor technology.

North Korea's nuclear weapons programme as a means for survival

North Korea has built an impressive nuclear weapons programme and practised a delicate act of brinkmanship in negotiating with the United States as a means for its own survival. In fact, for Kim, the nuclear option has virtually become an insurance policy and a "great equalizer" in dealing with South Korea and the United States,[6] as the gap in all other aspects between North and South Korea has steadily been widening. It is important to note that the North was continuing this programme even when it was negotiating a denuclearization statement with the South, permitting some ad hoc inspection by the IAEA, and having high-level talks with the United States throughout the period 1989–1994.

The history of North Korea's nuclear programme is a chequered one and its true transparency has yet to be proven. North Korea signed the NPT in 1985 but did not sign a safeguards agreement with the IAEA until January 1992, raising suspicions about the possibilities of diverting fissile material to weapons development. In September 1991 President Bush announced that all tactical nuclear weapons would be withdrawn from foreign bases and urged President Roh Tae Woo to forego any nuclear weapons development. On 8 November 1991 Roh publicly declared a denuclearization policy for South Korea. On 31 December 1991 the North and South did sign the joint declaration on the denuclearization of the Korean Peninsula, pledging that both sides would not possess, manufacture, or use nuclear weapons or plutonium-reprocessing facilities. In January 1992 US Undersecretary of State Arnold Kanter met with Party Secretary Kim Yong Soon in New York and told him that, if the North signed the safeguards agreement and began negotiation on a North–South Korean nuclear inspection regime, the United States and South Korea would cancel their annual Team Spirit military exercises for that year only and the Americans would continue their high-level talks with the North Koreans.

The North did ratify the long-delayed safeguards agreement in April 1992 but failed to implement it satisfactorily. From May 1992 to February 1993 the IAEA conducted six ad hoc inspections on the North's 14 declared nuclear facilities. Based on sample analysis, IAEA experts found some "inconsistencies" between Pyongyang's report that it had extracted about 90 grams of plutonium just once from the experimental 5 MW reactor in Yongbyon in 1989 and their own conclusion that the North must have extracted plutonium on at least three occasions in amounts ranging between 7 and 21 kilograms (sufficient to produce one or two bombs).

From September 1992, IAEA called upon Pyongyang to clarify these discrepancies, without success. Consequently, in February 1993 it demanded an unprecedented special inspection on two suspected sites believed to store nuclear wastes, and unlimited access to a large reprocessing plant called "the radiochemical laboratory", which IAEA's Director-General, Hans Blix, had visited one year before. The North then abruptly announced a withdrawal from the NPT on 12 March 1993, protesting about IAEA's lack of "impartiality" and the US–South Korean resumption of the Team Spirit exercise. IAEA referred this matter to the UN Security Council in May, with China abstaining on the resolution. The Council adopted a measure calling upon North Korea to reconsider its NPT withdrawal decision, again with China abstaining.

After consultation with South Korea, the United States decided to hold direct negotiations with North Korea to seek a diplomatic solution. US Assistant Secretary of State Robert Gallucci and North Korean Vice Foreign Minister Kang Sok Joo had their first series of high-level talks in New York. On 11 June 1993, just 12 hours before the 90-day grace period for a legal exit from the NPT expired, they signed a joint statement in which the North promised to "suspend as long as it considers necessary" its withdrawal from the NPT and in return the United States gave the North "assurances against the threat and use of force, including nuclear weapons" and a promise of non-interference in its internal affairs. At the second round of talks in Geneva held in July, the sides not only reaffirmed the New York agreement on the "impartial" application of full-scope safeguards by IAEA but also promised to discuss the conversion of the North's graphite nuclear reactors into light-water reactors. In this second agreement, Washington pledged to have a third high-level talk within three months, on condition that Pyongyang resumed IAEA inspections and a meaningful dialogue with Seoul.

But, in the event, Pyongyang did not keep these promises. In August 1993, it allowed an IAEA team only to change films and batteries in monitoring cameras and to check seals that they had previously installed in 1992. But, from September, the North refused IAEA requests for carrying out another round of routine inspections, thus reneging on the Geneva agreement. As a result, IAEA officials could no longer guarantee the continuity of safeguards because their cameras had run out of film, batteries were allowed to expire, and official seals went unchecked.

At this time, the Clinton administration's policy was that the North had to come back fully into the NPT and to accept the full IAEA safeguard inspection, including routine and special inspections, and to accommodate a mutual inspection with the South. President Clinton stated at the fateful "Bridge of No Return" at Panmunjom in July 1993 that, if the North develops a nuclear bomb and is tempted to use it, that will mean the end of the country. On 7 November he also made a public statement, saying that North Korea will not be allowed to develop an atomic bomb.[7]

But after Pyongyang issued a statement on 11 November 1993, proposing to negotiate "a package solution" so that the United States would renounce the nuclear threat and it would comply fully with the safeguards agreement, Washington began to retreat from its previous position and switched to a "comprehensive negotiation", including presumably issues of normalization with Pyongyang. Presidents Kim Young Sam and Clinton agreed on 23 November that they would now take a "broad and thorough approach" to the nuclear issue.

From January 1994, Washington began to ask that Pyongyang only suspend its withdrawal from the NPT and just grant access to the seven declared sites, thus dropping the demand for special inspection. It also offered to cancel the Team Spirit exercise for 1994 if Pyongyang accepted these inspections. On 15 February 1994 Pyongyang advised IAEA to send a team, but when it arrived in Yongbyon in March it was prevented from collecting samples of materials and making gamma ray scans in the plutonium-reprocessing plant. Once again, the UN Security Council issued a statement on 31 March, this time with China participating, calling upon Pyongyang to comply with all IAEA's requests and instructing IAEA to report to the Council on its progress by the end of May. But Pyongyang continued to defy IAEA's requests and this was duly reported back to the United Nations. On 30 May, the UN Security Council adopted its president's statement, which called for Pyongyang to segregate and secure fuel rods from its 5 MW reactor for later measurements by IAEA.

Ignoring these demands, Pyongyang began to remove the fuel rods from the only operating reactor at Yongbyon, after having restricted IAEA personnel from taking sample materials from these rods to determine how much plutonium it had reprocessed since 1989. IAEA Director-General Blix reported to the Security Council that his agency could no longer ascertain whether nuclear material from the reactor had been diverted for other purposes, and IAEA's Board of Governors adopted a resolution on 10 June 1994, ending technical assistance to North Korea. Only then did the Clinton administration start to explore some mild sanctions by the United Nations. US Defense Secretary William Perry said that these sanctions would be aimed at two goals – removing any nuclear weapons possessed by North Korea, and sustaining the integrity of the NPT,[8] which was up for renegotiation and extension in early 1995. When Washington revealed a draft UN resolution on sanctions, however, it was "so tentative and essentially meaningless that they conveyed hesitation rather than determination," according to Henry Kissinger.[9] On 13 June, Pyongyang announced that it would immediately withdraw from IAEA and that it would not allow any IAEA inspectors inside the country, and it issued stern warnings that it would regard any sanctions as an act of war.

Under these circumstances, Jimmy Carter carried out his "private" mediation in Pyongyang from 15 to 17 June 1994, and received a pledge from Kim Il Sung not to reprocess the removed fuel rods or to refuel the reactor, and to allow two IAEA inspectors to remain continuously in Yongbyon, if Washington resumed a third round of high-level talks with Pyongyang. Clinton detected some "hopeful signs" from this and decided to suspend the sanction move and to authorize the talks with Pyongyang in Geneva, starting on 8 July 1994. Clearly, Washington's position had been one of backtracking and diverging from its original goals by being reactive yet again toward North Korea, just as it has been when faced with the problems in Somalia, Bosnia, Haiti, and Rwanda.

The Geneva agreement and afterwards

It is apparent that Kim Il Sung wanted to strike a "package deal" with Clinton by freezing North Korea's current and future pro-grammes in return for the latter's action on providing light-water reactors, diplomatic normalization, and the "negative assurances" not to attack with nuclear weapons. Clinton, on the other hand, is interested, first, in preventing Pyongyang from reprocessing the removed fuel rods, and then in stopping two other graphite-mod-erated reactors from being completed. Once these aims have been achieved, he is willing to help Pyongyang get light-water technology, to grant security assurances, and to take concrete measures of politi-cal recognition, starting with liaison offices and leading eventually to diplomatic normalization. The Geneva agreement accommodated both of these positions so that they could be implemented by 2003. It is in this sense that the agreement represents a self-fulfilling prophecy, but it also has to go through a long process of reality testing.

Implicit in these two positions, however, is the fact that Pyongyang is determined to secure the *fait accompli* of attaining nuclear capa-bility by refusing to accept any special inspection, let alone mutual inspection, of its past nuclear record. Washington is apparently pre-pared to be at least acquiescent in what Pyongyang has already accomplished. This is something that Seoul can hardly tolerate: Pres-ident Kim Young Sam has been saying that even "one-half" of a nuclear weapon in the North is unacceptable as far as the South is concerned.

Judging from the Geneva agreement, Kim Jong Il has not revised the nuclear policy that his father initiated. He agreed to forgo the reprocessing of spent fuel rods and to halt construction of two nearly completed reactors, to seal the "radiochemical laboratory," to put these facilities under IAEA "monitoring," and to remain a party to the NPT. In return, the United States promised to provide North Korea with two 1,000 MW light-water reactors and assurances against the threat or use of nuclear weapons, to make arrangements for interim energy alternatives of 100,000 tons of heavy oil to compensate for the North's loss of the graphite-moderated reactors, and to establish diplomatic "representation" in each other's capitals.[10] Thus, Washington gave Pyongyang all that it had wanted.

This agreement, though, has two major weaknesses. First, and most importantly, it has allowed the North to delay special inspection by up to five years. The South is not going to supply their share of light-water reactors unless they can guarantee that there are no bombs in the North. Yet the agreement does not provide for inspection to prove this for some time to come. If the North should get the two light-water reactors, they would be able to produce even more plutonium than with the three reactors they are to replace. Second, the 8,000 highly radioactive fuel rods that the North is cooling can be reprocessed at any time, as long as they continue to be stored in the North.

Whether Pyongyang will implement its promises, therefore, depends on how Kim Jong Il acts on these issues. His domestic imperatives call for a political negotiation with the United States, in which Washington can agree to Pyongyang's demands for replacing the existing armistice with a peace agreement in such a way that the United States will be obliged to withdraw its troops from the South, even if in gradual steps. If the military does, indeed, perceive the nuclear weapons capabilities as a solid security guarantee against the United States and South Korea, it will be difficult for Kim Jong Il to make drastic concessions that might weaken any sense of security, especially during the consolidation period of his administration when he has to defer to the military as his major source of support. But his economic imperatives call for a basic reorientation of his foreign policy by accommodating the bulk of the United States' and South Korea's demands.

The moments of truth as to how he will act should come on three crucial occasions.

The present
The first decision concerns what to do about the 8,000 removed fuel rods that, if reprocessed, could yield up to five atomic bombs. The North agreed to "dry storage" of these first, and then to move them to a third country only eight years after the agreement. Technically,

these can be kept for a longer period if the water is chemically treated, as was reported to have been done in the United Kingdom. The United States wants the rods to be internationally controlled by the IAEA and to move them to a third country, possibly China. Under the NPT it is permissible for Pyongyang to reprocess them in the presence of IAEA inspectors, but so doing may be a violation of the North–South Korean denuclearization agreement. Yet it is by no means clear whether Pyongyang will, indeed, forgo reprocessing of the spent fuel rods. It should be pointed out here that plutonium in North Korea is believed to be solely for military purposes and not for any legitimate electricity generation (cf. the Japanese commercial programme, for instance).

The future
The second decision concerns whether Kim Jong Il will freeze future programmes. The North agreed to close down the 5 MW reactor and not to refuel it with fresh rods. There is another (50 MW) reactor, in Yongbyon, which would begin operations in early 1995, and a third (200 MW) reactor, in Taechou, which would begin by 1996. When these two reactors are in operation, they are capable of producing enough spent fuel for reprocessed plutonium sufficient to manufacture at least 12 or 20 bombs per year, respectively. Graphite-moderated reactors are designed to produce spent fuel containing plutonium, in contrast to light-water reactors, which can produce only non-weapon grade fuel and therefore are less dangerous. The North pledged to shut down the graphite-moderated reactors, provided that Washington supplies 500,000 tons of diesel oil annually. In addition to the three reactors, there is a plutonium-reprocessing plant, 600 feet (~ 183 m) long, which is almost completed. In March 1994, IAEA inspectors saw evidence that a second reprocessing line is being built in this plant; the North promised to seal this plant, too.

Thus, North Korea is on the threshold of becoming a major nuclear power. It remains to be seen whether North Korea will actually abandon all these facilities, costing more than $4 billion, in return for the pledge by the United States to supply light-water reactors, which cost about the same but take up to 7–10 years to be completed. Furthermore, dismantling these facilities will cost a huge amount of money. As far as light-water reactors are concerned, the South is supposed to play the leading role in not only finance but also construction, so that it can foster confidence and linkages by facilitating exchange of personnel and technology.

By law, the United States is banned from offering such aid. Only South Korea, Japan, Russia, and other international lending institutions can offer such funds and technology. North Korea is reported to favour Russian light-water reactors financed by the United States, Japan, and South Korea. And the North Koreans apparently told the Americans, in their informal contacts in New York, that they would continue to build their graphite reactors, including the 5 MW reactor, until the replacement light-water reactors became fully operational!

The past: Special inspection

The past concerns whether the North will allow special inspection of its past nuclear behaviour. The United States allowed the North to delay this by agreeing to the following provision: "When a significant portion of the light-water reactor project is completed, but before delivery of key nuclear components, the DPRK will come into full compliance with its safeguards agreement with IAEA"; this means that it may accept special inspection on unreported nuclear sites.

North Korea "preserves permanently the ambiguity around whether or not North Korea has already developed one or two nuclear devices." Having been concerned more with deterring the North from developing nuclear weapons, South Korea has made it clear to the United States that it cannot accept such ambiguity and, therefore, consistently called for special or mutual inspection of the suspected nuclear sites in the North. Having been more concerned with global non-proliferation, however, the United States seems to have adopted the approach of accomplishing such special inspection on North Korea's past record only after freezing the present and future programmes.

The US Central Intelligence Agency believes that North Korea has one or two nuclear bombs. Vladimir Kryuchkov, the former head of the KGB, reported in February 1990 to the Soviet Politburo that North Korea had already developed a nuclear device. More recently, on 27 July 1994, Kang Myung-do, a defector identified as the son-in-law of North Korean Prime Minister Kang Song San, told a news conference in Seoul that the North already possesses five nuclear weapons, is about to develop five more, and is thus trying to buy more time by stretching out its negotiations with the United States. Yet nowhere in the Geneva agreement of August 1994 is there any provision for special, let alone mutual, inspection on suspected nuclear waste sites. In effect, this agreement has the loophole of allowing North Korea to take advantage of the ambiguity about its past nuclear behaviour, and this is one reason why South Korea and Japan are not happy about it.

The reports cited above do indicate some possibilities that the North may have hidden some weapons or facilities. This is why transparency is so crucial to find out what it has really done with the plutonium. Some American strategists even suggest that the United States should unilaterally take out the reprocessing plants before it is too late. Obviously, the major reason why this cannot be done is that it may trigger another all-out war, which would cause enormous damage and sacrifices to the Korean people.

Just how Pyongyang will make these decisions on the present, the future, and the past of its nuclear programme will be revealed in the implementing process of the US–North Korean agreement announced on 21 October 1994 and subsequently amended.[11] Judging from Pyongyang's negotiation strategy, however, there is a real danger that the "package deal" for freezing the North's current and future programme may only enable it to get away with nuclear weapons capabilities and to gain more time in which to do it. Washington's offer of liaison offices at the first phase of negotiation for this purpose and for embassies at the second phase, and of taking up Pyongyang's past record after addressing such contentious issues as medium-range ballistic missiles and biochemical weapons, can actually enhance this danger. Washington sent experts to Pyongyang to discuss possible sites for a US liaison office, even before Seoul could establish such a liaison office in Pyongyang itself. Seoul has naturally feared that Washington might strike an independent diplomatic deal with Pyongyang by uncoupling its relationship with the North from its alliance relationship with the South. To persuade the United States to improve its relations with the North in parallel with improvements in North–South Korean relations, South Korean Foreign Minister Han Sung-joo made a hastily scheduled visit to Washington in September 1994. Washington did acknowledge the need that US–North Korean talks and parallel North–South Korean dialogue should complement each other, but made it clear that it would undertake its negotiations independently without making a formal linkage with progress in the Seoul–Pyongyang talks, thus departing from the previously held practice.

Some people go as far as to say that nothing can prevent Pyongyang from having nuclear weapons and that, therefore, we should be prepared to live with this possibility and hope that Pyongyang voluntarily gives them up after diplomatic normalization with Washington. Such a development has great potential to cause strains and stresses in US–South Korean relations.

The nuclear issue and North–South Korean relations: Globalization or Koreanization?

North Korea seeks to settle the nuclear issue only with the United States, which is more interested in global non-proliferation, whereas South Korea is more interested in local deterrence. North–South Korean relations are bound to suffer and stagnate. Naturally, South Korea is acutely fearful that it is being left out of the nuclear issue, in which it has vital stakes. Taking advantage of this, the North has actually treated its relations with the South only as a necessary adjunct to improving relations with the United States. Nevertheless, the civilian government launched in February 1993 under President Kim Young Sam was so concerned with the task of carrying out domestic reforms, in order to fight political corruption and to revitalize economic competitiveness, that its foreign policy, too, had to be reactive to changes in US and North Korean policies by improvising with short-term responses.

The South has stipulated that the United States must consult with it first, before conducting any negotiation with the North, and should make it clear to the North that, unless the North fully normalizes its relations with the South, the United States cannot do so with the North. Moreover, accomplishing a nuclear-free Korea requires North and South Korea to implement the denuclearization agreement that they reached in 1991. If it turns out that only the North possesses nuclear weapons, the South has no choice but to reconsider this agreement, for it can destroy deterrence and the prospects for reunification.

Once the North changes its internal politics sufficiently to abandon the nuclear option, it should be possible for the two Koreas to expand areas of common interests in the security and economic fields, before bringing about a reunited nation, either by mutual consent or by default.

The impact of North Korean nuclear weapons on South Korea: Erosion of deterrence and reunification

While the negotiations on the nuclear issue are being directly conducted between the United States and North Korea, South Korea cannot help but resent being excluded from them. Moreover, the impact of North Korea's nuclear arsenal on South Korea and on the North-East Asian region, including Japan, is far-reaching in terms of security and nuclear non-proliferation. Assuming that only the North possesses nuclear weapons and the South does not, this will certainly upset the military balance and deterrence between the two sides by eroding the US military presence and the South's ability to deter the North from undertaking military provocation. In particular, there is some doubt whether Washington would really keep its forward deployment intact after the North is fully equipped with nuclear arsenals.

The motivation for the North to develop nuclear weapons may well be defensive, but it is certain that the presence of such weapons will enable the North to blackmail the South in ways that cannot easily be ignored. Furthermore, the North's reactors are of the Chernobyl type and unsafe. More importantly, if the Kim Jong Il regime survives with nuclear weapons, it will make it quite difficult for the South to realize reunification by mutual consent through a gradual process of peaceful coexistence and confidence-building measures.

Considering these facts, a nuclearized North Korea will certainly cause South Korea to reconsider its denuclearization stand, and possibly Japan to do likewise and to build an equivalent deterrence with some delivery systems to cope with North Korea's nuclear weapons. Now that there is no nuclear power directly threatening the United States itself, "the sad fact is that extended deterrence – the ability of the US nuclear force to protect its allies – is dead." Neither is it realistic to expect that the United States can bring tactical nuclear weapons back into South Korea.

An additional factor is that North Korea can sell nuclear material and weapons to such countries as Iran, Libya, Iraq, and Syria. Such a denouement could irreparably damage the NPT, which was confirmed and extended indefinitely in 1995. At the present time, the United States is most concerned about this possibility. In short, by all accounts, the possibility of Kim Jong Il possessing a nuclear arsenal is perceived by many to be a nightmare, and this prospect will remain the most important challenge to South Korea. It is South Korea's firm stand that it cannot tolerate a permanent ambiguity about North Korea's past nuclear record and, therefore, cannot provide light-water reactors unless the North proves that it does not have nuclear weapons by accepting either special or mutual inspection on the suspected sites. Should the United States let North Korea get away with nuclear weapons, it will undermine the credibility of its security commitment and cause a greater degree of anti-American sentiment in South Korea.

After the Basic Agreement and the denuclearization declaration

It should be recalled that the prime ministers of North and South Korea put in force on 19 February 1992 two historic documents – the "Agreement on Reconciliation, Nonaggression, Exchange and Cooperation between North and South" (the Basic Agreement) and a "Joint Declaration of the Denuclearization of the Korean Peninsula." These are gentlemen's agreements in the sense that only when the parties voluntarily adhere to them can they be adequately implemented. Apparently, the sea change in the international environment after the end of the Cold War prompted Kim Il Sung to ratify these agreements. Had they been fully implemented, they would have really opened a new chapter of North–South Korean cooperation.

Unfortunately, the North dashed this hope the moment that the two sides tried to implement them. Beginning in June 1992, for example, Pyongyang refused to carry out the agreed mutual nuclear inspection and at the end of the year it broke off the Joint Nuclear Control Commission with Seoul. Kim Il Sung seemed to have concluded that fully implementing the two agreements, as hoped for by the South, would jeopardize the very legitimacy of his regime: for instance, it could open the door for the South to air the winds of capitalist ideas and democratic freedom in the North Korean political system.

And yet President Kim Young Sam genuinely set out to build a new relationship with the North in the spirit of nationalism. In his inaugural address, for example, he said: "No ally can be better than our nation; no ideology or thought can bring greater happiness than our nationalism." Subsequently, in March 1993, he allowed Li In-mo, a former North Korean war correspondent, to be sent back to the North out of humanitarian considerations.

Without displaying any reciprocal reaction to these gestures of goodwill, however, in April 1993 Kim Il Sung revealed a new "Ten-Point Program for Grand Union of All Korean People," with such preconditions as the suspension of US–Korean diplomatic cooperation, of the Team Spirit exercise, and of "reliance on foreign forces," coupled with the withdrawal of American troops. This new programme failed to mention either the Basic Agreement or the denuclearization statement, but called for the exchange of special envoys to discuss his proposal. Obviously, he had decided to make a breakthrough in North Korea's relations with the United States by openly playing the nuclear card.

After some resistance, President Kim Young Sam accepted Kim Il Sung's proposal for the exchange of special envoys so that they could discuss methods of realizing a North–South Korean summit. Four preliminary contacts were made at Panmunjom to prepare for the exchange, but with little progress. The North reiterated its unrealistic demands, that the South should suspend the Team Spirit exercise and its international collaboration with the United States, as a precondition for realizing such an exchange of special envoys. The South could not accommodate these overreaching conditions. It was at the last contact, in March 1994, that the Northern delegate accused the South of inciting war and made the ominous remark that, if war comes, "Seoul would be engulfed in a sea of flames."

Nevertheless, at the Clinton administration's urging, on 15 April 1994 Seoul did drop the idea of having an exchange of special envoys, to remove any potential obstacle to launch a third round of US–North Korean talks. Thus, Seoul had actually made every effort to avoid provoking Pyongyang, even to the extent of delaying Washington's plans for deploying the Patriot missiles. But after the war threat was made so menacingly, these missiles and other equipment were quickly brought in, without much opposition. Nationwide civil defence drills were resumed, and CNN-TV depicted these as if the entire Korean Peninsula was on the brink of another war.

After these ominous developments, the North unilaterally withdrew its officers from the Military Armistice Commission in April 1994, in clear violation of the Basic Agreement in which it had promised to "endeavor to transform the present state of armistice into a solid state of peace between the North and the South," and to "abide by the present Military Armistice Agreement until such a state of peace has been realized." Despite these promises, after North Korean Vice Foreign Minister Song Ho-kyong had met his Chinese counterpart, Tang Jiaxuan, on 2 September 1994, Beijing announced its decision to withdraw its representatives from the Military Armistice Commission at Panmunjom, thus abetting Pyongyang's quest for negotiation of a peace agreement with Washington, ostensibly to replace the armistice.

These actions by the North compelled the South to consolidate publicly its security cooperation with the United States by hinting at the possibility of resuming the Team Spirit exercise and other joint defence efforts. Meanwhile, tensions were rising after Pyongyang acted in open defiance of IAEA inspection and of the United States move for sanctions at the United Nations.

North–South summit?

It was against this background that US Ambassador James T. Laney is reported to have arranged the Carter mission to avert the possibility of imminent war. South Korean President Kim Young Sam immediately accepted Kim Il Sung's wish to meet him unconditionally, when Jimmy Carter conveyed it to him in Seoul. This paved the way for Deputy Prime Minister Lee Hong Koo and Party Secretary Kim Yong Soon to schedule what would be the first summit, for 25 July in Pyongyang, when they had their preparatory meeting on 28 June. Working groups from both sides busily cooperated on further details for the summit. There were considerable expectations for this historic event, for many people entertained rather high expectations that it could somehow contribute to easing the rising tension and to tackling the nuclear issue once and for all. But Kim Il Sung passed away suddenly on 8 July 1994 and the summit was postponed indefinitely by Pyongyang.

Upon hearing the news of Kim's death, President Kim Young Sam said that he regretted the missed opportunity of a summit, and ordered the entire armed forces to be placed on alert. Surprisingly, President Clinton sent a message of condolence to the North Korean people on behalf of the American people, departing from the previous practice by which an American president would first reaffirm the US commitment to the security of South Korea in times of uncertainty.

No wonder that a few national assemblymen of the opposition set out to urge the South Korean government to send a mission of condolence. But this triggered an outburst of protests condemning such attempts, because most South Koreans still regarded Kim Il Sung as a war criminal. Nevertheless, some radical students belonging to the so-called "*juch'e* thought faction" went as far as to post placards praising Kim Il Sung as a great nationalist hero and to stage a funeral service in his honour. These incidents prompted Prime Minister Lee Young Duck to make a cool public statement on 18 July: "History has already passed Judgement on Kim Il Sung as being responsible for a number of national tragedies, especially the perpetuation of

territorial division and the fratricidal Korean War." The Foreign
Ministry released some old Soviet documents forwarded by Russian
President Yeltsin, containing the new revelation that Kim Il Sung had
planned the Korean War with Josef Stalin and Mao Zedong in 1949–
1950.

Perhaps in response to these reactions in the South, Pyongyang's
propaganda machine resumed its bitter diatribes on the South
Korean government and on President Kim in particular. It focused its
verbal attacks on President Kim for having put the armed forces on
special alert and banning condolence activities. Meanwhile, in the
North, representatives of the army, the government, and the party
were pledging their allegiance to Kim Jong Il as their new Great
Leader.

Should this war of words continue, it will be difficult, if not impossible, for the sides to realize an early summit between Kim Young
Sam and Kim Jong Il. When Amnesty International disclosed, on
1 August 1994, a list of 55 political prisoners held in North Korea
that included Ko Sang-mun (a South Korean schoolteacher who had
mysteriously disappeared while in Norway in 1979), President Kim
Young Sam directed his cabinet to find ways of repatriating Mr. Ko
through international humanitarian organizations. Apparently, the
South wants to wait until the new ruler of the North proves that
he can hold onto his power more securely. Even if a summit is held,
it would be unlikely that the South would consider dropping its
demands for nuclear transparency and the mutual inspection to verify
it in the North.

In November 1994, Seoul announced its new policy on resuming
economic cooperation with Pyongyang by allowing businessmen to
visit the North and to make investments of up to US$5 million.
Pyongyang immediately refused to respond positively to this offer by
characterizing it as an evil design. In short, until the Kim Jong Il
regime can consolidate its power on a more secure basis, North–
South Korean relations are not expected to be greatly improved.

Reunification by consent or by default

The possibility of political change in the North has rekindled our
interest in the prospects for Korean reunification. Obviously, while
the Kim Jong Il regime continues there are serious differences in
philosophy and possibly insuperable barriers to real reconciliation.
The South sees reunification as a mutual process of peace, coopera-

tion, conciliation, and integration but the North sees it as an end to building a federal state. Unless the North finds some other means by which it can legitimize itself, other than the revolutionary cant derived from the *juch'e* ideology, it will be unrealistic to expect that the two sides could establish a Korean commonwealth or a national community of common interests and accomplish reunification by mutual consent. Even if such reunification is formally achieved, its sustainability would still be in doubt, as the recent tragic example of Yemen has demonstrated. In Korea, too, therefore, reunification may well come by default (as it did in Germany) rather than by design.

Whatever scenario of reunification actually materializes in Korea depends on what political changes take place in the North and on what decisions the North will make on the nuclear question. The late Kim Il Sung allegedly used to become almost hysterical about any "reunification by absorption." The South has also been wary of this possibility, for no other reason than that it will cost more than US$1 million million over 10 years, which it cannot adequately assume unaided. On the other hand, the two sides share another deep interest in common – neither wants reunification by war. China and Japan may secretly prefer a divided Korea and might see in "a modest North Korean nuclear capability a means to guarantee it," as Kissinger adroitly pointed out.

Given the present state of international affairs, therefore, the highest priority is to prevent nuclear weapons and war by peacefully managing North–South Korean relations. If the North comes to accept transparency as the first step to building confidence measures, it should be possible for these states to negotiate arms control in conventional forces. Once the nuclear suspicion is satisfactorily cleared up, they can carry out mutually beneficial economic exchanges, even though they differ in political ideology and system. Seoul is prepared to help Pyongyang to convert its graphite nuclear reactors into South Korean-style light-water reactors by bearing some financial and technological burden.

It is in the interests of South Korea that North Korea opens up its economy and joins such multilateral cooperation endeavours as APEC and ARF. Since the late Kim Il Sung visited China in November 1991, North Korea has been trying to emulate the example of the successful Chinese open policy by designating Rajin, Sun-bong, and Chongjin as "free trade zones" and by showing greater interest in the Tumen River development project being sponsored by the United Nations Development Programme (UNDP). Indirect trade between North and South Korea reached about US$200 million in 1992 but declined to less than US$180 million in 1993 because of the nuclear issue. Should North Korea open up, it will naturally be the South Koreans who would like to make investments there, just as the fabulously successful overseas Chinese have poured their investments and talents back into China.

This state of peaceful coexistence and economic cooperation is what the South genuinely wants to institutionalize as early as possible. But without some measure of compatible values between them, reunification by consent is unlikely to be achieved. In order for the North to meet these conditions, its political system must be sufficiently transformed to accommodate pluralism and interdependence. President Kim Young Sam declared on 15 August 1994 that his philosophy of unification is liberal democracy, and called upon the country to prepare for the advent of unification that may come at any time. In the short run, this was a clarification of his views on unification, especially when some radical elements advocating the *juch'e* thought of Kim Il Sung were raising their voice; in the long run, however, it set forth his vision for the direction of a reunited Korea. Unification, however, will probably not come by design; it is more likely to come by default, if at all.

Ultimately, reunification is for the Koreans to decide themselves, but it must be carried forward in a manner that does not harm regional stability. Hence, Korean efforts at peace and reunification need international support and guarantee from concerned powers and the world community. If a two-plus-four regional forum involving China, Japan, Russia, the United States, and the two Koreas, or a North-East Asian security forum, can contribute to these goals, it must be convened as early as possible. In this sense, *Koreanization* of the unification question (meaning normalization of North–South Korean relations) and globalization of it must complement each other as the goal of denuclearization between North and South Korea.

A regional approach to a nuclear-free Korea?

At this time of great uncertainty, when anything can happen in North Korea, what is most needed is a steady US–Japanese–South Korean partnership to make the newly emerging Kim Jong Il regime unambiguously give up a nuclear weapons programme and opt for peace and gradual reunification. When they do so, they can accomplish a regional approach to a nuclear-free Korea by establishing a strategic understanding with China and Russia that would help North Korea faithfully to implement the Geneva agreement and guarantee denuclearization on the peninsula.

Keeping North Korea from becoming a nuclear power requires the United States to exercise decisive leadership with clear goals, consistent policy, credible action, and timely decisions. First, the United States and South Korea must reaffirm the original goals of preventing nuclear weapons in the North and of ensuring denuclearization of the peninsula, not merely by freezing the current and future nuclear programmes of the North but also by fully accounting for its past records through transparent inspections by IAEA, as provided by the NPT, and through mutual inspection between North and South Korea. This is important because there has been real and lingering fear in South Korea that the Clinton administration was so preoccupied with keeping the North Korean threat off the front pages through the mid-term elections that it failed to hold out for more certain ways of preventing nuclear weapons in the North, thereby letting Kim Jong Il get away with nuclear weapons capabilities through permanent ambiguity.

Consistency must be restored in the policy of upholding the principle that only *after* the North allows unimpeded inspection by IAEA and mutual inspection by the two Koreas on its nuclear facilities and two undeclared waste sites can the United States actually establish diplomatic relations and South Korea construct light-water reactors. It is important to note that the US Senate unanimously passed a bill stating that "no funds appropriated under this or any other act may be made available to North Korea until the President certifies and reports to Congress that North Korea does not possess nuclear weapons, has halted its nuclear weapons program and has not exported weapon-grade plutonium." The Republican Congress may well prompt the Clinton administration to abide by this provision.

To prevent the North from continuing this brinkmanship game with impunity, we need some hard-nosed strategic thinking on making the North keep its promises. We must prepare for the possibility that implementation may fail, for as long as Pyongyang regards the nuclear option as a last means for regime survival it will be reluctant to give this up, unless on pain of losing something much more important than a few nuclear devices. According to a psychological school of international relations, people are generally more reluctant to give up something they already possess than to clamour for new things. States, too, tend to cooperate in order to avoid losses rather than to enjoy gains.

Washington needs to be particularly cautious not to transform the implementation talks with Pyongyang into what could be long and sterile political negotiations. The more the United States prolongs its direct negotiations with the North in this manner, the more the North will try to relegate its talks with the South to the status of being only ancillary to its talks with the United States. Such negotiations will definitely damage not only the chances for a basic political reconciliation between the two Koreas, on which an ultimate solution depends, but also the US–South Korean relationship, which is more important than the US–North Korean relationship.

It is time to take "a very firm stand and very strong actions," as US Secretary of Defense William Perry once suggested, to make the North comply with the requirements of global non-proliferation and North–South Korean mutual inspection. To cope with possible military provocation by the North, the United States must quietly prepare effective and "prudent defensive measures" (again in Perry's apt expression) along with South Korea, by enhancing their joint deterrence capabilities in the South and its vicinities.

Most importantly, the United States, Japan, and South Korea must enlist the support of China and Russia for a regional solution to the nuclear challenge. China has consistently opposed any pressure or sanction in favour of dialogues, without specifying how it can facilitate such dialogues. Now that the United States has reached a package deal with North Korea with China's help, it is incumbent upon China to help maintain this agreement as anticipated. And Russia is trying to sell its version of light-water reactors. While visiting Seoul on 25 July 1994, Tomiichi Murayama, Japan's first Socialist Prime Minister in 48 years, confirmed that his government will continue the foreign policies of the preceding governments. Japan may share the cost of light-water reactors with South Korea, provided that North Korea can account for its past nuclear records.

Since China is holding a key to persuading North Korea to enforce the nuclear agreement, the United States and Japan must stress the priority of resolving the North Korean nuclear issue in their bilateral talks with China. China must be told clearly that its failure to play a truly constructive role beyond merely advocating dialogues will irreparably damage its bilateral relations with the United States and Japan. If China can be swayed to join a "two plus four" forum on the nuclear issue, this North-East Asian security dialogue will have a better chance of realization.

Notes and references

1. Agreed Framework Between the Democratic People's Republic of Korea and the United States of America, Geneva, October 21, 1994, reproduced in full at appendix 3.
2. Byung-joon Ahn (1994) "The man who would be Kim." *Foreign Affairs*, November–December, pp. 94–108.
3. *Korea Herald*, 21 July 1994.
4. In this chapter, as throughout this volume, costs in dollars are US dollars, unless stated otherwise.
5. Ibid., 8 July 1994.
6. Andrew Mack, "North Korea isn't playing games, it wants the Bomb," *International Herald Tribune*, 3 June 1994.
7. *U.S.A. Today*, 8 November 1993.
8. *International Herald Tribune*, 6 June 1994.
9. Henry A. Kissinger, "Tell it straight to North Korea – but talking may not be enough," ibid., 4 July 1994.
10. *Korea Herald*, 14 August 1994.
11. See Joint DPRK–US Press Statement, Kuala Lumpur, 12 June, 1995, reproduced in full at appendix 4.

8

Defiance versus compliance: North Korea's calculation faced with multilateral sanctions

Peter Hayes

Introduction

In this chapter, I examine the application of American hegemonic power in the post-Cold War era to a major challenge to the global nuclear non-proliferation regime – the case of North Korea. By "hegemonic" power, I mean a peculiar and unique combination of (1) a consensual ideology, (2) institutional integration between the hegemon and its aligned and allied states, and (3) unique power capabilities (not merely military, but also political and economic, even environmental assets).

In the case of North Korea (DPRK), ideology has ruled supreme, as represented in the virtual isolation of the DPRK in UN General Assembly votes on its position on the Non-proliferation of Nuclear Weapons Treaty (NPT), as well as at the International Atomic Energy Agency (IAEA) Board of Governors and the UN Security Council. But non-proliferation values and norms have failed to bring North Korea back into the NPT and to observe its IAEA safeguards obligations. Institutional integration, as represented by its alliances with the Republic of Korea (ROK) and Japan, combined with its alignments and coordinated diplomacy with Russia and China, have also failed to make the DPRK conform. Finally, US nuclear threats and military forces have not compelled the DPRK to abandon its nuclear challenge, and to observe its international obligations to not allow the proliferation – or the threat of proliferation – of nuclear weapons.

In such a circumstance, the United States has drawn on a combination of its political and economic resources to reassure the DPRK that it does not intend to crush the post-Kim Il Sung state system, and that the regime's survival rests on its willingness to cooperate rather than to confront the international system. In this approach, the United States has relied more on its economic power and ability to create an international consortium of great powers capable and willing to provide major economic resources to the DPRK, along with important political and security assurances. To date, however, it remains unclear if this application of hegemonic power will suffice to achieve the goals of the United States and the international community.

This chapter examines why the economic instruments of American power may have been inadequate to date. Rather than focusing on the already obvious – the difficulties in orchestrating economic sanctions in a punitive campaign aimed at rolling back, weakening, or deterring North Korea from proceeding further with its nuclear proliferation activities – I concentrate on the more novel effort to wield "positive power" by offering the DPRK economic inducements, called often (and misleadingly) "carrots" by media covering the recent negotiations between the United States and the DPRK.

Method and qualifications

To understand why North Korea has simultaneously confronted and cooperated with the international community, one must examine the prospective losses and gains associated with its continued compliance versus defiance of the IAEA/NPT regime. The North Korean nuclear battering ram has forced the US leadership to clarify its intention over the last six months. The North Koreans correctly interpreted the US leadership in the latter half of 1994 as united as to what North Korea has to do to satisfy the international community, but divided, confused, and immobilized as to what the United States and the international community must do for North Korea. Now, specific inducements are being offered to North Korea that may be of very high political value to the North Korean leadership. In addition to the political–military assurances on the table and the prospective transfer of US\$4 billion worth of safer light-water reactors, the United States has indicated that it is willing to collaborate with North Korea on a range of non-nuclear energy problems, the overcoming of which would be of great political value to Pyongyang.[1]

In this analysis, I define a hypothetical North Korean calculation faced with sanctions on the one hand, and substantial inducements on the other.[2] Such a definition requires facing two tricky problems, namely (1) deducing what elements are contained in North Korea's calculation in evaluating the impact of sanctions, assuming North Korea to be a unitary, rational actor, and (2) calculating the approximate net annual costs to North Korea over the next few years of complying with versus defying the international community with respect to nuclear safeguards obligations.

These calculations and elements contained therein must be estimated relative to a meaningful baseline. I have adopted the current situation extrapolated for a year as the relevant baseline against which alternative scenarios are to be measured. This scenario is one in which North Korea is in non-compliance with its IAEA safeguards obligations, but is in an ambiguous status in that it has neither departed nor been evicted from NPT membership. This baseline itself entails costs and benefits for North Korea, but differs crucially with respect to the compliance and defiance scenarios in that no inducements are provided (but no sanctions are applied either).

Relative to this "status quo" baseline, I conclude that if North Korea encounters ambitious, multilateral sanctions as a result of its NPT non-compliance, then it could arguably lose up to \$1 billion/ year, or the loss of 5 per cent of its annual Gross National Product (GNP). The critical factors in this scenario are an ambitious set of economic sanctions, implemented multilaterally, that impose substantial direct costs on the North Korean economy.

In contrast, compliance with its NPT safeguards provides little marginal economic benefit to North Korea (relative to the status quo baseline scenario). This remarkable result underscores the importance of accounting for all the categories of costs and benefits, and the substantial savings in conventional force costs that a proliferating state can arguably accrue from a nuclear weapons programme – exactly the rationale of US nuclear forces in the NATO context for decades before the Cold War ended.

Readers should note a number of important caveats that apply to this essay. First, this analysis is static: it extends over only one year, and does not address the specific time horizons over which sanctions could be imposed on North Korea, or inducements delivered to and absorbed by North Korea. I assume also that neither side will escalate to war over sanctions; thus, no costs from a direct military confrontation are included. Nor do I address the political costs to the Clinton administration of undertaking the requisite arm-twisting at home and abroad to achieve multilateral sanctions or to deliver a substantial package of inducements. Also, the ongoing economic decline would be magnified by sanctions or continued under the status quo baseline scenario, but these indirect costs are not considered. Yet these indirect costs (or benefits) might be substantial in either of the alternative scenarios.

Three other considerations should be kept in mind before we explore this terrain. First, this exercise is strictly heuristic. The magnitudes used for costs and benefits are unofficial estimates, based on my own knowledge of the North Korean economy and the minimal published official data issued by North Korea itself, by international organizations, and by other sources, which often are of unknown or dubious authenticity. My main objective is to delineate the categories of costs and benefits; to determine whether they are positive or negative, whatever their magnitude; and to examine the overall economic logic of the starkly divergent options facing North Korea.

The advantage of this disaggregated approach is that it is transparent. Sceptics are welcome to change the categories, the magnitudes, and the signs, to determine the sensitivity of the overall impact of a scenario to a different combination of variables. The fact that the calculation can be decomposed points to a second important issue that arises from this analysis: hypothetical North Korean calculations are not simple but are complex, and the size and probability of many of the putative costs and benefits that enter the picture are highly uncertain. In spite of the Washington pundits, there are no simple truths as to what constitutes North Korea's advantage in ending the current stand-off. Even with the many simplifying assumptions used in this analysis, it is far from self-evident where North Korea's interests lie.

Third, I am not suggesting that any of these calculations are the actual intellectual constructs guiding North Korean decision-making, let alone the quantitative estimates provided here. North Koreans have complex motivations, including abundant historical and cultural factors that inform their behaviour, apart from economic concerns. Also, North Korea is not a unified, monolithic state, however totalitarian its political culture. Bureaucratic politics matter in Pyongyang, as anywhere else.[3] External pressures and circumstances have also changed radically, and generally to North Korea's disadvantage in the last decade, whatever the impact of domestic factors on decision-making. It would be a great mistake – albeit one often made in Washington – to reduce North Korean psychology and political culture to a crude "carrots and sticks" cost–benefit calculation, or to assume that North Korea's leadership exercises effective control over every aspect of North Korean behaviour.

In spite of these caveats, a number of important conclusions arise from this attempt to understand the North Koreans' dilemmas. Most obviously, North Korea faces a stark and inevitable choice between accelerating economic decline and the opportunity to revive its ailing economy (assuming that it takes the other requisite steps to commence an economic transition, requisite structural adjustments, and reforms of its command-and-control economy, all of which are largely responsible for its present economic crisis).[4]

Another noteworthy result is that developing and/or deploying a nuclear weapon may have substantial economic benefits for North Korea in the status quo scenario. That is, assuming that North Korea neither faces sanctions nor obtains inducements, having a nuclear force may allow the North Koreans to reduce their conventional military expenditure (or to avoid expanding it in the future). The implication of this cost-saving dimension of the nuclear weapons programme is that sanctions alone – or threats of sanctions – are unlikely to induce changes in its behaviour unless they are accompanied by very substantial – and highly credible – positive inducements to comply. Conversely, going nuclear may offer substantial savings that may be as large as inducements to comply. *For this reason, political benefits may be as important as (or more important at the margin than) economic inducements to comply.*

If this analysis is correct, then the North Korean cost–benefit analysis will tilt – eventually – toward compliance. Put another way, continuing defiance that results in the application of sanctions implies that North Korea's leaders value the political influence of nuclear weapons and the political control associated with high conventional force levels at more than $1 billion/year, and are concerned over the costs of "coming clean."

The analysis also has some important implications for the costs that the international community must bear for a peaceful resolution of the nuclear stand-off with North Korea. In particular, specific inducements that can be delivered very quickly and relatively cheaply may be needed to buttress the credibility of commitments concerning items that will take a long time to deliver to North Korea, such as the light-water reactors.

And finally, it may be as cheap (or much cheaper) to provide inducements to achieve North Korean compliance as (than) it would be to offset a North Korean nuclear weapon with US nuclear forces and upgraded conventional readiness levels – let alone to fight a war over the issue with North Korea. Buying the compliance of hard-core proliferating states may not be the neatest or most politically correct way to maintain and extend the global non-proliferation regime, but from a *realpolitik* perspective it may be the cheapest and only way to do so. But, worryingly, North Korean compliance is probably not for sale, given that defiance on the one hand and continued studied ambiguity on the other seem to offer virtually the same economic benefits to North Korea. From the economic perspective portrayed in this essay, there is not much to choose between the status quo and compliance options. The real choice is between these latter two options and the defiance scenario that would result in expensive sanctions.

Sanctions, however, are difficult to administer against North Korea. Short of sanctions, North Korea is not compelled to choose on economic grounds between full compliance and ambiguous defiance. This analytic result is consistent with the otherwise inexplicable behaviour on the part of North Koreans at this time; to many external observers who have not examined closely the actual situation, such behaviour appears to consist of irrational gyrations.

Thus, US negotiating strategy is unlikely to succeed unless economic inducements and threats are accompanied by credible and meaningful political and military assurances such as normalization of relations, negative security assurances, and the easing of North Korean entry into international institutions such as the World Bank and the Asian Development Bank.

The next two sections explain the derivation of the compliance and defiance scenarios in more detail.

The logic of North Korean nuclear compliance and defiance

In this section, I define plausible North Korean calculation for evaluating its defiance versus compliance options.

The net benefit of compliance is the sum of the elements of cost

Table 8.1 **The calculation of North Korean nuclear compliance**

Benefits
   B: Benefits of complying, that is:
   +B1: no sanctions
   +B2: inducements to comply
   +B3: avoided cost of bomb option
   +B4: reduced cost of conventional forces due to lowered tensions post
         compliance

Costs
   C: Costs of forgoing benefits of non-compliance, that is:
   −C1: political value of the bomb to North Korea
   −C2: political ignominy of admitting past errors or lies about programme
   −C3: nuclear substitution for conventional forces, no benefit if complies

Net benefit of compliance
   Equals the sum of:
   $B1 + B2 + B3 + B4 - C1 - C2 - C3$

and benefit shown in table 8.1. On the benefit side of the equation, these elements are (1) no sanctions, (2) the value of inducements to comply, (3) the avoided cost of developing nuclear weapons, and (4) the reduced cost of conventional forces due to lowered tensions after North Korea moves into compliance.

On the cost side of the equation, the costs of compliance and forgoing the benefits of non-compliance are (1) forgoing the political value of nuclear weapons to North Korea's rulers, both domestically and internationally, (2) the cost of truth, that is, admitting the truth in relation to past reprocessing activity or nuclear weapons programmes, and (3) the inability to substitute nuclear for conventional forces.

The equation for the net cost of defiance, on the other hand, inverts these costs and benefits, which are shown in table 8.2. On the benefit side of the equation, these elements are (1) the political value of nuclear weapons to North Korea, (2) not having to admit past reprocessing or weapons-building activity, and (3) substituting nuclear for conventional forces. On the cost side of the defiance equation are found (1) the cost of sanctions resulting from defiance, (2) forgone inducements, (3) the cost of developing nuclear weapons, and (4) the increased cost of conventional forces due to increased tensions in the light of defiance.

Table 8.2   **The calculation of North Korean nuclear defiance**

Benefits
   B: Benefits of defiance, that is:
   +B1: political value of the bomb to North Korea
   +B2: avoided cost of truth
   +B3: substitution of nuclear for conventional forces

Costs
   C: Costs of compliance and forgoing benefits of compliance, that is:
   −C1: cost of sanctions
   −C2: forgone inducements
   −C3: cost of developing the bomb
   −C4: increased cost of conventional forces due to increased tensions in light of
          defiance

Net cost of defiance
   Equals the sum of:
   $B1 + B2 + B3 - C1 - C2 - C3 - C4$

North Korea's calculation

In table 8.3, I list the elements contained in a posited North Korean cost–benefit calculation, with estimated values for each elements as derived in the rest of this section. These are described below.

Sanctions

The direct cost of sanctions at the end of a year is estimated to reach five per cent of North Korea's GNP, or about $1 billion/year. This estimate is based on the history of sanctions campaigns contained in Elliott's paper,[2] and my own unpublished estimates of the crippling effects of the current and prospective embargoes on North Korea's economy. The latter includes marginal impacts of tightened Coordinating Committee for Export Control (COCOM) restrictions on North Korea's imports, a partial constriction of yen flows from Japan, and a partial cut-off of Russian and Chinese trade and investment, assuming that Moscow and Beijing do not totally control provincial corporations involved with North Korea.

These are the costs to North Korea's economy of an ambitious set of sanctions applied multilaterally in the case of defiance. In the cases of compliance or continued ambiguity, there is no cost from sanctions to North Korea. (As noted earlier, relaxation of existing sanctions [benefit] or tightening of existing sanctions [cost] are not included in this calculation.)

Inducements

These are positive sanctions or post-compliance benefits that the international community would give North Korea for good behaviour. The rewards are political and economic in nature and would flow directly from successful conclusion and implementation of the US–DPRK talks and agreements. I have set the upper level of inducements at $0.4 billion/year, constituted by an annuity associated with the proposed transfer of a light-water reactor supported by a $4 billion loan at 5 per cent interest over 30 years (assuming that the North Koreans do not prepay interest or principal on this loan), and another $45 million of coal or oil to substitute for North Korea's non-operation of 255 MW of existing or forgone nuclear plant. This figure is 40 per cent of that committed in February 1994 to the Ukraine ($1 billion) to induce it to abandon a whole arsenal of strategic nuclear weapons. It is hard to imagine that the North Koreans can push the inducement package any higher than this prior benchmark of US "willingness to pay" for NPT compliance, although they tried to do so in the September–October 1994 talks with the United States by making meaningless demands for $2 billion compensation for their three decades of sunk cost in obsolete nuclear technology. (To repeat, the trade/investment impacts of lifting the existing US-led embargo against the DPRK are not included in this analysis.)

Cost of the nuclear weapon

This element is simply the cost of developing the nuclear weapon and related infrastructure over a five-year period, at 1 per cent of its annual GNP or $0.2 billion/year.

No current estimates of the cost of a DPRK-style, independent nuclear weapons programme exist in public sources. But based on mid-seventies estimates, $200 million/year for five years is a reasonable figure for a small nuclear arsenal employing missile and air-delivery systems.[5] (This cost estimate does not include all investments in nuclear fuel cycle capabilities, just those needed to extend these capabilities to include weapons-related capabilities based on an already established fuel cycle.)

Cost of conventional forces due to levels of tension

This element refers to North Korea's marginal investment in conventional forces in response to increasing/declining military tensions

Table 8.3 Net costs to North Korea and international community of North Korean nuclear compliance versus North Korean nuclear defiance if sanctions are ambitious and multilateral

Element in North Korea's calculation	Option 1: compliance scenario: North Korea complies with safeguards obligations	Option 2: defiance scenario: North Korea defies NPT and incurs sanctions	Baseline scenario: North Korea defies NPT but reaction is ambiguous
North Korea			
Sanctions	Zero, no sanctions	−5% GNP/y, accrued cost	Zero, no sanctions
Inducements	+2% GNP/y, accrued gains	Zero, no inducements	Zero, no inducements
Costs of nuclear weapons programme	+1% GNP/y, avoided cost	−1% GNP/y, incurred cost	−1% GNP/y, incurred cost
Costs of conventional forces due to level of tension	+1% GNP/y, avoided cost	−1% GNP/y, accrued cost	−1% GNP/y, accrued cost
Political–strategic value of nuclear weapons	?	?	?
Cost of truth	?	?	?
Substitution of nuclear for conventional forces	−2.5% GNP/y, accrued cost	+2.5% GNP/y, avoided cost	+2.5% GNP/y, avoided cost
Total, net cost or benefit to North Korea	~+1% GNP/y, circa + $0.2 billion/y	~−4% GNP/y, circa − $0.8 billion/y	~+1% GNP/y, circa + $0.2 billion/y
Total net cost relative to baseline scenario	Zero	−5% GNP/y, circa $1 billion/y	Not applicable

International community

US/ROK offsetting force posture	Circa + $0.5 billion/y force reductions	Circa – $0.5 billion/y force increases	Circa – $0.5 billion/y force increases
Impact on global NPT of North Korean non-compliance	+	–	–
Impact on regional nuclear proliferation of North Korean non-compliance	+	–	?

/y = per year.
+ = benefit to North Korea or international community.
– = cost to North Korea or international community.

157

in/around Korea due to its nuclear choice, estimated at ± 1 per cent of its annual GNP or \$0.2 billion/year, depending on whether tensions decrease following compliance and cooperation, or increase following defiance and confrontation. Crudely, 20 per cent of North Korea's approximately \$4 billion/year military budget might be cut without risking political or economic instability from resultant demobilization.

It could be argued that this effect is non-existent, as North Korea's conventional forces are largely for political control of the adult population and no reduction of force levels is likely in response to lower levels of tension resulting from compliance. However, the element is retained in this analysis.

Political value of the bomb option

This element is obviously the most difficult to "value" and no attempt is made to do so here. Whatever the realities, "the Bomb" is perceived to be a currency of great power, and to lend possessors the ability to exercise coercive diplomacy against adversaries and to reassure friends and allies.

Cost of truth

This element refers to the political cost of "coming clean" to the IAEA with respect to past reprocessing and other nuclear weapons-related activities in North Korea. One could argue that it might also rebound to their benefit, as in the case of South Africa, but it is probably not so perceived in Pyongyang. The political cost would be experienced internally (loss of faith at the top and middle level of the informed élite of the leadership) and externally (by reaffirming North Korea's reputation for gyrating and unreliable policies, even if it eventually settles on one preferred by the international community).

Substitution of nuclear for conventional forces

This element refers to the substitution of "cheap" nuclear deterrence/warfighting capabilities (which is already listed above ["Cost of the nuclear weapon"]) for expensive conventional forces. As this effect may (but may not) have the opposite sign to the element "Cost of conventional forces due to levels of tension," it is listed separately. I estimate this cost (benefit) to be about 10 per cent of current military expenditure; the latter is about 25 per cent of GNP/year. Overall, therefore, this factor is equivalent to about 2.5 per cent of GNP/year or $0.5 billion per year.

Like the tension-related cost of conventional forces, one could argue that this effect is non-existent in this category too, because North Korea's conventional forces are largely for political control of the adult population and no substitution of nuclear for conventional forces would occur if North Korea were to develop nuclear weapons. However, the element is retained in this analysis.

Each of these elements is shown separately in table 8.3 to allow the relative magnitudes in the posited North Korean cost–benefit calculation to be evaluated and compared between the two alternative scenarios (compliance versus defiance) and against the baseline scenario.

Conclusions

As is evident in table 3, the *net* benefit of compliance to North Korea after one year totals only about 1 per cent/year of North Korea's annual GNP, about $0.2 billion/year. But relative to the baseline scenario (whereby North Korea would reap some benefits from continuing with its defiant stand but not leaving the NPT), compliance would reap North Korea no net economic gains at all. This startling result is crucially affected by whether having a nuclear weapon would have allowed North Korea to reduce its conventional forces (or future force growth) by the estimated 10 per cent, as assumed in this analysis. If not, then the compliance scenario would appear much more attractive in the calculation relative to the projected baseline "ambiguous" scenario, and even more so relative to the defiance scenario.

Also, we have no way of estimating the value placed by North Korea's leaders on obtaining the political influence associated with nuclear armament. However, we *can* estimate its cost to the international community in terms of the cost to the ROK/Japan/United States of not reducing, maintaining, or increasing US forces to offset a North Korean bomb at the margin. In this regard, US–ROK military expenditure related to North Korea currently runs at about $12–14 billion. I assume a 5 per cent increase to respond to a North Korean nuclear capability, or about $0.5 billion/year. Over a 10-year period, the cumulative cost might amount to $5 billion.

To this must be added the cost of the damage to the global NPT non-proliferation system, the encouragement to other potential proliferators, and the harm to the East Asia-Pacific security architecture under the rubric of the "Pacific community." That is, North Korea could spoil the historic opportunity to construct a set of regional, multilateral institutions that would reduce the direct burden on the United States as regional hegemon for maintaining peace and security in the region.[6]

In the case of continued defiance, the elements contained in the equation for North Korea's calculation in the face of UN multilateral and ambitious sanctions are reordered. Relative to the baseline "ambiguous" scenario, the *net* costs of defiance to North Korea would be a fall of 5 per cent of GNP/year (or about $1 billion/year).

Thus, if North Korea opts to defy the international community and to develop nuclear weapons in spite of sanctions, then the net benefits derived from defiance in this calculation are substantially outweighed by the costs of defiance. As noted earlier, there is no way to value the influence of "the bomb" to North Korea's rulers in these calculations.

In sum, it appears that:
- In the case of compliance and on the assumption of forgone conventional force reductions, there are zero net gains relative to the baseline, plus or minus the international and domestic political impacts of compliance, that cannot be estimated quantitatively, and
- In the case of defiance, the net cost relative to the baseline would amount to as much as 5 per cent reduction of its GNP or about $1 billion/year, plus or minus the international and domestic political impacts of defiance that cannot be estimated quantitatively.

Of course, different weightings would produce different results. The values assigned to each element in this essay are plausible estimates, but different figures reasonably could be used. Some elements cannot be valued quantitatively, except in negative terms. In particular, North Korea's rulers would have to believe that its nuclear weapons option is worth forgoing up to 5 per cent of its annual GNP – a fall of about 30 per cent over five years – which would be a large but not insupportable cost in the short term during which negotiations will occur. (It should be noted that this fall of GNP would be in addition to the current GNP decline attributable to the existing embargo and internal problems, which might boost the overall GNP decline to a possibly insupportable 10 per cent per year.)

On the US side of the calculation, the cost of inducing compliance might amount to \$200 million/year (assuming that the United States shoulders half the burden of inducements) and ignoring gains that might accrue to the United States from lifting the existing embargo on trade, investment, and technology transfer, plus reduction of US military expenditure enabled by the lowering of tensions on the Korean Peninsula that would flow from a settlement of the nuclear issue. Over a decade, therefore, the United States might save directly at least \$2 in military expenditure to offset a North Korean bomb for every \$1 invested in an inducement package – and possibly much more.

Overall, therefore, the implementation of a credible, meaningful inducement package, such as that negotiated in September 1994 with North Korea, is a good deal for the international community, as long as North Korea complies. However, the fact that the status quo and the compliance options are similar in economic impact in the DPRK's posited calculation indicates that the DPRK's commitment to the deal may not be absolute. Obviously, if the inducement component were increased, that might result in a greater positive net gain compared with the status quo and, consequently, in greater chances of securing DPRK's lasting commitment. But the possibility of a low DPRK commitment, combined with the probable influence of the newly elected US Congress dominated by Republican hawks opposed to the deal, indicates that a rocky road lies ahead during implementation.

Notes and references

1. Possible cooperation along these lines is analysed in my papers "Should the United States supply light water reactor technology to the DPRK?" (to Carnegie Endowment for International Peace seminar on North Korea, November 1993); "Cooperation on energy sector issues with North Korea", "Cooperation on environmental issues with North Korea", and "Economic cooperation with North Korea" (three papers to Asia Society, 29 October 1993); and "Energy sector collaboration with the DPRK" (report to North-East Asia Peace and Security Network, 29 October 1993).
2. See the arguments made in this regard in a related paper by Kimberley Anne Elliott, "Will sanctions work against North Korea?", Report to North-East Asia Peace and Security Network, Nautilus Institute, Berkeley, December 1993.
3. A. Mansourov, Columbia University Center for Korean Research, "North Korean decision-making processes regarding the nuclear issue", North-East Asia Peace and Security Network Paper 11, April 1994.
4. See my "What north wants," *The Bulletin of the Atomic Scientists*, December 1993.

5. For bomb programme and fuel cycle cost estimates respectively, see G. Rochlin, "The development and deployment of nuclear weapons systems in a proliferating world," in J. King (1979) *International Political Effects of the Spread of Nuclear Weapons*, US Government Printing Office, Washington DC, p. 20; and L. Droutman (1979) *International Deployment of Commercial Capability in Nuclear Fuel Cycle and Nuclear Power Plant Design, Manufacture and Construction for Developing Countries*, Westinghouse Electric Corporation Nuclear Energy Systems report to Oak Ridge National Laboratory ORNL/Sub-7494/4, October.

6. See M. Valencia (1994) "Involving the DPRK in Northeast regional economic and environmental cooperation", North-East Asia Peace and Security Network paper, Nautilus Institute, January.

9

Russian strategic nuclear policy after the collapse of the USSR (1992–1994)

Alexei V. Zagorsky

Introduction

Since the collapse of the USSR, Russia faces three major sets of factors delimiting her nuclear policy. The first set is determined by loss of both nuclear potential and producing facilities in former Soviet republics such as Ukraine, Belarus, and Kazakhstan. The second set is shaped by the shift from the fourth generation of nuclear missiles to the fifth, which began in the late 1980s. The third is described by the decreasing military budget and drastic cuts in expenditure on new missile production.

By 1992 the former Soviet Strategic Nuclear Forces were composed of ground missile troops, strategic submarines, and strategic aviation. The overall number of missiles and warheads is represented in table 9.1.

Of these assets, the 39th Missile Army with 130 SS-19 Stiletto (RS-18 in Russian classification) and 46 SS-24 Scalpel (RS-22) missiles (90 SS-19 in Khmelnitsky, Khmelnitsky region; 40 SS-19 and 46 SS-24 in Pervomaysk, Kherson region), and the 46th Air Army with 43 heavy strategic bombers (16 Tu-160 Blackjack and 27 Tu-95 Bear in Uzin and Priluki, Kiev region) were deployed in Ukraine with a total of 1250 warheads and 650 aviation cruise missiles;[1] 72 SS-25 Sickle (RS-

Table 9.1 **Soviet nuclear strategic potential, 1993**

(a) Strategic ground missiles

Type	No. of missiles	No. of warheads
SS-11	326	326
SS-13	40	40
SS-17	47	188
SS-18	308	3,080
SS-19	300	1,800
SS-24	89	890
SS-25	288	288
Total	1,398	6,612

(b) Submarine-launched ballistic missiles

Submarine type	Missile type	No. of submarines	No. of missiles	No. of warheads
Typhoon	RSM-52 (SS-N-20)	6	120	1,200
Navaga (Yankee I)	RSM-25 (SS-N-6)	11	192	192
Murena (Delta I)	RSM-40 (SS-N-8)	18	216	216
Murena-M (Delta II)	RSM-40 (SS-N-8)	4	64	64
Navaga-M (Yankee II)	RSM-45 (SS-N-17)	1	12	12
Kalmar (Delta III)	RSM-50 (SS-N-18)	12	192	576
Navaga III, IV (Yankee III)	RSM-50 (SS-N-18)	2	32	96
Delphin (Delta IV)	RSM-54 (SS-N-23)	7	112	448
Total		61	940	2,804

(c) Heavy strategic bombers

Type	No. of planes	No. of bombs/cruise missiles
Tu-95	147	735
Tu-160	15	120

Source: *Izvestiya*, 20 November 1993.

12M "Topol") missiles were in Belarus (bases in Mozyr and Lida) with a total of 72 warheads,[2] and 108 SS-18 Satan (RS-20) missiles (deployed at Derzhavinsk and Zhangiz-Tobe, both Semipalatinsk region) and 40 Tu-95MS Bear heavy strategic bombers (deployed at Semipalatinsk) in Kazakhstan, with 1,400 warheads and 240 aviation cruise missiles.[3] Thus, 43 per cent of the former Soviet SS-19s, 35 per cent of SS-18s, 52 per cent of SS-24s, and 25 per cent of SS-25s, as well as all Tu-160s and 46 per cent of Tu-95s, were deployed outside Russia. According to some expert assessments, in 1992 a total of 27 per cent of the nuclear strategic potential was deployed outside Russia.[4] If the number of warheads only is counted as of mid-1993, Belarus had 1 per cent, Kazakhstan 12 per cent, and Ukraine 16 per cent of all nuclear warheads on the Commonwealth of Independent States (CIS) territory.[5] Many of these weapons, primarily SS-18 and SS-19 missiles in Ukraine and Kazakhstan, were due for scrapping in accordance with the Strategic Arms Reduction Treaty (START-1) signed by Presidents Gorbachev and Bush in July 1991. However, several types of missiles – the SS-24 Scalpel in Ukraine and SS-25 Sickle in Belarus, as well as heavy strategic bombers in Ukraine and Kazakhstan – are not covered by the START-1 control regime, leaving 460 warheads and 650 cruise missiles in Ukraine, 72 warheads in Belarus, and 240 cruise missiles in Kazakhstan.

Though the issue of post-Soviet missiles has occupied the international community ever since the Minsk agreement of December 1991 (Russia, Ukraine, and Belarus), the initial scheme preserving the Unified Armed Forces (UAF) of the CIS kept all nuclear weapons under de facto Russian control. This was mainly due to the fact that, in practice, neither Ukraine, nor Belarus and Kazakhstan, could use them as the launch codes were controlled from Moscow.

Moreover, all three post-Soviet "shadow" nuclear states proclaimed themselves as non-nuclear nations in October 1991. The initial Minsk agreement provided for the establishment of a unified nuclear command within the framework of the CIS UAF, with complete return of all nuclear weapons to Russia by the end of 1994. In early 1992 only Kazakhstan had joined the agreement.

It was the disintegration of the joint armed forces of the former USSR that produced new nuclear danger in the post-Soviet sphere. Russia can hardly be blamed for initiating that process. A strong national army was, and is, considered as a potent symbolic attribute of the new sovereignty in post-Soviet republics. Measures to establish their own armies (with conventional weapons) were initially taken by nations such as Ukraine, Moldova, Azerbaijan, and Georgia through putting under their command the troops and weapons already deployed there. In May 1992 Russia responded to these actions by creating the Russian Army Forces and included the strategic triad in their composition. The official formula was that Russia would take all nuclear forces under her command, and they would be subject to the Strategic Commandment of the CIS UAF as a Russian input to joint armed forces. From the point of view of former Soviet republics this step created a different political situation. As all three post-Soviet nuclear states – Ukraine, Belarus, and Kazakhstan – declined deployment of foreign troops or military bases on their territories, the situation turned out to be politically unacceptable for them. Furthermore, general issues of post-Soviet nuclear weapons were to be fundamentally reconsidered as the joint centre controlling them was rapidly disintegrating. In principle, the problem was settled at the Lisbon meeting in May 1992 where Ukraine, Belarus, and Kazakhstan joined the START-1 and also signed the Lisbon protocol pledging to accede to the Treaty on the Non-proliferation of Nuclear Weapons (NPT) as non-nuclear nations "within the shortest period."

The problem of managing nuclear issues is practically non-existent in Russia's relations with Belarus and Kazakhstan, which accept the idea of withdrawal in principle. Nevertheless, Ukraine is a problem. First, there is a certain perception of a lingering threat from Russian military potential; second, Ukraine sought to sell out her nuclear disarmament for economic assistance. Several steps taken by Ukrainian leadership in 1992–1993 have also aggravated the situation.

In February 1992 soon after the Minsk summit, Ukraine prohibited the transportation of tactical nuclear weapons from her territory to Russia, half of which were already withdrawn by that time. Deliveries resumed under American pressure on the eve of Ukrainian President Leonid Kravchuk's visit to Washington that May.

In June 1992 Ukraine established an "administrative control" over nuclear troops on her territory and created the Centre for Strategic Nuclear Forces Administration. This meant that she did not intend to use nuclear missiles and bombers; however, for everyday activities the staff was placed under Ukrainian command.

During 1992–1993 there were repeated statements by several Ukrainian leaders laying claim to the status of a "nation possessing nuclear weapons" and insisting on maintaining 46 SS-24 Scalpels not covered by START-1. In July 1993 the Ukrainian parliament proclaimed the nation a "possessor of nuclear weapons due to historical circumstances."

From July 1992 to January 1994, Ukraine refused to deliver up nuclear warheads to Russia. An interim agreement was reached by Presidents Yeltsin and Kravchuk in September 1993 at Massandra (Crimea), providing Russian uranium for Ukrainian power plants in exchange for delivery of Ukrainian warheads to Russia. However, Ukraine changed its interpretation, insisting on additional security guarantees, and the compromise was ultimately revoked by Russia.

The next stage of the confrontation was produced by the ratification of START-1 and the Lisbon protocol in the Ukrainian parliament in November 1993. The parliament stipulated that Ukraine did not accept article 5 of the protocol obliging her to join the NPT as a non-nuclear nation. It stated that only 36 per cent of delivery systems (missiles and bombers) and 42 per cent of warheads (cruise missiles included) are subject to reduction and scrapping.[6]

The issue was finally settled in January 1994 by the joint Russian–Ukrainian–American statement. Ukraine is to move to Russia 200 strategic warheads within the first 10 months in 1994. In exchange, Ukraine will get 100 tons of 4 per cent enriched uranium-235 for her power plants. The United States is to pay Russia US$60 million in advance as part of a Russian–American contract on the sale of the weapons-grade uranium to start financing Ukrainian disarmament. The same scheme is also expected to be adopted for the Kazakh and Belarusian cases. Russian Defence Ministry and Atomic Ministry officials are hoping to implement the nuclear disarmament of Ukraine within two years.[7]

The statement says that the three presidents are awaiting START-1 and the Lisbon protocol to take legal effect. Ukrainian President Kravchuk also repeated his pledge to join NPT as a non-nuclear state, although timing to join is not precisely set like a similar "best efforts" clause in the Lisbon protocol. The Russian and American presidents have further taken additional obligations to provide security guarantees to Ukraine after the START-1 acquires legal force and effect and Ukraine joins the NPT. In addition, Russia will provide technical services and will guarantee technical security of warheads, though Ukraine has not revoked the decision to treat warheads on her territory as her property.[8]

The trilateral joint statement proved to be the major factor in the practical implementation of CIS nuclear disarmament. Deliveries of

Ukrainian strategic warheads began in 1994 according to the agreed timing. By May 1994 Ukraine had already sent 120 warheads to Russia. Moreover, she took off military alert all her SS-24 and 20 SS-19 missiles, replacing nuclear warheads with dummy ones and stockpiling the liquid fuel of the SS-19s.[9]

Agreement on withdrawing missiles from Belarus was signed even earlier, in 1993. The first regiment (9 missiles) was taken out in 1993; four more regiments with 36 missiles are being taken out in 1994. The remaining 27 missiles are to be withdrawn in 1995, and the bases in Lida and Mozyr eliminated by 1996.[10]

In March 1994, Russia and Kazakhstan signed agreements on military cooperation and the status of strategic nuclear forces. Accordingly, all Kazakh missiles are to be taken down within 14 months in order to denuclearize Kazakhstan in 1995. Silos are to be dismantled within three years. Strategic bombers with cruise missiles are to be withdrawn to Russia by May 1994.[11]

Yet several crucial issues remain unsettled. First, timing for the withdrawal of all missiles is settled only with Belarus and Kazakhstan. In the Ukrainian case, precise obligations affect only 10 per cent of the warheads and do not really cover missiles and bombers. Furthermore, the detailed schemes of covering Russian expenditures for dismantling CIS warheads outside Russia and compensation for Ukrainian, Belarusian, and Kazakh warheads and missiles were never adequately discussed, except for the initial deal with the 200 Ukrainian warheads. It should be recalled that Ukrainian insists on compensation not only for strategic weapons but also for tactical armaments taken to Russia in January–May 1992. The third nuclear point relates to covering the expenditures for eliminating silos in Ukraine and Kazakhstan (with SS-24s in Belarus being mobile).

Changing generations of Russian missiles

Another complex issue for current Russian nuclear policy is that of replacing older missiles of the fourth (in NATO parlance or third per Russian classification) generation by those of the fifth (fourth) generation.

As of June 1993, Russia had seven types of ground missiles of the third to fifth (i.e. second to fourth in Russian terms) generations, as shown in table 9.2. In addition, four more types were under research: these were the SSX-26 (tested in 1986) – a heavy multiwarhead missile on liquid fuel – and the SSX-27, SSX-28, and

Table 9.2 **Russian ground missiles, as of 1 June 1993**

Type	NATO code	Russian code	Generation	Tested	Adopted	Deployment peak
SS-11	Sego	UR-100	3	1965	1967	1974
SS-13	Savage	RS-12	3	1965	1968	1970
SS-17	Spanker	RS-16	4	1972	1975	1980
SS-18	Satan	RS-20	4	1972	1975	1980
SS-19	Stiletto	RS-18	4	1973	1975	1984
SS-24	Scalpel	RS-22	5	1982	1987	1992
SS-25	Sickle	RS-12M	5	1983	1985	1993

Source: *Nezavisimaya Gazeta*, 4 August 1994.

Table 9.3 **Russian ground missiles as of 1 June 1993**

Type	Ground missiles Missiles	Warheads	START-1 Missiles	Warheads	START-2 Missiles	Warheads
SS-11	100	100	–	–	–	–
SS-13	40	40	–	–	–	–
SS-17	40	160	–	–	–	–
SS-18	302	3,020	154	1,540	–	–
SS-19	290	1,740	152	912	105	105
SS-24	92	920	46	460	–	–
SS-25	340	340	340	340	340	340

Source: *Nezavisimaya Gazeta*, 4 August 1994.

"Topol-M" (no NATO codes) – light monowarhead missiles on solid fuel.

As table 9.3 makes clear, during the series of START treaties, USSR/Russia tried to reshape its ground missile potential to the needs of the newer generations, at the same time reducing its missiles and warheads. START-1 eliminated the rest of Soviet/Russian missiles of the third generation – SS-11s (100 missiles with 100 warheads) and SS-13s (40 missiles with 40 warheads) – as well as SS-17s (40 missiles with 160 warheads) of the fourth generation. START-2 eliminates another fourth-generation class (302 SS-18s with 3,020 warheads) and one in the fifth generation (92 SS-24s with 920 warheads).

It is easy to understand the elimination of the fourth-generation SS-17s under START-1. Both SS-17 and SS-19 missiles were developed as competitive models to replace SS-11 and SS-13 missiles.

START-1 provides for the elimination of outdated third-generation missiles as well as an unnecessarily excessive replacement type, concentrating instead on SS-19 as a relatively light missile and SS-18 as a heavy missile of the fourth generation.

The same logic applies for START-2. It eliminates classes of missiles that anyway will be outdated by 2003 and would have been scrapped, irrespective of any agreement. The elimination of the SS-24 may be explained by the fact that it was developed as a Soviet analogue of the American MX Peacekeeper to replace the SS-18, but turned out to be less effective than the SS-18 and more vulnerable than a mobile SS-25.

On the other hand, START-2 is to some extent in advance of the logic for changing missile generations. Though a replacement of the light SS-17 was ready with the SS-25, no real alternative for SS-18 was in existence in 1992. In part, the logic may be explained by the fact that, in the early 1990s, Russian strategic planners assumed that under existing technologies the heavy multiple independently targetable re-entry vehicles (MIRVs) would become too vulnerable to be effective, and the strategic decision was made for lighter mobile missiles of the SS-25 and coming "Topol-M" types.[12] This logic is based on the fact that, where there are 1,000 warheads on 100 missiles placed in silos, an enemy may need only 100 highly precise hits to their location to destroy the whole potential, whereas if the same number of warheads is dispersed among 1,000 mobile missiles located all around Russia, the potential will be ten times less vulnerable. According to this logic, the Russian insistence on preserving 154 heavy SS-19 missiles was excessive.[13]

One more factor should be taken into account when discussing current problems of Russian ground missiles. From the outset the USSR traditionally relied upon competition between two major companies for developing its missiles. For the first third-generation missiles these companies were the Russian-based OKB-1 (Joint Construction Bureau-1, now NOP "Enegiya"), founded by S. Korolyov, and OKB-52 (now CKBM) founded by V. Chelomey. In the 1970s Korolyov's OKB-1 stepped down and its position was taken over by Ukrainian-based OKB-586 (KB "Yuzhnoye" in Pavlovsk, Dnepropetrovsk region), founded by M. Yangel and until recently headed by the current Ukrainian President Leonid Kuchma. In the 1980s the position of OKB-52 was taken by a new firm, MIT, headed by A. Nadiradze.

Among the missiles now in use in Russia, the light SS-13s are produced by OKB-1 (Korolyov's) and the SS-11s are produced by OKB-52 (Chelomey's) in the third generation; light SS-17 and heavy SS-18 missiles are produced by the Ukrainian OKB-586 (Yangel's) and light SS-19 missiles are produced by OKB-52 (Chelomey's) in the fourth generation. Of the fifth generation, heavy SS-24 and SSX-26 missiles are produced by the Ukrainian OKB-586 (Yangel's) and light SS-25, SSX-28, and "Topol-M" missiles are produced by MIT (Nadiradze's).

Since the 1970s, therefore, the USSR has substantially increased its dependence on Ukrainian-based missile production. Moreover, OKB-586 has grown to be the indisputable leader in producing heavy missiles, with a series of SS-7 and SS-9 (third-generation), SS-18 (fourth-generation) and SSX-28 (fifth-generation) missiles. Its main competitor, MIT, has concentrated on an efficient set of light missiles of SS-16 for the third generation, SS-20 for the fourth and SS-25 for the fifth. However, with the collapse of the USSR and the subsequent loss of Ukrainian production facilities, Russia was deprived of any possibility of ensuring a credible potential of heavy missiles. Such an option would have demanded a new research project to replace the Ukrainian-made SS-18 and SSX-26 missiles, as well as new production facilities. Therefore an option to eliminate all classes of heavy strategic missiles and to concentrate on MIT's mobile "Topols" was seen as the only possible solution to a difficult economic and political situation.

At present, the level of existing warheads on fifth-generation missiles is considered to be the best configuration for the current Russian geostrategic situation. In early discussions on the START-2 at the Supreme Soviet of the Russian Federation in February 1993, both committees on Defence and Foreign Relations insisted on further cutting the number of missiles allowed to some 600–1,000 pieces to prevent additional expenditure for building more modern missiles.[14] This was a little above Russia's current level of ground missiles of the fifth generation, modern submarine-launched ballistic missiles (SLBMs) of Typhoon and Delta IV classes, and heavy bombers.

Russian nuclear strategy under START-2

Since initiating in May 1992 a rather extended process of forming the Russian Armed Forces and then elaborating a new military doctrine for the 1990s, Russian has finally decided on maintenance of her strategic nuclear deterrent as the major guarantee for her security.

Referring to Russian nuclear facilities, Defence Minister Pavel Grachev indicates that currently Russian territorial security could be threatened only by another nuclear state.[15] The former commander-in-chief of the CIS UAF, Marshal Evgueny Shaposhnikov, was even more clear in setting priorities when he stated that "strategic nuclear forces should be regarded as the basis of Russian Armed Forces." He added that "if we have them highly ready, we will hardly expect any external threat."[16]

However, conditions set by START-2 impose a radically new situation on Russian strategic forces. Unlike previous Soviet–American agreements like the SALT (Strategic Arms Limitation) Treaties and START-1, the successor treaty not only limits the scope of any current arms race and cuts the number of missiles and warheads but also prompts Russia to reshape the whole structure of her strategic triad.

Traditionally, ground silo missiles formed the core of the Russian nuclear potential. SALT-2 as well as later intermediate range nuclear forces (INF) treaty provisions moved the Russian nuclear build-up towards heavy MIRVed missiles with the major stress on SS-18s. Naval forces and heavy bombers played a subordinate role in this structure, while Russia began acquiring mobile missiles (not covered by the INF treaty) only in the 1990s.

START-2 basically prohibits all major classes of missiles of the Russian core potential. Permission to keep 105 SS-19s does not really change the situation as they are to be de-MIRVed and lose their major advantage in attacking several independent targets.

Though START-2 does not set precise figures for warheads on each type in the strategic triad, they may easily be calculated. There is a major ceiling of 3,000–3,500 warheads of all types with a sub-ceiling of 1,700–1,750 warheads on naval missiles to be reached by the final stage at 2003. For Russia that will mean cutting naval missiles from 2,652 in November 1993[17] to 1,750, representing a 34 per cent cut.

Certainly, the first candidates for scrapping would have to be SLBMs of the first and second generations – Yankee I, Delta I, and Delta II classes adopted by the fleet in 1968–1973 and with terms of service expiring. The last type of the second-generation naval strategic missiles – a Yankee II class (adopted in 1980) – is deployed by only one submarine and is to be sacrificed, too. In addition, the Yeltsin–Clinton summit in September 1994 produced another pledge to cut at least 25 Russian submarines of Delta classes.[18] As Deltas I and II account for 22 submarines, it means scrapping at least three Delta III class units.

Russia is, therefore, allowed to keep the third-generation strategic submarines – Typhoons (adopted in 1983), Delta IIIs (adopted in 1983), and Delta IVs (adopted in 1986). But, even so, Russia still has up to 2,224 warheads aboard these vessels. To meet START-2 requirements, therefore, Russia may keep only six current Typhoon submarines with 120 SS-N-20 missiles (1,200 warheads), seven Delta IV (Delphin) submarines with 112 SS-N-23 missiles (448 warheads), and two Delta III submarines with 32 SS-N-18 missiles (96 warheads).[19]

From the point of view of the existing deployment of naval strategic forces, this means that Russia may preserve bases at Nerpichya with six Typhoons (the Northern Fleet) and at Olenya with seven Delta IV (Delphin) (Northern Fleet), with the remaining two Delta II submarines to be stationed between Yagelnaya (Northern Fleet, now with three of this class) or Rybachiy (the Pacific fleet, Kamchatka, now nine of this class). Meanwhile, preserving a special base of two submarines makes little sense, and an obvious solution would be to consolidate all Deltas at the same base.

An alternative approach may be seen in limiting the number of warheads to four on each SLBM, as provided by START-2. For Russia, it will affect the Typhoon class only (with 20 warheads per missile). In that case Russia would be allowed to keep 480 warheads on Typhoons, 448 warheads on Delta IVs, and 432 warheads on nine Delta IIIs, with a total of 1,360 warheads, or 390 warheads lower than the START-2 ceilings. One possibility filling this gap may be to build six more Delta IV submarines with 384 additional warheads to raise their level to 1,744. However, as no strategic submarine has been built in Russia since 1991, the chance of this happening is slim.

As far as the geographical deployment of strategic submarines under the second option is concerned, the marked correspondence between the Delta IIIs deployed now at the Kamchatka base and the same number allowed de facto by the Yeltsin–Clinton deal in September 1994, leads one to conclude that the Rybachily base at Kamchatka is to be preserved and the strategic facilities in the Sea of Okhotsk eliminated.

On the other hand, there are several considerations against maintaining a strategic base in the Far East. The first factor is that all Russian missile-loading facilities are located at the Kola peninsula.

The second point is that, of four Russian shipyards building and servicing strategic missiles, three have, in fact, closed their submarine-building programmes, including Komsomolsk-on-Amur, the only one in the Far East. The sole remaining submarine yard is at Severodvinsk in the Arkhangelsk Province near the Kola Peninsula. Therefore, in effect, any servicing of strategic missiles deployed in the Far East would be dependent on facilities around the home location of the Northern Fleet. The third factor can be explained by the characteristics of naval missiles of the third generation. The chief strategic significance in having a Russian naval base at Kamchatka was in bringing launches closer to the American Pacific coast, while evading submarine detection by the US anti-submarine weapons (ASW). This advantage was designed for the Yankee I class with a shooting range of 2,400–3,000 km and detectable by ASW within the range of more than 1,000 km in the open sea and within 100 km in shallow seas.[20] The base at the Sea of Okhotsk provided facilities for later classes of Delta I and Delta II with larger shooting ranges of between 7,800 and 9,100 km to ensure the coverage of the American Pacific coast with launches from within a closed Russian sea to evade ASW effects.

The third generation of Russian strategic submarines and naval missiles provides for new and better opportunities. With a shooting range of 8,000 km (Delta III) to 8,300 km (Typhoon and Delta IV) and a low detection range (see table 9.4), they could ensure the coverage of practically the whole American territory with launches from just the Arctic regions. It should be noted that the detection range indicated in the table assumes favourable weather conditions for ASW; under poor conditions the detection range decreases. For example, in the case of Delta IV the detection range in shallow seas with a wind velocity of more than 10 m/s is not more than 3–5 km.[21]

Of course, the situation is calculated as related to Russian–American balances (or it may be enlarged to assess the reaching range of any current nuclear power) and does not foresee a possible use of Russian naval nuclear potential in cases of local conflict rather remote from Russian borders. Two more considerations should be noted in this regard. First, at present the vulnerability of Russian naval nuclear potential is dependent solely on United States ASW capacities. Unless American assets are involved, Russian strategic submarines are able to penetrate any point, irrespective of their base affiliation. Second, major guidelines for current Russian defence strategy presume the use of armed force in three cases only:
– protection of sovereignty and territorial integrity, or other vital

Table 9.4 **Detection ranges (in km) by ASW for Russian strategic submarines**

Class of submarine	Open sea	Arctic	Shallow sea
Yankee I	>1,000	200	100
Delta I	<260–300	80	60
Delta II	<260–300	80	60
Delta III	<130–200	50	30
Typhoon	<130–200	40	20
Delta IV	<65	5–40	<15
Forthcoming 4th generation	<5	<5	<5

Source: *Nezavisimaya Gazeta*, 25 October 1994.

interests of the Russian Federation, in case of aggression against her or her allies;

– peace-keeping operations sanctioned by the UN Security Council or in accordance with Russia's international obligations;

– prevention of armed conflicts or any other illegitimate violence on the national border or another nation's border according to treaty obligations or within the Russian territory, endangering Russia's vital interests.[22]

From this, it is quite evident that the second case excludes the use of nuclear weapons. However, it remains a possibility in the other two instances, if the conflict occurs within the shooting range of Russian missiles. Therefore, the former objective of keeping Russian nuclear potential in the Far East is receding.

To calculate the allowed ceiling for Russian ground missiles we should first deduct the number of warheads on Russian strategic bombers from the combined ceiling of bombers and ground missiles. As of November 1993, Russia had 162 heavy bombers with 883 cruise missiles and nuclear bombs, including those in Ukraine and Kazakhstan.[23] As 43 bombers with 372 warheads were in Ukraine, and Russia may not realistically count on their use (their elimination is more likely), these should also be excluded from calculating Russian potential. That leaves the ceiling for Russian ground missiles allowed by START-2 at the level of 867 to 1,629 monoblock missiles with 105 SS-19s, with the rest covered by SS-25 and "Topol-12M" missiles. Starting from the baseline of mid-1993, that would mean scrapping 63 per cent of Russian missiles with a 74–80 per cent cut in number of warheads, and preserving only 36–51 per cent of the level of ground missiles allowed. Calculations by the Defence Ministry suggest that Russia should scrap 675–780 missiles and 3,775–3,880 warheads.[24] At the same time they envisage that the economic situation may permit only a level of 900 ground missiles by 2003, i.e. building about 450 new SS-25 missiles.[25]

Toward a new nuclear strategy

As a response to this situation, a new nuclear strategy is being contemplated. The basic idea provides for a reduced number of ground missiles to remain as the core of a Russian nuclear potential. Under this scenario, the SS-25 in two main modifications (mobile and silo-based) would form the basic type. The silo modification is supposed to incorporate 90 silos of SS-18s (which are being scrapped) and up to 400 silos of the earlier SS-11, SS-13, and SS-17. The base for the mobile SS-25 component would come from a withdrawal of units from Belarus and a redeployment of Russian missiles now in the Urals (Yoshkar-Ola, Nizny Tagil) and Siberia (Novosibirsk, Kansk, Irkutsk region). The ratio between silo-based and mobile modifications is estimated to be approximately 60–70 to 30–40.[26]

Nevertheless, the uncertain economic situation in Russia makes even this rationalization doubtful. Whereas the number of 900 missiles was considered to be economically sound in February 1994, the level was already reduced to 600–700 by June.[27] Bearing in mind that, in October 1994, about 95 per cent of the Russian military industry was curtailed owing to a lack of finance,[28] and with the strong likelihood of further cuts in the military budget in 1995, even this level seems quite unlikely.

The best answer, then, may lie in meeting START-2 requirements with the already existing potential (Typhoons and Deltas III and IV in naval forces and SS-19s and SS-25s in ground missile forces). That would radically change the structure of Russian nuclear strategic forces to increase naval strategic potential up to 70–75 per cent of her overall nuclear forces.[29]

Meanwhile, a fundamental contradiction should be noted in all current Russian discussions on new nuclear options. It is generally assumed that major possible threats to Russian security would be in local conflicts and wars within and around the CIS, as in Chechnya; such threats, however, would hardly need nuclear deterrence. This may ultimately prove a critical factor in connection with nuclear proliferation and the possibility of nations around Russia and the CIS acquiring nuclear and missile weapons of their own.

That possibility is considered quite plausible for Russian security calculations. At present, Russia is almost surrounded by a nuclear circle of recognized nuclear states and those belonging to the "grey zone," namely Belarus and Ukraine in the west; Kazakhstan, Pakistan, and India in the south; China and North Korea in the southeast; and the United States in the east.

In Moscow the issue is predominantly addressed as that of non-proliferation and strengthening the NPT regime and, consequently, as diplomatic rather than military. In practice, problems with Ukraine account for most of the rhetoric; however, the ultimate nuclear disarmament of Ukraine remains a major long-term aim of Russia's strategy on non-proliferation.

On the other hand, most technical considerations in discussions on the military side of nuclear problems are still measured through the traditional comparison of Russian and US nuclear capacities, as only the United States is considered to be a real nuclear match for Russia. Therefore, a wide gap remains between a diplomatic strategy of meeting issues of possible new nuclear states and a conservative defence policy still calculating the possible reaction to the perceived American challenge, while ignoring threats from the "grey zone."

International treaties and the role of international institutions

Summing up, we can find three major areas of Russian activities regulated by their own separate logic and specific international regulations: (1) the dimension of nuclear arms reduction; (2) the dimension of relations with CIS nuclear states, and (3) non-proliferation and related issues.

The first dimension is dominated by the extensive base of Soviet/Russian treaties dating from the 1970s. At present START-1 (1991) and START-2 (1993) are in force, with new Russian proposals to begin negotiations for a START-3 recently reiterated during the Yeltsin–Clinton summit in September 1994. Two more important agreements relating to the non-targeting of missiles at each other (between Russia and America, of January 1994, and between Russia and China, of September 1994) should also be added.

In these issues Russia obviously prefers bilateral negotiations and agreements, not leaving much place for international institutions. The former Soviet approach, based on weighing the possible input of every nuclear-possessing nation to global and regional balances, has definitely been abandoned by Russia. The current approach may be determined in terms of "balancing realism" according to Inoguchi's security model taxonomy.

Some additional observations should be added to this conclusion. First, as far as nuclear issues are concerned, the assumption is valid for the global system only. Peculiarities in regional nuclear balances, including the shape of nuclear potentials in Asia-Pacific, are not of major importance for Russia provided that they do not upset the global balance. Therefore, with any kind of regional situation, Russian attention is primarily drawn to issues of control over former Soviet nuclear facilities outside Russian territory (i.e. in Ukraine, Kazakhstan, and Belarus, in order of importance) and to non-proliferation issues at large.

Second, assuming that the balancing realism paradigm is to be taken for the global level of relations, only the United States represents a match for Russia's attention. Therefore, the process is to be led and dominated by bilateral Russian–American agreements until a level of nuclear arms similar to that of nations such as China, France, and Britain is reached.

The second dimension, that of relations with CIS nations, is regulated by the following instruments: START-1, as ratified by Ukraine, Belarus, and Kazakhstan; the Minsk declaration (Russia, Ukraine, Belarus, with Kazakhstan joining it in 1992); the Lisbon protocol (1992 – Russia, US, Ukraine, Belarus, Kazakhstan); Russian–Belarusian agreement of 1993, providing for withdrawal of SS-25s; Russian–Kazakhstan agreement on military cooperation and the status of nuclear strategic forces (1994); Massandra agreement between Russia and Ukraine on withdrawal of Ukrainian strategic missiles (1993); and Russian–Ukrainian–American joint statement on withdrawal of Ukrainian missiles (1994).

These vexed sets of relations with fractious neighbours are highly worrisome and tangible for Russia. No doubt, it would prefer to address them on a bilateral basis in negotiations with the specific republics involved, without admitting any new nation or body into the area of relations within the CIS. However, the Ukrainian position often tends to internationalize these issues, but the most Russia is prepared to accept is the American role of mediator/guarantor in the process of CIS denuclearization.

In this area Russia certainly would prefer a bandwagonning realism option in our security model taxonomy. Nevertheless, there is a distinct understanding that pending issues of Ukrainian nuclear weapons status may not necessarily be settled wholly within the CIS framework only. Therefore, Russia is eager to ensure periodic American involvement to ensure trilateral Russian–US–Ukrainian deals. However, such a tactic also induces and conditions Kazakhstan (and, to a certain extent, Belarus) to expect additional American assistance in settling their economic problems, as compensation for flexibility in nuclear issues. That factor leads to a distortion of the pure model for bandwagonning realism, by injecting the United States as a second major power in the system. Meanwhile, there would clearly be no chance for an institutional approach to these problems.

The third dimension of non-proliferation is to be addressed through traditional channels regulating the NPT regime. Its general strengthening and indefinite prolongation certainly corresponds to Russian interests, and one may expect to see the maximum degree of Russian cooperation in settling these issues. At the same time as the current Russian agenda in nuclear problems seems to be overloaded by issues related to the two initial dimensions, it would be hard to expect from Russia anything but mere declarations instead of the detailed initiatives to settle broader aspects addressed primarily by the international institutions. Therefore, in this context, the non-proliferation problem does fairly match the "institutionalization paradigm" proposed by Inoguchi's model.

Notes and references

1. *Segodnya*, 22 December 1993; *Nezavisimaya Gazeta*, 25 January 1994.
2. *Nezavisimaya Gazeta*, 19 November 1992.
3. *Izvestiya*, 22 December 1993; *Izvestiya*, 4 May 1994.
4. *Nezavisimaya Gazeta*, 6 August 1992.
5. Calculated from data in *Izvestiya*, 20 November 1993.
6. *Izvestiya*, 20 November 1993.
7. *Segodnya*, 19 January 1994.
8. *Moscow News*, 16–23 January 1994, No. 3.
9. *Izvestiya*, 4 May 1994.
10. Ibid.
11. Ibid.
12. *Nezavisimaya Gazeta*, 4 August 1994.
13. "SNV-2 ukreplyaet bezopasnost, Rossii (START-2 strengthens Russian security)." *Izvestiya*, 10 April 1993.
14. *The Moscow Tribune*, 12 February 1993.
15. "Voyennaya doktrina i bezoposnost, Rossii." (Pavel Grachev: The military doctrine and Russian security). *Nezavisimaya Gazeta*, 9 June 1994.
16. "Osnovnye napravleniya voyennoy reformy v Rossii" (Evgueny Shaposhnikov: Major guidelines for the military reform in Russia). *Segodnya*, 24 June 1994.
17. Official data of the Russian Defence Ministry. *Izvestiya*, 20 November 1993.

18. *Segodnya*, 15 November 1994.
19. A Typhoon submarine has 20 SS-N-20 missiles with ten warheads each; a Delta IV (Delphin) submarine has 16 SS-N-23 missiles with four warheads each; a Delta-III submarine has 16 SS-N-18 missiles with three warheads each.
20. For technical data on Russian strategic submarines see *Nezavisimaya Gazeta*, 25 October 1994.
21. Ibid.
22. "Osnovnye polozheniya voyennoy doktriny Rossiyskoy Federatsii" (Major guidelines of the military doctrine of the Russian Federation). *Izvestiya*, 18 November 1993.
23. Data of the Russian Defence Ministry. *Izvestiya*, 20 November 1993.
24. *Segodnya*, 1 June 1994.
25. *Izvestiya*, 9 February 1994.
26. *Izvestiya*, 9 February 1994; *Segodnya*, 9 February 1994.
27. *Segodnya*, 1 June 1994.
28. *Izvestiya*, 30 October 1994.
29. *Nezavisimaya Gazeta*, 18 March 1994.

Conclusion: A peace-and-security taxonomy

Takashi Inoguchi

Introduction

In the Conclusion to this volume, I would like to revisit themes that Immanuel Kant first broached in his classic work, *For Perpetual Peace*.[1] This is appropriate not only because of the lasting relevance of the Kantian categories: we are also reminded of Kant's landmark study of conflict and conflict avoidance, because 1995 marked the 200th year since the publication of *For Perpetual Peace* in 1795.

Kant was a personal witness to the wars that devastated Europe at the end of the eighteenth century and that were to climax in the massive blood-letting of the Napoleonic conquests. Kant believed that war would be a recurrent feature of modern life unless the means were devised to ensure "perpetual peace." In place of the cycle of diplomacy, conflict, and defeat, he wished to substitute a cycle of institution-building, *embourgeoisement* (the inculcation of middle-class attitudes and comfort), and democratization. Kant believed that such a virtuous cycle would stifle impulses to war. The question was then, and still is, how to make the Kantian cycle of "perpetual peace" work.

Kant's principal concern was with the means of averting conflict. He identified three strategies of peace building – institutionalism, economic interdependence, and democracy. These he counterpoised to traditional statecraft based on an exacting calculation of power, describing the latter as realism.

To the realists, Kant was a bitter critic. As Kant viewed the statesmen of his own day, they were primarily concerned with schemes to maximize national interests through the pursuit of power, wealth, and prestige. War and diplomacy were simply tools to these ends.

Today, Kant's ideas are almost embarrassingly familiar. Generation upon generation of political scientists, historians, strategists, and economists have reflected upon the Kantian categories and incorporated them into their work. For that matter, Kant borrowed generously from a long tradition of European analysis of the art of government, from Thucydides to Machiavelli and Thomas Hobbes. Kant's view of the state, for example, is essentially Hobbesian. When he writes about realism, the actors that he has in mind are states. Expanded by one level, states interact with each other in larger alliances and coalitions.

Similarly, Kant's concept of institutionalism leaned heavily on the work of Hugo Grotius, the seventeenth-century scholar who laid the foundations for the contemporary practice of international law. Kant argued that subnational and transnational institutions could foster an atmosphere of mutual confidence that would gradually erode the rationale for war based on the conflict of national interest. Thus, international institutions, non-governmental organizations, and the private sector could become major actors in the pursuit of "perpetual peace." The troublemakers – the realist statesmen – would have to cope with people who were unwilling to go to war because they worked effectively with each other across national borders.

A second Kantian strategy – owing a large debt to Adam Smith – was to foster peace through open markets. The more closely linked national economies became, the less benefit would accrue from the mercantilist practices that were endemic in eighteenth-century Europe. Adam Smith and his disciples believed that peace would follow free trade. In this second Kantian approach, economic entities, such as businesses and banks, can serve as the major actors in the peace process.

Finally, Kant argued that democracy was in itself a force against war. In a democracy, he said, governments are held accountable to their citizenry. The commitment to democratic values makes it more difficult for political leaders to order up troops: they have to explain their actions. Kant was among the first thinkers to realize the awkward position of the realist-statesman in a democratic society, and clearly the first to view individual citizens as actors on the world stage. It is the latter perception that we mean when we describe an approach or viewpoint as "Kantian."

The twentieth century has been called the century of war. The accumulated death toll of the century's conflicts has far surpassed that of any other century. Small wonder, then, that each of Kant's various strategies for conflict manipulation and conflict avoidance have their modern arbiters.

The realist school has been especially active in the twentieth century. I would like to highlight just two of its proponents – Henry Kissinger and Robert Gilpin. Why these two? Because they are representative of two radically opposed realist strategies to achieve peace. One is through a *realpolitik*, or cynically calculated balancing of power. In his latest work, *Diplomacy*,[2] Kissinger takes up the classic argument that peace is a by-product of a stand-off between major powers. Gilpin, on the other hand, proposes in *War and Change in World Politics*[3] that peace emerges when one power effectively asserts hegemony over the others.

The twentieth century has seen its fair share of institutionalists, as well. Robert Keohane, in his *After Hegemony*, and John Ruggie, in *Multilateralism Matters*,[4] both argue that institution building and confidence building are essential for global peace. Keohane is also a proponent of the Kantian and Adam Smithian notion tying together peace and free markets. Keohane's *Power and Interdependence*,[5] written with Joseph Nye, outlines the thesis of global interdependence through economics. Bruce Russett and others have shown the basic empirical validity of this proposition.[6] Finally, Russett's *Grasping the Democratic Peace*[7] offers a contemporary update of the Kantian thesis on peace and democracy.

Towards a security model taxonomy

Now, let us try to imagine the security environment in North-East Asia around the year 2005. I would like to propose five Kantian-inspired models of the way that peace might be waged, a decade hence.[8]

For each of these five models, I have identified six features in order to flesh out my taxonomy. These six features are as follows: (1) the structural properties of each – especially whether relations between the major actors are roughly relations of equals, or isomorphic; (2)

behavioural rules, or the norms that guide the major actors; (3) the role of international institutions; (4) potential outcomes, or scenarios, based on the model; (5) model preference, or how major actors rate the model; and (6) plausibility, or the adequacy of the model to explain probable outcomes in the year 2005.

With each of these models I have paid close attention to two sub-terranean themes. One theme is the extent to which the growing wealth of North-East Asia may affect the security and the behaviour of each of the major actors. Secondly, I have tried to track in each model the degree to which it is based upon interaction between equal actors or entities. Relationships between institutions, for example, are inherently isomorphic, or equal, whereas relations between weak and strong states can be anything but equal.

Balancing realism

The main thesis of balancing realism is that peace is an outcome when major states manage to check each other's assertiveness through power balancing. The more even the power balance, the more permanent the peace.

Structural properties
The major powers of North-East Asia could potentially enter into an isomorphic relationship, or relationship of equals. This would depend on the five powers of the United States, Japan, China, Russia, and the Association of South-East Asian Nations (ASEAN) remaining much as they are now – independent actors with converging ideologies.

Behavioural rules
The balancing realists view war and diplomacy as two means to the same end, of peace. The fact that major actors agree on broad norms of diplomacy, deterrence, and war serves as a natural restraint on unilateral assertions of national interest. This is a world of relatively homogeneous norms.

Role of international institutions
Realists want to keep the role of international institutions minimal: they regard them as non-essential. The realists look with disfavour on any supranational authority, actors, or institutions. No US admin-istration of either party has ever been overly enthusiastic about the idea of a United Nations Armed Force with its own general staff.

The realists tend to view international institutions as merely another venue where they can observe and calculate the movements of other actors. Hence the realists' enthusiasm for the ASEAN Regional Forum (ARF), which was formally launched in 1994. Although institutionalists have their own reasons for approving the ARF process, realists find ARF's regular meetings and confidence-building processes acceptable as long as the organization refrains from addressing any difficult issues.

Scenarios
The balancing realism scenario is all shadows or light: if the major powers attain equilibrium, the result is peace; if they do not, equilibrium is not working and all manner of trouble is bound to result.

Model preference
Balancing realism is overwhelmingly the popular viewpoint in writings on security issues in China. Strategic thinkers in the United States and ASEAN are also fond of this model.

Assessment
Many policy makers instinctively subscribe to the perspective of balancing realism. This lends the model a certain credibility, although what is meant by balance and balancing differs from strategist to strategist. The outlook for North-East Asia in 2005 based on this model is disturbing. US isolationism, Chinese assertiveness, the expansion of Japanese political and economic influence, and the re-emergence of Russia are all factors tending to break the present equilibrium. Even so, there are forces at work sustaining the balance, including China's need for regional stability to pursue its goals for economic growth, and the rising prestige and affluence of ASEAN.

The real question is how quickly the Chinese economy is growing. Caution is necessary here, as there is a common tendency to overestimate China's development prospects. Even so, China's rapid growth runs counter to US policy to integrate its economy with Asia-Pacific economies. Runaway growth in China might tempt balancing realists in the United States to discourage market and democratic reforms that might strengthen China too much. At a minimum, the balancing realists would argue against free transfer of technology to China. The result, they would say, is that China will end up with the most sophisticated weapons technology outside the United States and Russia.

Bandwagonning realism

The basic idea of bandwagonning realism is that hegemony is conducive to peace. The bandwagoners argue that the eras of Pax Britannica and Pax Americana, when British and American power was predominant, offer proof that the global system ticks along smoothly when a single power dominates.

Structural properties

In the event of United States predominance (at least on the basis of past experience), the lesser players in this model are relative equals, or isomorphic. This would be less true if either Japan or China became predominant: both are inward-looking cultures that to some extent deny the universality of their values or institutions. Neither would be likely to construct rules that applied equally to both the hegemonic power and lesser powers, as both Britain and the United States have done during their pre-eminent periods.

Behavioural rules

Smaller players are supposed to confine their manoeuvres to the hegemonic framework. As hegemonic shifts take place, successful players will lean to the dominant side. An image of strength is just as important as the reality. Again, rules are relative as the hegemonic power shapes most of the rules, including cultural values.

Role of international institutions

The bandwagonning realists look upon international institutions with the same suspicion and reserve as the balancing realists.

Scenarios

As to North-East Asia in 2005, the bandwagonning realists think that peace will prevail as long as (1) the United States retains its vigour and high degree of engagement in the region; (2) Japan maintains its economic dynamism, preserves a low profile, and continues to open its markets, particularly to Asia; and/or (3) China successfully opens its market to Pacific Asians at the same time as preserving its access to global markets. The worst scenario is US retrenchment combined with Japanese economic collapse and Chinese mercantilism. The result would almost certainly be some form of assertion and conflict.

186

Model preference
Bandwagonning realism is the dominant view in the United States. Even proponents of alternative models are subconsciously influenced by it.

Assessment
The strength of this model is its seeming correspondence with history. Looking back over the past few centuries, one can see a clear lineage beginning with the Pax Sinica of the Manchus in the seventeenth and eighteenth centuries, through the Pax Britannica of the nineteenth and early twentieth centuries, Japan's abortive Pax Nipponica, and the successful Pax Americana of the post-war period.

The problem is in pinpointing when each hegemonic cycle comes to an end. I would wager that, 10 years from now, the United States will still be the regional hegemon. If so, the implications for US policy are that Washington should (1) preserve Japan as its major regional ally, (2) engage China in as many ways as possible, and (3) keep ASEAN busy acting as a mediator or articulator.

Institutionalism

Institutionalists argue that the process of building institutions is also one of building mutual confidence. Both lead inexorably to peace.

Structural properties
The more numerous the institutions engaged in networking, and the more extensive the networks, the more isomorphic this model becomes. In other words, as institutions become familiar with their international counterparts, or extend themselves globally, institutions themselves become the common denominator of the international political economy.

Behavioural rules
The basic notion is to build a sense of community that cuts across national borders. The "community" can be at the regional or international level; actors may be interest groups or nation-states. The "growth triangles" that have become a prominent feature of East Asian and South-East Asian development can also become the focus for institution building. Participants foster a communal sensibility through cooperation and transparency.

Cooperation and transparency are particularly critical in the building of communities in the security field, such as the North Atlantic Treaty Organization or the ARF. Institutionalists assume that the principal actors – institutions – willingly share the same rules, norms, and organizational procedures.

Role of international institutions

As far as the institutionalists are concerned, the sun never sets on international institutions. For example, the French look at the European Union (EU) as a means to achieve global as well as national goals. By constructing legal institutions in the Napoleonic spirit, they believe that they will be able to restrain other actors more effectively. At the same time, the French argue that the EU as a whole will have far more power to influence global events than France on its own.

Similarly, the United States has stressed rule making and institution building in the Asia-Pacific Economic Cooperation (APEC) forum. This has become a political issue within APEC, with its opponents arguing that market forces matter more than rules and regulations. APEC, the opponents of institutionalism say, should adopt a "loose and open regionalism," the consensual style of ASEAN rather than the rules-based approach of the EU.

Such arguments aside, both APEC and the EU are close to the ideal sought by the institutionalists. They are communities across nations, mostly neighbours, which meet on specific policy matters whose parameters have gradually deepened and widened.

Scenarios

As long as no single institution or network goes too far, according to the norms and perceptions of its time, peace should prevail. For example, taken too far in the direction of rules and codes, APEC would conflict with the World Trade Organization; the ARF might alarm China and force it into a defensive posture; ASEAN's flirtation with Europe through the Asia–Europe Meeting (ASEM) might frighten the United States into adopting a more protectionist and bloc-like model within the North American Free Trade Association (NAFTA).

Model preference

The United States, Australia and New Zealand, and Russia are enthusiastic institutionalists. ASEAN and Japan, however, are sceptics, because of their dislike for the type of legalism that institutionalism often represents. China is particularly averse to participating in any form of rules-based organization that would impose legal restrictions on its sovereignty.

Assessment

Institutionalism is compatible with both realism and idealism. Realists, like institutionalists, expect the principal actors in global affairs to share common norms and values. Idealists look at institutions as having the power to spread common norms and values through the force of example. Institutions help to build confidence, according to idealists, because the main actors learn each other's values. Knowledge is the antidote to fear.

The US perspective on institutionalism has elements of both realism and idealism. One current thrust of US policy emphasizes soft power. The idea is to nurture global institutions based on the US norms, rules, and institutions. By reflecting US values, such institutions maximize US "soft power" – or so the thinking goes. The policy implications for the United States are to enmesh as many actors as possible in such schemes, led by the United States.

Interdependence

Architects of interdependence argue that shared economic interests, based on open markets, lead to peace.

Structural properties

This model becomes isomorphic as more and more national and regional markets subscribe to free-market capitalism. The more global players share a common economic system: in other words, the more economic actors become the common denominator of the global political economy.

Behavioural rules

The free marketeers have a simple creed: stay market friendly for greater profits; stay fit and nimble; carry out structural adjustments quickly when needed; and strike a sensible balance between market liberalization and social disintegration. The creed accepts that wealth creates the basic conditions for peace: the wealthy have a vested interest in keeping the peace, whereas the dispossessed have nothing to lose in times of war.

Role of international institutions

Free marketeers approve of international institutions as long as they are market friendly. They see as particularly useful international organizations that monitor market forces and government policy. Both the Organization for Economic Co-operation and Development (OECD) and, more recently, APEC carry out such monitoring. Some free marketeers, however, object that institutions may obstruct market forces from functioning freely. For example, some Pacific Asians are reluctant to fix rules and standards of international organizations – APEC in particular – at an early stage in ways congenial to the current market leader.

Scenarios

For North-East Asia in the year 2005, the risks of this model seem slight. The two dangers are protectionism, which could create rifts in the growing network of interdependence, and income inequality resulting from drastic market liberalization. Otherwise, peace is likely to be the outcome of the region's growing affluence.

Model preference

Japan is the most enthusiastic proponent in the region of economic strategies for conflict reduction. ASEAN, the United States, and Russia offer milder endorsements.

Assessment

Technological progress has brought nations together into a global economy where interlinkages and interpenetration are increasingly the norm. Greater interdependence fosters peace, especially when it leads to prosperity and alleviates inequality within a given country. The challenge is to expand the network of interdependence while ensuring that prosperity and equality go hand in hand. Unless the latter challenge is met, economic growth may trigger social collapse, protectionism, and political instability.

Democracy

Democracy requires government accountability and responsibility. Consequently, it is harder for governments to resort to war, especially with other democracies. Empirically, democracies rarely fight each other.

Structural properties

The belief and anticipation that democracy will become widely prevalent fosters this model's isomorphism: even if authoritarian regimes remain, democrats assume that they will eventually join the ranks of democracies. Democrats believe that democracy itself will transform the international system into a club of equals.

Behavioural rules

The principles of democracy are widely known and understood, although rarely applied with any consistency. Democrats argue that democracy leads to the peaceful evolution of civil society, in which inequality is minimized. Peace will grow out of continued democratization in Pacific Asia, according to this model.

Role of international institutions

Democrats look to international institutions to champion democratization and human rights. In recent years, a number of international institutions, foreign ministries, and non-governmental organizations (NGOs) have begun to monitor and assess freedom and democracy in order to facilitate democratization. Democrats sometimes argue that stronger measures are necessary. A classic example is the imposition of restrictions on concessional lending to China by the international financial institutions after Chinese troops killed students and workers in Tiananmen Square in June 1989. Currently, US President Bill Clinton's UN advisors have argued in favour of intervention to maintain, advance, or restore democracy in Haiti and elsewhere.

Scenarios

Under this model there are risks that democratization might trigger instability of an extreme kind or cause the loss of confidence in a government that is non-democratic or imperfectly democratic. Otherwise, in a variation on the interdependence model, peace is an outcome of democracy coupled with economic prosperity.

Model preference

Americans, Australians, New Zealanders, and the Japanese are strong proponents of the democracy model; acceptance is growing among the élite of ASEAN. Yet there are senior Asian statesmen who disagree vehemently and noisily. The policy élite in China reject the democracy model as US propaganda.

Assessment

Democracy has made steady progress throughout the twentieth century, especially in the last three decades. If one can imagine a world populated with egalitarian democracies, one can also accept the notion that democracy is conducive to peace. The implication for US policy is to do everything it can to facilitate democratization. One role the United States may play is to smooth the way for states that are in the process of transition from authoritarian to democratic regimes. Specifically, the United States and its allies should facilitate the smooth transition of China, North Korea, and Viet Nam into the democratic family of nations.

Summary of the role of international institutions

The importance of international institutions depends very much on viewpoint. Realists minimize the role of international institutions; perhaps it is tautological to note that institutionalists maximize it. The interdependence and democratic perspectives both want institutions to perform as ombudsmen of the international system: one is concerned with economic, the other with political criteria. However, the appreciation of international institutions by proponents of economic interdependence and democracy is little more than opportunism. Neither is committed to international institutions as the most effective agents to scrutinize adherence to free market or democratic practices.

Pressure points: Threat perception in North-East Asia

Now that I have laid out my taxonomy for peace building, I will summarize the major threats to North-East Asian peace and stability. These threats have been covered by my colleagues in the preceding chapters. My contribution is to outline the major themes of threat perception in the region – territorial disputes, national unification problems, and nuclear non-proliferation.

Territorial disputes

In our volume, Song Yimin, Cheng-yi Lin, and James Tang deal with the South China Sea issue, centring on territorial disputes over the barren Spratly Archipelago. Lau Teik Soon offers a view on possible mediation roles that might be played by ASEAN, the ARF, and other entities.

192

The territorial fight over ownership of the Spratly Islands has dragged in China, Taiwan, Viet Nam, and all the ASEAN countries, except for Thailand and Singapore. Each country has its sovereignty claims to individual islands, and many have fielded naval forces to protect them. China claims sovereignty over most of the region, backing up its claim with an increasingly powerful navy. Although ASEAN countries continue to hope that China will compromise, so far no such offer has been forthcoming.

International institutions are severely limited in what they can do to ease tensions over the Spratlys, but there are important issues of international law at stake. First, and most obviously, is the territorial issue, which raises the question of how conflicting claims may be arbitrated when there is no historical or legal precedent for arbitration. Second, the conflicting claims have jeopardized the right of innocent passage through the sea, supposedly guaranteed by the Law of the Sea convention, as well as common practice. These conflicts could potentially threaten the economic prosperity of much of Pacific Asia. Third, the conflicts threaten to interrupt another important economic activity – the search for oil. The Spratly waters have proven potential for oil and other resources.

National unification issues

Song Yimin, Cheng-yi Lin, and James Tang also deal with the contentious issue of Chinese unification. The chapters by Byung-joon Ahn and, to a lesser extent, Peter Hayes deal with North-East Asia's other flashpoint – the trauma of Korean unification.

The ghost of the nineteenth century lingers on in national unification issues, where nineteenth-century notions of national sovereignty and non-interference in matters of territorial integrity prevail. Unfortunately for North-East Asia, the neighbourhood is burdened with two of the world's most complex and emotional unification dramas – one between China, Hong Kong, and Taiwan; the other between North and South Korea.

The issue of the two Koreas has its roots in the closing days of World War II. The two halves of Korea were created in 1945, when Soviet troops occupied Korea north of the thirty-eighth parallel and US troops held the south, and reaffirmed in the truce of 1953, following the Korean War.

The cleavage between the two client republics was put into play, then frozen by the Korean War. The Korean War, in which UN forces led by the United States clashed with Chinese troops aiding the North, made the issue far more complex than the original Soviet–US rivalry. Tensions ebbed after the Democratic People's Republic of Korea (DPRK) obtained UN membership. The problem now is that the four big powers that maintain a stake in the Korean Peninsula – the United States, China, Russia, and Japan – are committed to the status quo. Their idea of conflict resolution is to provide some fine-tuning in the international environment, such as emergency aid for North Korea, which reduces the chance of a sudden collapse of the Pyongyang government. Their passive response to the unification issue has left its resolution to the whims of domestic politics in the two Koreas.

All the same, there are some new and more promising aspects to the Korean situation. For example, the recently established Korean Energy Development Organization (KEDO) may provide a vehicle for substantial economic interaction between North and South. The ARF may suddenly attempt to engage the DPRK in its expanding circle of participants, perhaps to startling effect. The big powers could launch a scheme of their own, perhaps revisiting former US Secretary of State James Baker's proposal for big-power mediation of Korean unification.

The China–Hong Kong–Taiwan issue is immensely complex and often irrationally emotional. The return of Hong Kong to China in 1997 is the simplest side of the triangle, because the Sino-British Joint Declaration of 1983 addressed fundamental legal issues. Some observers argue that "Hong Kong 1997" has come and gone already, as the Chinese and Hong Kong economies become increasingly interdependent. British and Chinese authorities have laboured to prevent surprises in the period leading up to the reversion, which is, at 14 years, the lengthiest of the post-colonial transitions. Thus, the main significance of the transfer of sovereignty will lie in the precedent and message it sends to Taiwan. In a major policy speech in January 1996, Chinese Premier Li Peng said that Beijing would focus on reunification with Taiwan after the return of Hong Kong in 1997 and Macau in 1999. Some Chinese officials have set 2010 as a deadline for regaining Taiwan. If the international community moves to guarantee the human and civil rights of the people of Hong Kong, it will be a reassuring signal to Taiwan and perhaps a chastening one to China. If the international community takes a hands-off posture – as is perhaps most likely – Taiwan's anxiety is bound to increase.

China's tangled relationship with Taiwan is far more worrying than its straightforward claim to Hong Kong. The Taiwanese government came into being in 1945 with Japan's defeat in World War II and the end of Japanese colonial rule. For the first half of its existence, the Western world, with the exception of Britain, gave unstinting support to the Chinese Nationalist government on Taiwan. The international community supported Taiwan's claim that it continued to rule all of China after the Communist victory in 1949. But in 1971, when the United Nations ousted Taiwan and replaced it with China, against US protest, the seeds of the current conflict were laid.

Since then, the United Nations and the majority of UN member states have accepted Beijing's territorial claim over Taiwan. Only 30 countries recognize Taiwan and its population of 21 million, despite an aggressive campaign by Taiwan's government to raise its diplomatic profile that began in the early 1990s. Taiwan has also lobbied vigorously for re-admission to the United Nations; during a controversial visit to the United States in June 1995, President Lee Teng-hui offered the United Nations a gift of $1 billion in exchange for membership. The gift was politely declined.

In March 1996, as China was conducting large-scale military exercises off the coast of Taiwan, UN Secretary-General Boutros Boutros-Gali expressed the hope that "all concerned will exercise restraint" to "avoid tensions in the area," but otherwise reaffirmed the United Nations' post-1971 stance on the matter. The Secretary-General emphasized that Taiwan is a "province" of China and that any military exercises by either side constituted "an internal matter." There was no effort to call the UN Security Council into session, despite the largest mobilization of Chinese troops since the Sino-Viet Nam War of 1979 and a crisis atmosphere that caused the United States to send two aircraft carrier battle groups into nearby waters.

In fact, the United Nations has paid remarkably little attention, given its usual concern with self-determination of peoples, to the self-determination of Taiwan. The real problem began when the Nationalist government began to democratize its political system, in order to secure the loyalty of the post-mainland generation of Taiwanese. At the same time, the Taiwanese economy began a new growth spurt. By the mid-1990s, Taiwan was No. 1 or No. 2 in the world in its foreign exchange reserves, mostly US dollars. Taiwan's Democratic Progressive Party (DPP), with a platform based on Taiwanese autonomy, was gaining in popularity. Even the nationalist Kuomintang Party became increasingly sympathetic to Taiwanese interests and aspirations under the leadership of Lee Teng-hui, President since 1988 and Taiwan's first native-born leader.

Thus, Taiwanese democratization and liberal capitalism have both become elements heightening the potential for collision with China. Beijing has been alarmed by the steady progress of the DPP in recent elections in Taiwan. In July and August 1995, China conducted live-fire military exercises in the Taiwan Straits in the run-up to parliamentary elections in December 1995, in which the DPP won 35 per cent of the popular vote, campaigning on a platform of independence for Taiwan from China.

The December parliamentary elections appeared to convince the Chinese leadership that they needed to make an even stronger statement prior to Taiwan's first presidential election in March 1996. In early February, Beijing announced a second round of "military action," aimed at discouraging Taiwan's voters from a repeat performance. In this second round of exercises, China showed that it was ready to go to war to keep Taiwan from leaving the fold. Following hard on Premier Li's declaration on reunification in January, Beijing made no secret of its intention to influence Taiwan's first general election on 23 March. The exercises began on 12 March and continued until 25 May, just after the election.

As an intimidation tactic, the military drills worked only half-way – President Lee was re-elected with a solid 54 per cent majority. The DPP's candidate, Peng Min-min, got 21 per cent, and two reunification candidates got the remaining 25 per cent of the vote. But, as a demonstration of Chinese power, the exercises were a spectacular success: in 18 days of land and sea exercises, China managed effectively to blockade the Taiwan Straits by firing rockets off the key ports of Kaohsiung and Keelung. The exercises deployed 150,000 élite troops and some 300 warplanes, missile-launching craft and attack vessels. The arsenal on display included some of China's recently purchased advanced Sukhoi-27 fighter jets and four of China's Scud-type M-9 missiles, fired into "splashdown" areas near the two ports.

After the election, President Lee rather ostentatiously proposed holding a summit meeting with Premier Li of China to begin discussions on reunification. The overture was rejected. But the March crisis did produce some palpable changes in the China–Taiwan reunification drama. Taiwan's voters may be less likely than before to raise a direct challenge to Beijing's sovereignty; for many, emigration and capital flight may represent the best short-term solutions. The United States may have to rethink its strategy of deliberate ambiguity – effective in the small-scale posturing that has characterized Beijing–Taipei relations up to now, but risky when whole divisions are on the move.

The most important question of all remains unanswered. Will it be possible to work out a compromise along the lines of Hong Kong – one China, two economic systems? As the economies of China, Hong Kong, and Taiwan become integrated, the shadow of "Greater China" looms large over the rest of Asia. The Chinese bloc may well stifle growth in neighbouring Pacific Asian economies if it closes its own market and uses its vast labour force to drive export competitors out of business.

So far, China has managed to block most efforts by international institutions to soothe tensions. China insists that both Taiwan and Hong Kong are exclusively domestic issues. It has refused to allow the ARF, for example, to address either domestic or bilateral issues at meetings. Nor has China joined any of the United Nations' treaties on human rights or maritime resource development. Yet, from the perspective of the international community, there will be inexorable pressure on China to surrender partial sovereignty over a number of economic, civil, and political issues. First among these will be its treatment of civilians and the environment.

Nuclear non-proliferation

Nuclear non-proliferation is a critical issue in North-East Asian security. If nuclear non-proliferation is widely perceived to be a hollow or broken promise, North-East Asia could become a nuclear theatre more frightening, in its way, than the Cold War arena of confrontation between the Soviet Union and the United States.

In a nuclearized North-East Asia, the major powers would each possess nuclear weapons, or, falling short of an existing arsenal, would have the unambiguous capacity and will to develop one. This scenario is none too far removed from the present situation in which the American "nuclear umbrella" offers the main rationale to such nuclear-capable powers as Japan and South Korea not to develop their own nuclear weapons. Japan, of course, would have to overcome the obstacles presented by its constitution and by deep-seated public opposition to the use of nuclear weapons.

None the less, there is a dangerous tendency to overestimate the moderating influence that the United States can provide. Ideally, an international agency would exist with the clout to implement sanctions against the violators of international conventions against non-proliferation. In its absence, the international community has left the difficult and thankless job of imposing sanctions to a reluctant United States. Now that domestic support for international police work is weakening, Washington's will to accept such a role by default may also waver. Without cooperation from the United States, there is no question that the International Atomic Energy Agency (IAEA) cannot fulfil even the most basic of its tasks, the monitoring of all diversions of weapons-grade and weapons-potential nuclear material by nuclear energy states from peaceful uses, such as power generation, to the arms trade.

In this volume, Byung-joon Ahn and Peter Hayes have dealt with non-proliferation issues on the Korean Peninsula; Alex Zagorsky has covered the current thinking on nuclear strategy in Russia, while Atsuyuki Suzuki explored the economic rationale for Japan's reliance on plutonium-generating fast-breeder reactors. Suzuki has also considered the need for a regional nuclear energy agency similar to that of Europe.

The most topical and controversial of North-East Asian nuclear non-proliferation issues is the narrowly averted nuclear crisis of the spring and summer of 1994, when the DPRK refused access to IAEA inspectors to two nuclear power plants under construction. Washington and South Korea accused the North of conducting a covert nuclear weapons programme. The plants were supposed to have the capability to produce enough plutonium for one or two nuclear warheads. At the same time, the DPRK was firing off tests of its Rodong missile series in the Sea of Japan. By June 1994, Washington's hawks were preparing for war.

For a host of reasons, not least the sudden death of DPRK's paramount leader, Kim Il Sung, the crisis cooled down, and after tortuous negotiations the United States agreed to supply the North with US$5 billion worth of light-water reactors, the by-products of which do not include weapons-grade nuclear material. The October 1994 accord, as revised, stipulates that the United States and its partners, primarily Japan and South Korea, will supply light-water reactors to North Korea over a 10-year period and that the North will allow international inspections of its facilities after five years. An international consortium (KEDO) has been set up to construct the reactors.

In many ways, the KEDO deal illustrates both the power and the limitations of the current US role as regional policeman for nuclear non-proliferation. The United States wants to prevent all nuclear-capable states from developing nuclear weapons programmes. The rationale is both to keep the world safe from nuclear wars and to sustain the US position of global leadership into the foreseeable future. The quid pro quo that the United States can offer such states varies from light-water reactors and advanced fighter aircraft, to theatre missile defence systems.

North Korea, on the other hand, has two motives for continuing its nuclear programme. One is the non-controversial need to develop new energy resources when the supply of oil at "sweetheart" prices from China and Russia becomes impossible; the KEDO deal has addressed this problem. But North Korea's strategic interest in developing a nuclear weapons programme will not go away so easily. Its paranoia leads it to see a South Korea and United States perennially on the verge of invasion. It views Japan's fast-breeder reactor programme with deep suspicion, as does South Korea. From a DPRK perspective, the KEDO deal has done nothing to solve its main problem – its vulnerability to hostile neighbours. Thus the situation on the Korean Peninsula remains unstable.

A similar US strategy is visible in its efforts to limit Japan's technological potential for producing weapons-grade plutonium. The United States has started to wind down its technological cooperation. Meanwhile, Washington has urged Japan to consider joint development of a theatre defence missile system. The programme could build upon, and improve, Japan's own troubled scientific rocket programme. The main rationale is to offer Japan reassurance that the United States remains committed to its defence. The Scud missile attacks on Israel during the Gulf War created intense anxieties in Japan, which is in missile range of both China and North Korea. At the same time, the United States may be using such high-technology defence cooperation as a carrot to woo Japan away from any inclination to develop its own weapons capability.

Japan has responded to international criticism of its fast-breeder reactor programme by developing the technology to produce and use plutonium without actually extracting it from the reactors. Tokyo's leaders are aware that it has been able to sustain its nuclear power programme, which uses uranium as well as plutonium, only with the cooperation of the US, France, and Britain.

While the North Korean nuclear crisis and Japan's large-scale imports of plutonium have tended to grab headlines, Russia is no less problematical. Indeed, Russia's threat to the nuclear non-proliferation regime is global. Nuclear facilities are poorly managed, Russian nuclear scientists and engineers are flocking abroad (some to states with open nuclear ambitions), and smuggling of nuclear materials and components has become big business. Observers may tend to overlook the problem because it is so massive and, apparently, insoluble. Russia's arsenal of nuclear weapons is second only to that of the United States. Political instability, regional insurgencies, and a state of near-economic collapse exacerbate the potential for nuclear crisis. Behind the scenes, the Group of Seven (G7) countries have been trying to help Russia improve its management of nuclear facilities, but with little success. Plutonium-smuggling plots were recently uncovered in Germany. Clearly, the flow of nuclear-related materials and personnel has not been staunched.

Against this backdrop, South Korea is a nervous bystander, accustomed to firm US commitment to its defence but not always happy about the results. Leaders in Seoul spend much of their time plotting the various scenarios of response and reaction between North Korea, Japan, and the United States. Their worst nightmare is that the KEDO deal will give the North a free hand to develop nuclear weapons and that Japan will go nuclear in response: non-nuclear South Korea would be caught in between. At a less paranoid level, the South was not pleased with the nuclear inspection moratorium granted to the North under the terms of the KEDO deal. Nor does it find it pleasant to watch the United States prop up the DPRK regime by supplying oil for its factories and installing light-water reactors. Under US pressure, the South has abstained from using the controversial fast-breeder reactor technology, and it worries about Japan's intentions.

At present, there seems little scope for international institutions, other than the IAEA, to play a role in nuclear non-proliferation issues in North-East Asia. The United States and its allies have too much at stake, including front-line US troops stationed in Japan and South Korea, to invite the United Nations or anybody else to manage the show. Any experiment with a multilateral insurance scheme would probably have to come from the United States itself. The present role of international institutions is confined to important but limited tasks such as international monitoring and safeguards, encouraging the smooth installation of light-water reactors, and pouring a great deal of money into Russia and North Korea for nuclear facilities management.

Yet, even in a limited way, international organizations have played a positive role in North-East Asian security. There is potential for an expanded role. The minimal contributions of international organizations so far have at least helped to build confidence in the concept and practice of nuclear non-proliferation. The diligence of the IAEA was instrumental in drawing attention to the potential for weapons production in North Korea and ultimately in persuading Pyongyang to moderate its nuclear programme. In managing the Russian nuclear arsenal, the G7 countries have at least been able to obtain the co-operation of a distracted Russian government.

Applying the taxonomy

Finally, our shared goal has been to investigate the usefulness of our models to explain current and future trends in North-East Asian security.

Institutionalism

International precedents
The successes of ASEAN, APEC, and ARF suggest that these arrangements, or subregional variations based on them, may have a role to play in resolving at least some of the security dilemmas facing North-East Asia. Among the most encouraging developments is the membership of the "two Chinas" and Hong Kong in APEC. China, Taiwan, and Hong Kong joined APEC simultaneously at the Seoul meeting in 1991.

We see a number of lessons that can be distilled from these pan-Asian or South-East Asian multilateral experiences, including the following:
1. Do not force consensus.
2. Go at the speed of the slowest common denominator, but do not accept the low standards of the least-developed member.
3. Set gradual and realistic deadlines and allow opting out for the hesitant.
4. Try to maintain the greatest amount of flexibility without sacrificing clarity.
5. If circumstances change or one party becomes dissatisfied, be prepared to renegotiate the arrangement in order to keep participants engaged.
6. Never embarrass or threaten your partners.

7. Broach difficult topics in private or with adequate warning.
8. Ensure that you obtain complete agreement on the agenda ahead of time, and that only the appropriate topics are referred to discussion.
9. Recognize that certain sensitive matters must still be dealt with bilaterally, or with second-track or secret diplomacy.

Some of these lessons, of course, are not entirely unique to Asia or to our times. For example, after the initial enthusiasm for joint policy wore off in the European Union, members discovered that they needed some means of holding back from more ambitious policy resolutions. Europeans quickly discovered the notion of "subsidiarity," or opting out. Even Australia, which usually prefers multilateral and quasi-legal solutions to its diplomatic dilemmas, went in for private negotiations to settle its differences with Indonesia over undersea resources rights in the Timor Gap. The Indonesia–Australia agreement subsequently survived a challenge at the World Court.

Possible faster convergence in technical areas
Based on the experience of APEC and China–Taiwan relations, one of the lessons for institution builders is to start small. Among the most successful aspects of APEC is the region-wide work now on narrow technical issues, ranging from Customs regulations to safety rules and tourism. APEC working groups are actively sharing information, tackling standardization issues, and providing regional officials and experts with chances to get to know each other better. This represents institution building at a fundamental level.

Technical experts and professionals have achieved a head start on building a genuine multilateral spirit within APEC. In relations between China and Taiwan, as well, the Taiwan-based Straits Exchange Foundation and the Association for Relations Across the Taiwan Straits of the People's Republic of China (PRC) have made substantial progress on such matters as mail delivery and the verification of documents.

Whatever the reason, the success of such interaction is a signal to expand the circle of technical cooperation in the region. Atsuyuki Suzuki proposes the establishment of a regional agency to conduct nuclear non-proliferation work, complementing the IAEA. Another promising area for regional cooperation would be in the area of environmental protection regulations and technologies.

It is something of a mystery to me why it should be the case that technicians and professionals are better at multilateral institution building than are, say, political scientists. Perhaps the political leaders tend to overlook technical issues in their enthusiasm for grappling with larger policy issues, ignoring the opportunities for a meeting of minds over clearly defined and unemotional aspects of their diplomatic relationships. Perhaps it is just that some fields are so obscure that the technicians welcome somebody else – anybody – to talk to. Whatever the reasons may be, we should accept such gains as a positive trend.

Interdependence

Asians believe that markets and economies are best left alone. They distrust both managed trade and the type of forced march to market liberalization favoured by the World Bank. Asians see trade and investment flows as almost impossible to control or direct, along with illegal immigration and smuggling. Some of the most rapid growth in the region is taking place in the so-called "growth triangles," which succeed despite the fact that they cut across state boundaries as well as ideological divisions.

Even so, the region displays an inexorable trend towards liberalization. ASEAN and APEC both are committed to reducing trade barriers over the next few decades. Such commitments reflect an innate trust in the virtues of free markets fostered by a homogeneous merchant class. Each step towards liberalization has been accompanied, however, by high levels of anxiety over the potential for social disintegration. This can be seen in the paternalism of Singapore, which in the spring of 1996 became the first nation to introduce official screening of the Internet. It can also be seen in the periodic drives against "spiritual corruption" in China, which target pop culture and the sexual revolution.

Democracy

Democracy continues to be a tangled issue in Asia. Wherever it is practised in the region, democracy has an "Asian face." Asian democracies do not always meet the criteria associated with Western-style democracy. The rest of the world is gradually becoming accustomed to the differences, although not smoothly. The continuing debates over the nature of Asian values and Asian democracy may actually have produced set-backs for democracy in countries whose leaders feel threatened by Western criticism. China, for example, regards with suspicion the genuinely inspired democracy movements in Hong Kong and Taiwan, seeing them as attempts by the West to undermine or destabilize their political system.

None the less, in 1995, the release from house arrest of Myanmar's most prominent democracy activist, Aung San Suu Kyi, attests to the enduring power of democracy.

Balancing realism

The Chinese favour this most traditional of models, along with the proponents of *realpolitik* in the United States, Japan, and ASEAN. The strategy suggested by this model is to maintain the current status quo. The risks to it lie in China's rapid military build-up and in US isolationism triggered by anger over the perceived unfair tactics of Asian trading partners. The latter could lead to the withdrawal of US troops from Asia. Song Yimin argues that the PRC does not seek military dominance and wants to be a good neighbour. The views from Taiwan and Hong Kong are more sceptical. Nevertheless, most of our Chinese scholars believe that the United States will eventually wind down its military presence in Asia and become either an engaged or distant balancer, depending on the domestic environment and administration.

Bandwagonning realism

As we have noted, few now expect US hegemony to survive in the region. The two most likely challengers to US hegemony – China and Japan – are both unknown quantities in this particular role. If either rises to hegemony, all bets are off: neither country's behaviour can be readily anticipated or predicted, and the isomorphic structure of our model breaks down.

I have listed the preferences of each of our contributors, within our taxonomy of security models:
– Lau (Singapore): Institutionalism
– Clements (Australia): Institutionalism/Democracy
– Song (China): Realism
– Tang (Hong Kong): Interdependence/Democracy/Realism
– Lin (Taiwan): Interdependence/Democracy
– Zagorsky (Russia): Institutionalism/Realism

- Suzuki (Japan): Institutionalism
- Ahn (South Korea): Interdependence/Realism
- Hayes (United States): Realism

If nothing else, this volume demonstrates that Pacific Asian scholars cannot easily be fitted into one dominant model or methodology. Whether this remains a short-term phenomenon will be one of the more interesting questions for academicians and practitioners.

We revere Kant's memory for his encouragement to examine the issues of peace and security at a structural and philosophical level. Like us, he lived at a time when blind forces were breaking down the old systems of war and peace and new systems had yet to emerge. The sweeping regional and global changes of the post-Cold War world have put the traditional tools of diplomacy to test and found them wanting. War and intimidation lose some of their efficacy when neither ideologies nor national borders are the principal assets at stake in international conflict. At the same time, confidence building takes time – and crises will certainly not wait until the institutions are at hand to defuse them.

How should nations organize their political systems and economies to nurture peace? And how can we expand the construction of systems to nurture peace to the regional and global level? Perhaps, because of the criticism directed at efforts to build peace structures across nation-states, we should for the time being emphasize interdependence and democracy. At the same time, we can prepare ourselves for an unknown future by constructing our models and scenarios. If we have constructed them well, they may alert us to the blind spots in our vision and help us toward the ultimate goal of perpetual peace.

Notes and references

1. Kant, Immanuel. (1795) *For Perpetual Peace*, as selectively reproduced in Howard Williams, Moorhead Wright, and Tony Evans (eds) (1993) *A Reader in International Relations Theory and Political Theory* (Buckingham: Open University Press) pp. 112–121.
2. Kissinger, Henry A. (1994) *Diplomacy*. New York: Simon and Schuster.
3. Gilpin, Robert. (1983) *War and Change in World Politics*. New York: Cambridge University Press.
4. Keohane, Robert O. (1984) *After Hegemony: Cooperation and Discord in the World Political Economy* (Princeton: Princeton University Press); John G. Ruggie (1993) *Multilateralism Matters* (New York: Columbia University Press).

5. Keohane, Robert O., and Joseph S. Nye, Jr (1977, 1989) *Power and Interdependence: World Politics in Transition*. Boston: Little, Brown.
6. Russett, Bruce, and William Antholis. (1992) "Do Democracies Fight Each Other? Evidence from the Peloponnesian War." *Journal of Peace Research* 29(4): 415–434.
7. Russett, Bruce M. (1993) *Grasping the Democratic Peace*. Princeton: Princeton University Press.
8. This taxonomy was first presented in Inoguchi Takashi (1994) *Sekai hendo no mikata* (Global changes) (Tokyo: Chikuma Shobo); and Inoguchi (1994) "Five scenarios for Asian security: Affluence, amity and assertiveness in its changing configuration," paper presented at the Council on Foreign Relations, 17 October 1994.

Appendices

Appendix 1

Treaty of Amity and Cooperation in Southeast Asia

Preamble

The High Contracting Parties:

CONSCIOUS of the existing ties of history, geography and culture, which have bound their peoples together;

ANXIOUS to promote regional peace and stability through abiding respect for justice and the rule of law and enhancing regional resilience in their relations;

DESIRING to enhance peace, friendship and mutual cooperation on matters affecting Southeast Asia consistent with the spirit and principles of the Charter of the United Nations, the Ten Principles adopted by the Asian-African Conference in Bandung on 25 April 1955, the Declaration of the Association of Southeast Asian Nations signed in Bangkok on 8 August 1967, and the Declaration signed in Kuala Lumpur on 27 November 1971;

CONVINCED that the settlement of differences or disputes between their countries should be regulated by national, effective and sufficiently flexible procedures, avoiding negative attitudes which might endanger or hinder cooperation;

BELIEVING in the need for cooperation with all peace-loving nations, both within and outside Southeast Asia, in the furtherance of world peace, stability and harmony;

SOLEMNLY AGREE to enter into a Treaty of Amity and Cooperation as follows:

Chapter I
Purpose And Principles

Article 1

The purpose of this Treaty is to promote perpetual peace, everlasting amity and cooperation among their peoples which would contribute to their strength, solidarity and closer relationship.

Article 2

In their relations with one another, the High Contracting Parties shall be guided by the following fundamental principles:

a) Mutual respect for the independence, sovereignty, equality, territorial integrity and national identity of all nations;
b) The right of every State to lead its national existence free from external interference, subversion or coercion;
c) Non-interference in the internal affairs of one another;
d) Settlement of differences or disputes by peaceful means;
e) Renunciation of the threat or use of force;
f) Effective cooperation among themselves.

Chapter II
Amity

Article 3

In pursuance of the purpose of this Treaty the High Contracting Parties shall endeavour to develop and strengthen the traditional, cultural and historical ties of friendship, good neighbourliness and cooperation which bind them together and shall fulfil in good faith the obligations assumed under this Treaty. In order to promote closer understanding among them, the High Contracting Parties shall encourage and facilitate contact and intercourse among their peoples.

Chapter III
Cooperation

Article 4

The High Contracting Parties shall promote active cooperation in the economic, social, cultural, technical, scientific and administrative fields as well as in matters of common ideas and aspirations of international peace and stability in the region and all other matters of common interest.

Article 5

Pursuant to Article 4 the High Contracting Parties shall exert their maximum efforts multilaterally as well as bilaterally on the basis of equality, non-discrimination and mutual benefit.

Article 6

The High Contracting Parties shall collaborate for the acceleration of the economic growth in the region in order to strengthen the foundation for a prosperous and peaceful community of nations in Southeast Asia. To this end, they shall promote the greater utilization of their agriculture and industries, the expansion of their trade and the improvement of their peoples. In this regard, they shall continue to explore all avenues for close and beneficial cooperation with other States as well as international and regional organizations outside the region.

Article 7

The High Contracting Parties, in order to achieve social justice and to raise the standards of living of the peoples of the region, shall intensify economic cooperation. For this purpose, they shall adopt appropriate regional strategies for economic development and mutual assistance.

Article 8

The High Contracting Parties shall strive to achieve the closest cooperation on the widest scale and shall seek to provide assistance to one another in the form of training and research facilities in the social, cultural, technical, scientific and administrative fields.

Article 9

The High Contracting Parties shall endeavour to foster cooperation in the furtherance of the cause of peace, harmony and stability in the region. To this end, the High Contracting Parties shall maintain regular contacts and consultations with one another on international and regional matters with a view to coordinating their views, actions and policies.

Article 10

Each High Contracting Party shall not in any manner or form participate in any activity which shall constitute a threat to the political and economic stability, sovereignty, or territorial integrity of another High Contracting Party.

Article 11

The High Contracting Parties shall endeavour to strengthen their respective national resilience in their political, economic, socio-cultural as well as security fields in conformity with their respective ideas and aspirations, free from external interference as well as internal subversive activities in order to preserve their respective national identities.

Article 12

The High Contracting Parties in their efforts to achieve regional prosperity and security, shall endeavour to cooperate in all fields for the promotion of regional resilience, based on the principles of self-confidence, self-reliance, mutual respect, cooperation and solidarity which will constitute the foundation for a strong and viable community of nations in Southeast Asia.

Chapter IV
Pacific Settlement of Disputes

Article 13

The High Contracting Parties shall have the determination and good faith to prevent disputes from arising. In case disputes on matters directly affecting them should arise, especially disputes likely to disturb regional peace and harmony, they shall refrain from the threat or use of force and shall at all times settle such disputes among themselves through friendly negotiations.

Article 14

To settle disputes through regional processes, the High Contracting Parties shall constitute, as a continuing body, a High Council comprising a Representative at ministerial level from each of the High Contracting Parties to take cognizance of the existence of disputes or situations likely to disturb regional peace and harmony.

Article 15

In the event no solution is reached through direct negotiations, the High Council shall take cognizance of the dispute or the situation and shall recommend to the parties in dispute appropriate means of settlement such as good offices, mediation, inquiry or conciliation. The High Council may however offer its good offices, or upon agreement of the parties in dispute, constitute itself into a committee of mediation, inquiry or conciliation. When deemed necessary, the High Council shall recommend appropriate measures for the prevention of a deterioration of the dispute or the situation.

Article 16

The foregoing provisions of this Chapter shall not apply to a dispute unless all the parties to the dispute agree to their application to that dispute. However, this shall not preclude the other High Contracting Parties not party to the dispute from offering all possible assistance to settle the said dispute. Parties to the dispute should be well disposed towards such offer of assistance.

Article 17

Nothing in this Treaty shall preclude recourse to the modes of peaceful settlement contained in Article 33(1) of the Charter of the United Nations. The High Contracting Parties which are parties to a dispute should be encouraged to take initiatives to solve it by friendly negotiations before resorting to the other procedures provided for in the Charter of the United Nations.

Chapter V
General Provisions

Article 18

This Treaty shall be signed by the Republic of Indonesia, Malaysia, the Republic of the Philippines, the Republic of Singapore and the Kingdom of Thailand. It shall be ratified in accordance with the constitutional procedures of each signatory State.

It shall be open for accession by other States in Southeast Asia.

Article 19

This Treaty shall enter into force on the date of the deposit of the fifth instrument of ratification with the Governments of the signatory States which are designated Depositories of this Treaty and of the instruments of ratification or accession.

Article 20

This Treaty is drawn up in the official languages of the High Contracting Parties, all of which are equally authoritative. There shall be an agreed common translation of the text in the English language. Any divergent interpretation of the common text shall be settled by negotiation.

IN FAITH THEREOF the High Contracting Parties have signed the Treaty and have hereto affixed their seals.

DONE AT DENPASAR, Bali, this Twenty-fourth day of February in the year one thousand nine hundred and seventy-six.

For the Republic of Indonesia, President, (sg d) Soeharto.

For Malaysia, Prime Minister, (sg d) Datuk Hussein Onn.

For the Republic of the Philippines, President, (sg d) Ferdinand E Marcos.

For the Republic of Singapore, Prime Minister, (sg d) Lee Kuan Yew.

For the Kingdom of Thailand, Prime Minister, (sg d) Kukrit Pramoj.

Appendix 2

ASEAN Regional Forum (ARF)

CHAIRMAN'S STATEMENT
THE FIRST MEETING OF THE ASEAN REGIONAL FORUM (ARF)
25 JULY 1994, BANGKOK

1. The First Meeting of the ASEAN Regional Forum (ARF) was held in Bangkok on 25 July 1994 *in accordance with the 1992 Singapore Declaration of the Fourth ASEAN Summit*, whereby the ASEAN Heads of State and Government proclaimed their intent to intensify ASEAN's external dialogues in political and security matters as a means of building cooperative ties with states in the Asia-Pacific region.

2. Attending the Meeting were *the Foreign Ministers of ASEAN, ASEAN's Dialogue Partners, ASEAN's Consultative Partners, and ASEAN's Observers or their representatives*. The Minister of Foreign Affairs of Thailand, served as Chairman of the Meeting.

3. Being the first time ever that high-ranking representatives from the majority of states in the Asia-Pacific region came to specifically discuss political and security

ASEAN consists of Brunei Darussalam, Indonesia, Malaysia, Philippines, Singapore, and Thailand. ASEAN's Dialogue Partners are: Australia, Canada, the European Union, Japan, New Zealand, Republic of Korea, and the United States. ASEAN's Consultative Partners are China and Russia. And, ASEAN's Observers are Laos, Papua New Guinea, and Vietnam.

cooperation issues, the Meeting was considered *a historic event for the region. More importantly, the Meeting signified the opening of a new chapter of peace, stability and cooperation for Southeast Asia.*

4. The participants of the Meeting held a productive exchange of views on the current political and security evaluation in the Asia-Pacific region, recognizing that developments in one part of the region could have an impact on the security of the region as whole. It was agreed that, as a high-level consultative forum, the ARF had enabled the countries in the Asia-Pacific region *to foster the habit of constructive dialogue and consultation on political and security issues of common interest and concern. In this respect, the ARF would be in a position to make significant contributions to efforts towards confidence-building and preventive diplomacy in the Asia-Pacific region.*

5. Bearing in mind the importance of non-proliferation of nuclear weapons in the maintenance of international peace and security, the Meeting *welcomed the continuation of US-DPRK negotiation and endorsed the early resumption of inter-Korean dialogue.*

6. The Meeting agreed to:

   a) *convene the ARF on an annual basis* and hold the second meeting in Brunei Darussalam in 1995; and

   b) *endorse the purposes and principles of ASEAN's Treaty of Amity and Cooperation in Southeast Asia, as a code of conduct governing relations between states* and a unique diplomatic instrument for regional confidence-building, preventive diplomacy, and political and security cooperation.

7. The Meeting also agreed to entrust the next Chairman of the ARF, Brunei Darussalam, working in consultation with ARF participants as appropriate to:

   a) collate and study all papers and ideas raised during the ARF Senior Officials Meeting and the ARF in Bangkok for submission to the second ARF through the second ARF-SOM, both of which to be held in Brunei Darussalam. *Ideas which might be the subjects of such further study include confidence and security building, nuclear non-proliferation, peacekeeping cooperation including regional peacekeeping training centre, exchanges of non-classified military information, maritime security issues, and preventive diplomacy;*

   b) *study the comprehensive concept of security,* including its economic and social aspects, as it pertains to the Asia-Pacific region;

   c) *study other relevant internationally recognized norms and principles pertaining to international and regional political and security cooperation for* their possible contribution to regional political and security cooperation;

   d) *promote the eventual participation of all ARF countries in the UN Conventional Arms Register;* and

     e) *convene, if necessary, informal meetings of officials to study all relevant papers and suggestions to move the ARF process forward.*

8. Recognizing the need to develop a more predictable and constructive pattern of relationships for the Asia-Pacific region, the Meeting expressed its firm conviction to continue to work towards the strengthening and the enhancement of political and security cooperation within the region, as a means of ensuring a lasting peace, stability, and prosperity for the region and its peoples.

Appendix 3

AGREED FRAMEWORK BETWEEN
THE DEMOCRATIC PEOPLE'S REPUBLIC OF KOREA
AND THE UNITED STATES OF AMERICA
GENEVA, OCTOBER 21, 1994

Delegations of the Governments of the Democratic People's Republic of Korea (DPRK) and the United States of America (U.S.) held talks in Geneva from September 23 to October 21, 1994, to negotiate an overall resolution of the nuclear issue on the Korean Peninsula.

Both sides reaffirmed the importance of attaining the objectives contained in the August 12, 1994 Agreed Statement between the DPRK and the U.S. and upholding the principles of the June 11, 1993 Joint Statement of the DPRK and the U.S. to achieve peace and security on a nuclear-free Korean Peninsula. The DPRK and the U.S. decided to take the following actions for the resolution of the nuclear issue:

I. Both sides will cooperate to replace the DPRK's graphite-moderated reactors and related facilities with light-water reactor (LWR) power plants.

1) In accordance with the October 20, 1994 letter of assurance from the U.S. President, the U.S. will undertake to make arrangements for the provision to the DPRK of a LWR project with a total generating capacity of approximately 2,000 MW (e) by a target date of 2003.

– The U.S. will organize under its leadership an International consortium to finance and supply the LWR project to be provided to the DPRK. The U.S., representing the international consortium, will serve as the principal point of contact with the DPRK for the LWR project.

217

    – The U.S., representing the consortium, will make best efforts to secure the conclusion of a supply contract with the DPRK within six months of the date of this Document for the provision of the LWR project. Contract talks will begin as soon as possible after the date of this Document.

    – As necessary, the DPRK and the U.S. will conclude a bilateral agreement, for cooperation in the field of peaceful uses of nuclear energy.

  2) In accordance with the October 20, 1994 letter of assurance from the U.S. President, the U.S., representing the consortium, will make arrangements to offset the energy foregone due to the freeze of the DPRK's graphite-moderated reactors and related facilities, pending completion of the first LWR unit.

    – Alternative energy will be provided in the form of heavy oil for heating and electricity production.

    – Deliveries of heavy oil will begin within three months of the date of this Document and will reach a rate of 500,000 tons annually, in accordance with an agreed schedule of deliveries.

  3) Upon receipt of U.S. assurances for the provision of LWRs and for arrangements for interim energy alternatives, the DPRK will freeze its graphite-moderated reactors and related facilities and will eventually dismantle these reactors and related facilities.

    – The freeze on the DPRK's graphite-moderated reactors and related facilities will be fully implemented within one month of the date of this Document. During this one-month period, and throughout the freeze, the International Atomic Energy Agency (IAEA) will be allowed to monitor this freeze, and the DPRK will provide full cooperation to the IAEA for this purpose.

    – Dismantlement of the DPRK's graphite-moderated reactors and related facilities will be completed when the LWR project is completed.

    – The DPRK and the U.S. will cooperate in finding a method to store safely the spent fuel from the 5 MW (e) experimental reactor during the construction of the LWR project and to dispose of the fuel in a safe manner that does not involve reprocessing in the DPRK.

  4) As soon as possible after the date of this Document, DPRK and U.S. experts will hold two sets of experts talks.

    – At one set of talks, experts will discuss issues related to alternative energy and the replacement of the graphite-moderated reactor program with the LWR project.

    – At the other set of talks, experts will discuss specific arrangements for spent fuel storage and ultimate disposition.

  II. The two sides will move toward full normalization of political and economic relations.

  1) Within three months of the date of this Document, both sides will reduce barriers to trade and investment, including restrictions on telecommunications services and financial transactions.

2) Each side will open a liaison office in the other's capital following resolution of consular and other technical issues through expert-level discussions.

3) As progress is made on issues of concern to each side, the DPRK and the U.S. will upgrade bilateral relations to the Ambassadorial level.

III. Both sides will work together for peace and security on a nuclear-free Korean Peninsula.

1) The U.S. will provide formal assurances to the DPRK against the threat or use of nuclear weapons by the U.S.

2) The DPRK will consistently take steps to implement the North-South Joint Declaration on the Denuclearization of the Korean Peninsula.

3) The DPRK will engage in North-South dialogue, as this Agreed Framework will help create an atmosphere that promotes such dialogue.

IV. Both sides will work together to strengthen the international nuclear non-proliferation regime.

1) The DPRK will remain a party to the Treaty on the Non-Proliferation of Nuclear Weapons (NPT) and will allow implementation of its safeguards agreement under the Treaty.

2) Upon conclusion of the supply contract for the provision of the LWR project, ad hoc and routine inspections will resume under the DPRK's safeguards agreement with the IAEA with respect to the facilities not subject to the freeze. Pending conclusion of the supply contract, inspections required by the IAEA for the continuity of safeguards will continue at the facilities not subject to the freeze.

3) When a significant portion of the LWR project is completed, but before delivery of key nuclear components, the DPRK will come into full compliance with its safeguards agreement with the IAEA (INFCIRC/403), including taking all steps that may be deemed necessary by the IAEA, following consultations with the Agency with regard to verifying the accuracy and completeness of the DPRK's initial report on all nuclear material in the DPRK.

Kang Sok Ju
Head of the Delegation of the
Democratic People's Republic of Korea,
First Vice-Minister of Foreign
Affairs of the Democratic People's
Republic of Korea

Robert L. Gallucci
Head of the Delegation of the
United States of America,
Ambassador at Large of the
United States of America

Appendix 4

Joint DPRK-USA Press Statement

The delegations of the Democratic People's Republic of Korea (DPRK) and the United States of America (U.S.) held talks in Kuala Lumpur from May 19 to June 12, 1995, with respect to implementation of the DPRK-U.S. Agreed Framework of October 21, 1994.

Both sides reaffirmed their political commitments to implement the DPRK-U.S. Agreed Framework, and with particular regard to facilitating the light water reactor (LWR) project as called for in the Agreed Framework, decided as follows:

I

The U.S. reaffirms that the letter of assurance from the U.S. President dated October 20, 1994 concerning the provision of the LWR project and interim energy alternatives continues in effect.

The Korean Peninsula Energy Development Organization (KEDO), under U.S. leadership, will finance and supply the LWR project in the DPRK as called for in the Agreed Framework. As specified in the Agreed Framework, the U.S. will serve as the principal point of contact with the DPRK for the LWR project. In this regard, U.S. citizens will lead delegations and teams of KEDO as required to fulfill this role.

II

The LWR project will consist of two pressurized light water reactors with two coolant loops and a generating capacity of approximately 1,000 MW(e) each. The reactor model, selected by KEDO, will be the advanced version of U.S. origin design and technology currently under production.

220

III

The Commission for External Economic Relations representing the DPRK Government and KEDO will conclude a supply agreement at the earliest possible date for the provision of the LWR project on a turnkey basis. On the basis of this statement the DPRK will meet with KEDO as soon as possible to negotiate the outstanding issues of the LWR supply agreement.

KEDO will conduct a site survey to identify the requirements for construction and operation of the LWR project. The costs of this site survey and site preparation will be included in the scope of supply for the project.

KEDO will select a prime contractor to carry out the project.

A U.S. firm will serve as program coordinator to assist KEDO in supervising overall implementation of the LWR project: KEDO will select the program coordinator.

A DPRK firm will enter into implementing arrangements as necessary to facilitate the LWR project.

IV

In addition to the LWR project, the two sides decided to take the following steps towards implementation of the Agreed Framework.

Experts from the two sides will meet in the DPRK as soon as possible in June to agree on a schedule and cooperative measures for phased delivery of heavy fuel oil in accordance with the Agreed Framework. KEDO will begin immediately to make arrangements for an initial delivery of heavy fuel oil, subject to conclusion of the above agreement.

The DPRK-U.S. Record of Meeting of January 20, 1995, on safe storage of spent fuel will be expeditiously implemented. In this regard, a U.S. team of experts will visit the DPRK as soon as possible in June to begin implementation.

Appendix 5

**Peace Mechanism Should be Established on Korean Peninsula
without Delay**

MEMORANDUM OF DPRK FOREIGN MINISTRY

The Foreign Ministry of the Democratic People's Republic of Korea on June 29 published a memorandum on the 20th anniversary of the adoption of a resolution on the Korean question at the 30th UN general assembly session.

The document says the Foreign Ministry of the DPRK publishes a memorandum to make clear the stand of the Government of the DPRK concerning the question arising in implementing the UN general assembly resolution on the Korean question.

In the first part the memorandum elaborates on the sincere efforts of the DPRK Government to implement the UN resolution.

The Government of the DPRK has put forward reasonable ways and proposals and did all its possible efforts to implement the resolution of the 30th UN general assembly session and achieve a lasting peace on the Korean peninsula, the memorandum says, and continues:

The Government of the DPRK has paid a primary attention to talks with the United States. In 1974 it proposed the U.S. side for talks to replace the Armistice Agreement with a peace agreement and on January 10, 1934, it proposed to have tripartite talks among the DPRK, the U.S. and the south Korean authorities.

With a view to easing politico-military tensions between the north and south of Korea, though it is not a package solution to peace guarantee, the DPRK Government set forth a new proposal on December 30, 1986 to hold high-level political and military talks between the north and south.

On July 23, 1987, the DPRK Government proposed to reduce the troops in the north and south to less than 100,000 each with three phases and, accordingly, called for a phased withdrawal of the U.S. forces from south Korea. And it took a positive step to discharge 100,000 soldiers by the end of 1987 as a well-intentioned step. On November 7, 1988, the DPRK Government brought forward a comprehensive peace proposal to realise the principle of guaranteeing peace, U.S. troop pullout in parallel with arms reduction of the north and the south and verify them, which came in a concrete form of the phased arms cut proposal, and a wide-range proposal for universal and complete arms reduction and peace on the Korean peninsula on May 31, 1990.

Thanks to the sustained generosity and sincere efforts of the DPRK, "Agreement on Reconciliation, Non-aggression, Cooperation and Interchange between the North and the South" was adopted in December 1991 and the North-South Joint Military Committee was organised to supervise the implementation of the agreed non-aggression. As a result, a substantial foundation for preserving peace between the north and the south has been laid.

The questions remain only to be resolved between the DPRK and the U.S. in implementing the UN General Assembly resolution for a durable peace on the Korean peninsula.

If the U.S. had accepted the fair and aboveboard proposals of the DPRK, the UN resolution would have been implemented long ago, a danger of war removed from the Korean peninsula and a lasting peace settled in this region.

In the second part the memorandum says that to establish a new peace mechanism in place of the outdated armistice system in the Korean peninsula is an important matter which brooks no further delay.

The United States, a signatory to the Korean Armistice Agreement, far from observing it, has systematically wrecked and violated it.

Shortly after the Armistice Agreement was signed and its implementation began, the U.S. set out to unilaterally abrogate Paragraph 13 d, a nucleus of the agreement.

Paragraph 13 d of the Korean Armistice Agreement requires to "cease the introduction into Korea of reinforcing combat aircraft, armored vehicles, weapons, and ammunition" and stipulates that the Neutral Nations Supervisory Commission, through its Neutral Nations Inspection Teams, shall conduct supervision and inspection of the implementation in this respect.

When the shipment of its operational materials had been brought into light one after another, the U.S. side forced neutral nations inspection teams to withdraw in June 1956 and declared an abrogation of the observance of the paragraph 13 d of the Armistice Agreement at the 75th meeting of the Military Armistice Commission (MAC) on June 21, 1957.

In fact, the Armistice Agreement and the ceasefire mechanism had since had no influence and the Neutral Nations Supervisory Commission had nothing to do in actuality.

The U.S. side abrogation of the paragraph of the Armistice Agreement at its disposition means the abrogation of the paragraph 61 of the agreement which is stipulated to be revised and supplemented only under the agreement between the two sides; it is destruction of the legal foundation for maintaining the Armistice Agreement.

Moreover, in March 1991, the U.S. side paralysed the MAC by appointing to the post of "senior member" of the MAC a "general" of the puppet army of south Korea which is not a signatory to the Armistice Agreement but doggedly went against its signing itself and has no real power in the maintenance of the ceasefire.

Under such condition, the Korean People's Army side took a step for recalling its members from the MAC and getting delegations of the Chinese People's Volunteers and the Neutral Nations Supervisory Commission withdrawn.

Owing to the irresponsible acts of the U.S. side in the past, the Korean Armistice Agreement (KAA) has now become a mere scrap of paper with no content but form, and the armistice supervisory mechanism, a tool for fulfilling the agreement, has remained like a house with no pillars.

The armistice system has been unable to be rehabilitated and revived and there is no other way to replace it with a new system.

To provide an institutional machine to prevent the recurrence of a war in Korea is an immediate task assigned to the real signatories to the Armistice Agreement.

The "UN Forces" present in south Korea, a legal party concerning the KAA, are an anachronistic creature produced by the United States by abusing the name of the United Nations to justify the Korean war after unleashing it. The United States must remove the cap of the "UN forces" from its forces present in south Korea.

The "UN Forces Command" in south Korea is a camouflaged one made by the United States at its disposition, not by any resolution of the United Nations.

The "UN Forces Command" in south Korea means the U.S. Forces Command, and the "UN Forces" are the U.S. Forces.

Peace cannot be guaranteed on the Korean peninsula by the old armistice system with the "UN Forces" as a party concerned.

The "UN Forces Command", an aggressive tool in the era of the cold war, must be dissolved without delay. Its dissolution is a resolution of the UN and a requirement of the international peace forces.

The DPRK put forward a proposal for a new peace mechanism in April 1994, the DPRK-U.S. Framework Agreement was adopted in October and has entered into the stage of implementation. Under this condition, it is considered that measures and conditions have matured to dissolved the "UN Forces Command".

The United States should make a resolute decision to withdraw its forces from south Korea as demanded by the UN resolution and sign a peace agreement with the

DPRK, and thus fulfill its responsibility and role in ensuring peace on the Korean peninsula.

If the United States is not in a position to do so at once, it should dissolve even the "UN Forces Command", as mentioned in the resolutions offered by two sides.

If the United States turns its back on the DPRK's just demand which it must accept, the DPRK government will have no other choice but to take unilateral steps one by one to clearly liquidate the remains of the era of the cold war in Korea.

Appendix 6

European Atomic Energy Community (EURATOM)

On March 25, 1957, a treaty was signed in Rome establishing the European Atomic Energy Community (EURATOM). The treaty was executed by Belgium, France, Germany, the Netherlands, Luxembourg and Italy. The function of the Community, according to the treaty, is to create the conditions required for the speedy formation and development of nuclear industries in order to help raise the standard of living in the Member States and to promote trade with other countries.

European Atomic Energy Community

Summarized below are excerpts from the official resume of the treaty which established the European Atomic Energy Community, which has its own Council and its own Commission.

1. The Development of Research

The Commission must promote and facilitate research. Research and training programmes, which may not exceed five years, will be approved by a unanimous decision of the Council taken on the proposal of the Commission, which will consult the Scientific and Technical Committee. The Economic and Social Committee will be kept informed of the programmes. In order to accomplish the aims laid down in the Treaty, the Commission will: set up a Community Nuclear Research Centre, organize and develop the exchange of knowledge and information, complete the research conducted in Member States by means of measures of coordination, may conclude research contracts with Member States, and may extend its financial and technical assistance to the research work.

2. Dissemination of Information

The Commission shall do its utmost to obtain or have obtained, by amicable means, licenses to exploit patents, provisionally protected claims, patent applications or working models covering inventions of use to the Community.

3. Personal Security

Basic standards concerning the personal security of the population and workers against the dangers resulting from ionizing radiation will be established in the Community.

4. Development of Investments

(1) The Commission will publish programmes indicating the production aims for nuclear energy and the capital investment thereby implied.

(2) The Commission will be notified of projected investments, it being the duty of the Council of Ministers to define the nature and importance of the projects.

5. Community Enterprises

Community enterprises will be deemed to be enterprises: which are of outstanding importance for the development of nuclear industry in the Community, which the Council of Ministers will decide to set up, and whose statutes and rules of operation are governed by some specific principles.

6. Supplies

The supply of ores, raw materials and fissile matter will be ensured on the principle of equal access to resources, and by pursuing a joint policy of supply. For this purpose the Commission will set up a commercial Agency, which will be a corporate body vested with financial independence and will possess an option to purchase ores, raw materials and special fissile matter produced in the territories of the Member States, and the exclusive right to conclude contracts for purchase or sale outside the Community.

7. Security Control

The Commission must ensure, on the territories of its Member States: that ores, raw materials and special fissile matter are not diverted from their intended use as declared by their consumers; and that the arrangements for their supply and any special control measures accepted by the Community in an agreement concluded with a third State or an international organization are observed.

8. Ownership of Special Fissile Materials

Special fissile materials will be the property of the Community. The Community's right of property will extend to all special fissile matter produced or imported by a

Member State, an individual or an enterprise, which are subject to security control regulations.

9. Common Market in Nuclear Materials

The common market in nuclear materials will seek to: repeal import and export duties or taxes on Treaty products (The non-European territories of Member States may continue to levy duties or taxes solely of a fiscal character); apply a common tariff to third countries; facilitate the free movement of persons engaged in nuclear work; set up an insurance scheme against atomic risks; and facilitate the transfer of capital needed for nuclear projects.

10. External Relations

The Commission will be responsible for any liaison needed with the various international organizations.

Contributors

The contributors to this volume have fairly diverse backgrounds. As authors approach their respective issues from the mix of theoretical perspectives and taxonomy that they find most congenial, it might perhaps be instructive to present the following brief biographical sketches as an aid to our appreciation of each one's contribution.

Kevin Clements is the Director of the Institute of Conflict Analysis and Resolution, George Mason University, Virginia, USA. Prior to 1994 he was Director, Peace Research Centre, Australian National University.

Lau Teik Soon is the Chairman of the Singapore Institute of International Affairs. He is also a member of Parliament, Republic of Singapore. Prior to 1994 he was also Professor of Political Science, National University of Singapore.

Song Yimin is a senior research fellow at the China Institute of International Studies. She was a research associate of the United Nations Institute for Disarmament Research.

Atsuyuki Suzuki is a professor in the Department of Quantum Engineering at the University of Tokyo, Japan. He specializes in nuclear energy utilization.

James T.H. Tang is a professor in the Politics Department of the University of Hong Kong. His latest book (as editor) is *Human Rights and International Relations in the Asia-Pacific Region*.

Cheng-yi Lin is a research fellow at the Institute of European and American Studies, Academia Sinica, Taipei. One of his latest papers has appeared in the *China Quarterly*.

Byung-joon Ahn is a professor in the College of Social Sciences at Yonsei University, Seoul, Korea. He has published many books and articles on the topic of North-East Asian security.

Peter Hayes is the Director of the Nautilus Institute for Security and Sustainable Development, Berkeley, California, USA. He has published many books on energy and environment issues.

Alexei V. Zagorsky is head of the Centre for Japanese and Pacific Studies at the Institute of World Economy and International Relations, Moscow. His work focuses on Japan and North-East Asia.

Takashi Inoguchi is the Senior Vice-Rector at the United Nations University, Tokyo, Japan. Prior to 1995 he was Professor of Political Science at the University of Tokyo. His latest book (as co-editor) is *United States–Japan Relations and International Institutions after the Cold War*.

Grant B. Stillman was a programme associate in the area of peace and security at the United Nations University. At present he is a consultant at the Organisation for Economic Co-operation and Development (OECD) in Paris.

230

Index